"You think

"Doubtful," Mack B_____ _____
and he's not that bright.

"Well, it sounds like you've got this under control."
As an afterthought he added, "It's just too bad that
innocent people have to pick up the pieces when
tragedy strikes."

"Not this time," the Executioner said, making no
effort to hide the rancor in his tone. "I'm about to
shut down this operation—permanently. I'm going
forward with this mission as planned and will turn
off the pipeline at its source. Carillo and the FARC
pose a significant threat to security, more right now
than Shui. The KLCT is still licking its wounds after
our last bout."

"But it sounds like the triad is the real threat."

"Agreed, but destroying the drug source destroys
demand for weapons or territories."

"Okay, then what?"

"Then I finish the remaining rats as they retreat,"
the Executioner promised.

***Other titles available in
this series:***

Backlash	Terror Spin
Siege	Judgment in Stone
Blockade	Rage for Justice
Evil Kingdom	Rebels and Hostiles
Counterblow	Ultimate Game
Hardline	Blood Feud
Firepower	Renegade Force
Storm Burst	Retribution
Intercept	Initiation
Lethal Impact	Cloud of Death
Deadfall	Termination Point
Onslaught	Hellfire Strike
Battle Force	Code of Conflict
Rampage	Vengeance
Takedown	Executive Action
Death's Head	Killsport
Hellground	Conflagration
Inferno	Storm Front
Ambush	War Season
Blood Strike	Evil Alliance
Killpoint	Scorched Earth
Vendetta	Deception
Stalk Line	Destiny's Hour
Omega Game	Power of the Lance
Shock Tactic	A Dying Evil
Showdown	Deep Treachery
Precision Kill	War Load
Jungle Law	Sworn Enemies
Dead Center	Dark Truth
Tooth and Claw	Breakaway
Thermal Strike	Blood and Sand
Day of the Vulture	Caged
Flames of Wrath	Sleepers
High Aggression	Strike and Retrieve
Code of Bushido	Age of War

Don Pendleton's Mack Bolan

Line of Control

Frontier Wars

BOOK I

A GOLD EAGLE BOOK FROM

WORLDWIDE.

TORONTO • NEW YORK • LONDON
AMSTERDAM • PARIS • SYDNEY • HAMBURG
STOCKHOLM • ATHENS • TOKYO • MILAN
MADRID • WARSAW • BUDAPEST • AUCKLAND

First edition July 2003

ISBN 0-373-61491-8

Special thanks and acknowledgment to
Jon Guenther for his contribution to this work.

LINE OF CONTROL

One usually dies because one is alone, or because one has got into something over one's head. One often dies because one does not have the right alliances, because one is not given support.

—Giovanni Falcone,
Italian judge,
1939–1992

Whether it's drugs for guns, guns for terrorism, or terrorism for terror's sake, I will use any methods necessary to rid the world of it. And even if I die alone, without allies, I will ultimately make sure the enemy goes with me.

—Mack Bolan

To the members of the Drug Enforcement Administration—
who risk their lives every day to keep poisonous death
off the streets and out of the hands of our children.

PROLOGUE

Toronto, Canada

"We are taking our art to a new people," Lau Ming Shui announced. "The Americans."

Silence fell on the room as the faces ranged around the large conference table expressed surprise and confusion. To anyone outside that room, this was the annual stockholder meeting of the Shui Films & Arts Corporation. But it was something else entirely to those present. It was the bid for ultimate power that Lau Shui had been planning for years. His proclamation afforded any of the present members in the Kung Lok Chinese triad the opportunity to dispute his claims.

No one did because no one was that foolish.

Ing Kaochu, leader of the Scarlet Dragons, cleared his throat to break the taut silence. "We are not artists, Lau. We are warriors...like our ancestors."

Shui smiled. "That is true. And you are our prized possession, our front line of defense and enforcement. Nonetheless, we have monopolized the entertainment industries in Hong Kong, Vancouver and Toronto. There is nothing left to be had here. Thusly we are compelled to seek new forms of revenue because we are also men of business. Like any business, we must continue to show profits. All kinds of profits."

Nobody protested Shui's observations. As a matter of fact, they were nodding in agreement with him, looking to one another for support and unity. That excited Shui, because he was speaking the truth—they knew it and believed it. Unity was their most important asset. Without it the Kung Lok triad had little real power.

While the triad controlled the politicians in China, a move that was ostensibly simple after the reversion of urban ownership to the Chinese by the British, there were still issues to be addressed. The Kung Lok influence spread far and wide throughout the world, but the Americans had managed to keep large parts of the triad at arm's length. It was time to change that relationship.

"We must become more intimate with American money," Shui continued.

"And why is that so important?" one of the members asked.

It took Shui only a moment to recognize the wary features of Dim Mai, head of the Asian Pacific arms theater. Mai had served with the Kung Lok as the major supplier of guns from Mongolia to New Guinea. His operation was one of the largest in the world, and very few guns sold couldn't be traced to Mai as their source.

"It is important because American money is spent freely, frivolously and without thought of consequence. Particularly in the area I think we should focus. Lights, please."

The lights were dimmed by one of Shui's Scarlet Dragon enforcers and bodyguards, on loan from Ing Kaochu. The screen behind Shui filled with a map of the United States, and the entire Southwest region was shaded in red. Major cities from Los Angeles to San Antonio were highlighted with red-and-yellow dots—the primary colors of the Kung Lok. There were black stars situated on San Diego, Las Vegas and El Paso.

"Two things prevail in the American Southwest, like nowhere else in the country—sex and drugs. Both are plentiful, cheap and popular enough that we can control them with ease."

"And how do you propose to do this?" Mai challenged with a snort.

"That is the beauty of this plan." Shui looked at Kaochu, adding, "And the art. You see, my friends, it has already been done for us."

"By whom?" another member of the group inquired.

"By the Americans themselves!" Shui cried triumphantly, raising his finger to signal for attention. "We have discovered through our political contacts that there is a major pipeline recently opened. With an increased demand for heroin and the drug Ecstasy has come an increase in profit. The money is already being made. We must simply implement measures to transfer it from the pockets of those making it into our own. And we must do it without their knowing about it."

"Your plan sounds profitable," Mai interjected, "but I'm not convinced it is practical in theory. How do you propose to do this?"

"I am glad you asked, my esteemed colleague. The ability to control this situation is dependent on mutual cooperation. We already have the cooperation of our own people in China. Namely, our political friends who have solicited cooperation from certain officials within the American government. This will provide culpability of others should anything go wrong."

"And then?"

"The drugs are already present, or at least the raw materials," Shui continued. "With the assistance of Ing and yourself, we should have no trouble protecting our assets. We must ensure that our involvement is swift, decisive and ultimately ambiguous enough to escape detection. The Kung Lok is well-known by American law enforcement for gang-related activities, but this is something I do not think on which they will count."

"The American police are many," Kaochu said. "We are few."

"And that is precisely how we will accomplish our goals with invisibility. Your people must be like shadows, something that is already within the realm of your specialization."

"You do not foresee this to be a burden on my resources?"

"Of course not," Shui replied with a smile. "That is because your task is strictly administrative. There will be little need for open violence—of this I am certain. The suppliers and distributors in America are known for their history of eliminating competition for the sake of self-preservation. When this is done, we will simply move in at an appropriate time and acquire the goods. As I have alluded, you see, the work has already been done."

"You have discussed your angle on the drug products," one of the others said. "You have not described the angle on sex."

"Sex is for sale where drugs are for sale," Shui stated frankly. "We have already reaped tremendous profits from our export sales to both the legitimate and underworld American markets. The demand for films and videotapes is at an all-time high, regardless of the sexual content. The mixture of drugs and sex has proved to be profitable before, and it will once again. Whites, blacks and Hispanics in the Southwestern U.S. will pay heavy prices for such graphic and explicit material. The addition of drugs creates a parity of astounding magnitude, and will prove more than equitable to our overhead.''

Shui stopped a moment to let his words have effect. He had always prided himself on his eloquence. His ability to woo others with his words and grandiose speeches was renowned throughout the Kung Lok society. Yet, at the same moment, he could be obtusely brutal toward the competition. It was these traits that had elevated him to his present stature as self-proclaimed leader of the Kung Lok triad in the West. No one on this side of the world would have dared oppose his authority.

The others seated in the room were influential and extremely powerful in their own right, to be sure. But none of them wielded the power in North America like Shui—he knew that and so did they. His plan would have sounded preposterous and been taken as an insult anywhere else; not here and not in this setting. All members of the Kung Lok triad considered such behavior unethical. It was truly an organization that believed in honor and heritage over personal gain, and Shui was proud to be part of it.

"All of this *sounds* good," Mai said. "However, I find myself skeptical about your methods, Lau. I would like to hear more about how exactly you plan to do this."

"Of course," Shui said. "Allow me to explain how we shall take our art to the Americans."

CHAPTER ONE

Brownsville, Texas

Mack Bolan was rigged for war.

He lay in the weeds on top of a small hill that overlooked an abandoned parking lot, dressed in his blacksuit, his face smeared by combat cosmetics. An LBE harness supported several tools of his trade, including M-26 grenades. A Beretta 93-R was holstered in shoulder leather, and a .44 Magnum Desert Eagle hung in leather at his right hip.

A Heckler & Koch PSG-1 was set up on a bipod, locked and loaded. The highly precise bolt-action sniper rifle came with a 6×42 scope, and was chambered in 7.62 mm NATO ammunition. The soldier loved this rifle for its versatility and accuracy, an invaluable combination in his line of work. It also used an illuminated graticule in the scope, which made it perfect for this operation.

One thing had brought the Executioner to Brownsville: drugs. He had fought many battles to keep them off the streets of America, but this particular mission held importance because it was affecting kids. They called it Ecstasy, aka Adam or XTC, and it was taking

American youth by storm. Intelligence had it that Brownsville was one of the major entry points for 3-4 MDMA, the major synthetic ingredient used by meth labs to manufacture the stuff. Once it was cooked and distributed, it brought many of the risks of cocaine or amphetamines—an epidemic quickly finding its way into schools and gangs across the nation.

The Executioner was going to close this pipeline by utilizing a tried-and-true weapon in America's arsenal— the Bolan blitz.

Up to this point, both the DEA and Border Patrol had been helpless against the onslaught of Ecstasy. It didn't just bring death to America, but it also brought pornography, white slavery, guns and violence. The profit the drug generated was high enough that the dealers would go to considerable lengths to get 3-4 MDMA into the States, and even further to protect their investment.

Well, they were in for a surprise this night.

Bolan lowered the night-vision goggles as truck headlights swung into the parking lot and winked off. The soldier set the NVDs aside and drew up closer to the PSG-1. He put his cheek to the stock and removed the lens caps from the scope. A flick of the switch and the night was lit in a brilliant gray-green through the viewfinder. Bolan could see two men seated in the cab of the truck, one of them smoking a cigarette. The pinpoint glow increased in intensity as the passenger inhaled deeply. After a few moments, the smoker climbed from the cab and left his *compadre* behind the wheel. He was dark haired, probably Hispanic, although it was difficult for Bolan to tell from his position almost one hundred yards away.

The sound of additional car engines reached the Executioner's ears, and he lifted his head just above the scope to view the arrivals—a pair of light gray BMWs. It looked as if all of the players were in the game, and Bolan returned to the scope to get a better view of the other half of this transaction.

Two hardcases dressed in suits and toting machine pistols emerged from the first sedan and approached the truck passenger. The guy raised his arms and a quick frisk apparently satisfied them. Bolan took a moment to study the hardware: Finnish-made Jatimatics. They fired 9 mm Parabellum rounds, weighed less than five pounds and had folding forward grips and 30-round magazines. They were the perfect weapons for those in the business of dealing death.

Bolan took a deep breath and let out half as he sighted on the first gunman. He'd take out the guys with the grease guns first, the truck driver and then the passenger. That way, the drugs wouldn't go anywhere before he had a chance to neutralize the vehicle. Any additional troops in the BMWs he could deal with on a first-come, first-served basis.

His finger curled on the trigger as he fired the first round. The high-velocity slug caught one of the gunmen in the neck, tearing out his throat and nearly severing his spinal column. Bolan worked the bolt and had a round chambered before the guy hit the ground. The few seconds of panic allowed him to align his sights on the second hardcase. The guy took the round high in the chest before lights suddenly flooded the parking lot and a whistle sounded.

Bolan pulled away from the night scope, closing the eye that had been flooded with a bright haze and opening the other. A mass of agents clad in body armor rushed the meeting area, the back of their vests adorned with bright, yellow letters that read DEA. Screamed warnings by many of the agents went unheeded as about eight more gunners poured from the BMWs, rushing from the vehicles like cockroaches and taking up firing positions.

The Executioner swore under his breath. He killed the infrared scope and then sighted on the passenger who was trying to climb into the truck while obviously yelling at his cohort that they should get the hell out of there. Gunfire rang out as Bolan switched targets, putting two rounds into the head of the driver. The window exploded as the bullets drilled through his skull and blew out the other side.

The passenger now turned to look through the windshield, seemingly uncertain from where the offending rounds had come. Bolan used the momentary lapse to take down the drug pusher, triggering a single round that exploded the guy's heart.

With that finished, Bolan abandoned his weapon, drew the Desert Eagle and burst from cover. He sprinted down the hill to join the melee already well in progress.

THINGS WEREN'T OFF to a good start.

Agent Lisa Rajero screamed at her people to take cover even as several armed men exited the BMW sedans and opened up with machine pistols. The night was filled with a cacophony of automatic weapons' fire as several of her agents responded quickly to the threat and began to return fire.

Rajero dropped to the asphalt and rolled away from the gunfire directed at her. She brought her MP-5 submachine gun to bear and returned the fire of one of the bodyguards protecting the real target. The 9 mm rounds spat from the muzzle of her SMG and cut down the gunner before he could find his mark.

The strangest thing was that it didn't appear as if their quarry were attempting to escape. They were actually standing, making a fight, and that surprised Rajero. It wasn't that these purveyors of death were anxious to get caught. She was beginning to wonder why they hadn't simply jumped in their cars and beat it the hell out of there. Perhaps they had more to lose than she had originally thought, and they weren't about to let the DEA just take their drugs.

Rajero also wondered if the drug dealers actually had a fighting chance. Despite the body armor, two more of her men fell under head shots. Rajero grimaced as she jumped to her feet and raced for the cover of the truck that was supposedly carrying several hundred pounds of 3-4 methylenedioxy-methamphetamine, the primary ingredient in Ecstasy. She could hear the hammer of weapons' fire as 9 mm Parabellum rounds chewed the pavement at her feet.

She was just nearly diving for cover when a large hand grabbed her and pulled her off track. Only a millisecond passed before the *tink-tink* of more enemy fire hit the truck where she had been standing. Her body continued in a circle, and she was slammed against the back of the truck. It stung, but it wasn't hard enough to harm, and it was certainly better than the alternative.

Rajero turned and glanced at the profile of her saving angel. He was tall, muscular, and dressed in black from head to toe. Combat cosmetics covered most of his face, and he was dressed like a soldier. She recognized the M-26 grenades hanging from his load-bearing web belt, the result of her training in ordnance and explosives at FLETA, and he clutched a .44 Desert Eagle in his left fist. He still had one hand on her shoulder, his own back pressed to the tailgate of the two-and-a-half-ton truck.

"Who the hell are you?" she snapped, shrugging away his hand.

"No time to explain," he replied.

Rounds whined through the air as they ricocheted off truck and pavement. Bolan risked a glance around the corner, then jumped onto the tailgate and took a quick look inside. He got down, his face a mere shadow in the lights of the parking lot, and yanked one of the grenades from his web belt. He gestured at a fenced generator and a stack of pallets. "On my count, you head for the back of that store."

"Who do you think you are?" she demanded. "I'm the agent in charge of this operation."

The man whirled on her now, the determination and ferocity in his ice-blue eyes evident. "You *were* in charge. Your move should draw enough fire from the others and still provide good cover. Now go before you lose every man you've got out there."

Rajero bit her lip, fighting further protests as she nodded her understanding. The man yanked the pin and ordered her to take off. The agent burst from the back of the truck, firing the MP-5 one-handed as she ran for the stacked pallets. She actually managed to hit one of the enemy gunmen, but she noticed the bodies of DEA agents strewed everywhere. Even as she reached the pallets, autofire raked the area around her. She dived behind cover and then turned to look for her benefactor, but he was no longer behind the truck.

A moment later, the vehicle erupted into a fireball as the highly explosive chemicals went up in flames.

THE EXPLODING TRUCK created the brief moment of surprise and pandemonium for which he had hoped. The Executioner risked exposure just long enough to kneel and draw a solid bead on the closest enemy gunman. The Desert Eagle thundered, barely bucking in his two-handed grip, and a .44-caliber missile burst the target's head like a cantaloupe. The booming report not only signified the power of the handgun, but it also had an added psychological effect. Bolan took the next gunman in a similar fashion, then rolled away from a hail of bullets triggered by two others.

One of the DEA agents apparently felt he had a chance—he burst from the cover of a steel garbage Dumpster and returned fire. The last two hardcases jumped into the rearmost BMW. The sedan backed away from the carnage with a squeal of tires, gaining about one hundred feet before the driver put it into a J-turn and rocketed away from the scene.

The driver of the other sedan leaped from his vehicle and put his hands in the air. Several DEA agents rose from the pavement and rushed forward to take the wheelman into custody. They were seemingly ignorant of the Executioner, who decided it was time to split.

Bolan made a quick estimate as he retreated and realized that many of the DEA agents had fallen under enemy fire. Damn! If they had just let him handle this, it wouldn't have gone sour. The soldier could only assume that they had been onto this deal from the start, probably having spent months to gather the same intelligence he'd solicited with one phone call.

That was the most important element in Bolan's war; it was what separated him from law enforcement. The Executioner had resources that the DEA and FBI couldn't even begin to comprehend, much less more covert agencies such as the CIA or NSA. Never mind that he also didn't have to operate within the "rules" of fair play. Members of sanctioned groups couldn't just shoot first and ask questions later. He didn't have to operate within the parameters of the law, and so much the better. Nonetheless, Bolan understood the reason for rules and he respected anyone who *could* operate under those rules. That didn't mean he had a license to just go out and waste everyone who looked at him sideways. He wouldn't have done that even if he was able, and that was the difference between any psychopath with a gun and the Executioner. Bolan did what he did out of duty. And the way he saw it, he had a new duty.

To find out who had been on the receiving end of the shipment, and left nearly a half-dozen good men lying dead in that parking lot.

AT ABOUT 10:00 a.m. the following morning, Lisa Rajero was leaving the Brownsville, Texas, DEA office when she encountered the tall stranger on the steps leading from the building.

"I ought to arrest you," she snapped.

"Good to see you, too," the Executioner replied.

She turned away and continued down the steps. The Executioner had to take longer than normal strides to keep up with her as her heels clacked along the sidewalk. It was much easier to appreciate her good looks in contrast to the body armor and fatigues she'd been wearing last night. She had long, brown hair with eyes to match. She wore a pink blouse that accentuated full breasts, and a white denim skirt that rode just above shapely calves.

"I'd like to explain," Bolan said, "if you'd slow it down a minute."

"Yes, well, you're about twenty minutes late."

"What do you mean?"

She stopped in the middle of the sidewalk and whirled to face him. "I mean that I just barely got out with a three-day suspension and part of my ass missing. No thanks to the fact that you couldn't even bother to show up and verify my story. If it hadn't been for a couple of my own guys doing the stand-up thing, I probably would have lost my job. The chief here is just looking for a reason to get rid of me."

"I don't think it would have been a good idea for me to do that."

"Oh, really?"

"Really."

There was a long silence before Rajero finally retorted, "Where's your utility belt with all of that hardware, Batman?" Some of the edge was gone from her tone.

"I left it in the bat cave. Listen, I'd like to talk to you."

"You're talking to me."

He shook his head. "Let's find some place quieter. I'll buy you breakfast."

"I don't eat breakfast," she said as she turned from him and continued down the sidewalk. "But I know where you can get a hell of a good cup of coffee."

"Where's that?"

To his surprise, the Executioner found her place quite

comfortable. And only a fifteen-minute walk from where she worked, which had to be damn convenient. She confirmed it was as she put on a pot of coffee and then sat down with him at the small table in the dinette of her spacious studio apartment.

"All right, you've got fifteen minutes."

"Is that the going price for the life of a DEA agent?"

"Hey, let's get something straight! I did my job the best I knew how, and it wasn't my damn fault anyway. Metzger promised me backup, and then he didn't come through. Then the dumb ass threatens to lock me up because he thinks I'm making up this whole thing about you showing up and ruining the gig! Not to mention the fact that whole flipping shipment went up. There's a ton of evidence gone, no thanks to you!"

"I needed a diversion," Bolan replied simply.

"At the cost of helping us make our case."

"Those guys were only the tip of the iceberg, and you know it."

"Maybe so, but they could have led us—"

"Nowhere, so let's put it to rest. The only reason any of you are alive is because it was more important for them to give whoever was behind this deal a chance to split. If they had wanted to, they could have brought a lot more guns down on us than they did."

"How do you know?" Rajero shot back challengingly.

"Because it's my business to know."

To his surprise, the woman didn't have anything to say to that. He'd already studied her file before contacting her. The Executioner had guessed from her profile that she wouldn't turn him into her people and so far, she'd proved him right.

"Just like I know who *you* are. Lisa Marie Rajero… age, thirty-six. You joined the USMC at seventeen and did six years as an MP before resigning and attending college. You hold a Bachelor of Science in chemistry, which led you to biochemical consultation with the DEA, then eventually a position as a field agent. Your specialties are heroin and amphetamines of any kind. You've blown some major drug labs wide open posing as a chemist, and your work in the field has earned you several high marks, as well as a handful of commendations."

Rajero didn't say anything, but stared hard at Bolan for some time. She finally rose and poured each of them a cup of coffee, offering him sugar and cream, which he waved off, and then indulging in three cubes in her own. The stuff was mud, to say the least, but Bolan wasn't about to complain. He'd had a lot worse, some of which he'd made himself.

"So, you know a lot about me," Rajero said. "I still don't know anything about you."

"And we should keep it that way."

"Can you at least tell me if you're with the DEA?"

"Not exactly."

"You're part of the internal-affairs division, then, right?" She slapped her thigh and said, "Damn it, I *knew* they were looking at me."

"No," Bolan replied with a chuckle, "no one from the DEA is looking at you. I'm on my own."

That statement caused her to raise her eyebrows. "Freelancer?"

"Of a sort."

"So how is it you got turned on to my operation?"

"I used to work for the government," Bolan replied. "Once. On occasion, I still do favors..."

"But this one is strictly freelance."

"Yeah. Any idea who was behind that shipment?"

"Maybe," she said, looking at him with obvious interest over the rim of her coffee mug. She took a sip and added, "Why do you want to know?"

"The same reason you do," he said. "There's entirely too much Ecstasy on the streets lately. It's filling the morgues faster than we can count the bodies. I'm tired of watching others make money from the death of our youth. American kids have enough to worry about today without adding drugs to the equation. My intelligence tells me that there's a pipeline coming through Brownsville. I'm here to close the valve."

Rajero let out a laugh of disbelief. "In that case, you're up for a fight."

"What do you mean?"

"We're not just up against the drugs," she said quietly. "We're also up against people who will go to any lengths to protect their product. The one behind the dope itself is a man named Jose Carillo. Have you ever heard of him?"

"The one they call Panchos?"

She nodded.

"Yeah, I've heard of him. I've even tangled with some of his people on occasion. So he's the one pushing this stuff through?"

"Oh, yes." As she rose and poured herself another cup, she continued, "But he's not doing it alone. Our informants tell us that he's operating in conjunction with several other parties. We know one of the parties is south of the border, and supplying Carillo with the weapons and manpower necessary to protect the shipments.''

''Mexican mafia?''

''Possibly, although they've managed to latch on to some pretty heavy hardware. Did you notice anything unusual about the weapons carried by our friends last night?''

''Yeah. They looked like Jatimatics.''

''Exactly. Weapons made in Finland, and yet here in bulk. We've made other busts in the recent past along this area of the border, and there have been some strange similarities in the weapons department. Everything from Steyrs to FMKs, and even AR-15s and M-16s.''

''Which means someone bought them on the black market,'' Bolan deduced. ''That usually means large, cash deals. With the risks to get that kind of hardware into the country, it's not going to be for a few bucks here and there. These arms dealers will only risk large shipments because there's no money in piecemeal sales.''

Rajero nodded, visibly impressed. ''I would have to say it looks like you *have* done your homework.''

''I try to keep up.''

''Several team members who are in my corner promised they would begin a concerted effort to trace those firearms recovered at the busts. I don't know if we'll get anywhere with them, but it'll be a start.''

''And maybe bring you one step closer to finding out who else is involved.''

''Precisely.''

It did seem strange to the Executioner that there was such a variance in the weaponry. He began to consider the fact that Rajero might actually be on to something.

So many different weapons caches could only suggest one of two things: terrorists or a paramilitary group. That left countless groups in Central and South America that might stand something to gain by assisting Carillo. But there was still a piece of the puzzle missing.

"You mentioned some other parties that might be working with Carillo."

"Yes," she said, lighting a cigarette. "We think that he has someone on the inside of the DEA or the Border Patrol. I'd like to think the latter, but one can only hope. If there's someone dirty inside my organization, they're higher than me and they're damn good at covering their tracks."

"Time will tell."

The phone rang. Rajero appeared startled by it at first, then laughed and picked up the receiver. "Yeah." After a moment she said, "Already? Okay, that sounds real good, Pete. No—" she looked at Bolan "—no, don't do anything with the information right now. That's right, you heard me. Just sit on it. I'll get back to you when I know something." Another pause, and then, "Don't *worry* about it, Pete. You know, you worry too much. It's less likely they'll be watching me now that Metzger suspended me. Just hang tight, and I'll be back in touch. And Pete? Don't talk to anyone else about this. Got it? Thanks."

She hung up the phone and smiled at the Executioner triumphantly.

"I take it you caught a break."

"You bet your ass we did. One of my people managed to trace that gun off a ballistics match for a murder committed less than three weeks ago. You'll never guess where the hit went down."

"Where?"

"El Paso."

The Executioner nodded. El Paso was as good a place to start as any.

CHAPTER TWO

Chihuahua, Mexico

Jose "Panchos" Carillo gently set the antique telephone receiver into its cradle and then slammed his fist on the table.

He tried to contain his anger, but he simply couldn't suppress the quiver of hatred and loathing that ran through his lithe, athletic figure. Beads of sweat formed on his face and soaked the collar of his yellow polo shirt. He took several deep breaths, shoved his hands into the pockets of his tailored khaki slacks, then turned and left his study. He crossed the room and walked through the open double doors onto the veranda of his home.

The hacienda-style mansion overlooked the deep Rio Grande valley surrounding the city of Ciudad Juárez. This was *his* city. The fact that it bordered El Paso, an Americanized version of the gorgeous metropolis, was a small price to pay. After all, this unusual relationship had profited him so greatly.

Ciudad Juárez sat more than thirty-five hundred feet above sea level, at the intersection of three major highways. Known as the twin cities of the border, the two urban sprawls shared an equal affinity for transportation as a main source of revenue. Whether it was by truck, rail or waterway, the economy prospered on both sides of the border from the transport of goods and services. Sometimes those goods and services weren't wholly legal—if at all—but Carillo had founded his empire on this fact.

Carillo had begun his career as a mule, slipping unmolested between the two cities, first carrying marijuana and other items of smaller value, and eventually graduating to cocaine and heroin. Born and orphaned in Chihuahua, and raised by Ciudad Juárez's mean streets, Carillo learned how to survive and prosper. Searching for a better life in the U.S. had never been one of his aspirations. He'd never considered crossing the Rio Grande and not returning. Part of the thrill had been the chase itself, evading dope-sniffing dogs and Border Patrol agents. He'd been caught once and deported back to Mexico, although not before making his delivery. It was actually an easy process—the INS had made it so— to pose as a poor Mexican alien searching for a better life. It was a role to which he was well suited.

Before he knew it, Carillo was the personal bodyguard and chief enforcer to Don Placido Flaminiez, a heavy hitter in the Mexican mafia and a major player with the Blanco crime family. Eventually, somebody decided that Flaminiez had become too old or too lazy for the game, and snuffed him. By that time, Carillo had moved on and so Don Placido's blood wasn't on *his* hands. Carillo was now moving into previously charted territory. With an iron hand and singular purpose, Carillo meticulously eliminated the competition through various devices. Now, he stood on the brink of an un-

precedented alliance with the Colombian revolution-
aries.

Carillo took another deep breath of the humid air, and
it made him feel only a little better. A quarter million
in street value had gone up in smoke, the reason for the
phone call, and now he was left without even a trace
return on his investment in the stuff that had gone into
Brownsville. It seemed his contacts in the DEA hadn't
been privy to the fact he was making the shipment, and
now he didn't have so much as a dime in profit for what
had proved a very profitable area in the past.

So what the hell was he paying Sapèdas all of that
money for? To sit on his sorry ass while hundreds upon
thousands of dollars of *his* profit went up in flame? Not
to mention the loss of two of his most reputable and
trusted mules. In some sense, Carillo was equally puzzled by the events in Brownsville. His contacts had spo-
ken of a sniper and the use of heavy explosives to destroy the shipment. That didn't sound like typical DEA
tactics, especially considering that the destruction of the
shipment was also a loss of hard evidence.

Yes, that had him very disturbed. But he couldn't let
on to his guest—whose arrival was pending—what had
taken place. He had to keep quiet long enough to find
out who had betrayed him. He had to discover where
the leak was at, and plug it once and for all. It wouldn't
do for Nievas to find out.

As if on cue, Carillo observed the arrival of an inconspicuous wreck of a car that had stopped at the front
gate and was awaiting permission to enter. Carillo
smiled with satisfaction. It was good to let the new arrivals wait. He didn't want to seem anxious, but the truth
of the matter was that he was very excited. This newly

formed alliance with the Colombians was already turning out as one of the best things he'd ever contrived, not to mention what it would do for his reputation. None of the other dons would dare oppose him now. It was as if the rich aristocrats of nineteenth-century California had returned.

Carillo whirled and walked purposefully but unhurried through the house as the beater car made its way up the long, circular drive, which was flanked by gardens. Birds sang, their tunes echoing through the spacious house, as he descended the wide spiral staircase of his mansion. Three of his bodyguards snapped to attention at his appearance, two toting machine pistols on shoulder slings. His chief enforcer and personal assistant, Conrado Diaz, wore a .40-caliber semiauto pistol in shoulder leather.

Carillo still carried a pistol himself, a little Taurus .380 in an ankle holster. He'd learned at a very young age that one couldn't be too careful. He was considered a dangerous man, but he was also a wanted man, and it was his money and reputation for hard-nosed business that kept the Mexican police and U.S. federal agents at bay, thus the nickname Panchos. He had no false sense of security or invulnerability. Carillo had survived this long by being careful and seizing the advantage when it seemed easy for the taking. He wasn't about to let his guard down by thinking that twenty or thirty men on the grounds were adequate protection.

Anybody could be hit if the hitters wanted it badly enough.

Diaz opened the door and stood aside to let his men accompany Carillo onto the porch, the roof of which served as the base of the veranda Carillo had stood on a minute earlier. Carillo threw up his hands in welcome as the visitor emerged from the old rust-bucket that came to a stop in front of the house.

It was the first time that Carillo had ever set eyes on the man in the flesh. His name was Colonel Amado Nievas, and he was the leader of one of the most powerful insurgent organizations ever assembled against a South American government. The Revolutionary Armed Forces of Colombia—FARC—was perhaps one of the best equipped and trained fighting forces ever established. It had begun as a pro-Soviet army in 1964, growing exponentially to a force that now exceeded 15,000 active members. In addition to its attacks against foreign and domestic Colombian targets, primarily dignitaries and politicians, it was extensively involved with narcotics traffickers. It provided protection, cultivation, manufacture and transport of drugs. It worked cheap, thrived on spreading terror and was in need of continuous financial support from outside sources.

Seeing an opportunity, Carillo had moved on that need.

"Colonel Nievas," Carillo greeted him in a warm, congenial tone. "Welcome to this, my humble abode in a jungle paradise. Mine is yours."

Nievas stepped forward and studied Carillo a moment in a stiff, perfunctory manner. The Mexican had only seen pictures of the man in uniform, and he looked taller and more astute in these. In actuality, however, he was much shorter than Carillo had imagined. But there was no mistaking the tough, leathery skin and dark, piercing eyes. He had a clipped mustache that dipped past the corners of his mouth, and wrinkles lined his eyes and forehead. A pert nose jutted from his dark skin, but his chin was square and strong. Carillo could see Nievas had a mind and body hardened by fighting in the harshest, most inhospitable and most unforgiving environment on Earth—the jungle.

After a long and stern appraisal, a faint smile broke Nievas's granitelike features. "It is indeed a pleasure to meet you face to face at last, comrade."

Nievas reached out and grabbed Carillo by the neck, touching either cheek to his new ally before anyone knew what was happening. The guards stepped forward immediately, reaching for their machine pistols, and the driver came out of the car, SMG in hand, rushing to get in front of Nievas to protect his own master.

Carillo raised his arms and shouted a few terse obscenities at his men. "What is wrong with you! Put down your weapons. Colonel Nievas is my guest and you will treat him with the respect you treat me, or you will not live to see sunset!"

All parties calmed and lowered their weapons.

"I am very afraid that was my fault," the colonel replied, turning to assure his own bodyguard. "I should have warned you of the custom of my people."

"You have nothing to apologize for, Colonel," Carillo replied smoothly, staring daggers at Diaz. He added, "Trust is the foundation on which we should and *must* build our partnership."

"I am completely in agreement."

"Good. Let us proceed inside. I would like to show you the rest of the estate, and then we may enjoy some refreshment and discuss our business."

Nievas whispered something to his assistant, who perfunctorily saluted, and then he followed Carillo into the mansion. The Mexican led his Colombian counterpart on a grand tour of his hacienda, showing him the guest rooms and the master suite. He described the history of the place, which allegedly dated back to the time of the Franciscans, and showed him some of the most prized art pieces in his Spaniard collection. Included was a fully restored version of conquistador dress, helmet, flintlock pistol and sword included, which stood in grandeur along the main hall.

Once they had returned to the downstairs, Carillo ushered Nievas into a dining area that looked onto the rear grounds. Levels of gardens, fed by stone-lined fountains, terminated at a central rock bottom pond. Multicolored fish swam there, fed by insects, worms and other morsels dredged from the continuous flow of water. A steamy haze covered the entire area, but not so much that the brilliant oranges, reds and purples of exotic flowers didn't come through crisp and bright under the noonday sun.

"A veritable paradise," Nievas observed as they sat and sipped iced tea dashed with lemon and sassafras. "Just as you described it."

Although the patio was fully shaded from the sun, Carillo squinted and replied, "I was born to live here. I will die here."

Nievas frowned over his glass. "A seemingly macabre statement, Don Carillo. Under the circumstances, of course."

"Please, you may call me Jose."

"And me, Amado."

"It truly is a pleasure to have you here, Amado. I have so longed to meet you. Word of your exploits reaches even this part of the world."

"Really?" Nievas appeared impressed with this revelation. "I was under the distinct impression that our struggle against the Colombian government was an old story."

"Old, true, but *not* forgotten. Your struggle represents everything that is right about the quest for freedom, and everything that is upside down about democracy and politics."

"You take a strange viewpoint for a man who was brought up in a democratic bureaucracy."

It was Carillo's turn to smile. "Yes. A bureaucracy that has brought nothing but hatred and dissension among its people. Do you know why my country is so poor, Colonel? It is because of this crass democracy in which we live. The government taxes everything. *Steals* everything, in other words, from the people who most rightly deserve it. What I do in my work tends to return some of that wealth to the people. I want to restore the glory of Mexico when it was at the height of its potential. I want freedom from repressive laws and governmental interference, just as you do from yours. Thus, there are parts of my struggle that could be paralleled with those of your own. And there are parts that I feel are just as important."

"My dear Jose, you would compare the struggles of the Carillo family with those of the people's revolutionary forces?"

"Only as an allegory…never out of disrespect," Carillo replied smoothly and quickly. He sat forward, tapping the frosted-glass table with his finger and added, "That is why I called you here. I know that you need more support, particularly in the area of weapons and demolitions. I, on other hand, need support from a more practical aspect. I need protection for my shipments.

That is why I think we could help each other, Amado. I have a plan that will astound you. When you have heard what I have to say, you will find it very hard to turn me down."

"Then perhaps you should indulge me."

Now was the moment for which he had waited almost six months. He had obviously made a good impression—otherwise a man like Nievas wouldn't still be seated here. Here, in his home! He couldn't blow it now by acting as some impudent child. It was of paramount importance that he convince Nievas of the promise in his words and the totality of his vision.

Carillo took a deep breath before speaking. "When my former employer was eliminated by competing families, without reason or justification, I made the realization that one does not survive in my world without friends and allies. Powerful allies, to be certain. I am persuaded you have come to understand this, as well."

Nievas nodded.

"It occurred to me," Carillo continued, "that the single most important factor in profitability falls back on the laws of supply and demand. The demand in America for drugs is higher than it has ever been. The very fabric of economics in my business is built on who can efficiently supply the highest quality product in a fast and inexpensive manner. In the past, various competitors have cornered this market because of their ability to distribute large quantities through multiple channels. I, my friend, am now in the position to do such a thing. With your assistance, I can control the entire pipeline between America and my own country."

"And if I were to supply you with this 'assistance,' what is my reward?"

Carillo sighed deeply, savoring the moment of triumph. "You are in desperate need of firepower to continue your struggle, yes?"

"Of course."

"I can supply you with that, as well. America is a veritable gold mine of weapons. There are numerous military suppliers in the market, not to mention those weapons that come from the outside by other means. The idea of guns for drugs and vice versa is not a new concept. In controlling the borders, I can just as easily pipeline weapons into Mexico as I can the drugs into America. Do you see?"

Nievas took a long sip of his tea and set the glass gently on the table. He looked onto the rich, colorful foliage and fauna spreading across the grounds. Carillo could tell the wheels were turning inside the head of his Colombian ally. It was a tremendous deal, and the very concept sold the idea itself. The magnitude of such an operation might have seemed spurious to most, but not to a great man like Nievas, and certainly not to an ambitious builder of fortune such as Carillo.

Finally, Nievas said, "What you propose has merit. However, it is a much riskier venture for my people than for yours."

"Not if you look at the bigger picture, Amado."

"What do you mean?"

"Let us just suppose that you *did* choose another avenue. Let us pretend you do not wish to take me up on my offer, for which I would not begrudge you this even a moment. You would still be tasked with protecting your own investment, irrespective of the source of the guns. The beauty of what I'm proposing lies in the fact that I have already gone to great lengths to protect my investment. A considerable amount of funds has already been put into the hands of those in the American government who have conspired with me for the sole purpose of finding their own fortunes.''

"How much money?''

"Two and a half billion dollars.'' Nievas sat in stony silence. "They are blinded by greed.''

"And that, Jose, is what makes them so dangerous,'' Nievas countered.

"Perhaps. But I would remind you that it is also what makes them beholden to us. We smuggle drugs, and I pay the American authorities to look the other way. In return, they get what they wish, and I bring back firearms while they continue to look the other way. The other half of the money is being supplied by the arms dealers and distributors. It requires nothing more from you than the support and manpower to do it.''

"And to deter any competition?''

Carillo laughed, an almost sinister laugh. "That might be part of the game, but it will still hold true in any respect. The difference here, my friend, is that you will control your own destiny, and that of your cause.''

"I control it now.''

"Ah, but you are still faced with a crisis. You are being shorted and ripped off by those who have gained your trust. They continue to skyrocket the price for your freedom.'' When Nievas glanced at him out of a corner of his eye, Carillo added quickly, "I have done my homework, you see. I know that you continue to pay more and get less. Here you can pay nothing, and I can give you *every*thing. More supplies and munitions than you will know what to do with!''

"It is a tempting offer,'' Nievas admitted. But his

tone lacked any malice as he added, "You are a fork-tongued devil, I think."

"You know it is true, what I say."

"I must consult with my advisers," Nievas said, rising to signify that the meeting had ended. "I will require a telephone and complete privacy."

"Of course. The grounds and facilities here are at your disposal."

"Excellent." As he turned to leave, he stopped and looked at Carillo. "You would not violate my trust by listening to my conversations, would you?"

Carillo grinned. "As I have said before, Amado, trust is the foundation on which we must build our partnership."

"Then I will take that as a no."

With that, Nievas turned and walked into the house.

BORDER PATROL CHIEF Ramon Sapèdas was walking on air.

The deal was being finalized today, and before anybody knew what had happened he would be sunning himself on some forgotten tropical beach, sipping champagne and toasting his own ingenuity. That was if he could get rid of the dark-haired stranger who now sat across from his desk and watched him with cold blue eyes.

There was something frightening about this man. He carried himself with an air of calm authority that was rare in men. Sapèdas didn't like him the moment they shook hands, and now the big guy who called himself Mike Belasko of the DEA was asking some very pointed questions that the Border Patrol chief didn't really feel like answering. Perhaps the air this guy carried wasn't authoritative as much as it was impertinent. Well, whatever the hell it was, Sapèas didn't like it.

"Who was it that you said sent you here again, Belasko?"

"Charlie Metzger," Bolan said quietly. "He's head of the DEA office in Brownsville."

"I know Charlie," Sapèdas said. "As a matter of fact, he's a friend of mine. I'm just a little surprised he didn't call ahead of time to let me know you'd be here."

"He had to go to Washington at the last minute," Belasko said.

"I see."

Well, the guy *seemed* harmless enough, but Panchos was paying him quite a bit of money to keep the DEA from nosing around. There was something that Sapèdas didn't quite understand about this whole deal, though. Some of the cash he'd seen was being funneled to other officials in different areas. He was certain someone higher up in the DEA was on the payroll—definitely higher than Metzger or this Belasko clown. He'd have to let Carillo know what was what and get some of the heat out of his backyard.

"So what brings you to my neck of the woods?"

"Guns, primarily."

"What about them?" Sapèdas asked, trying to maintain a nonchalant expression and not squirm in his chair. It was those damn eyes, and if this guy would just quit scrutinizing him like a specimen under a microscope, he might be able to lie his way out of this one.

"There was a murder committed here two weeks ago," Bolan continued. "Somebody hit a known drug pusher and then disappeared."

Sapèdas scoffed at the federal guy. "This is El Paso,

guy. Drug pushers get whacked on a daily basis here. You want to try and be more specific?''

Bolan pulled out a small pad of paper, glanced at it briefly, then put it away and said, "The victim was Randy Lovato, age twenty-nine. He was a member of the Rosarez crime organization.''

"Oh, yeah, I remember that. But my people didn't have anything to do with that. You'd need to talk to the FBI on that one, Belasko. We're strictly in the business of 'nab them and ship them back,' if you know what I'm saying. We don't get involved too much in the organized-crime part of this game.''

"No, but your team was the first to arrive there and take possession of the murder weapon. It was a driveby shooting, and the reports say you checked the weapon into evidence.''

"What's your point?''

"My point," Bolan replied coolly, "is that the weapon turned up in a major drug bust that went sour the night before last. It was a machine pistol, Finnish made, and not legal for import. It killed quite a few of our people before we brought down the user. Since your guys checked it into evidence, we'd like to know how you could explain it being back on the streets.''

"As far as I know," Sapèdas replied, "it's still in evidence. Unless the FBI came and got it later. I don't keep track of everything that goes into and out of my station, Belasko. I don't have the time. Now, if you're accusing me of something, perhaps we should take this up with Metzger. Otherwise, I would suggest you talk to the boys in Washington about this and keep the Border Patrol out of it. You guys are always trying to make us take a bite out of the shit sandwich. Well, you ain't gonna do it in *my* jurisdiction. You got that?"

The big guy stood up and leaned forward on Sapèdas's desk. "Last time I looked, we were all on the same team. Keep that in mind the next time someone comes and asks for a little cooperation. Otherwise, those people you're calling an enemy may not be there to scratch your back when you need them."

"Go talk to the FBI, Belasko, and stay out of my face, will you?"

"Don't bet on it." Bolan turned and left the office.

Sapèdas sat in contemplation for a minute or two, then picked up the phone and dialed an unlisted number in Mexico. On the third ring, he said hoarsely, "Tell the man I need a meeting…ASAP."

CHAPTER THREE

"It's me," Mack Bolan said. He was in a pay phone a half block from the Border Patrol building, watching the front doors as he talked with Lisa Rajero.

"How did it go?" she asked, skipping the small talk.

"About the way I figured."

"Do you think he knows something about the guns?"

"Of course. But he's not about to tell me anything."

"What did he say?"

Bolan paused a moment, trying to decide if it was a good idea to tell her where it was at this early in the game. From one perspective, he still didn't have any real reason to trust her. It was entirely possible *she* was on Jose Carillo's payroll, and doing everything she could to throw him off track. Somehow, though, his instincts were telling him differently. He couldn't buy Rajero being in bed with the Mexican mob—something about that idea just didn't wash.

"He's blaming the FBI, of course. Claims because it was an OC hit that they're the ones in charge of this thing."

"That's very possible. You want me to look into it?"

"No," Bolan snapped. There was a curt silence on the line but he couldn't be worried about her sensitivity.

"I don't want you to make a move on that for the same reason I wouldn't let you tag along. I'm suspicious someone's watching you."

"Then that means someone's watching you."

"I can handle myself. Just stay cool and I'll be in touch again when I need something more."

"Like to keep your women at home, barefoot and pregnant, eh?" she quipped good-naturedly.

"No," he said, unable to contain a smile. "I like to keep them alive."

Bolan clicked the receiver a moment, got a dial tone, then dialed a second number he knew very well. There were whirs and clicks on the line, the sound of several numbers being dialed by a computer and then finally a voice broke through. It was a man who probably knew the Executioner better than anyone, a man who had been with him from nearly the beginning in his war. Someone who gave a damn about the same things he did, and was willing to go the extra mile any time his friends were in need.

"Brognola," the familiar gruff voice answered.

"Hal, it's Striker."

"Are you okay?" Brognola asked without hesitating a moment.

"Yeah, I'm fine."

"Where are you?"

"In Texas. I've got something serious cooking down here. Something that started out simple and got a lot more complicated."

Brognola chuckled. "That's usually the way it goes with you."

"I suppose. Look, I need you to get me some information. I may be out of touch for a while, but you can expect a callback for this.''

"Talk to me."

"First, I need all of the intelligence you can get on Jose Panchos Carillo."

"Carillo of the Mexican drug cartel?"

"If what I was told recently is true, he practically *is* the cartel now, Hal," Bolan replied. "I took down a shipment last night that had Carillo's paw prints all over the thing, according to the DEA. Which brings me to another little favor. Pull what you can on Ramon Sapèdas, chief of the Border Patrol troop in El Paso."

"How do you spell it?"

Bolan gave it to him.

"How does the Border Patrol figure into this?"

"I don't know yet," Bolan said as he glanced at the front of the building.

Sapèdas was descending the stairs. The Executioner watched him as he crossed the busy street, maneuvering between the cars of angry drivers leaning on their horns, and then disappeared inside an underground parking garage.

"I'm going to have to see how this plays out," the Executioner continued, talking quickly now. "Just have Barb and Bear get on it, and I'll touch base again."

"Will do. Anything else you need and you call me, Striker."

"Bet on it. Out here."

Bolan hung up the receiver and trotted quickly to a convertible he had parked in an empty space across from the Border Patrol building. He climbed behind the wheel, adjusted his rearview mirror so he could see the exit ramp of the parking garage, and then started the engine. A BP sedan appeared a moment later, and the Executioner caught a clear glimpse of Sapèdas behind the wheel. He waited for the guy to drive past, ducking in his seat to make sure he wasn't seen, then put the rental car in gear and edged into traffic a few car lengths back.

Bolan knew that he would have to be cautious. After all, the guy was a cop and could probably pick out a tail with relative ease. Underestimating an opponent was something the Executioner learned could be fatal.

He followed Sapèdas as he headed south, watching his side and rearview mirrors for anyone who might pose a threat. The Border Patrol chief got on the I-25 interchange that would take him to Mexico 45. He was probably bound for Ciudad Juárez. Bolan began to consider this new turn of events. There was no question in his mind now that Sapèdas was headed to meet whoever it was that pulled the strings. If his theory proved correct, and the lawman was dirty, then he'd apparently applied just enough pressure to cause Sapèdas to panic. That was what he was hoping for.

The thing that had Bolan most puzzled was the connection between the illegal guns and drugs. Dope running was Carillo's line of business, and Bolan couldn't figure where the guns came into that deal. It was feasible that Carillo was trading drugs for guns, but the hardware used by the guys in his last encounter wasn't there in quantity for a trade. Maybe the money from the drugs was being used to purchase the weapons, although that didn't make any more sense than the first theory. There was no shortage of black-market arms in Mexico. If Carillo was trading drugs for guns, why not do it in his own territory instead of risking the transaction in the States?

Was Carillo doing it to prevent any connection between him and the guns? That was possible but not probable, and Bolan was frustrated that he couldn't find a reasonable answer. He was certain of one thing, though—there was more to this than met the eye. And the Executioner couldn't help but wonder just how big this thing was.

The sun was setting, painting the horizon with shades of red and orange. Traffic was light at this time of the evening, but it was Friday and before long the social crowds and border-crossing weekenders would be out to play.

As they passed through the border checkpoint and entered Ciudad Juárez city limits, the hairs stood on the back of his neck. Something in the warrior's sixth sense, something elusive and dark, began to tingle in his subconscious. He focused on every nuance of his immediate surroundings even while he kept one thought on Sapèdas'-vehicle ahead of him. They were still on Mexico 45, a divided four-lane highway, maybe two miles from the checkpoint.

Bolan realized there was trouble a moment before he actually spotted the two Plymouth Reliants rapidly approaching from the rear. One occupied the left-hand lane, visible in his side mirror—the other was on the shoulder and skirting a sports car that was tailgating him. The front-seat passenger of the vehicle in the fast lane held a sawed-off shotgun.

Bolan took a calculated risk, slamming on his brakes before jerking the wheel hard left. The driver of the sports car did the only thing he could, stomping on his own brakes and swerving to the right to avoid a rear-end collision. The Plymouth on the shoulder skidded to avoid hitting the sports car. Bolan continued across the left lane, cutting off the other Reliant before power sliding his convertible into the grassy median.

The Executioner unleathered the Beretta 93-R into play and snap-aimed at the driver of the Plymouth as it sped past him, selector switch set to 3-round bursts. The Beretta barked in his hand. Two of the rounds missed but one found its mark. The driver's head exploded inside the Reliant and the car skidded off the highway, flipping several times before coming to rest on its wheels.

Bolan double-clutched and threw the gearshift into reverse, his vehicle never coming to a full stop as he stomped on the accelerator. He yanked the wheel and backed the car onto the highway again, bringing it to a stop on the backside of the Plymouth that had nearly hit the sports car. He holstered the Beretta and reached under the front seat to grasp the cold butt of the Desert Eagle.

The Executioner went EVA, shouting a warning at the sports-car driver to get the hell out of there. He didn't want innocent civilians getting wasted during a shootout with the enemy. The guy didn't need to be told twice, putting his car into gear and taking off as several gunners poured from the Plymouth and took up firing positions.

Bolan crouched behind his open door, whipped the Desert Eagle into play and aligned his sights on the first available target. The big weapon boomed twice as he fired on the closest gunman. The .44 Magnum slugs punched twin holes in the gunner's chest, blowing out parts of his heart and spine. The man spun, the Beretta Model 12S SMG he'd been toting flying from his grasp. The remaining three gunmen from the sedan dived for cover, opening fire simultaneously and riddling Bolan's convertible with high-velocity rounds.

The firing ceased a moment as all three of the enemy troops paused to reload. The Executioner reached under the console and ripped away an M-26 he'd taped beneath the steering column. He yanked the pin and tossed the explosive charge overhand. The grenade bounced off the trunk of the Plymouth and exploded before the enemy could recover.

Two were caught in the immediate wave of the blast, razor-sharp shrapnel shredding their flesh. The concussion disoriented the survivor long enough for Bolan to seize the advantage. The Executioner crossed the expanse in three long strides and raised the Desert Eagle. Flame spit from the barrel as he pumped a round into the stunned gunner.

As the echo of the shot died in the evening air, the sound of sirens took their place. Bolan reached down and scooped up the Model 12S. He trotted past the frightened but curious onlookers who were slowly driving past and continued onto the second Plymouth. Nobody moved inside the crunched vehicle, but he could hear a moan. He walked to the passenger side and looked in the front window. The guy he'd seen in his mirror carrying the shotgun was barely alive, his face mangled by broken glass and razor-sharp metal.

Bolan raised the Desert Eagle. "Who are you working for?"

There was something about the guy's ramblings that sounded all too familiar to the Executioner. Was it Japanese? It was hard to tell, but there was something about the facial structure—or what remained of it—that marked him as Asian. His words were unintelligible, but the accent left no doubt. Then one of the words rang true in the Executioner's psyche, and he realized it was a Cantonese dialect. The man was Chinese!

Blood bubbled up from between the guy's teeth, and a moment later the man let go a death sigh. The sirens were getting louder, and Bolan knew he had only a few minutes to split. He reached into the dead man's coat pocket and found a wallet there. He opened it and noted the ID. It was a Nevada driver's license listed to a Danny Chang, and an ID card in a clear casing above the license identified him as security for a Las Vegas casino.

None of this was making any damn sense, but he knew Bolan would have to sort it out later. The most aggravating thing was that Sapèdas had escaped, and he didn't have the first clue where the guy was headed. He was right back where he started. But at least he'd acquired something out of the deal. He had a name and he had a location. It looked as if it was time to pay a visit to the Sunset Strip.

And with that, Bolan disappeared into the night.

Brownsville, Texas

AFTER LISA RAJERO HUNG UP with Belasko, she turned her attention to other important matters. Her primary concern was for her safety and that of her team. Rajero hadn't told Belasko of her real feelings about Charlie Metzger, and the possibility that he was one of the players who had thrown in with Carillo. There was a rumor that internal agents of the DEA had Metzger under investigation, but rumors ran far and wide in the organization.

But that didn't bother her nearly as much as keeping her team alive. Most agents wouldn't have been so skittish, but Rajero had been involved in just such an undercover operation against another officer three years earlier. She'd done things she wasn't proud to admit during that time, but they were things for which she wasn't about to apologize, either.

A dirty lieutenant at her office on the East Coast had been sexually harassing the female agents assigned to him. Rajero's mission had been to penetrate the organization as a young and impressionable rookie, and then sway the guy's affections any way she knew how. She did that…and a whole hell of a lot more. By the time Rajero had finished with the guy, not only was his career over, but also his marriage was destroyed, he landed in federal prison on a ten-year wrap and several incidents of graft were brought to light.

For her actions, Rajero received a commendation, promotion to lieutenant and her choice of a new duty-assignment location. The daughter of career police officers, Rajero wanted to be where the action was. And for the DEA, Brownsville was the biggest drug-smuggling hotspot next to Miami. Now, after almost five years here, Rajero could tell she was close to cracking this case wide open. Just as soon as she could figure out who was involved in helping Jose Carillo maintain his hold on the Brownsville pipeline, and whether Charlie Metzger had anything to do with it or not.

Besides, Metzger was her problem, not Belasko's. She wasn't sure yet that she completely trusted the dark-haired stranger who fought like a demon and could freeze someone in his or her tracks with one glance of those blue eyes. Well, that wasn't completely fair—hc *had* pulled her out of a scrape that might have cost her life. Not to mention the fact he seemed genuinely interested in helping her figure out where the heavy doses of 3-4 MDMA were coming from. She couldn't fault the guy for that, right?

After a shower and coffee, Rajero drove across town and rendezvoused with one of her team members, Peter Willy. Willy was one of those of guys who could be trusted with just about anything, and he'd been with Rajero since her first steps with the Brownsville office. Willy had even stood up for her against Metzger after their bust went bad. During the fighting, he'd been winged by an enemy bullet, so now he was playing desk jockey for a couple of weeks while recuperating. It provided them the perfect opportunity to dig further into the case without Metzger being the wiser. The meeting place was a nondescript, out-of-the-way diner about a half mile off the interstate leading out of Brownsville and heading northwest to El Paso.

After she ordered a bagel with cream cheese, Rajero watched Willy wolf down half of his deluxe cheeseburger while she waited.

"So, what else did you find out about those guns?"

"Nothing really," Willy said around half a mouthful of food. He sucked the grease off his thumbs and wiped ketchup from his mouth before adding, "The gun *was* allegedly signed out by somebody from the FBI, but when I called to confirm the identity of the agent, the EPIC office said they had never heard of him."

"So we now have another piece to this mystery puzzle," Rajero replied absently.

Willy shook his head and gulped from a large glass of milk. He set the glass on the table roughly and said,

"I don't know *what* the hell is going on, Lisa, but I know I don't like it."

"You and me both."

"What about the information I already gave you? What did you do with that?"

Rajero paused for a moment, trying to decide if she should spill the beans about Belasko. She'd promised the guy she'd keep quiet about his involvement, but that was under the assumption she was going to go on living. If something happened to her, she couldn't justify at least not letting someone else know about a new player in the game, and she didn't want to see him gunned down because he didn't know the play. She took a deep breath and decided to tell Willy.

"Can I trust you, Petey?"

He looked at her with surprise. "What kind of a question is that?"

"I know, I know, but just humor me. Can I trust you?"

"You know it."

"Okay, then here it is. After I left the office yesterday morning, that guy I said I had seen at the bust made a second appearance. His name is Mike Belasko. He claims he's a former government agent, although I'm not sure who he worked for. Now he's freelancing and he was onto that bust before we broke in and screwed things up for him."

"God, Lisa, why didn't you tell me? Why didn't you at least have him come back and explain himself to Metzger?"

"I almost did," she replied, "but he asked me not to. And there's something about the guy I trusted."

"I think you're letting the fact he pulled us out of a scrape cloud your judgment."

"Maybe, but just listen to me for a minute. He knew about that transfer going down the other night, Pete. He knew everything about me and Carillo, and he even seemed to buy my theory that someone higher than us inside the DEA is offering cooperation to the Mexican mafia."

Willy looked at her sideways. "Well, you know how I feel about that theory."

"I know you think it's bullshit," Rajero said quickly, "but what if it is true, Petey? What if I'm right, and Metzger or, God forbid, somebody higher is playing footsies with the Carillo crime cartel? Can you imagine what would happen if this kind of information went public? Nobody in this country would ever trust the DEA or U.S. Border Patrol again."

"They don't now," he said matter-of-factly with a shrug.

"Come on, Pete, you don't really believe that any more than I do."

"I guess you're right."

"Let's just look at this a moment. Carillo has doubled his activity in shipping drugs across the borders. There are reports coming in all over the place, and have been for the past month. Ecstasy use and sales are higher than ever, and the stuff just keeps turning up. We shut down one pipeline in Miami, another one opens in El Paso. We shut that down, another opens in Mexicali. We close *that* down and the one in Miami is open again. It seems like there's no end to this story."

"Welcome to the DEA, Lisa."

"That's not what I'm talking about," she snapped,

shaking her head emphatically. "I'm talking about the fact that the stuff just keeps coming through, no matter how much pressure we put on the Mexicans or Colombians or whoever. They get it in, the gangs and pushers get it out on the street and the criminals continue to make money while we continue to watch our efforts turned into profit for death." She sighed and added, "Sometimes I get tired of this war."

"Me, too."

She smiled, noticing his downcast expression, then reached out and grabbed his hand. "Listen, I know how cynical you are but you have to trust me. I think this Belasko's on our side. I just wanted you to know about him in case something happens to me."

"Why?" he asked suspiciously. "What do you think is going to happen to you?"

"I don't know. I just wanted to protect this guy. I don't want him caught in the cross fire."

"Jeez, Lisa, what the hell has come over you? You're like some schoolgirl with butterflies over this dude. Is he that important?"

Rajero smiled as she said, "I think he's more than that. I think he could be the answer to this problem. There's something about Belasko that... Well, it's just damn frightening. I mean, you saw the way he fought those guys that night."

"Yeah. I have to admit, he's good. And I'm damn sure glad he's on our side."

"Yes," Rajero whispered, talking more to herself now than Willy. "So am I."

CHAPTER FOUR

Las Vegas, Nevada

When Mack Bolan entered his suite on the ninth floor of the Windfall Hotel & Casino, he immediately sensed another presence in the room. He didn't turn on the lights, realizing that if he wasn't alone then his attackers would be less effective in the dark.

The first assailant approached his rear flank, trying so hard to be silent that his footfalls were like elephant steps to the Executioner's attuned senses. Massive biceps encircled the soldier in a futile attempt to pin his arms to his sides. Bolan crouched, dropping his center of gravity as he drove an elbow into his opponent's solar plexus. Air whooshed from the man's lungs. Twisting his body, the soldier executed a hip toss before his attacker could recover. The guy landed on the carpeted floor hard and groaned as he went unconscious.

Bolan reached into his suit coat and withdrew the Beretta 93-R, thumbing the selector switch to single shot as he reached behind him and flicked on the lights.

Two more Asian attackers appeared from the master bedroom. They stopped short and reached for their own hardware upon seeing Bolan was armed, but they were a moment too late. The Executioner had loaded the Beretta with 120-grain subsonic cartridges, and the Italian-made pistol barely coughed a report as Bolan squeezed off his first shot. This round took one of the pair in the face, blowing out part of his jaw and windpipe before depositing the guy on the floor in a crumpled heap.

The second gunner had unleathered a 9 mm pistol and dived for cover behind a padded chair. The Executioner beelined for a nearby wall as the guy started firing wildly in his direction. He made it to cover alive but not without cost. One of the would-be assassin's stray rounds found its mark, tearing a furrow in the Executioner's left shoulder. He ground his teeth at the pain, then raised his weapon, selected burst-fire mode and squeezed the trigger. The 9 mm Parabellum rounds ripped through the back and continued into the Chinese gunman, dropping him dead and depositing the shredded chair on top of him.

A fourth attacker emerged from the closet behind Bolan, the door striking him in his wounded arm as the guy raced out of the hotel room. Bolan pushed the door away and rushed after the hood. The chase continued down a long hallway that terminated at a set of stairs. Bolan could see this guy was smaller than his comrades, but he was lithe and extremely fast. He pumped his arms and legs, willing his body to go more quickly. By the time he'd reached the door and began to descend the stairs three at a time, his quarry had a one-flight lead. Bolan could feel his heart pounding, and they reached the bottom floor within a couple of minutes. He pushed through the closing exit door and emerged in the crowded hotel lobby.

The jingle of change hitting trays, coins being fed into

slots and the fiery excitement of the gamers thundered in his ears. A few women screamed at the sight of a bleeding, almost breathless Bolan as he scanned the crowd for his runner. He spotted the man pushing impatiently through the crowd and lurched onward, intent on bringing the guy to his knees. He noted that security was also headed into the game, and he cursed himself for the mistake. It hadn't been his intention to involve any innocents—even armed security—but he wasn't about to lose his prey.

Bolan circumvented the crowd, carefully ducking and dodging waitresses with trays. His maneuver paid off, and he met the runner on the other side of the crowd as the guy was pushing his way through. The Executioner had holstered his Beretta a moment earlier, not wishing to attract further attention. His quarry had no such conscience. As he sprinted for the exit, he reached into his jacket and produced a .38-caliber S&W Model 60. He popped off two shots, forcing the Executioner to dive out of the way and drag down a woman with him.

Undaunted, Bolan was quickly on his feet and through the revolving glass doors. He burst onto the sidewalk of the Las Vegas Strip, looked both ways, and then spotted the guy directly across the street. He'd been joined by several more Asian hoodlums, dressed completely in black except for scarlet headbands with Chinese characters, all having just emerged from a sedan. There was no mistaking the intent behind the Model 12S SMGs in their hands. Bolan shouted a warning at the sidewalk of pedestrians. The Chinese gunners raised their arms and sprayed the area with a hail of Parabellum rounds at a cyclic rate of 550 rounds per minute.

Bolan popped the nearly spent magazine as he rolled

away from the onslaught of 9 mm stingers. He shoved
a fresh load into the pistol and got to his feet on their
right flank, heading across the Strip full of logjammed
automobiles as he fired. The Beretta cracked now, Bolan
having changed out the subsonic cartridges for 158-grain
hardballs. He took down two of the five attackers before
they could realign their sights. One gunman was tossed
against the vehicle, and the second staggered into the
middle of the street and tried to hold on to protruding
intestines where Bolan's rounds had ripped out part of
his stomach.

The remaining Chinese gunners attempted to cut him
in two, but Bolan had already secured cover behind a
large delivery truck. Panicked citizens were now racing
away from the combatants locked in a heated trade of
autofire. Bolan dropped another SMG-toting hood who
foolishly tried to charge him, ventilating the man's chest
moments after the gunner left cover.

The pistol-carrying hood Bolan had chased onto the
Strip and his remaining partner apparently decided it
was a hopeless effort. They abandoned the sedan and
raced from the scene, pushing aside fleeing citizens who
got in their way. Bolan opted to give up the chase. He
was already winded, pumped on his nine-floor descent
and evasion of death by only a fraction of a second. He
quickly glanced at the dispersing or hiding people and
realized that nobody had been hurt.

Bolan quickly frisked the guy who had tried to charge
him, but found no identification. He studied the characters on the headband a moment, then pulled away the
man's collar. Three odd marks were tattooed on the dead
man's neck. Chinese writing, certainly, but it was the
location and the type of characters that had Bolan's pri-

mary interest. He quickly memorized them, then rose and headed for the nearest alleyway.

The Executioner had been in Las Vegas less than an hour, and somebody had already tried to kill him. As he holstered his pistol and trotted down the alley, Bolan realized that he had finally identified his mysterious Asian enemies.

Mack Bolan was up against a Chinese triad.

IN HIS MANY TRAVELS, the Executioner had made acquaintances and established connections all over the world. He knew of an FBI safehouse in a residential section of Las Vegas, and it was still in operation. The place was a brick, ranch-style home maintained by a retired U.S. marshal named Vittorio Rosetti. An ex-undercover agent for the Justice Department's OC task force, Rosetti had penetrated the Marconi crime family, an organizational part of the Chicago Four that ran the numbers racket in the late 1970s. For six years Rosetti lived the life of a mobster, but ultimately put away a dozen or more of the heavy hitters who made up the Marconi hierarchy.

Unlike most agents who spent that much time undercover, Rosetti never let the glamour and money blind him from his goal. He did what they told him when they told him, and he'd watched many of the Marconis' criminal competitors turn up dead in trunks, or as permanent parts of the aquatic life in Lake Michigan. But he never wavered and it eventually paid off. He was as hard as they came and willing to lend a hand any time an ally was in need. He was Mack Bolan's kind of guy and one of the toughest sons of bitches Bolan knew. He'd never changed his name or identity after putting the Marconis into federal penitentiaries throughout the country.

Rosetti had always said, ''Hey, if they really want to come and get me, then they know where to find me. Right?''

The Executioner couldn't argue with that logic. Particularly since he was now asking the guy's help, and under the mercy of Rosetti's suturing talents. In addition to his skills as a former federal agent, Rosetti was also a very talented Army Reserve medic. He completed his task in record time and then shared an ice-cold beer with the man he hadn't seen in over fifteen years. Rosetti was one of the few men alive who really knew Mack Bolan was still alive and well, and hadn't died in the war wagon that fateful Saturday night in Central Park so long ago.

''So how goes it, brother?'' he asked the Executioner.

Bolan shook his head. ''It goes hard, Vito. I'm onto something that's bigger than I first thought.''

''Care to talk about it?''

Bolan shook his head. ''No. You've put your neck out far enough. I made sure I wasn't followed, but that doesn't mean anything if I'm right about those behind my little welcoming reception.''

''Fair enough. I won't push it.''

A long silence fell between them. The two men looked at each other, then looked away and were lost in their individual thoughts for a time.

The Executioner was still trying to put it all together. If he was up against a Chinese triad, he needed to find out which one. He also couldn't put his finger on why they would have any association with the Mexican mob. There seemed to be an extraordinary amount of drugs floating around, not to mention the hardware he'd seen used by all of the parties involved to date. And then there was the issue of perhaps one or more of Ramon Sapèdas's men being involved in covering the tracks of a nameless enemy. Bolan knew enough to realize that Sapèdas might have arranged a meet with Jose Carillo. It was no secret Carillo ran his empire from Ciudad Juárez, since he owned a dozen or more "legitimate" companies that actually served as fronts so he could peddle his junk.

Could it have been an alliance formed between the Chinese and Mexicans? Bolan found that very hard to believe. There was no real benefit he could see in the two groups merging, and no credible reason for them to work together. Yet it had seemed that the Chinese he'd encountered near the border were actually trying to protect Sapèdas. That was assuming, of course, that they hadn't been watching him before he'd ever contacted Sapèdas. And since Bolan was freelancing this one, a government leak couldn't be part of the answer.

The more he thought about it, the stranger it became. He checked his watch and realized it was time to contact the Farm. Rosetti pointed him to a phone in his office where he could have privacy. The guy obviously realized that Bolan really didn't want him to know what was happening in this latest episode in the Executioner's war. It seemed to be enough for Rosetti that he could simply help his longtime friend.

Barbara Price answered her office line on the first ring. Bolan knew the line was scrambled.

"It's me."

"Hi," she said, a hint of interest detectable in her otherwise efficient tone.

It was her way of saying she missed him and hoped he was all right, and he knew it. He couldn't help but smile.

"What did you guys pull on Ramon Sapèdas?"

"Hold on a moment. Hal and Bear are both here, too, so I'm going to put you on speaker."

There was a click and then Brognola's voice broke in. "Striker, we pulled everything we could find on your man. Sapèdas was born here in the U.S. after his parents emigrated from Spain. Fairly normal childhood, although his family didn't live high off the hog. He enlisted in the Marine Corps at eighteen, served six years and was honorably discharged. He immediately entered college under the GI Bill, majored in criminal justice and law enforcement and then joined the Border Patrol after graduating. They were happy to have him. This guy speaks four languages and knows six Spanish dialects. His primary job in the corps was as a linguistics expert in cryptoanalysis."

"He has a military background?"

"Yes, and get this. His entire tour was done stateside, part of the time at Fort Hood and the remainder at Fort Huachuca."

Bolan nodded to himself. "So he's been around that area his entire life."

"Exactly," Price interjected.

"Plenty of time to strike up various acquaintances on the other side of the border," Aaron Kurtzman remarked.

"That was my thinking exactly," Bolan said. "Was there anything else?"

"Not really, no," Brognola replied. "This guy's background seems pretty straightforward. He's never been under investigation for any kind of criminal activity, and never known to take a bribe. The people of his command hold him in the highest regard, and he's a highly decorated officer with the Border Patrol."

"I know I'm not barking up the wrong tree here, Hal," Bolan said. "This guy is definitely connected with someone on the other side of the border."

"And you suspect it's Jose Carillo?"

"That I don't know. I don't have much more right now than a strong suspicion."

"Frankly, Striker, I'd trust your hunches before those of most."

"Does Sapèdas have any family?"

"His mother is in a nursing facility in El Paso. Her health is apparently failing. His father died of a heart attack six years ago."

"Okay. Listen, I had a little encounter here in Las Vegas. Barb, what do you know about the Chinese triad and their activities here?"

"Well, they definitely have an active role there, but I wouldn't say it's a large one," she replied.

"Would it be large enough that they might feel some need to protect it with automatic weapons and trained soldiers?"

"It would depend on which group you were talking about. The Chinese primary involvement in Las Vegas has been money laundering and check fraud. For the past few years, several groups across the country have been sending mules from all over the country to kite or cash forged checks. They then take the money and pull their people out before any action can be taken. The police have caught maybe a few offenders over the years, and those who will talk say they were put up to it by known members of local Chinese criminal organizations. But if a Chinese triad does have a major operation running there, it's probably a relatively new one.''

''Well, I managed to get an SMG I took off a hit team in Mexico and sent this to Cowboy. He's next on my list to call. I'm hoping he'll have some answers.''

John ''Cowboy'' Kissinger was the Farm's resident weapons expert. Most firearms of this nature were modified in one way or another to make them untraceable. Many times, special acids were used or polymer fills to alter serial numbers, while others were reworked with generic bolts and special reloads. Kissinger knew many signature techniques well.

''Yes, perhaps Cowboy will be able to figure out where these weapons are coming from,'' Price said.

''Or at least what group would have potentially had access to them,'' Kurtzman added.

''Yeah,'' Bolan said. ''So far, none of this makes any sense. I can't find any sensible link that would connect Carillo's organization with the Chinese, or vice versa.''

''You've got your work cut out for you on this one, Striker,'' Brognola said.

''Tell me about it.''

''Is there anything else we can help you with?'' Price asked.

''Not right at the moment.''

''Well, you know we're here if you need us,'' Brognola said.

''Thanks. You guys take care of yourselves. Out here.''

Bolan disconnected the call and sat for a moment in silent contemplation. Stony Man had come through with the information and he didn't really know much more than he had before. Kurtzman had hit the nail on the head when he'd remarked about Sapèdas having time and opportunity to create allies in the Mexican drug trade. The pieces to the puzzle were starting to fall in place, but Bolan wasn't wholly convinced all the players had shown their hand. If he were going to put it together, he'd have to wait for them to make their next move.

And when they did, the Executioner would make his.

Toronto, Canada

LAU SHUI SAT in stony silence and listened carefully as Ing Kaochu reported their failure. An unknown party had interfered with the observation team they put on the Border Patrol officer. This mysterious American had single-handedly dealt a crippling blow to Ing Kaochu's Scarlet Dragon enforcers in Mexico, and subsequently foiled attempts by a second team to capture him alive in Las Vegas. As Kaochu concluded his report, Lau Shui maintained his silence, opting to stare at the head of the Kung Lok soldiers with a mixture of disappointment and distaste.

"What do you make of this man, Ing?" Shui finally asked.

Kaochu cleared his throat before replying, "I do not know what to make of him, and I do not know who he is."

"Obviously, he is proving to be a formidable opponent," Shui replied. "From what you've told me thus far, I would have to conclude he is quite well trained."

"It is possible he works for the American government," Kaochu interjected. "Perhaps the CIA or DEA."

Shui considered this a moment but quickly dismissed

the idea with a wave of his hand. "It is possible but highly unlikely. American agents are not so bold. They do not engage in open firefights in such a manner, and they most certainly are not trained in military tactics of this kind. This man fights like a soldier."

"Then you think he is military?"

"I think he is on his own," Shui replied, shaking his head. "Maybe receiving intelligence from a more unorthodox source. Let us consider this logically a moment, Ing." Lau Shui rose and began to walk around the room, his arms folded and a finger touching his lips in contemplation. "He operates independently, with apparently little or no outside support. He is proficient with both firearms and with his bare hands and he will avoid any encounters with law enforcement when possible."

"What makes you think that, Lau?"

Shui stopped in his tracks, turned on his heel and smiled at his longtime associate and friend. "If he was operating under sanctions, then why not wait for the American police to arrive? What does he have to fear? Why does he run away? Come now, Ing, you of all people should know that in order to defeat a strong enemy, you must understand him. You must know his strengths and weaknesses, and you must manipulate the situation to your advantage. Only then will your knowledge allow you leverage against an opponent and facilitate your victory over him."

"As always, I am shamed by your wisdom," Ing said with a bow.

"One day, I will be the head of the entire Kung Lok organization. I intend for your authority to become second only to my own. Perhaps you may even step up to take my place."

"I am honored by your confidence in my abilities. Do you wish me to handle the elimination of this man personally?"

"No, I need you for other things more worthy of your talents," Shui replied quickly. "For the time being, we should watch this man and nothing more. You will know when the time is right."

"It shall be as you wish," Kaochu said. "What do you want me to do?"

"My sources tell me that Jose Carillo has enlisted the help of the Colombians. Namely, the leader of the FARC, Colonel Amado Nievas. I do not think I need to remind you, Ing, that this man is competent and very dangerous. He has as many as ten thousand men at his command, and could do considerable damage to our plans for the U.S. However, we have one advantage."

"And that is?"

"The majority of his people have their hands full of problems. Between fighting the Colombian government, battling various international law-enforcement agencies and protecting the drug product, Nievas will only have limited resources. Nonetheless, Nievas poses the greater threat. Do you understand?"

"Of course."

"Therefore, if our plans to dominate the drug and sex trade in America are to succeed, this alliance can never come to its full potential. We need Carillo, of course, because he supplies the product that will make us wealthy beyond our wildest imagination. But Nievas is interested only in guns. He cares little for Carillo's profit, and that could become rather detrimental to our investment."

"But we have arranged for our people to supply the guns."

"Those are only tools of convenience. I am certain that Dim Mai is still somewhat resistant to increasing the supply demands necessary to fill these outlandish orders for firepower. It's too risky for him right now, and he stands to lose a considerable amount of profit if our plan doesn't work. I don't completely have his support, and I'm certain he has gone back to Hong Kong to run me down to the council. I have to prove that this can work to our mutual benefit."

"Are you saying that we should not supply the weapons for Carillo in order that we may squash this alliance?"

"Not exactly. I am simply suggesting that we do not fill the orders in the quantity that they are asking. It's too risky, and we should make them understand this. Carillo is not a foolish man, mind you, and we would both be prudent to keep that in mind. He does not realize that we are actually on the receiving end of profit from both sides of this. But he's also intelligent enough to realize that his ability to move his drugs across the border is dependent upon two things. First, that he can find ways of keeping the American officials looking the other way. Second, that he is able to keep the competition to a minimum."

"But as you have said," Kaochu interrupted pointedly, "he does not know that we are both friend and foe."

"But he could find out, and that is why upon securing the full trust and dependence of Nievas, you will be the one to do the honors. I believe that time may come sooner than either of us would believe."

"What are you saying?"

"I'm saying that when we have complete control of the situation, I want you to kill Colonel Nievas. And eventually, we will eliminate those involved in the American government, as well. Then, and only then, will we truly have complete control of every major city in the United States. And then the Kung Lok will be all-powerful."

CHAPTER FIVE

Las Vegas, Nevada

Within a few hours of talking with Stony Man, Bolan had his answers.

He'd reached John "Cowboy" Kissinger—or rather the weapons expert had located him—and discovered the gun had signature reworks that pointed toward the Kung Lok triad. That explained a lot to the Executioner, and brought him one step closer to discovering what the connections were between the Kung Lok and Jose Carillo. To Bolan's way of thinking, the answer was that there really wasn't a connection between the two groups—at least none other than a coincidental one.

Kissinger was convinced that the weapon was the handiwork of the Kung Lok, and that could only mean one thing: Dim Mai was involved. Everyone who was anyone in intelligence circles across the globe knew that Dim Mai controlled every firearm imported by the Kung Lok, and those supplied or traded in the Asian Pacific. For this very reason, there was no arms dealer or supplier in Southeast Asia more powerful than Dim Mai. From southern Russia to Indonesia, weapons were in high demand, and Mai was one of the select few capable of meeting that demand. Almost all suppliers, regardless of nationality, location or creed, got their guns and munitions from Dim Mai in one way or another. That made him a very dangerous man—it also made him a most likely candidate behind this new and seemingly endless cache of weapons mysteriously appearing in drug smuggling and dealing.

Nonetheless, something told the Executioner that Mai wasn't the only one behind the Kung Lok initiative. Bolan knew enough about the Kung Lok to know that it was highly irregular for the triad to operate so openly as he'd seen here. The Kung Lok was run by a group of wealthy politicians in what most were calling the "new Hong Kong." These men were actually controlled by the underbosses, who allowed the politicians to think they were running the show. Two others had major operations: the eastern and western underbosses. Frankly, Bolan found it hard to believe that the underboss of the eastern triad, Yi-chang Shen, would have dared attempt to muscle into the U.S. or any of its neighboring territories. That left only one possibility, and Bolan was betting it was a strong one.

Lau Ming Shui, sometimes known derogatorily by his competitors as "Merciless Ming," was just the kind of triad gangster who might actually try to insert himself into the American drug scene. After all, where there was gambling there were vices, and where there were vices there were drugs. Popular designer drugs, just like 3-4 MDMA, PCP and the date-rape drugs. There was also the standard stock of cocaine and heroine, bought with sex, hot merchandise or by any other means that could be dreamed by animal man.

Like the Jamaicans had done in the late 1980s, much

to the dismay of the Italian and Latino crime families, Shui might possibly envision a ripe market just there for the taking. This wouldn't sit well with Mexican mafia, and Bolan knew it. So did Shui, if his reputation was anything like the intelligence community gossiped it was, and he would definitely have a need to protect his newfound interests. So it seemed more than feasible that they would start such an operation here in the sex-and-drug capital of the American Southwest. They take all the peddlers and competition off the streets, they insert Danny Tang's men instead, then they have Mai supply weapons to the Scarlet Dragons. That could mean only one thing: war was coming to America in a way no one could have foreseen. A war that would take an unimaginable toll if someone didn't step in before things got worse. Mack Bolan was just the one to do the stepping. And he was going to start by stepping on the neck of Danny Tang.

He lowered the miniature night-vision goggles, stowing them in his satchel. He was attired in the skintight blacksuit, the special woolen material insulating him against the cold evening rain that was falling softly on the roof where he was keeping his vigil. The streetlights below reflected off the rain-swept streets and sidewalks separating the two buildings, gleaming like an oily sheen.

The Beretta and .44 Magnum Desert Eagle were both in place, but the satchel took the place of the LBE suspenders he normally wore. There was an HK-53 submachine gun slung across his right shoulder. One of the most versatile and accurate SMGs in the world, the HK-53 was perfect for a soft probe like this. While some argued that this compact version of the HK-33E didn't really qualify as an SMG because it was chambered for the 5.56 mm NATO cartridge, Bolan disagreed. He'd used the weapon many times before, and aside from the Fabrique Nationale FNC, it was one of the most reliable. The Executioner knew that given the amount of resistance so far there was a good chance things could go hard in a hurry. He was hoping the sound suppressor—customized by Kissinger—would buy him some time before shots alerted the police while not compromising firepower.

He had a specific target in mind. Through some of Vito Rosetti's contacts, Bolan knew that the particular house he was watching, a veritable mansion in a neighborhood like this, was owned by Linghup "Danny" Tang. Tang was a major player in the Asian bride game, which was still in demand in places like Las Vegas. It was open season for American men seeking "little China doll to keep house happy and bed warm." Oh yes, it was still big business, and Tang had the contacts to keep it profitable. But a small part of the cut had to be going into Lau Shui's pocket. Bolan wanted to know exactly how much and where it was going.

The Executioner stepped onto the slippery parapet and raised his subgun into position. The weapon had been modified by Kissinger. Attached by rings around the barrel and muzzle was an aluminum tube that contained a single propellant charge. Protruding from the tube was a sharp, five-hooked steel claw attached to a length of thin, galvanized aircraft cable coated by foam rubber. Bolan extended his arm, took careful aim and then tapped another hook attached to the back of the tube and just in front of the trigger guard. There was a pop and small hiss before the special climbing cable arced gracefully across the chasm and attached itself to the eaves on the far side of the house. Bolan then detached the tube, wrapped the cable twice around the chimney of the roof, and snared the hook against the cable. Without hesitation, he ventured out and shimmied hand over hand twenty feet above the rain-slick pavement. He reached the other side in less than thirty seconds and dropped almost soundlessly onto the roof. Between the pitch and shingle material, the roof was very slippery, and the Executioner had to hold on to the cable with one hand while he ascended one side and came down the other on his belly.

Bolan reached the deck and slowly lowered himself onto it. It extended halfway around the house, and the room beyond the sliding glass doors was dark. Billowy curtains whipped inward under the gentle wind. The Executioner was surprised to find that only the screen door was attached. He yanked his Colt Combat knife from the sheath at the small of his back and quickly cut away the thin screening material. He pushed it aside, creating an opening large enough to crawl through.

The room, which looked like an office or study, was vacant. The hallway door stood slightly ajar, letting just enough light into the room that Bolan could make out the shapes of a desk, some chairs and a rather large bookcase that took up one wall. He allowed himself another moment of orientation before moving to the door. He unslung the HK-53 before catfooting to the door and peering into the hallway. Everything seemed quiet—a little too quiet to suit the Executioner's tastes.

The soldier stepped into the hallway and walked its length until he reached stairs descending to the first floor. He backtracked, quietly opening the door of each room, checking for Tang's gunners before moving on to the next one. He didn't want to get outflanked by enemy troops because he'd been too lazy to check for their presence.

The last room held a surprise.

The woman was tall; he could tell even though she was lying beneath bright white linen sheets. Dark hair cascaded to her shoulders, as silky smooth as the cleavage into which it dipped. She had brown eyes, not quite almond-shaped in contrast to the high cheekbones, with creamy shoulders and ruby-red lips heavily coated with lip gloss. There was some sort of strange aroma in the room—maybe jasmine or cinnamon, but definitely a spice. There was also something attached to her wrists, and Bolan quickly recognized they were leather restraints manacled to the bedposts with thick ropes.

He closed the door and moved quickly to the bed as the woman started to scream. The soldier jammed a rough palm against her mouth and shook his head. Finally, she nodded her understanding. Bolan didn't release his hand from her mouth immediately, waiting a moment or two until he felt something wet on his hand. She was crying and the muffled noises coming from her mouth weren't screams, but rather whimpers.

"Keep quiet and keep breathing," the Executioner warned her sternly. "Understood?"

She nodded and he finally released her. She nearly choked on her spit and blurted, "Th-thank God. Who are you?"

"You first," Bolan told her, even as he was pulling his knife and cutting the leather restraints from her wrists.

"Noreen Zahn. I'm an agent with the DEA, assigned

with undercover operations three months ago to penetrate Danny Tang's outfit.''

Bolan eyed her suspiciously as he replaced his knife. The muzzle of the HK-53 hadn't moved from being trained dead center on her chest. One wrong move and he could trigger a sustained burst with hardly a sound. His mission could still be accomplished with her alive or dead, and until she provided a more reasonable explanation for being tied up and naked in what was obviously the master bedroom, Bolan wasn't taking any chances.

''Get into your work?'' Bolan commented.

She rubbed her wrists self-consciously and snapped, ''Two nights ago, he came in here and started to ask a lot of strange questions. I knew just by the way he was acting that I was blown. The only thing I couldn't figure was who he'd talked to.''

''Tang has a lot of friends. No idiot in his right mind would have put you into a cover role like this. Especially not as a supposed girlfriend.''

''What do you mean?''

''I'll explain later. You have clothes?''

She nodded and pointed to a nearby dresser.

''Get into them, quickly and quietly. And if you play any games with me, I'll figure you for one of them and take care of business.''

She indicated she understood as she got off the bed and went quickly to the dresser. The Executioner took an appreciative look and then returned his attention to the door. He kept one eye on it, the other on his new discovery. Her story sounded legit anyway, and he didn't bother to get into any of the details with her. God only knew what she might have suffered at the hands of a maniac like Danny Tang. It wasn't his place and it wasn't his problem. He needed to complete his mission and get the hell out of there before things became even more complicated.

Zahn was dressed in less than two minutes. She didn't have any shoes, but a pair of flip-flops in the bathroom did the trick. She was rather lithe and agile looking in her loose-fitting blue jeans and red sweater. Well, it wouldn't do much good keeping to the shadows now. They were alone on the second floor, which meant Tang and his men were on the first floor and apparently preoccupied with something more important.

Within five minutes, the Executioner knew what that something was. There was an indoor pool—actually more like a very large Jacuzzi whirlpool—on the first floor off the kitchen. The lights were on, music was blaring and it appeared Danny Tang was entertaining some lady friends. There were also several other men in the Olympic-sized hot tub, and these gentleman were also being swarmed by topless Asian and American escorts.

Bolan let his eyes rove over the scene, more concerned with the numerous hardcases ranged around the whirlpool, pistols and machine pistols within easy reach. He took a brief count, the numbers running in his head, and he realized that he would have less than thirty seconds to neutralize any resistance. Longer than that could result in disastrous consequences.

So he would just have to do it in under that.

Bolan whispered quick instructions to Zahn, advising her to find a way out and wait for him in his rental car. She nodded, stopped to give him a brief expression of thanks and then disappeared around the corner. With the woman out of the way, Mack Bolan knew it was time to get down to business. He needed to talk to Tang.

The Executioner was like a ghostly wraith as he pulled a flash-bang grenade from his satchel and slid aside the steam-covered door. No one immediately looked toward the entrance or took notice of him, as the music was loud enough to mask the sound of his entrance. By the time the first few pairs of eyes realized someone had entered the room, the flash-bang was already sailing through the air and descending toward the middle of the hot tub.

Bolan raised his HK-53, thumbed the selector to 3-round-burst mode and squeezed the trigger. The only sound above the *phut-phut-phut* of the suppressor was the ratcheting noise of the rolling bolt mechanism as 5.56 mm shell casings were extracted from the chamber. The soldier took the first two before anyone actually realized what was happening. The bullets chopped holes and ripped flesh from the two thugs carrying Jatimatics, throwing them against the far wall and leaving gory streaks on the wall.

Bolan then closed his eyes, opened his mouth and covered his ears as he rolled away from a hail of slugs spitting from other guns throughout the room. The flash-bang made short work of most of the whirlpool's occupants, and even took a few of Tang's gunmen by surprise. The women began to scream, clawing at the men who were either stunned by the blast of the concussion grenade or scrambling to get clear of the steaming water.

One gunner tried to angle for a better shot as Bolan was now behind the cover of the above-ground hot tub, but the guy was a moment too late. The Executioner had switched to full-auto and now triggered the HK-53. An ugly corkscrew pattern ripped through the man's belly and chest, tearing flesh from his body and slamming him into a portable wet bar positioned against one corner.

Bolan now leaned back against the hot tub and turned in time to see another gunner appear. There was no time to bring the SMG to bear. He unleathered the Beretta and squeezed the trigger at the moment he had target acquisition. The first 9 mm subsonic round hit Tang's man in the hand, tearing off several fingers and knocking his weapon from his grip. The man screamed as he turned away from the shots and reached for an automatic pistol shoved into the front of his pants. Bolan shot him a second time, this bullet puncturing his lower back. The guy staggered forward and crashed through a sliding glass door.

The Executioner jumped to his feet and lurched around the tub, heading in Tang's direction. He needed to get the high-priced pimp in a vulnerable position. When men like Tang were in a vulnerable position, they started to sing like canaries if they thought for even a second they might walk away and turn a bad situation good. Had it been an actual soldier from the Kung Lok triad, or a member of the Scarlet Dragons, things might have been different. But Tang was soft and Westernized, and the Executioner planned to use that to his advantage.

Nobody in the whirlpool apparently even noticed Bolan, seemingly more intent on getting out of there. Only two remained standing from Tang's protection team. The two goons tried to split up, giving Bolan two separate targets to worry about, but the soldier wasn't buying it.

He raised the HK-53, the muzzle of the SMG tracking the gunman trying to split from his partner. The

5.56 mm NATO rounds found their mark, punching holes in the guy's head and shoulders. He dropped from view behind the hot tub. The barrel of the subgun continued on, taking out the second guy with well-placed head shots.

Bolan calmly walked to where Tang was still trying to leave the hot tub. He was obviously stunned by the ferocity of the Executioner's surprise attack. His eyes moved fast as he tried to recover from the blinding light of the flash-bang grenade. Bolan slung the subgun, then dragged Tang's body from the water by a handful of hair. The pimp stumbled from the hot tub and fell onto his knees. Water splashed from his body, soaking the floor around the Executioner's combat boots.

"Who the fuck are you?" Tang spit.

"Judgment," Bolan said, his eyes narrowing as he drew the .44 Desert Eagle. The hood's eyes rolled to look at the large gun, and the Executioner knew immediately he was having the desired effect. "You've been riding the free train for entirely too long, Danny boy. I'm here to punch your ticket."

"Who sent you? Did Rosarez send you?" Tang stammered.

"If you're referring to drug-running slime Benny Rosarez, then the answer's no. I'm done answering questions. Now you're going to answer mine."

"And if I refuse?" Tang challenged him.

The Executioner produced a frosty smile and pressed the muzzle of the pistol against his forehead. "I'll get my information elsewhere."

Tang gulped. "I see your point. What do you want to know?"

"Who keeps tabs on you, Tang?"

"What do you mean?"

"Just what I asked. You don't expect me to believe you're on your own. Members of the Scarlet Dragons paid me a visit this morning. I think you sent them."

"No, I swear. I don't even know you," Tang pleaded.

"Wrong answer," Bolan said, pressing the muzzle tighter against his forehead for emphasis.

"Wait! I swear to God, man, I don't know what you're talking about."

"Then if you didn't send them, who did? They were Chinese triad goons, and that has your fingerprints all over it. Everyone knows you control the porn action in Vegas." Bolan had played the guy's ego; now he would deal the final hand. "But someone gets a cut of the action, don't they? You're going to tell me who, and if I believe you I'm going to let you live. It's a good deal, Tang. Don't pass up a good deal."

"Who says I major in the action here, pal?" Tang said, trying one last time to play the role of victim rather than victimizer.

"You must think I'm stupid, Danny boy," Bolan replied. He jerked his head in the direction of the now empty hot tub and added, "This place looks like a Bangkok bathhouse. Not to mention the woman you had tied up was ratted out by someone within the DEA. You honestly think I don't know what you're into?"

"Okay, okay," he stammered, raising his arms. "You promise to let me live?"

"I promise zip. But you have nothing to lose, either."

"Okay, it's a guy named Ing Kaochu. He heads up the Scarlet Dragons, and they pick up the cut once a month. I used to pay some of Rosarez's guys to mule for me, but that's all changed. Someone pushed him out. That's all I know."

Well, that cinched it. That explained why Randy Lovato, a major pusher for Rosarez, left Las Vegas and got killed in El Paso. Now, Rosarez was out of the action. Compared to the Carillo crime cartel, Rosarez was small-time and it probably hadn't been hard for a group the size of the Kung Lok to bring him down. It was all starting to make sense.

"Does this Kaochu work for Lau Ming Shui?"

"I don't know. Maybe. Let's face it, *everyone* in the trade works for Shui."

Bolan shook his head. "No dice. Vegas has always been owned and operated by the Mob, and I don't think the Kung Lok triad has enough guts to muscle into their territory."

"You fool! The Mob's been about gambling here and little else. They leave the other shit to us. They keep their hands clean, while we work the streets for the sex and the dope. That way if it hits the fan, it's the yellow man who goes down and not them."

"Then why are the Scarlet Dragons here in force?"

"Rumor has it Merciless Ming is making a play for the big time."

"Gambling?"

"No, but all of the drug and skin action. We've been paying him protection, and now he's actually turning on us. It could start a war, you know. There are some who just won't take it."

"Like the Mexican drug cartels?"

There was a flash in Tang's eyes, and Bolan nodded. It was the information he'd been looking for, and it confirmed beyond a shadow of a doubt that the Kung Lok triad was involved. Moreover, it told him they were making a play for stuff that had primarily been controlled by Carillo and others within the Mexican mafia groups. That could only mean trouble down the line.

"You tell Kaochu to take a message back to his master," Bolan demanded. "You tell him that *nobody* is going to poison American kids. Not while I'm alive. You hear me?"

"I hear you."

"Get out of this business, Tang. While you still can."

Once he'd escaped from Tang's place, it only took Bolan a few minutes to reach his rental parked a few blocks away. He used the time to mull the new information as he jogged to the sedan. There was a very serious situation brewing, and he knew it was about to go sour. Time was against him, but he now had enough information to act.

With the Kung Lok triad obviously vying for a solid position in Las Vegas—and probably other hot spots—war was imminent. Bolan knew there was only one way to slow it down, and that was to take out one side of the conflict first. He would have to concentrate on the triad, since it was the more immediate threat. What had been going on with the Carillo cartel had been going on for some time. For the moment, he would have to let the DEA and Border Patrol handle that.

Which brought the Executioner to Lisa Rajero and her people. Bolan was betting whoever had blown the whistle on Zahn was also playing two ends against the middle with Rajero and the Kung Lok. The Executioner couldn't do much more at the moment than warn her. He'd see what information Zahn had, and maybe help Rajero come one step closer to finding out who in the

DEA, be it Metzger or someone else, was friendly with the enemy. The more he thought about it, the more Bolan realized he was going to have to fight a war on two fronts. A war that was going to get very hot.

CHAPTER SIX

"You need to drive for a while," Bolan told Zahn.

"What's wrong?"

"I'm bleeding."

The Executioner hadn't detected it at first, but he had to have pulled enough skin away to foul up Rosetti's stitch job. Nonetheless, the middle of the desert in the late afternoon, even on a road as busy as U.S. Highway 95, was neither the place nor the time to bleed to death. Bolan was an accomplished medic in his own right, so he would have to just deal with it here and now.

He pulled off the road and traded places with Zahn. She got behind the wheel, quickly adjusted her seat and then turned to look at him and cleared her throat. "You know, I didn't properly thank you back there for pulling my bacon out of the fire."

The Executioner shook his head. "Forget it. Maybe you'll get to repay the favor some time."

"I can think of many ways I'd like to repay it now."

"I'm sure you could," Bolan replied with a grin. "But I need to keep my mind on business and you need to keep your own on the road. We have to get back to Brownsville before something else goes wrong."

She nodded her understanding although she didn't

hide the disappointment in her expression. As she put the car in gear and pulled onto the highway she asked, "Wouldn't it have just been faster to fly?"

"Yeah, and it would have made it ten times easier for the Scarlet Dragons to track us."

She looked at him with disbelief. "Did you say the Scarlet Dragons? I mean, are we talking *the* Scarlet Dragons of the Kung Lok triad?"

Bolan had to admit he was impressed with Zahn's insight. As a matter of fact, he was beginning to wonder if she weren't a little too insightful. The Drug Enforcement Administration was thorough in its training, but unless things had changed in recent times, he wasn't aware that training went extensively into Chinese triads and tongs. Ostensibly, local law-enforcement agencies and federal groups like the FBI and BATF were more likely to encounter Chinese triad activity than the DEA.

On the other hand, it was quite possible Zahn had acquired the knowledge on her own. He wasn't sure he bought that story, but it wasn't enough to think she was a mole that the enemy had put purposely in his path. Even if members of the Kung Lok were onto him, they wouldn't have had any reason to think the Executioner would hit Danny Tang. Everyone knew about the Scarlet Dragons, but not many people were up to snuff on Chinese organized crime factions like the Kung Lok. For Zahn to immediately tie the two together was a clear sign of her training—or perhaps her allegiance.

In either case, Bolan would have to keep an eye on her.

It took him only a few minutes to re-dress the wound. The bleeding was minimal, as only two of Rosetti's stitches had pulled loose. Bolan gritted his teeth as he managed to pull the silk thread tight to close the wound, then dressed it with fresh bandages he'd bought at a grocery store on the outskirts of Vegas.

"Looks like that's going to leave a scar," Zahn noted, glancing occasionally at him with an expression of concern.

"It won't be the first," Bolan replied matter-of-factly.

"So you think the Kung Lok has something to do with Danny Tang?"

For some reason, she had abruptly changed the subject again. Bolan had noticed in his previous conversations with her that Zahn did this frequently. Some people would have said it was a sign of high intelligence, but the Executioner couldn't help but be a bit annoyed by it. Still, she'd proved herself an insightful companion so he could overlook the little personality quirks.

When he'd completed his patch job, Bolan removed the Beretta from his shoulder holster and quickly set to the task of cleaning the weapon. He retrieved a military cleaning kit from the glove compartment, keeping the Desert Eagle close at hand beneath the pull-down console of the rental. It wouldn't do to have an attack come with his only means of defense sitting in pieces on the dashboard.

Bolan pulled a can of gun scrubber from beneath the seat and then placed a paper bag he'd acquired from the grocery store on the floor mat between his feet. He quickly disassembled the moving parts of the 93-R with practiced efficiency, and sprayed them with the gun scrubber. The cleaning material acted like a liquid freon, instantly neutralizing the powder residue and metal fouling of the weapon. It allowed Bolan to simply use a toothbrush to strip away what resembled little more than hamster droppings. The entire process took less than five minutes, and after a light coat of oil the Beretta was back in place and ready for action.

"You mentioned something before that piqued my interest," Zahn said, breaking the silence in which she'd left him to his work.

"What's that?"

"You said that nobody in their right mind would have put me into Tang's operation in an undercover role. What did you mean by that?"

Bolan didn't answer immediately, wondering if he should bring up Lisa Rajero. It was still too early for him to completely trust Zahn, but he was convinced she was definitely a legit member of the DEA. He just wasn't sure if that was the only place she was collecting her pay. He didn't want to be paranoid, but he didn't want to compromise innocents, either. Then it occurred to him that Zahn had been one of the victims of whoever was trying to sabotage DEA efforts against the Mexican drug cartel.

"You said you were sent out of the Brownsville office to penetrate Tang's operation?"

She nodded. "We had informants who told us Tang was getting into the drug scene in Las Vegas. The local office there was concerned that with Tang's connections, one of their people would get blown the minute we made contact. So my superiors asked for a volunteer and I stepped up."

Bolan shook his head and scowled. "Then somebody tried to blow you."

"I don't understand, Mike," she said with a shrug. "What would anyone within the DEA in Brownsville have to gain by blowing my cover in Las Vegas?"

"I don't have the answer to that question...yet," Bolan remarked. "I'm not even sure it's someone in the DEA."

"Then what were you doing in Vegas?"

"Following a hunch," he told her flatly. "There's a definite connection between the U.S. Border Patrol in El Paso and the Kung Lok triad. I don't know what that connection is, but it could be related to something Tang told me. The Scarlet Dragons are basically in Vegas to stomp out competition and prepare for a large movement by the Kung Lok organization. I don't know which cities they plan to hit, but I do know they're cutting into major holdings of the Mexican crime cartel."

Zahn whistled with disbelief. "That could get damn ugly. Maybe we should let our people know when we get back."

"No dice," Bolan countered, shaking his head emphatically. "If someone in your department *was* trying to get you out of the way, you'll be safer if they think Tang killed you. Do you know Agent Rajero?"

"Yes. Lisa and I worked together on a sting operation once before. I have nothing but respect for her."

"Her boss suspended her after a bust they had set up went sour. I think the only one set up was Rajero. She's convinced he had something to do with it."

"Are we talking about Charlie Metzger?"

"Yeah."

"He was the one who assigned me to Tang."

"You have any reason to think he's dirty? Or to think that possibly he's the one who blew your cover?"

"No. I like Charlie...always have." She smiled, tossing Bolan a wink and a knowing look before adding,

"He's a pain in the ass at times, like most bosses can be, but on the whole he likes his people."

"He doesn't seem to have much like for Rajero."

"Well, you probably wouldn't, either, if you knew what Metzger does. A few years ago, Lisa took down a corrupt lieutenant who was sexually harassing female members of his staff. That was the sting she involved me in, as I worked for this jerk and put up with his sick advances. I was glad when they finally brought him down."

"So Metzger knows Rajero was involved. He's got nothing to worry about if he's on the level, so why hold it against her?"

"You don't understand much about the DEA. It's like any law-enforcement agency. People get close. These people watch out for your ass and you watch out for theirs."

"I understand loyalty and friendship much better than you might think," Bolan reminded her.

Something flashed in Zahn's eyes—something that alternated between surprise and hurt—but then it disappeared as quickly as it had come. Bolan was watching for a further reaction but it never came.

"You're right, of course," she said quietly. "I'm sorry."

"No need to be," he replied. "What we need to do now is get back to Brownsville and contact Rajero before the Scarlet Dragons figure out where we went and give chase."

"Do you think they'll come after us?"

"They'll certainly try, after I left the message I did with Tang and told him to give it to his superiors."

"That's pretty brave of you, Mike," Zahn observed,

"considering what you're up against. Are you crazy or just suicidal?"

"I'm just setting the bait."

"And what if they decide to take it?"

There was a hard edge in Bolan's voice as he replied, "I'll be ready."

Stony Man Farm, Virginia

HAROLD BROGNOLA, director of the Sensitive Operations Group and head of the ultracovert agency known as Stony Man Farm, was angry. Mack Bolan, friend and ally, was out there on his own and risking his life to clean up the streets of America. Brognola owed more than just his life to the Executioner—he owed the man the lives of his family, as well. So when he knew that his longtime friend and ally could be in trouble, he would pull out all of the stops and do whatever was necessary to help him. Except in this case, Brognola had been given a direct order from the President of the United States just fifteen minutes earlier that he was *not* to interfere.

"Not under any circumstances, Hal," the President had said. "Am I being clear?"

"But, sir, Striker needs support on this one. There's a very strong possibility that members of our own government could be involved in this. Members high up in the Border Patrol…or possibly even in Justice."

"The federal agencies under the DOJ are your domain, Hal. If you have some strong evidence to support such an accusation, then I'm willing to grant carte blanche and open a full investigation. But Stony Man's tactics are just too radical on such premature assumptions.''

"I'd like to put Able Team on standby.''

"You can run your outfit however you think is best, Hal. You know I won't interfere in that respect. However, I will caution you that no activation is to occur unless you have my express permission. Your men have been in this position before. I understand your concern, but I'm not sure I understand the level thereof.''

"The reason I'm concerned about this situation is because Striker hasn't been able to clearly identify the enemy.''

"From what you've told me so far, it sounds like he may have more than one,'' the President observed. "And then again there may be none at all. I'm sorry, Hal, but I just don't see enough evidence there to give the go-ahead to move. If you can bring me something more tangible, then I'm willing to get the ball rolling. Now, I have to meet with the Joint Chiefs.''

"I understand, sir. Thank you for your time. I'll be in touch.''

"You do that, Hal.''

And that had been it. Brognola thought he knew why the President was hedging on this one, but he wasn't sure he understood it. Mack Bolan had saved the country more times than anyone cared to count. To ask that Stony Man support him now—even when the guy was on his own on an unsanctioned mission—wasn't too much to ask. At least not as far as the head Fed was concerned. In fact, Brognola couldn't believe the Oval Office was taking this stance.

Well, the President was at least willing to look at any new or solid evidence that could prove Bolan's theory of operation between the Mexican drug cartel and officials in the Border Patrol. It was an old story, sure, but it wasn't as common as it had been in the early 1980s. The scandals surrounding the Noriega syndicate, not to mention the Iran-Contra arms affair and other such incidents, had certainly turned America on its ear. The number of investigations into corruption in American politics during this hotbed of activity had been equaled only by those of the McCarthy era.

Brognola just couldn't stand by and do nothing. He had opted against putting Able Team on full alert. They could be called up if needed when that time came, but this wasn't that time. Not that they wouldn't have raced to Vegas, Brownsville—or halfway across the globe for that matter—to assist Mack Bolan if called upon to do so. And in a pinch, Brognola wouldn't hesitate.

Nonetheless, it wouldn't improve the Executioner's situation to act impulsively or to waste the resources of a valuable team without first having something more solid to go on. The best they could offer Bolan right now was support and intelligence. And Stony Man had plenty of resources to handle that job.

"What do we know?" Brognola asked Barbara Price as soon as she entered the War Room.

"Not a lot," Price replied.

She sat and crossed her shapely legs. The Stony Man mission controller was the kind of woman who could do just about anything and look good doing it. But beyond her fashion-model looks was a depth and intelligence unrivaled by any woman he'd ever known, except, perhaps, his wife. A former member of the NSA SIGINT group, Price had many contacts in the intelligence community. This, coupled with the facts she was hardworking, respected by the others and efficient to a fault, made Price an invaluable member of the Stony Man team.

"We have narrowed down who we believe may be working with the Mexican drug cartel." She opened a file folder and took out a color still that was sharply defined. "A CIA agent in Ciudad Juárez took this photograph three days ago. Aaron's people had to really clean it up before we could make heads or tails but we've positively identified him as Colonel Amado Nievas."

Brognola looked up from the picture with total surprise, hardly able to believe his ears. "The head of the FARC?"

"Well, he's one of them. His primary position is military commander of the FARC joint forces, which involves factions from several different arenas within Colombian territory. He's a formidable opponent, and the Colombian government admits that all efforts to apprehend him have been unsuccessful. He's very well protected, and we were a bit troubled to find him operating so close to U.S. borders."

"Operating in what way?"

"He's considering formation of alliances with Jose Carillo."

"Good God," Brognola breathed.

"And that's not all," a voice interjected.

They turned to see Aaron "the Bear" Kurtzman wheel himself into the War Room. The expression on Kurtzman's face left little to guess that he didn't have any more good news for them than Price had.

"We think that Carillo is looking for a lot more than friendship," Price continued. "We think he's looking to strike a deal with Nievas for protection. Both sides stand to benefit tremendously if the Carillo crime cartel can seize control of the drug trafficking between Mexico and the States."

"And lots of them," Kurtzman answered, rolling himself to a nearby terminal.

Credit-card transactions, banking and funds movements, corporate NASDAQ ratings and other financial information all went through Stony Man Farm. The information was processed, batched and stored by a program designed specifically by Kurtzman.

Kurtzman's job was one that went 24/7, and he never let them down. There were other important features in his database program. Information on every known terrorist organization, past and present, was available at the push of a button; as well as technical schematics on everything from firearms to bicycles. The supercomputers at the Farm's annex were technological marvels, processing, sorting and even—in some case—disseminating information in impressive quantities.

"What else have you come up with, Bear?" Price inquired

"This might get uglier than we had originally thought," Kurtzman replied. He fixed Brognola with an askance expression, adding, "And a whole lot deeper."

"How so?" the Stony Man chief asked.

"Two weeks ago," Kurtzman began, "members of the BATF intercepted a weapons cache being smuggled in aboard a Chinese freighter. Most of them were standard-issue variants of Kalashnikovs, but a small number were Italian-made Jatimatics and some other easily concealed machine pistols. Do you remember when Striker said that he'd sent one of the guns he'd lifted off that Asian hit team to Cowboy?"

They both nodded.

Kurtzman tapped a computer key to dim the lights and then another to project an image on a large screen integrated into the wall. "This is an image of the weapon that he sent to me less than an hour ago. It's a Model 12S, 9 mm submachine gun manufactured by Beretta. We stock some in the armory. According to Cowboy, this has signature machining on it that would suggest the work of Dim Mai's people."

Price nodded in remembrance. "Head of the Kung Lok's arms supply."

"Exactly," Kurtzman acknowledged.

"That's why Striker had asked us about the Chinese operating in Las Vegas," Price said. "They're trying to smuggle arms into the country to help subsidize whatever major operation they're preparing to undertake."

"Okay, let's say you're right," Brognola said. "What does that have to do with any alliance formed between the Colombian FARC and Mexican drug cartel?"

Price looked at him a moment, and then her expression became downcast. "I'm not sure. But I think Mack was onto something here. All other things being equal, he mentioned he couldn't find any logical reason for Carillo and the Chinese to be connected."

All three of them now sat in silence and pondered the issue. Brognola was troubled by the new turn of events. He realized that they were probably barking up the wrong tree, that there really was no relationship between the two entities. Yes, perhaps that was it. Perhaps these incidents were unrelated and the fact that the events had unfolded like they had was pure coincidence. But Brognola wasn't about to buy that line, either. There was some connection here, and it was going to be up to them to figure it out and get the information to the President so he could act.

Or at least get it to Mack Bolan so *he* could act.

"Wait a minute," Price finally said, breaking the long silence. "The two main seats of power in the Kung Lok have always been in China and Canada. They literally control the entertainment industry from a power base in Toronto. Intelligence reports indicate the Western underboss is Lau Ming Shui."

"Head of the Shui Films & Arts Corporation," Brognola acknowledged. "Are you proposing that they might be thinking of breaking new ground here in the States?"

"That's exactly what I'm proposing," she replied.

"That's all well and good in supporting Striker's theory, Barb," Kurtzman reminded her. "But how does it tie into the Colombian-Mexican connection?"

"Hold on, Bear," Brognola chided him. "I'm beginning to understand this. Kung Lok decides it wants to hit the Vegas scene. Now in order to gain control, the triad's going to have to take some things by force. That means eliminating the competition."

"The Mexican drug cartel," Kurtzman said with a nod of understanding. "I see where you're going now, Barb. They smuggle in weapons and use them to take by force what they can't take by attrition."

"Naturally," Price replied. "And when Carillo starts losing his foothold, he calls in Nievas to help him."

"In return for what?" Kurtzman asked.

"Guns," Brognola announced slowly.

"Oh, my God," Price said with a gasp. "War between the FARC and the Kung Lok triad? Here in America?"

"The ramifications of something as heavy as that are

astounding, Hal,'' Kurtzman announced. "We're talking untold loss of lives, property damage in the millions and full-scale chaos for law-enforcement agencies all across the U.S. Lord knows that about the only ones prepared for that kind of conflict would be the National Guard.''

"It's unthinkable, Hal,'' Price added. "We're talking war in our streets. Martial law would have to be declared in the larger cities. And Phoenix Force and Able Team couldn't be everywhere at once, even if we knew where to start.''

Brognola turned to pick up the phone and call the President. "I'm going to let the President know what we think we could up against.''

"What do you need from us?''

"Find Striker. Pronto!''

CHAPTER SEVEN

Brownsville, Texas

Bolan and Zahn arrived without incident.

The Executioner was now behind the wheel, and he drove them straight to Lisa Rajero's place. It was early afternoon—nearly twenty-four hours since Bolan had hit Danny Tang's place—so he was counting on the fact that the high-priced pimp had passed on his message to his masters. It was only a matter of time before the Scarlet Dragons took another shot at him.

In the meantime, however, it was important that he get this information to Rajero. He didn't have the connections in the DEA that she did, and he was going to need her help whether or not he liked it. With his discovery of the connection between the Mexican mafia and the Kung Lok, Bolan didn't have time to pursue the connection between the guns and Border Patrol chief Ramon Sapèdas. He would have to let Rajero handle that; there just wasn't enough time.

Bolan pulled into the parking lot of a small apartment complex one block over and crossed through a backyard with Zahn to reach Rajero's place. He'd already contacted Rajero to tell her they would be arriving, but she was the only one who knew. Unless the enemy had the phones or interior of the house bugged, which Bolan seriously doubted. Rajero wasn't a big enough player to be a threat to those inside the DEA who might be corrupt, and she definitely wasn't a threat to the Kung Lok. As far as the Executioner was aware, they didn't even know she existed.

Bolan hoped to keep it that way.

He knocked on the back door of her house, and a moment later she opened the door. They entered, and the two women glanced at each other just a moment before embracing. The Executioner let out a mental sigh of relief. At least they were on friendly terms—that would make him feel better about leaving Zahn with Rajero. She would be in friendly hands, anyway.

"My God, I thought you were dead!" Rajero said breathlessly.

"So did I," she said, jerking her thumb at Bolan, "until this guy showed up. If it hadn't been for Mike, Danny Tang probably would have raped or beaten me to death by now." She let out a visible shudder.

"Or both," Rajero said with an emphatic nod.

She looked at Bolan and said, "Thanks, Belasko."

"Forget it," he told her. "Sorry to break up your little reunion, but we've got a serious problem."

"Well, come on into the kitchen and I'll pour us some coffee. You guys hungry?"

"I'm famished," Zahn said. "I could use something. And a bathroom."

Rajero nodded, gesturing for Bolan to take a place at the kitchen table and ushering Zahn to the bathroom. She returned a few minutes later and poured both of them some coffee. She said something about Zahn wanting to clean up and then put her chin on her hand and studied the Executioner. She was a damn beautiful woman; one at which Bolan found it easy to stare.

"So, what's the story with Las Vegas? And how did Noreen's cover get blown?"

"I don't know," Bolan replied. "Somebody in your agency probably ratted her out to Tang. Maybe one of the locals in Vegas."

"They didn't know about the operation."

"Somebody had to have known," he countered with a shrug. "She was there at the request of the DEA office."

"The commander of that bureau knew," Rajero said. "As well as myself and Charlie Metzger. That's it."

"I don't know what to tell you," Bolan said. "Either somebody turned her out, or she gave herself away. In either case, at least I happened on to her before the worst."

"Amen to that."

"I'm going to have to leave her here with you. Nobody can know she's still alive until I get a better handle on the situation."

"Is there trouble in Las Vegas?"

"There's trouble all over. When I pulled Zahn out of there, Danny Tang and I had an informative chat. It seems that the Kung Lok triad has decided to move its operations into the desert strip. The triad's starting to hit Mexican drug rings all over the Southwest. That gun I lifted off those hitters in Mexico was what made the connection for me. These guys are muscling into Carillo's action, which is why you ran into trouble the other night on that bust. The fact those guys were ready for you and toting that kind of hardware was no coincidence.''

"What about Chief Sapèdas?" she asked.

"I'm not sure how he figures into this yet, but I'm sure he does," Bolan answered. "I think he may be working for Carillo."

"No chance he's with the Kung Lok? You said on the phone they were the ones who tried to hit you when you were tailing Sapèdas."

"I don't think they were as concerned with me as they were with Sapèdas, true. But after what Tang told me, there's no question they have a hidden agenda. Maybe they were planning to take out Sapèdas and I got in the way."

"Do you really believe that?"

"No, but it's just as believable as my original theory."

"And what if Sapèdas has nothing to do with the Kung Lok?"

"Then he's not my worry."

The Executioner wasn't sure what he'd said wrong, but something went flat in her expression. Rajero's eyes narrowed and she studied him for a moment. He knew what was coming, and he had hoped it wouldn't. This was the chief problem with involving outsiders in his missions, and the very reason why he preferred to work alone. When Bolan was trying to be efficient, others thought he was being cold and heartless.

"This guy may be associating with known criminals and taking payoffs from a Mexican drug lord like Jose Carillo. Now you're telling me that's not your problem?"

"Not when a more serious one presents itself," Bolan

said. "You're more than capable of pursuing Sapèdas, and if that's what you want to do, then I say go for it. As a matter of fact, I'd encourage it. But I'm trying to stop a full-scale war that's about to explode right on the streets, lady. Some things take priority, and this is one of them."

Rajero's expression softened as his words registered. She finally nodded. "You're right, Belasko. I'm sorry I got so hot under the collar."

"Forget it. Where I need to focus now is on the Kung Lok triad. I'm betting that it'll go one step at a time, slowly working its way across the bigger cities, then take care of the smaller fish."

"I agree," Rajero said. "If the triad can control the major distribution pipelines, the other stuff will be a cakewalk. The little dealers and runners don't really give a shit who they pay the cut to, as long as they're treated fairly."

"I can guarantee there won't be any of that."

"What do you mean?"

"If the Kung Lok is like other triads, it believes in a strict monopoly. Profit motive is the driving factor, and competition is costly. Those weren't pop guns being carried by those Scarlet Dragon troops in Vegas. We're talking the real thing here."

"So you think they'll cop a winner-takes-all attitude?"

"I'd bet on it." He stopped a moment to consider their discussion and then asked her, "What areas would you think that they stand to benefit the most by controlling?"

"As far as the drug trades are concerned?"

"Yeah."

"No doubt they'll hit Carillo in Houston. That's where most of the money changes hands and where they bankroll their laundering and distribution operations."

"Easy to hide because of all the money in the oil industry there?"

"Precisely. As far as sales and movement of the drugs themselves, Carillo has known pipelines in El Paso, Brownsville and Nogales. Very little gets run across the Rio Grande. At least not enough that we can't handle it through the agency."

"Looks like quite a bit of territory. I'll have to get some wings."

"Okay, so how do you want to handle this? And how can I help?"

"You've done everything you can. I have ways of getting intelligence, other sources with means not at your disposal."

"I want to be involved," she protested.

"If you really want to help, then find out everything you can about Carillo and Sapèdas," he told her. "And see if you can determine who blew Noreen Zahn. We need to keep her alive in order to find out."

"Can you at least tell me your plan?"

"It's better you don't know. You're alive, and I want to keep it that way."

She did nothing to hide the disappointment in her expression.

"Listen, kid, I just can't take the liability. I've got enough blood on my hands, and I'm not about to add any more."

"I can take care of myself."

Bolan smiled, amused by the woman's spunk. "I know you can. That's why I'm leaving the mission on

Sapèdas all to you. You've got a knack for bringing down dirty cops. You did it before and I think you'll do it again.''

''Where will you start?''

''I think El Paso. From there, I'll have to beat tracks to Houston, Vegas and possibly Phoenix. California will be last on the agenda.''

''You think this Kung Lok triad will actually go that far?''

''They would have to. The Baja strip is a site of major action for both drugs and sex-for-hire. Tang indicated that the Chinese figure these two go hand in hand. That's as close to the truth as it gets.''

''Sounds like a big job.''

Yeah. Bolan meant to retaliate in full; that meant he wasn't going to wait for them to reassemble. He needed to hit the enemy while they were still off balance, and he'd learned long ago the best way for a soldier to do that was swiftly and decisively. Throughout his War Everlasting, the Executioner's policy hadn't really changed. Yet it still seemed the most effective against the savages that preyed on the unsuspecting innocents.

The plan was simple.

Infiltration!

Target identification!

Confirmation!

Destruction!

It was a plan that had served Bolan time and again— one that sent the enemy reeling every time. And that was how he would do it this time. He would bring this war down on top of their evil heads, and he would make them eat the fire of vengeance and retribution. It would be a destructive conflagration like they had never seen before. And when it was all said and done, the Kung Lok and Carillo crime cartel would suffer a debilitating and final blow it wouldn't forget.

Because the Executioner was on the warpath. And it was lined with fire and brimstone.

Chihuahua, Mexico

JOSE CARILLO WATCHED the sun setting on Ciudad Juárez from his porch.

He'd been awaiting Amado's answer for several days now, and the Colombian soldier hadn't responded. Carillo was becoming impatient. He wasn't accustomed to waiting on others, but he knew there wasn't a thing he could do about it. Nievas would do things in his own way and on his own time, and Carillo was just going to have to wait.

The sound of a car approaching woke him from his state of self-pity. He immediately recognized the engine sounds of the jalopy in which Nievas had ridden upon his first visit. The ugly economy car came into view from around the flowers and rock beds lining the winding drive of Carillo's estate.

The Mexican crime lord could barely contain his excitement as he left the porch, sloshing liquid from his tumbler as he quickly descended the stairs. He arrived at the front doors in time to see Nievas emerge from the car. There was a broad grin that immediately spread across the FARC leader's face, and Carillo knew the answer before Nievas even opened his mouth.

"Welcome back to my home, my friend," he said, hugging Nievas in the colonel's traditional fashion.

"Thank you, Jose. I come bearing excellent news."

"You have agreed to my terms?"

"Yes," he said, raising his finger, "but on one condition."

"And that is?"

"I can provide you approximately one hundred of my best men. In return, we ask a small fee in addition to the weapons."

Carillo was a little suspicious now, and he knew his expression had given it away. So they wanted a cut of the action now. That hadn't been discussed as part of the original agreement, and he was wondering just exactly how much this "small fee" would amount to. Still, he had to maintain appearances until he could determine if the offer was reasonable.

"I can see your reticence," Nievas said with a smile. "And believe it or not, I can understand it. But you must understand that I fought against this. The revolution is already getting a considerable amount from this alliance. I did encourage them to accept your terms as offered, Jose, but they would not heed my advice. I hope you understand."

Carillo lent him a wan smile. "I will understand more when you stop apologizing and tell me just exactly how much we're talking about."

"Ah, we come to the point on this. That's what I admire about you, Jose. It is one of the first things I admired when I met you, and I told my people so."

"How much, Amado?"

After he looked down and sighed, he returned his attention to his new ally and replied, "Five percent."

Carillo had to consider it only a moment before he realized it was more than fair. He had thought they were at least going to try for double digits, but they hadn't, so he wasn't going to argue over that. A mere five per-cent in an annual multibillion dollar industry wasn't go-ing to break the bank. And he was even less prepared for what came next.

"And you can keep the books on it. We will trust you to disburse to us whatever this amount will be on a quarterly basis. We'll take cash or product, as long as it's untraceable. This will be payable directly to me and only me, and I will in turn get it to my superiors."

Carillo stuck out his hand and said, "I accept your terms."

The two men shook hands, hugged and then finally entered the air-conditioned house together. They moved through the halls, drinking, smoking Cugan cigars and discussing their plans for the future. It was a good time for celebration, and a good time for talking business. Carillo had something on his mind, though, and he was trying to find a way to tell Nievas. He'd thought seri-ously about simply keeping it to himself, but he knew it was too important to ignore. If Nievas found out that he'd lied, he could pull the plug on the whole deal.

Carillo didn't fear the Colombians—particularly not the FARC—but he damn sure respected them. He knew that Nievas had the resources and firepower to put down ten empires like Carillo's cartel, but it was more a ques-tion of willingness to divert those kinds of forces. After all, only one hundred men wasn't exactly generous when one considered the amount of territory to be covered. Still, the Colombians had their own battles to fight, and that would always take place above Mexican mob prof-its.

Nonetheless, Carillo could live with it. And while maybe he didn't trust all of the Colombians, he trusted this one and he felt it was necessary to maintain that trust by being forthright in certain matters. Particularly when it served the greater interest of his people and his business.

Carillo took a deep breath and said, "A new problem has arisen in your absence. One I could not have foreseen until it reared its ugly head."

"And what is the nature of this problem?" Nievas asked with a tone of genuine interest.

"One of those American authorities I'm financing came to see me a couple of days ago. It would seem that an unidentified U.S. agent is getting closer to the operation in Brownsville."

"And how did this happen?"

"Just before we talked, I received a call that a major shipment had been hit by the DEA in Brownsville."

"You didn't advise me of this."

Carillo shrugged. "You had no reason to know at the time. You hadn't yet accepted my offer, so I saw nothing provoking me to discuss business. Besides, these things happen now and again."

"So where is the problem?"

"The DEA attempted to seize the drugs, but they were destroyed before that could take place. We have not been able to identify exactly who was responsible for this, but the next afternoon there was a DEA agent in the office of this American in my employ. He was asking questions. Questions about guns and how they were found and supposed to be impounded."

"I think I understand now."

Carillo nodded. "We're very concerned that this man could become troublesome to us. As I said, we haven't been able to identify who it was that destroyed our shipment, but we think that the man who showed up in El Paso is a likely suspect. He tried to follow our American friend from the Border Patrol, but somebody stopped him before he could track my man here.''

''And who were these mysterious saviors?'' Nievas asked with suspicion now.

''That we do not know, either. We think that perhaps they were others that this man from the DEA had crossed. He has apparently made many enemies.''

''Then I'm afraid I must recant my original statement. If he's no longer of any concern to us, I do not understand your problem.''

''He's still alive. And we've begun to suffer losses both along the border and in Las Vegas.''

''Surely this one man couldn't put so much pressure on you?''

''We don't know if he's behind it all. There have been no witnesses to any of the hits in Las Vegas and Houston so far. We think that is by design, and perhaps if this man is behind it then he's operating without the sanctions of his government.''

''A freelancer?''

''Possibly, or maybe a mercenary they use to cover their own asses and facilitate plausible deniability.''

''Well, he's only one man so I don't really see how he could be any kind of true threat.''

Carillo wasn't so sure, but he chose not to comment on that. If what Ramon Sapèdas had told him was true, then he had every reason to think it was the same man behind all of their losses to this point. There was no other reasonable explanation.

The American Mafia presence wasn't hcavy enough in Houston to make any notable difference, and drug running wasn't its thing. As a matter of fact, the major players in U.S. organized crime were more business executives, softened by years of luxury and easy money, than the hard-nosed gangsters of the 1960s. And while they might have had the resources to pull off something like this, they didn't have the balls. Carillo knew the Sicilians wouldn't have risked starting an all-out war of rivalry with the Mexican crime families when a peaceful coexistence had worked all of this time. They had tried that with the Jamaicans to no avail.

So there wasn't anything left in his mind, other than the American government. And whether this particularly elusive individual was rogue or sanctioned by the Americans didn't matter.

"I'm convinced that if we eliminate this man, these attacks on our product will stop altogether."

"And if it doesn't?"

"Then we haven't spent considerable resources to destroy the threat. He's only one man, after all."

"Which is why I'm not convinced he's the threat behind these attacks you talk of. Have you considered the possibility of an outside threat?"

"What do you mean?"

"I mean, it's possible that this is another organization looking to take over your business. Perhaps even one of your local competitors."

"I suppose it is possible, Amado, but I consider it highly unlikely."

"Why?"

"Because none of my competitors has those kinds of resources. Moreover, I don't think they would risk standing against me."

"If I'm not mistaken," Nievas shot back with a

crooked smile, "I believe there were those you've put down who probably said the same thing."

"Your observations both flatter and humble me."

"I have to acknowledge that you might be right," Nievas said. "But I still wouldn't rule out anything until you have more evidence."

"But I'm spread thinly enough as it is. I cannot risk spreading myself out to pursue one man."

"If he is behind these attacks, as you suspect, then I imagine he will come to you. Besides, you forget that my people will be here tonight. We may then distribute them at our leisure. I can guarantee you that this man will not last long against soldiers of the revolution."

Carillo chuckled. "I have no doubt of that, my friend."

"I do not want you to worry about this anymore, Jose. We will take care of it when the time is right. If it will make you feel better, I can immediately divert a detachment to Las Vegas to protect your interests there."

"Thank you, my friend. That will certainly ease my conscience. In following your line of thought, there are rumors that a Chinese triad could be involved in this. I do not have any tangible evidence, only suggestions from my intelligence network. For that matter, it could be information being supplied to them by one of my own. But I'm sure eventually we will know who is behind this, and then you may take care of them."

"The triads, eh?" Nievas said thoughtfully, stroking his chin. Finally he added, "That's an interesting theory. I'm certain you are correct. Eventually, you will find out what's going on, and then we may deal with it in an appropriate manner. Now, what are our plans for moving the drugs into America?"

"I have set up three entry points, and two major centers of operation. We presently control the pipelines in El Paso, Brownsville and Nogales. There is still Mexicali to worry about and then how to move the product up safely to San Diego once it is across."

"The areas through the Sonora Desert will not be easy. Particularly around the Baja. That could become a major task. It might be better to forget this altogether, and utilize the other pipelines to their fullest potential."

"I cannot do this, Amado," Carillo said, shaking his head. "That territory is entirely too large to relinquish. The success of this plan is rooted in the idea that we control the *entire* border, not just bits and pieces. Anything less would result in total anarchy among those working under us. This is how we will maintain control."

"And increase profits?" Nievas said, raising his eyebrows.

"Naturally."

"When is the next shipment scheduled for crossing?"

"Tomorrow night. We will be able to test your people firsthand in a real situation. I have connections that are awaiting the shipment on the other side in El Paso. We will move the drugs under the noses of the U.S. Border Patrol agents, then arrange to ship them to our distribution area. From there, the people who tried to pick up the last shipment will get them. This will be much safer, I think. Plus, we will have real soldiers helping us to protect it."

"You refer to revolutionary forces of my people?"

"Of course, my friend. Make no mistake, my men are excellent. But they are not veterans like yours. They lack the experience to handle these operations for any extended time period. The involvement of your troops will change the tide of my operations forever. While others might entertain the idea of opposing Mexican cartel protection, they would think twice about attacking or stealing shipments guarded by crack combatants.''

''It is an ingenious plan, Jose,'' Nievas admitted with genuine awe. ''The American drug police won't know what hit them. And your competition? There will be none once they hear you've allied yourself with a veritable army of hardened soldiers. My people are the very best at what they do.''

''And they will be amply rewarded.''

''I see a long future filled with rewards.''

Carillo stopped and raised his glass. ''I'll drink to that.''

CHAPTER EIGHT

Brownsville, Texas

Mack Bolan didn't waste any time in contacting Stony Man Farm.

Shortly after his departure from Rajero's home, Barbara Price reached him over a special paging device that Bolan carried with him. If he was ever captured by an enemy, the pager had a fail-safe heating element in it that would fuse the circuits if it was tampered with or operated incorrectly. The circuitry used was untraceable to the Farm, let alone any manufacturer in the United States—even the best hackers would have considerable trouble tracing slag metal anyway.

The intelligence that Price and Kurtzman laid on him got his attention. Brognola still hadn't been able to convince the President that action by either of the Stony Man teams was imminent. So far, all they had was a plausible theory that happened to fit the facts at hand. That wasn't proof in the Man's book, and quite frankly the Executioner couldn't blame him.

Bolan stood inside a darkened phone booth, its door open as a torrential rain beat on the roof. His car was nearby with the engine running and the lights off. "Is there anything else I need to know?" he asked Price.

"No, that's about all we have right now. We can definitely start monitoring Kung Lok activity in the major cities where we know Jose Carillo has a presence. We also plan to keep tabs on Amado Nievas and his continued dealings with the Mexican drug cartel. We'll just have to feed you the intelligence as you go."

"That'll work. Now, I need a favor. Is Hal around?"

"Sure, hang on."

"I'm here, Striker," Brognola's voice boomed. "What do you need?"

"I need JG here, and I need him in a bad way."

Jack Grimaldi was Stony Man's ace pilot and one of Mack Bolan's few close friends.

"No problem," Brognola told him. "As a matter of fact, he's not too far from you. He's taking a little R and R, but I'm certain he'd curtail his plans to work with you."

"Good enough. Tell him I'll meet him at that private airfield in Houston—" he glanced at his watch "—by 1100 hours tomorrow. He'll know the place I mean."

"Understood." Brognola cleared his throat and said, "Will you be needing additional help?"

Bolan smiled into the phone. There was no putting one over on the head Fed. The most powerful man in Justice was offering anything he could, even if it meant breaking a few rules. The Executioner didn't want to do anything to compromise Stony Man's security or their good graces with the Man. While the Oval Office strongly appreciated the Farm's efforts, the President could be pushed too far. Brognola sometimes did that pushing and, in so doing, narrowed the window through which executive privileges flowed. Still, the Stony Man chief knew what he was doing.

"Anything in the supply arena you think Jack can tote with him would be good. But let's keep other personnel out of it for the time being."

Brognola was silent for a time, but finally said, "Okay. You're calling the shots on this one. Still, you know we're ready to do what's necessary."

"I know, and I appreciate it. By the way, Lisa Rajero from the DEA mentioned that Jose Carillo might have an attorney in Houston who takes money for laundering. Could you look into it and see if you can find out who it is? I'll need a name and address next time I call."

"Done."

"Thanks."

"You take care of yourself, Striker. You hear me?"

"Always."

Bolan hung up the phone and hurried to his car. Once inside, he put the shift selector into gear and slowly accelerated from the curb.

Thanks to intelligence provided by Rajero and her team, Bolan knew exactly where to start his blitz. Carillo had a manufacturing warehouse on the southeast side of Brownsville. Once the raw MDMA or coca product was smuggled here, they converted it and then sent out the processed junk for distribution. The DEA believed the Brownsville facility also served as a money clearing-house, but Carillo's political connections had so far prevented authorities from closing the place for good. Allegedly, the money was then shipped up the Intracoastal Waterway off the Gulf of Mexico, dropped in La Porte, Texas, and then trucked into Houston to be laundered.

According to Rajero, the DEA had been trying to

close down the factory for years, but every time they turned up enough evidence to make their move, either a bribed judge, corrupt politician or the mysterious disappearance of that evidence got in their way. It sounded like a sweet deal for Carillo and an irresistible takeover for the Kung Lok. Bolan planned to end that deal.

Permanently.

The warrior negotiated the light weeknight traffic and soon found himself on a nearly deserted road that passed by the warehouse. The road was actually a hundred yards or better above the raised dock where the small, lone factory stood. It looked like a legitimate operation from the exterior, one that would have left most with the impression it was some kind of small lumber or machining factory. But Bolan knew better. The old cliché "Can't judge a book..." came to mind as he pulled off the road, hid the car in some tall weeds and made his way to a wooded promontory overlooking the factory.

The Executioner studied the lay of the land for a few minutes through his NVDs, then returned to his car and grabbed his equipment. He slid into the LBE suspenders he'd worn on his first night in Brownsville, and applied combat cosmetics. He replenished his ammo pouches with 30-round magazines for the now unsuppressed HK-53, then closed the trunk and carefully proceeded down a slippery embankment that led to a tree line on the backside of the factory.

Once he was at ground zero, Bolan stopped to study the place again in more detail. Off the main building, there were two outbuildings and a thirty-foot water tower that the Executioner estimated at about a thousand gallons. There was also a nonfunctional waterwheel attached to an old-fashioned pumping house and a dock that led directly from the main building. The Executioner nodded with satisfaction as he let his eyes rove the length of the dock and come to rest on a boat.

That was probably the money boat being readied to leave for La Porte. A stroke of fortune had accompanied the Executioner on his first mission, and it appeared his plans to meet Grimaldi in Houston would pan out nicely. Now it was simply a matter of figuring out which group was running this actual operation. Nothing in Rajero's intelligence led Bolan to believe that the Kung Lok triad had moved on this place yet, or that they even knew about it. Chances were good that Carillo's men were still in charge of the site.

Time would tell.

Bolan flicked the selector switch on the HK-53 to full-auto, and then broke cover and sprinted across the open field. It was risky, exposing himself for the some fifty yards to the back doors of the factory, but he wasn't about to take out the opposition while hiding behind the trees. He had no explosives other than the two M-26 fragmentation grenades that remained from his previous battle in Brownsville. That was hardly enough to bring the factory crashing to the ground.

The Executioner reached the doors without incident but found them locked. The flat handle of the door was the pull kind, and a quick measure gave the soldier an idea. He detached one of the frags from his LBE, yanked the pin and inserted the bomb between the handle and the door. He stayed low, holding it in place while he pounded on the door with his fist, then rose and dodged around the corner.

A moment later, he heard the door pop open and the footfalls of at least two men, possibly more. Bolan hoped that the use of one of the only two precious grenades would help do his work for him. He risked a glance around the corner and counted four shadowy forms as they emerged from the open doorway. The unmistakable shapes of SMGs held low were evident, even in the darkness. The soldier ducked out of view a moment before the grenade exploded. He could feel the heat of the blast as some of the fragments whooshed past his head.

Bolan came around the corner, the HK-53 tracking for targets. All four of his opponents lay on the ground. One was actually missing a leg, another was dead and the others were spread out in a bizarre fashion. Bolan knew they were suffering, but he couldn't risk mercy rounds at this stage of the game. He kicked one weapon out of reach from those who were still alive and then proceeded through the door.

The Executioner shoulder rolled in time to avoid being chopped to shreds by a pair of gunners firing AK-74s. He came to one knee and fired the HK-53 on the rise. The weapon echoed a thunderous report in the cavernous construction of the factory. A burst of 5.56 mm NATO rounds took the first gunner in the chest, tearing holes through his back and ripping apart heart and lungs. The drug pusher left his feet and crashed against a metal pole. The second gunman tried to avoid Bolan's fire, the initial volley missing vital organs and catching him in the legs as he dived for cover. He hit the floor hard and died under a fresh salvo before he could recover from the assault.

Bolan moved through the factory now, looking for new targets. Thus far, he'd seen only Caucasian or Hispanic faces among the opposition. No Scarlet Dragon types, which meant Carillo was still in charge of the operation here. At least for a few minutes longer.

The Executioner met two more attackers on the far side of the factory as they crashed through a side door and ran toward the front. Both men were dressed in nice clothing, wearing sport jackets and carrying oversize gym bags. How they had expected to get far toting the heavy bags remained a mystery, but Bolan didn't wait for introductions. He took the first one high in the chest as the guy ran past him and reached inside his jacket. The high-velocity slugs slammed into his body, seemingly pinning his arm inside his coat and spinning him away. The bag flew from his fingers as he landed face first, his arm still pinned beneath him.

The other guy unloaded his baggage, obviously in favor of self-preservation, and tried to draw a bead on the Executioner from one knee. Bolan rushed to cover behind a pole in time to avoid being ventilated by a hail of .45-caliber slugs from the shooter's semiautomatic pistol. Bolan waited until the guy had stopped firing and he heard the pop of a magazine before emerging from cover just enough to snap-aim the HK-53 and blow him away. The man's head exploded under the impact of several 5.56 mm rounds.

Bolan crouched and turned to his rear flank at the sound of boots slapping concrete. Four more gunmen appeared from the other side of the warehouse, emerging from a room bathed with light. He could see the multiple levels of glass vials and vats, attached to layers of tubes. It was the stepping room, the area where they processed the chemicals necessary to refine their product into street-ready drugs. The Executioner knew the processes required copious amounts of flammable chemicals—this was a perfectly happy alternative.

As the quartet of protectors armed with Uzis charged his position, the chemists and cleaners working in the makeshift laboratory burst from their hiding positions and tried to make good their escape. Bolan dealt with the armed opposition first, taking out two with a controlled burst from the HK-53 before they could get a fix on him. He made a beeline for another pole, reaching the cover even as the remaining pair fanned out and tried to flank him. Bolan kept moving, confident these guys weren't up for a confrontation with a combat-hardened warrior.

The Executioner's assessment was correct.

He charged the closer guy in a game of human chicken, surprising an enemy who didn't know what to make of this big madman dressed like a commando. Bolan waited until he was less than ten yards from the gunner, then knelt and opened fire, cutting down his opponent. The remaining gunner turned to escape, realizing the odds had been evened. Bolan raised his weapon and took the guy out, reluctant to leave a surviving hardman.

Bolan waited another moment or two, steeling himself and preparing to defend against any further attacks. He'd learned long ago that impatience was the number-one killer of soldiers. Professionals waited for the enemy in most cases, because it was in the haste of their movement that they usually made fatal mistakes. The Executioner knew that next to assumption and underestimation, impulsiveness on the part of his opponents could be used to great advantage.

After nearly a minute of silence, Bolan rose from his

position and moved toward the lab. He quickly scanned the room and took in the death. An almost euphoric feeling swept over him, and he realized he was being exposed to the chemicals used by Carillo's people to peddle death throughout the American youth culture. Another very large batch of stuff was being processed, and it would never hit the streets.

Bolan uncapped a small cylindrical tube on his LBE harness and withdrew a single wooden match from inside the case. He clasped the stick between his fingers and struck the white tip with his thumbnail. The chemical vapors were beginning to overpower him, so he tossed the match onto the first flammable area he saw and immediately left, closing the doors behind him. The heat would build enough inside the high-ceilinged room to where eventually it created a flashover and blow the place sky-high.

He went back to the two dead men wearing suits and quickly inspected their bags, which held both with money and heroin. The money was probably for the attorneys in Houston to launder. The drugs? Probably for the attorneys themselves. The Executioner hoisted both bags onto one shoulder and made haste for the front exit.

Bolan left the factory and trotted along the dock toward the boat, sweeping the muzzle of the HK-53 side to side, ready for more enemy troops. He reached the small cabin cruiser unchallenged, unloaded the bags on a cushioned seat in the main hold and then proceeded to the controls. The Executioner eyed the panel with a practiced eye, finally locating the starter switch. It turned over several times before the engine finally coughed to life. He untied the mooring lines, shoved the power stick forward and steered away from the dock.

The nighttime sky was suddenly lit with a brilliant flash as the lab exploded. Glass shards blew from the darkened windows, the echoes of secondary explosions rolling through the air. Bolan glanced back with satisfaction. It was just another battle won, but he knew it would infuriate Jose Carillo. Eventually, the Executioner knew he would have to deal with the Mexican drug lord, but for now he had damaged him severely. Rajero indicated this was probably a major processing center; now it was ashes. Let Carillo chew on that for a while.

Bolan kept to the center of the Rio Grande, preventing any trouble from flanking him out of the riverside brush. The tree branches grew outward, well away from the shore, and it would have been foolish to open himself to attack from above—especially in the dark. There were pirates on both sides of the border to worry about, as much as enemy troops.

Everything had gone like clockwork so far, but the numbers were running down and he knew there would be a limit to his effectiveness. Time could be the great enemy or supreme ally, depending on how the Executioner used it. In either case, he would move the drugs across the Rio Grande and up the path they usually went. It was highly improbable that he'd make contact with law enforcement, particularly if Rajero's allegations about the Carillo bribery network were true. In any case, Mack Bolan could find satisfaction in one thing.

Another arm of the Carillo drug empire had officially been severed.

MANY OF La Porte, Texas, still slept when Mack Bolan arrived. The lights of the bay town burned brightly, serving as comforting beacons for the Houston Ship Channel. La Porte was a town of more than forty thousand people, but it still had a friendly small-town atmosphere. Many areas were green and lush, fed by the waters of the Gulf of Mexico.

Founded by French settlers in 1889, La Porte was very similar to the coastal towns of Louisiana and those along the Eastern Seaboard. There were commercial and private fishing boats, steamers, commercial ocean liners and cargo ships, and an assortment of recreational boats scattered all along its shore.

The Executioner was counting on moving the drug money he'd acquired off the boats and into Houston without trouble. It would be time to put in another call to Stony Man to see if intel had turned up that established Carillo's legal contact in Houston. Then he would implement a little role camouflage and see what information he could squeeze the guy for. He needed to know Carillo's other major points of distribution. Rajero's information was good, but he didn't know how reliable. Especially since most of it had been obtained by street snitches and government informants some time back.

Drug dealers regularly moved their operations to keep anyone from getting too close or too comfortable with the information. Personnel were kept to a minimum. Chemists who worked in the labs made good money, only because they knew the risks were high and it was always possible they could become expendable. It was ironic yet sad how drug processing had become such a science. There was no point in dealers and drug lords like Carillo putting junk on the streets that wasn't cut correctly. Enough customers were lost to drug programs and overdoses, or wound up in jail. Good dealers would generally go to great lengths to make sure the product they disbursed was of decent quality and safety. Drug dealers figured dead users were unprofitable.

Bolan moored his boat at an inconspicuous dock and disembarked, both bags slung over his shoulder. One of the duffels now contained the full stash of drugs and money. He had the Beretta within reach beneath a light blue windbreaker, which he'd donned during his trip up the waterway. He'd cleaned the combat cosmetics from his face, and stashed the HK-53 and LBE harness in the other bag. The blacksuit would have looked suspicious in broad daylight, but given the windbreaker, bags and the time of morning, the few people he did pass didn't give him more than a cursory glance and a smile.

The Executioner had learned that much of role camouflage was appearance. He'd learned success came when he could appear to be what someone expected him to be rather than trying to pull off an act. His tactics had proved effective time and again throughout his war against the Mafia, and now they were going to aid him once more.

Bolan quickly located a phone booth and called Stony Man. He glanced at his watch: 0524 hours. They would already be up and moving at the Farm by now. At least Kurtzman was, because he answered the phone.

"Bear, it's Striker."

"Yeah, we've sort of been keeping tabs," Kurtzman replied in a sheepish voice. "Mark one for the good guys."

"What did you find out about Carillo's lawyer?"

"We got a name and address for you, and the information seems pretty reliable. Carillo got nailed on a petty charge for illegal possession of a firearm when he was visiting here in the States. He has some pretty powerful friends in the Mexican government, so they managed to get him a slap on the wrist and back to Chihuahua before the ink was dry on the judge's order. The attorney used was a guy named Mario Ibanez.''

"What do we know about him?''

"He's a slick, high-priced legal eagle for some large Houston law firm, but known to consort with some pretty shady characters, including several oil and industry tycoons.'' Kurtzman gave him the address. "He once got popped for an open-and-shut drug charge, but his father's a judge and his cousin a well-known attorney. I'm sure you don't need the details.''

"Sounds like our guy.''

"That was our assessment, as well. But Hal wanted me to tell you to be extracareful.''

"Yeah?''

"Ibanez apparently travels with a consortium of bodyguards and lowlifes. No big surprise, given his clientele. You'll be lucky to even get close enough to deliver your message.''

"We'll see,'' Bolan told him. "Thanks for the information, Bear. And thank Hal for me, too.''

"Sure thing. If you need anything else, call.''

"Understood. Out here.''

Bolan hung up the phone. Now he had a name.

CHAPTER NINE

Houston, Texas

Two hours and a change of clothes later, Bolan stood in the lobby of Ibanez's Houston law offices wearing a three-piece suit and carrying a very large briefcase.

The blond bombshell behind the desk was calling her boss now to announce him. Bolan tried to look seemingly enamored by the very visible cleavage staring back at him. The curves of her breasts dipped low into the V-shaped collar of her white cotton blouse. It was almost stereotypical, the soldier thought, that a dirtbag like Ibanez would hire such a beauty to tend to his affairs. Nonetheless, despite the round hips under a red skirt and her soft eyes, she seemed professional enough.

She looked at him, the phone pressed to her ear, and said, "Mr. Ibanez would like to know who sent you, Mr. Belasko."

"Tell him Panchos."

The woman repeated the name, listened a moment, nodded and then set down the phone. "He'll see you right away."

"Thanks," Bolan said, tossing her a disarming grin.

She inclined her head and showed him into Ibanez's office.

The place was spacious and filled with expensive furniture. There was a huge desk just in front of a large, tinted window that offered a tremendous view of the city. A bookshelf lined one wall, crammed with classics and law books. Bolan had to admit that the attorney spared no expense to keep up appearances. He was directed to a seat in front of Ibanez's desk, which had a plaque that read Mario Bonafacio Y Rosperanza Ibanez, Esq. There were various certificates, degrees and other honoraria adorning the walls throughout the room, in addition to some very rare and expensive paintings, including one Picasso.

The man who entered a moment later from a side door was well dressed, with manicured fingernails and gelled black hair. His skin was very dark, as were his eyes, and there was no mistaking his Hispanic descent. The man was unusually tall and moved with self-importance. The Executioner had to admit that Ibanez wasn't what he'd expected.

Bolan stood as the guy came over and reached out a hand. As they shook, Ibanez said, "So, Mr. Belasko... Panchos sent you?"

"Yes."

He directed Bolan to sit and then took a seat behind his desk. Bolan pretended not to hear the two men who had entered from another door and were now standing behind him. He could generally sense their presence, although he didn't dare risk a glance to size them up. As long as he could play the inferior, and act as if he were there on friendly terms, he didn't pose a threat.

That would keep Ibanez off guard long enough to get the information he needed.

"I'm a bit surprised you're here," he said. "After all, Panchos doesn't generally tend to send his people directly to me in this fashion. We usually meet somewhere a bit more, how would you say, neutral?"

"Okay, so he changed his plans."

"And how is he?"

"He's not good."

"Really?"

The Executioner could already see where the conversation was going. Certainly, Carillo knew by now that someone was hitting his businesses all over the Southwest. He obviously wasn't going to be happy about that, and Bolan knew if he acted too chummy that Ibanez would immediately become suspicious. Especially given the fact that the attorney was probably one of the few who knew about Carillo's operations at large. It would only stand to reason that Carillo might suspect Ibanez as being behind the hits. A meeting like this would have then been arranged, and Bolan could play the part of a Carillo lackey looking to feel out each of the drug lord's associates.

"Someone has been very unpleasant toward Mr. Carillo," Bolan replied easily, producing a slight frown as if the very thought of it were distasteful.

"And he suspects me?"

"He suspects everyone at the moment, Mr. Ibanez," Bolan said. "Even me."

"I know about the trouble he's had," Ibanez stated matter-of-factly, "but I have no idea who's behind it."

"Mr. Carillo figured you would say that."

"And?"

"And he told me that if you said that he would know it was the truth."

This comment seemed to please Ibanez immensely. It was entirely possible that just the opposite was true. The Kung Lok triad was an extensive organization, with its fingers into every imaginable aspect of the underworld. But that didn't mean it had information on all of Carillo's operations. The triad's intelligence was coming from somewhere—the network it had on the streets wasn't that considerable. Barbara Price had indicated that until recently, the Kung Lok triad wasn't very active in the States. It hadn't occurred to the Executioner until just that moment it was possible the triad already had its claws into Ibanez, who was providing inside information. But if the attorney was nervous about being discovered, he had a pretty good way of covering it.

"You can assure Panchos that we're behind him one hundred percent, Mr. Belasko. If he needs anything, you let him know that I'm at his disposal."

"I'm certain he'll be pleased to hear that," Bolan replied. "Now, let's dispense with the nice-nice and talk business. You know why I'm here?"

The lawyer nodded at the briefcase. "You have a delivery to make, I assume."

"Yes, but I'll get to that in a moment. There's another issue we should discuss first. It has to do with the punks who are cutting into Mr. Carillo's business. I assume you know who I mean?"

"Well, I don't know who it could be, but I know they've been troublesome," Ibanez said, studying his fingernails.

Bolan had to wonder how much more perfect the crooked attorney's hands could get. The guy probably already had a manicurist on twenty-four-hour call, but he seemed to have a fetish about his nails. He kept looking at them, becoming distracted and distant as he talked to his visitor.

"Troublesome doesn't even come close. Last night, somebody cancelled the operation in Brownsville. There's not much left of it except a smoldering pile of ashes. I barely got out alive."

Something in Ibanez's expression changed, and there was an edge to him now. *That* was a particular piece of news he hadn't expected. This told Bolan two things: the guy knew about the Brownsville plant, but he had expected to hear someone had taken it over, not destroyed it. Now Bolan was very suspicious that perhaps Ibanez *was* working for the Kung Lok triad. It was time to sweeten the pot with an offer he just couldn't refuse. An offer that wouldn't only bring the triad to him, but also set the stage for knocking out two birds with one stone.

"This is only one part of the actual take," Bolan said. "The rest of it ended up in El Paso, since we couldn't risk bringing it directly here. I'm taking a big chance sending you this much. You'll also find a little extra set aside for your trouble."

"What trouble?" Ibanez said, splaying his hands in an attempted gesture of innocence.

The Executioner wasn't buying it. "Mr. Carillo needs you to take yourself and some of your people and pick up the rest of the stuff tonight in El Paso. He's left it in the care of our Border Patrol friends. I assume you know who I mean?"

"Yes, of course. But why does he need me to go?"

"Because you're one of the few he trusts," Bolan

snapped. He could sense the increased tension of the men behind him, but he didn't hear them make a move. He added quickly, "Mr. Carillo is finding it difficult to put faith in any of his business associates right now. Consider yourself one of the lucky ones."

"I understand. I will take care of it personally."

"I'm sure you will." Now it was time to get some answers. "Mr. Carillo wanted me to ask you something."

"What is it?"

"He wanted to know where else you think they might hit him. He wants to get your take on this thing." Bolan was really into the role now, stroking Ibanez's ego. He was treating the guy as if Carillo thought he was important; as if his opinion really mattered and as if he walked on water where Carillo was concerned. "He wants to know what other locations might be threatened."

"Well, I'm certain the operations in Las Vegas are in trouble, particularly where much cash is trading hands."

"Like?"

"Like the Milburn House and the Del de Lox Casino."

Bingo.

"What about some of the remote locations, such as El Paso?"

"That's possible, although I think it's too close to his home operations." He looked at his fingernails and continued, "However, there are the major holdings here in Houston, although I think those are safe."

"For the most part anyway," Bolan said quietly.

Ibanez nodded his agreement. "Of course. Then let

us not forget San Luis Rio Colorado, Laredo, Nogales and Mexicali. Ah…blessed Mexicali."

The Executioner found the man's behavior strange now. He couldn't determine what was so special about Mexicali, although the capital city of the Baja was a major traffic route for narcotics. Everyone knew it, but nobody seemed to want to do anything about it. It was easier for the DEA to protect the high-profile areas, such as Miami, because of the natural boundaries of water. But the Baja California–U.S. border didn't enjoy that much fortune, and the natural maintenance of such a large area naturally required a high number of personnel.

Nonetheless, Bolan knew that whoever controlled that part of the border controlled every bit of the drug trafficking that found its way into San Diego and the distribution pipelines that ran from it. Most of the dope that found its way across the northern part of the Southwest strip, from Los Angeles to Denver, could claim its source through Mexicali and the surrounding areas.

"I'll pass on your observations to him." Bolan left the briefcase on the desk and got up to leave. "The meet is scheduled for eleven o'clock tonight. Be on time. Mr. Carillo doesn't want a repeat of the incident a few days ago in Brownsville. He doesn't yet know about what happened last night. I get the privilege of having to break the news upon my return to Mexico."

"I've never met you before," Ibanez said, standing, as well. His eyes narrowed. "Conrado has always handled these kinds of things for Panchos. Just who exactly are you?"

"You can ask Mr. Carillo tonight, although I doubt he'll tell you."

Ibanez raised his eyebrows. "You mean he's going to *be* there tonight?"

Bolan cocked his head and tried to look irritated. "You have a hearing problem? I already said that Mr. Carillo doesn't trust anybody right now. He'll be there to oversee the operation and make sure nothing goes wrong."

"Okay, I understand."

"Good." Bolan turned to leave, then stopped to say, "Just a friendly bit of advice, Counselor. Don't do anything foolish tonight. My boss is trusting, but he's no fool."

"I wouldn't think of crossing him, Mr. Belasko."

Bolan smiled. As he turned, he made a show of acting startled to see two rough-looking bodyguards standing near the office doors. Their muscular chests and broad shoulders pressed against the tailored suits, which threatened to burst at the seams. In addition to their menacing expressions and general size, Bolan also had to assume they were carrying hardware beneath the jackets.

"You guys are good," Bolan said as he opened the door between them. "I didn't even hear you come in."

With that said, Bolan left the office of Mario Ibanez. He knew within just twelve hours, he would be dropping the hammer on the very same man. Hopefully, if fate was with him, he'd strike his first blow against the Kung Lok, triad as well. Although they didn't know it, the Scarlet Dragons were about to experience the Executioner's fury for the very first time.

And it would be an experience they wouldn't soon forget.

JACK GRIMALDI BROKE into a wide grin when he saw the Executioner entered one of the T-hangars at Ellington Field at 1100 hours sharp.

Serving as a both a civil and military airport, Ellington Field had more than sixty years of history, and was acquired by the city of Houston in 1984. In addition to passenger shuttle flights for a major commercial airline, it also catered to the U.S. military, NASA and a worldwide package-delivery company. And now it was working to serve Mack Bolan.

The two men shook hands, and then Grimaldi quickly led the Executioner through the terminal and out to where a plane awaited. It wasn't the Gulfstream 21C that Bolan had expected, but instead a Bell Cardoen 206L-3 Bichito helicopter. A civilian version of the Bell OH-58A Kiowa, the Cardoen 206L-3 was fast, reliable and very popular for commercial use. It would serve its purpose perfectly, and Bolan mentally commended his friend for the choice.

Grimaldi had to have sensed the Executioner's appraisal. "She's not fully armed like an Army chopper, but Hal figured you wanted to keep a low profile."

Bolan nodded at his friend. "I do. It's perfect, Jack."

"Thanks. Where to?"

"Our first stop's El Paso, but I've bought us a little time. This thing is much bigger than I imagined. That's why I asked Hal to bring you in on it. I hope you don't mind cutting short your R and R."

"Not at all," Grimaldi said, shrugging. "I was just sitting around a hotel room and cooling my heels with a tumbler of Scotch. Frankly, I was pretty bored. Now I know why Lyons and McCarter are always bellyaching about never enough action."

"Yeah, well, Lyons and McCarter should learn how to relax once in a while," Bolan said with a grin.

Grimaldi chuckled, lighting a cigarette as he replied, "Exactly right. So, what's the gig?"

"Well, I don't know how much Hal told you, but I hope you signed on for some action, because you're going to get it."

Grimaldi eyed his friend a moment with a cocksure expression, then through a cloud of smoke asked, "Blitz play?"

"In a nutshell. You brought the maps?"

"In the chopper," he replied with a jerk of his thumb.

Bolan stepped into the cramped cargo area of the Cardoen and quickly located an ammo can that contained a score of U.S. maps in different versions, including sectional, regional, topographical, and aerial-satellite reconnaissance. He yanked a topographical from the labeled folders inside the can and spread it out on his bags. Grimaldi stepped onto the strut and leaned inward, careful to keep his cigarette outside the confines of the plane.

"Here's the plan," Bolan said, tracing his finger on the path as he described it. "We're going to head into El Paso first. I've set the bait in a parking area across from the Border Patrol offices, inside an underground parking facility. Once I've got the enemy inside, they're all mine."

"Barb mentioned something about the Kung Lok triad," Grimaldi interjected. "What's all that about?"

"That's only part of this deal. Do you remember my mission a few years ago against the Mexican drug cartel?"

"Who could forget it? We were all over the countryside, both in Central America and here. I don't think I've ever clocked so many hours on a single mission. We bounced all over the map."

"Yeah, well, not much has changed," Bolan replied grimly. "The new guy in town is a dope dealer by the name of Jose Carillo. His influence seems to stretch pretty far, and he's got his fingers deep in a lot of pies. The action has apparently proved profitable for him. Profitable enough to turn heads in the Kung Lok."

"How high does it go?"

"I don't know yet, but I have a name. The Kung Lok operation is being enforced by the Scarlet Dragons under the leadership of a guy named Ing Kaochu. His people are being supplied with weapons by Dim Mai."

Grimaldi's eyebrows rose and he whistled. "The Asian arms dealer? Those are some pretty heavy hitters, Sarge."

"Well, it seems they've turned their eyes on Carillo's business. I guess the profit outweighs the risks."

"So Kung Lok is prepared to do war with Mexican mafia," Grimaldi observed.

Bolan nodded with a grim expression. "And they've picked this country as the battleground. The Kung Lok controls the entertainment industry in Canada. If memory serves, the head of the organization is a guy named Lau Ming Shui, aka Merciless Ming."

"I've heard the name," Grimaldi replied. "Although I was never sure of the connection before. So where else are you planning to hit?"

"In addition to El Paso, I know they have operations in Las Vegas and San Diego. Although I'm betting the payload is going to be somewhere along the border. Any ideas?"

"Well..." Grimaldi began. He paused, looking at the map and scratching the back of his head. "If it were me, Nogales and Laredo wouldn't be worth it. They're small potatoes.''

''Agreed. There's no evidence Carillo has a major influence in these areas anyway. The attorney that handles his business here in the States said that they have operations there, but there's no evidence to prove these are major locations. There has to be a central pipeline.''

''Okay,'' Grimaldi said, ''so that leaves either El Paso, San Luis or Mexicali…or maybe all three. Hell, I don't know, Sarge. That's a lot of area for just the two of us to cover.''

''Mexicali *is* the California pipeline, more or less. But that might seem too obvious to law enforcement. This attorney talked about it like it was the be-all, end-all. But if we're going to shut down this operation, we'll have to shut it down for good. That means I'll have to go up against both Carillo's people and the Kung Lok.''

''But we aren't sure who has what right now,'' Grimaldi reminded him.

''Maybe not, but Carillo obviously has influence in El Paso. It's possible he might try the same play in Mexicali, but I don't have enough intelligence to make that assumption with certainty. We'll have to see how it goes, Jack. The more intelligence I have, the easier this will be.'' He looked hard at Grimaldi and added, ''For both of us.''

The Stony Man pilot shrugged. ''Like I said, Sarge, I'm in this for the long haul. I'll be here as long as you need me.''

''Thanks, Jack.'' The Executioner looked at his watch and realized he hadn't slept in a while. ''How long do you think it will take us to get there?''

"How much time you need to spare?"

"Say fifteen minutes from drop-off."

The pilot shrugged. "Range on this thing isn't that great, so there'll be one fuel stop in San Angelo. With a cruising range of about 118 mph, I'd guess probably five hours, give or take."

'That gives us about five hours to catch some shut-eye. It's going to be a long night, and I especially don't want *you* falling asleep at the wheel."

"Shucks," Grimaldi quipped, "I didn't know you cared."

As THE CLOCK STRUCK 2230 hours, Bolan broke out the two crates of gear Grimaldi had brought with him. He began to inventory their contents as the pilot sipped on the thermos of coffee they had acquired in San Angelo. Grimaldi had managed to put together quite a bit of stuff on his alleged "short notice." Among other basics like MREs and standard supplies, there was an impressive amount of weaponry. One box contained an MP-5 SD-6, the silenced counterpart of the MP-5 line of SMGs. Not only was this one of the best weapons available in the Stony Man arsenal but it was also an extremely accurate weapon. There were also twenty loaded 30-round magazines of lead-cored 9 mm ball ammunition for the weapon.

The other box contained various tools, including twenty-five pounds of C-4 plastique, a spare Beretta 93-R with shoulder holster and ten Diehl DM-51 grenades. Weighing less than a pound each, and containing PETN high explosive, the DM-51 had a special feature: it could be used as an offensive *or* defensive grenade. When Bolan operated in offensive mode, the grenade generated a significant blast with very little fragmentation. A hollow plastic sleeve, which was filled with more than six thousand 2 mm steel balls, could then be added for a defensive effect. The high-velocity fragments propelled by the explosion would decimate any enemy soldiers within its twenty-five-square-meter effective range.

"Nice job on the equipment, Jack," Bolan remarked through the headphone set in back that linked him with Grimaldi in the cockpit.

"My pleasure," the Stony Man pilot said. The Executioner checked his watch. True to Grimaldi's words, it had taken them just over five hours to get to El Paso. Bolan nodded, well aware the approaching lights visible through the cockpit window signaled their proximity to the city. He'd make the meeting on time, barring any unforeseen trouble. The plan was to spring the surprise on the Kung Lok, and he was certain they would show. There was very little doubt that Carillo wasn't the only one from whom Ibanez took payments.

At least now he had some answers; he knew where the major holdings were. These would undoubtedly be the targets for the Kung Lok triad. The only question remaining was where would they hit. It might have been better to simply let the triad do away with Carillo, and then he would only have to bring war against a single enemy. But if there was to be violence and bloodshed on American streets, then the Executioner had a responsibility to make sure the destruction was kept to a minimum and the bloodshed was kept to the enemy.

Bolan wouldn't let this war get out of control. He couldn't just stand by idly and watch these devils cut down innocent bystanders. Hardworking men and women, looking to just survive or support and protect their children, were no match against heartless savages armed with automatic weapons.

"Four-minute ETA, Sarge," Grimaldi informed him through the headset.

Bolan threw the pilot a thumbs-up and then armed himself. He slid into the double holster for the Beretta 93-Rs and shoved the weapons with extended magazines into their respective spots beneath his armpits. He then slung the MP-5 SD-6 and filled his fanny pack with several DM-51 grenades. The Desert Eagle rode in military webbing on his hip, and a Colt Combat knife was sheathed on his thigh.

Grimaldi held up a finger. "One minute to ground zero."

Bolan nodded as the chopper dipped toward the city lights. The Kung Lok triad wouldn't just stand around the parking garage and wait for his assault. He would have to seek them out and then implement his plan. And that plan spelled out only one thing: complete annihilation. A moment later, the chopper landed on the rooftop helipad of the U.S. Border Patrol parking garage.

And Mack Bolan jumped from the chopper, prepared to meet his destiny.

CHAPTER TEN

The Executioner shoved his six-foot-three, two-hundred-pound frame against the roof door and splintered it off its hinges.

He descended the stairwell, tracking the area ahead with the MP-5 SD-6. With standard ammunition, the MP-5's sound suppressor reduced muzzle velocity in such a way that the sound was no louder than the air brakes on a panel truck. In single-shot bursts, the sound was unrecognizable to the untrained ear as a silenced machine pistol, and single-shot accuracy was high within one hundred meters.

The soft neoprene pads glued to the soles of Bolan's combat boots would further enable him to maintain some covert movement. That would prove to his advantage, since his first encounter with four Kung Lok ambushers didn't occur in quite the way they were expecting. The Chinese gunmen turned just in time to see Bolan come around the corner of the stairwell landing, lower the muzzle of his weapon and squeeze the trigger.

The first two 9 mm Parabellum rounds chewed through the closest gunman's jaw, splattering flesh onto his Scarlet Dragon brothers. He staggered backward, signals no longer going to his brain as his autonomic reflexes took over. The weight of his body toppling backward interfered with the remaining trio since they had foolishly clustered themselves on the stairwell.

Bolan seized the advantage, pressing forward and shooting another Dragon gunner who was trying to push his dead cohort away while simultaneously clawing shoulder leather for his pistol. The bullet plowed through the guy's chest, puncturing his lung and leaving him wheezing for air.

The other pair tried to retreat down the stairs. One got his hand on the door handle before Bolan fired twice, both rounds going through the gunner's right kidney and exiting his belly to lodge in the metal door. The Dragon was slammed face first into the door by the force of Bolan's slugs. He slid to the ground, his deadweight now effectively blocking the only exit.

The remaining Dragon paused a moment, obviously torn between the decision to run or fight. He chose to fight, managing to clear a Jatimatic from beneath his long leather trench coat and aim it in Bolan's direction. The Executioner was already triggering his weapon, but then a very familiar and very bad sound reached his ears. The weapon's extractor jammed on the shot, the bullet straying low and effectively locking out further fire until the breech could be cleared.

Bolan dived for the stairs, the bodies of the fallen saving him from a very painful landing and broken bones. The report of the Jatimatic was cacophonous within the stairwell as the 9 mm rounds whizzed past the Executioner's ear. He completed a roll and got to his knees, the Colt Combat knife now cleared from its sheath. The warrior drove the blade into the Kung Lok terrorist's solar plexus, sinking it to the hilt. A half gasp, half cry issued from his opponent's open mouth before the guy dropped his weapon and hit his knees. The body fell prone onto the landing after Bolan yanked the knife from its belly. The blade was wiped clean, then returned to its sheath. He picked up the MP-5 SD-6 and expertly cleared the double feed—a quick inspection of the breech revealed no visible damage. The weapon was safe to continue using.

The Executioner keyed up the microphone to the wireless headset that kept him in communication with Grimaldi.

"Eagle One, this is Striker."

"Go ahead," came Grimaldi's clear voice.

"I ran into trouble here. The cat's out of the bag, so I won't meet you topside. Go to Plan B for our rendezvous point."

"Roger, Striker. Eagle One out."

Bolan could hear the concern in Grimaldi's voice, but he knew the pilot would follow instructions. Anytime they had a mission together, an alternate plan for pickup was chosen. This was usually predetermined, and then Grimaldi would await the Executioner's signal. In the event Bolan got out of contact and didn't show at the scheduled rendezvous point, Grimaldi would automatically proceed to the alternate area and wait for an agreed amount of time. If still a no-show, Grimaldi was to assume that Bolan was either dead or unavoidably detained, and he was to beat feet out of the LZ and cool his heels until it was established the Executioner was alive or dead.

Now Bolan was less than three minutes into this mission and he already had trouble. Even within the concrete-and-steel confines of the stairwell, somebody was sure to hear the Jatimatic fire. If the enemy could pinpoint the Executioner's location before he could complete the mission, everything would end right there. That would undoubtedly put finality on the situation, and whether Brognola could take over with Able Team or Phoenix Force was anybody's guess. Still, the Executioner wasn't planning to give up just yet on his plans. The mission was still salvageable—as far as Bolan was concerned—and there were numerous Kung Lok gunners in that garage who needed to be dealt with.

Bolan decided to take each level one at a time. He'd left instructions for the meet to take place on the ground floor, so the Scarlet Dragons he'd encountered on level four had obviously been posted as sentries. He reached a door labeled L-3 without incident and entered the garage proper, sweeping the darkened parking area with the muzzle of the MP-5. Most of the spaces were empty, giving the Executioner a clear line of sight. He sprinted across the open space and had almost reached the center partition of the ramp when the sounds of squealing tires and a powerful engine reached his ears.

A moment later, a van rounded the corner and raced toward him as he sought cover behind a concrete support. The van screeched to a halt and a half-dozen Scarlet Dragons jumped from the rear and side doors. They wore black fatigue pants, scarlet T-shirts and combat boots. The gunners fanned out, machine pistols and automatic rifles held at the ready.

Bolan turned the selector switch to 3-round bursts, leveled the MP-5 S-D6 and opened fire on the gunmen. Most of them ducked, keeping low and in motion. Two immediately fell under the Executioner's crack marksmanship. A burst of 9 mm Parabellum rounds spit from the muzzle, tearing through one Dragon hardman and continuing into the guy immediately behind him. Bolan squeezed the trigger repeatedly, laying down a hail of autofire that took the gunners by surprise.

The remaining four continued moving, spreading themselves as far apart as possible and returning Bolan's fire with a fury of their own. The Executioner ducked behind the pillar as enemy rounds whistled past, some of them chewing concrete chips from the pillar while others scored deep gouges in the slick pavement. Bolan yanked one of the DM-51s from his harness and pulled the pin. He poked his head around the corner, fired off a few 3-round bursts, and then rolled the grenade in the general direction of the enemy troops.

The Scarlet Dragons realized their mistake, the smooth outside walls offering no suitable cover from the blast. The best they could do was hit the pavement and press themselves flat as the DM-51 exploded, showering the area with the superheated pellets. Another gunman died immediately, too close to the grenade to escape its deadly blast. The others were far enough out to escape the deadly fragments, but the concussive blast was disorienting in the confines of the garage.

Bolan emerged from cover and knelt. He tracked the MP-5 on to the nearest Chinese enforcer and squeezed the trigger. One round connected with the gunman's shoulder, flipping him onto his side, and the remaining pair of slugs decimated his face. The Executioner was already aiming at the second gunner who was trying to align his sights on the him. The Executioner found his mark before the guy could pose any real threat. The bullets split open his skull, cracking bones and shredding brain matter on the way through.

The remaining Scarlet Dragon got to his feet, shooting wildly in Bolan's direction, the shots going high and wide. The gunman was trying for the door where Bolan had made his entry. The Executioner raised his weapon, took a breath and squeezed the trigger as he let half out and steadied the chattering weapon. The 9 mm Parabellum rounds caught the Dragon at the small of his back just as he was opening the door. The force of the bullets pushed him through the opening, depositing him onto the floor in a dead heap. The door closed, propped open maybe a foot by the pair of lifeless legs protruding from the doorway.

The Executioner started to rise but paused a moment when the flash of movement registered in his peripheral vision. He turned in time to see the driver and a passenger in the van raise their weapons—in time to hear the crack of their pistols as they opened fire—in time to realize he'd made a fatal mistake.

In time to feel the first round punch through his body...

MARIO IBANEZ SAT in the back seat of his rented limousine and glanced nervously at his watch.

The limo was parked a half mile up the street, the entrance to the parking garage in view. The Kung Lok Scarlet Dragons were inside the structure right at that moment, checking things out and clearing any potential threats. Despite his early-morning visit from the guy who claimed to be an employee of Carillo, Ibanez wasn't stupid. He wouldn't put himself in any position that could result in getting his ass shot off unless he first knew the place was secure.

Ibanez hadn't been able to reach either Carillo or Sapèdas; that wasn't unusual, considering it was Saturday. It might not have even meant a thing, but Ibanez wasn't going to take that chance. If this was a legit meeting, he'd find out soon enough. Not to mention the fact that his business partners were anxious to get their money. Ibanez had decided not to mention the fact he'd gotten his cut, and then some. Why slit his own throat? He was the key to Carillo's laundering operation anyway. And if what this Belasko character had said was true, Carillo was still as trusting and foolish where it came to Ibanez's loyalties as the Mexican drug lord had ever been.

Besides, Ibanez really did have a good thing going here. He wouldn't throw it away on the word of just anyone. Let Kaochu's people take the heat if there was going to be trouble. For all he knew, it was Carillo or Sapèdas who had set up this whole thing. Perhaps Belasko had been sent to lure him into a hit. After all, Panchos had as big a reputation for taking care of traitors as he did for rewarding loyalty. Frankly, Ibanez was just about ready to get out of the business altogether anyway. Just as soon as the Kung Lok triad was in control, and he had the rest of what was coming to him, Ibanez was going to disappear. Forever.

The sound of a chopper passing overhead caused him to stiffen. He peered up through the heavily tinted windows of the limo and watched as the low-flying chopper passed overhead. He continued to watch it move away and then relaxed and let out a sigh when he realized he'd been holding his breath.

"Relax, Mario," he whispered to himself. "You're being paranoid. Everything's cool."

The attorney reached into the wet bar and poured himself a drink. Weekend traffic was pretty heavy, but not so much that he felt out of place. Once this meeting went off, or maybe if it went off, he'd have the boys take him out for a late dinner somewhere. But there was a plane awaiting him at the El Paso airport...well, screw those bastards. They could wait, too, as far as he gave a shit, and that was that. Ibanez sucked down the full tumbler of Scotch, and then poured another half-full and set it on his lap.

Bertie Gutierrez opened the back door of the limousine and squeezed his large frame into a seat across from his boss. The attorney's chief enforcer was a loyal companion. He was the only one Ibanez trusted, and even in that light he didn't trust the big bruiser any farther than he could throw him. In some respects, Ibanez resented the fact that despite all of his money and power he spent most of his time with this secret fear for his life. Thus, he'd been required to surround himself with guys like Gutierrez. But then he slowly became afraid and distrusting of his own men, despite the fact they had never given him any reason to take such a position.

Ibanez's therapists, and he'd been to many, had all basically said that his kind of fear was unhealthy and unnatural. Well, what the fuck did they know? he thought. Bunch of overpriced peons who had never amounted to anything in life, pedantic kooks who didn't have a shred of common sense and sat so pious in their million-dollar offices, hiding from the real world and charging hardworking men like Ibanez a hundred-plus dollars an hour to tell them how screwed up they were. Which reminded him that he had to schedule another appointment with Dr. Kingston. Perhaps when hc'd concluded his session with the four-eyed, pimply faced college intern he'd have Bertie put a bullet in Kingston's chest.

"Any word yet?" Ibanez asked his bodyguard.

The man shook his head. "Nothing yet, Mario."

"Well, I'm getting sick and tired of sitting on my ass. I'm hungry and I'm tired. How long does it take to check out that garage? It's only four levels, for God's sake."

"I don't know, sir. Do you want me to take a walk down there?"

"No, I don't want you to do anything but sit here and keep me company," Ibanez replied with irritation. "What did you think of that Belasko guy?"

Gutierrez shrugged. "Seemed all right."

"You think he's really working for Carillo? Or do you think it's a setup?"

"Sheesh, Mario, you've asked me that a hundred times already. I don't know who the guy is—"

"Well, I'm asking you again!" Ibanez could feel his face go flush, and Gutierrez promptly shut his mouth. He knew they hated him when he was in this kind of mood. Hell, he didn't like himself when he was in this kind of mood. But damn it to hell, that just didn't really matter right now. "I'm sorry I lost my cool, Bertie. Let's just forget it. Okay?"

"Okay, boss. It's forgotten."

Gutierrez fell silent and Ibanez fell back into another vigil of self-pity. He continued to think about how he needed to get away from the psychologists he was seeing. But not until he'd made one last appointment with Kingston, and let Bertie plug the guy. After all, he couldn't risk it if word of his treatment got out. He couldn't risk having Kingston shoot off his big mouth and say something Ibanez would regret. Ibanez wouldn't show weakness, not to colleagues or friends, and especially not to his enemies. Such a thing could prove disastrous for a man in his business.

Not to mention how disappointed his father would have been, as pride ran deep in the Ibanez family. Every man in his bloodline was to be a strong leader and above social reproach. The pressure was so high to conform to these standards that usually most of the Ibanez men turned into social pariahs. Not in the sense of social mingling—since they were well connected to some of society's most prominent people—but generally in their innate abilities to cope with others. Ibanez men tended to be rather domineering when it came to their women, antisocial and ethically dysfunctional. It was a family curse, but Ibanez wasn't going to wear it as a stain. Better to wear such a mark proudly, stay wealthy and happy and never forsake or betray the Ibanez name. To do so would mean dishonor, and death.

And that's what it was all about. So Ibanez knew he would just have to sit here and wait for word from the lieutenant leading the Scarlet Dragons. He'd have to answer nicely when he got the report, and kiss the man's ass because he worked directly for Ing Kaochu, and Kaochu just happened to be Ibanez's meal ticket for the time being. Well, that was just fine with him. Because soon, very soon, he wouldn't need anyone.

FATE, OR SOME UNKNOWN deity, had been with Mack Bolan. Because while his movements might have been fatal, the bullets that ripped across his body didn't hit areas that would result in death. One grazed the small of his back and the other pierced his left calf. The subgun flew from Bolan's fingers as he stumbled and fell. He managed to execute a half-decent shoulder roll, clenching his teeth and growling against the pain in his leg and back.

The Executioner got to one knee, both of the Berettas now clutched in his fists. He fired in succession, the weapons barking with thunderous reports as the 158-grain 9 mm lead-core slugs rocketed across the garage and struck his enemy.

Two rounds from one of the pistols punched neat little holes in the driver's chest, ripping through lung and heart tissue and blowing out part of the gunman's spine. His body convulsed with the impact of the bullets before he did a short pirouette and collapsed to the pavement. The passenger took twice as many rounds from the Executioner's pistols, his body doing a similar dance to that of his comrade's as the 9 mm slugs blew out his kneecap, intestines, throat and the top of his skull.

Bolan climbed to his feet, scooped up the machine pistol and tucked it under his arm, and then hobbled to the van. He knew the fight wasn't over, but he didn't have time to worry about further enemy troops until they presented a threat. It was entirely possible there were Scarlet Dragon reinforcements on their way, but he couldn't allow that fact to divert him from his mission. He still had Ibanez to deal with, if he could lure the guy, and the van would provide him the opportunity. Plus, it wouldn't be long before he'd have to get some medical attention. It wouldn't do him any good to stay and fight longer only to die of infection perhaps a day from now—or even a week.

The Executioner stepped gingerly but quickly into the van, put it in gear and swung the vehicle into a one-eighty. He powered down the garage ramp, thankful that his left calf had taken the brunt of the trauma, leaving his right one free for the drive. His shoulder was throbbing, and both wounds hurt like hell. Despite the fact he'd been shot dozens of times and come closer to death more times than he could count, familiarity with injury didn't seem to numb the pain.

Bolan reached the ground level and started to accelerate as he saw several Kung Lok hardmen attempting to wave him down. He then thought better of it and decided to play along with their game, applying the brakes as he pulled up to the closest man. He stuck his arm out the window, one of the Berettas in his fist, and shot the triad gunner in the face. The man next to him fell a moment later as the next bullet from Bolan's pistol entered through his chest and blew apart his heart.

The last Dragon stepped onto the running board on the passenger side while the vehicle was still moving and tried to shoot Bolan through the open door. Bolan ducked back in time to avoid being decapitated by a 3-round burst from the guy's machine pistol. The soldier brought the other Beretta 93-R into play, flicking the selector switch to 3-round burst as he stomped on the brake pedal. The enforcer lost his balance, holding on to the mirror to save himself. The distraction was enough for Bolan to pump three rounds into the Dragon before he could regain his balance. He fell from the van and Bolan stomped on the accelerator.

The van emerged onto the street, and the Executioner stopped, looking both ways. The sudden flash of lights from a limousine parked a half mile down the street caught his attention. Bolan turned the wheel in the other direction and quickly drove to the next intersection.

He'd driven these roads a few days earlier and was familiar with them. Circled the block, he drove past the intersection where the limo was parked. He proceeded one block farther and then turned at the next intersection so that he could move in behind the vehicle. Bolan was making an educated guess that either the head of the Kung Lok was inside the limo, or it was Ibanez himself. In either case, they would be expecting the van to contain friendly troops. The Executioner was counting on that fact to give him an edge.

After he made a left onto the street one block to the rear of the limousine, Bolan detached the remaining two Diehl DM-51 grenades from his harness. He removed the sleeves from them to reduce the risk of endangering civilians. The limo was parked in front of a darkened building, there were no passersby on the street and he was going to double park the van to protect passing traffic.

As the van drew close, one of the big men Bolan had seen earlier that morning in Ibanez's office emerged from the driver's door. Well, at least he knew which enemy occupied that vehicle. The Executioner didn't slow, instead choosing to increase speed until he was practically on top of the limo. He couldn't see the fear in the bodyguard's eyes because they were covered with dark sunglasses—oddly enough—but there was no mistaking the sudden shout of surprise and the fact nearly all color drained from his face. The van smashed the bodyguard between the limo and front fender of the van.

Bolan yanked the pins on the DM-51s and tossed them through the open window of the van. They landed on the exposed front seat of the limo. He then jumped from the van and limped away from the scene. A moment later the limousine erupted with a tremendous blast, the windows shattering under the impact of the concussion as a bright orange ball of flame and black smoke emerged from the new openings. The second grenade exploded a moment later, nearly lifting the limousine off the ground.

The Executioner took the first alleyway and headed in the general direction of the rendezvous point.

At least the first stage of the operation was complete: no more money would be laundered in Houston, no more dope processed in Brownsville, and a message had just been sent to the Kung Lok, Sapèdas and, with any luck, Jose "Panchos" Carillo. A message that basically told the story of how the purveyors of death would find only death as their lot; that he who lived by the misery of American citizens would die under a blanket of fiery destruction. But most of all, a message that the Executioner had come to settle just debts in a most permanent fashion—once and for all.

CHAPTER ELEVEN

Las Vegas, Nevada

Ing Kaochu could hardly believe his ears when he was told of the death of a respected lieutenant and more than a dozen of his Scarlet Dragon brothers. He sat in brooding silence in the office of his new home—a home under considerable remodeling after its surrender by Danny Tang. Leave it to a half-breed to screw up a perfectly suitable place with what amounted to little more than the American version of ancient Chinese art. Well, Tang would no longer present a problem since he had joined those in the afterlife of eternal damnation. This was his punishment for allowing the enemy to steal Zahn, and for agreeing to serve as messenger for the man called Belasko.

Now he'd lost fifteen more good men, along with any known connections to the operations being conducted in Brownsville and El Paso. Moreover, rumor had it that a firebombing down the street from the Border Patrol parking garage might have been Mario Ibanez, an attorney who provided laundering and distribution services for Carillo's Houston operations.

That now meant three major services had been destroyed, which would effectively cut the Kung Lok profits by half. It would've been easier to take these operations like they had those here in Las Vegas, and slowly phase out Carillo's people once they had an overall handle on the situation. Even as Kaochu now sat here thinking about it, Lau Ming Shui's plans were falling down around his ears. It was time that they took matters into their own hands.

Kaochu picked up the telephone and immediately called Shui's private home telephone number. He would probably be reprimanded for waking the mastermind from his sleep, but it was important for Lau Ming Shui to know the situation immediately. As the first ring buzzed in his ear, Kaochu smiled with the thought of the man known throughout the triad as Merciless Ming. It was a derogatory moniker, albeit an accurate one, and yet Kaochu was still unafraid—actually felt privileged and honored—to be in the employ of such a brilliant man. In some respects, Lau Ming was everything Kaochu could ever hope to become, had attained everything he could ever hope to attain.

Their meeting hadn't been the event of chance. A specific introduction was arranged for Kaochu when he was a young, upstart lieutenant in the Scarlet Dragons. Lau Ming Shui was scheduled to attend a special banquet in Hong Kong, a ceremony of the independence of the city and a dual celebration for his daughter, who was graduating from one of the political universities. In all the ranks, Kaochu was chosen by Dim Mai to provide personal security for the daughter of the great Western underboss. Sure enough, someone tried to maul the beautiful young Win-Sunglow Shui, only to face the business end of the ambitious Kaochu's pistol. The actual assassination of the would-be assailant had taken place in the hospital after the festivities. During the actual attack, Kaochu could only beat the man senseless because of too many witnesses.

Because of his actions, not only protecting Win-Sunglow but also restoring her honor and the honor of Lau Ming, Kaochu was promoted to second in command of the Scarlet Dragons. Soon, his cunning and bravery began to outshine that of his employer, which most certainly would have resulted in his death had Lau not warned Kaochu his life was in danger. The Western underboss brought the young soldier into his home, hiding and protecting him while simultaneously training him for even more greatness. Eventually, Ing Kaochu was allowed to revisit the head of the Scarlet Dragons, mete out retribution and rightfully take his place as head of the largest enforcement arm in all of the Chinese triads.

Nearly two thousand troops strong, the Kung Lok Scarlet Dragons were the most feared triad power group in the criminal underworld. They were as well equipped as some small armies, thanks to the connections of men like Dim Mai, and they all answered to Ing Kaochu. However, Kaochu had to answer to Shui, and it was only Shui's love for Kaochu that kept him in the criminal leader's good graces.

"I would assume that you're calling me at this hour for a good reason?" Shui answered, his voice cracking with the high-pitched sound of grogginess.

"I'm very sorry to wake you, but this is important."

"What has happened?"

Kaochu hesitated a moment, but then thought better of it. It wasn't a good idea to keep Shui waiting. "The American that we discussed has struck again. This time, he killed more than a dozen of my men and destroyed the processing facility in Brownsville. He may also have killed that attorney who was working for Jose Carillo.''

There was almost a minute of dead air—a minute that seemingly lasted so long Kaochu wondered if his master had fallen asleep or simply hung up the phone. These weren't the times that Kaochu relished his position, despite Shui's long-suffering attitude and patience toward his ward and future heir. Kaochu had earned this right only because he was closer to the underboss than anyone, and Shui had never been able to sire a son—not that he didn't keep trying, but the man was aging rapidly. And it went against Shui's personal belief system to take more than one wife.

''What are you planning to do about this situation, Ing?'' Shui finally asked.

''I wasn't sure I would do anything,'' Kaochu said. ''Your last advice was to wait. You said that he would come to us.''

''I would say that he has. What do we know about this man?''

''We know his name is Belasko, and that he is a competent warrior,'' Kaochu said quietly. ''If I were to have my own way with him, I would recruit the American dog to fight with us. He also seems to have unlimited resources at his disposal, given the firepower with which he has resisted us. There is already talk among some of my men that he's not real, but rather a spirit that looks real and fights like a demon from the grave.''

''You must squash those rumors immediately, Ing,'' Shui warned him. ''Such things can be much more dangerous to you than the actual threat.''

''I understand, and I will deal with this. I know that

he is just a man and you know the same. However, he is a formidable opponent and, as I believe we previously discussed, he is dangerous to both the physical and mental well-being of our organization.''

"Not to mention the radical amount of interference he's created in both my plans and the established operations we meant to acquire.''

"My feelings exactly.''

"I will leave this in your hands. This man has become a thorn in your side, and I feel your need to exact vengeance. You may deal with him as you wish, provided it does not alter our timetable.''

"My sources tell me that they think this is the next place he will come.''

"It's possible. But I think to be on the safe side, you should provide him some incentive.''

"What do you mean?''

"Send your men to capture the two women that aided him. The Zahn bitch he took from Tang, and the other one that we know helped him in Brownsville. They've been troublesome to us, and I'm sure he has some loyalty to both of them now.''

"Do you think he'll actually worry about them?'' Kaochu asked with disbelief. "Belasko is a professional soldier of some kind. Their lives may not matter to him.''

"Perhaps, but I'm not inclined to think so. His hits against Carillo's people and ours have been precisely timed and carefully orchestrated. Innocents always appear to be out of the way. Even our failed hit in Mexico resulted in no loss of life by those uninvolved. I think he actually cares for people.''

"I think I see. You're going to use this as leverage.''

"Precisely. You see, Belasko is on the offensive, and he apparently likes to keep it that way. We must change our tactics so that the hunter becomes the hunted, and we put as many of what he considers innocents in the way to keep him on the run. Eventually, he must retreat so far that he can go no farther and then he is trapped. It is an old art form in war, but still a very effective one."

"I understand."

"I hope you do, Ing. I hope you understand that the Kung Lok cannot and will not tolerate this man's interference any longer. We've suffered losses that we're already feeling, and I'm sure news of this incident in El Paso will get back to Hong Kong. That will not be good. We must put an end to this now."

"I will not fail you, Lau. I promise."

"I'm going to hold you to that." A long silence followed before Shui added, "Find Belasko and finish him."

El Paso, Texas

GRIMALDI SHOOK his head as he stood in the emergency room of the El Paso Trauma Center and studied the Executioner's wounds.

There was a large patch on the back of his calf and a second covering his shoulder. Grimaldi had met Bolan at the arranged alternate point, picked him up and flown him straight to the trauma center. He'd even called ahead to let them know he was bringing the soldier in via helicopter and was planning to land on their roof pad. They used their credentials as DEA agents to get past all of the uncomfortable questions. A chopper bringing in a shot DEA agent in the middle of the night in El Paso probably wasn't the most unusual sight to the hospital staff, and it was certainly explainable if the local authorities showed up. Any details of the incident would be taken care of later by Stony Man, including the erasure of all records from the hospital, DEA and police databases if necessary—thanks to the handiwork of Aaron Kurtzman.

"You should stay for a few days," the doctor told Bolan when he'd completed suturing the wounds and administering tetanus and antibiotic shots.

Bolan shook his head. "Sorry, Doc, but no dice on that. I've got work to do."

"I'm sure your colleagues can handle that."

"No, they can't."

"I'd really prefer you stay."

"I'm not staying. Okay?"

And something in the Executioner's eyes had told the doctor it was better to just nod and leave the room from the large and commanding presence as quickly as possible. Particularly one with cold blue eyes, who was dressed head to toe in a blacksuit and who'd been shot. The man's entire presence read, "Don't argue with me."

Now Grimaldi watched as the Executioner quickly removed the blacksuit and rapidly dressed in the street clothes the pilot had brought him from his pack in the chopper: blue jeans, a red plaid shirt and a black leather jacket. Bolan had donned one of the holsters and Grimaldi passed the Beretta over to him to holster. The other holster he slung over his shoulder with nonchalance.

With things wrapped up there, they headed for the

helipad. Bolan looked at his watch and scowled. It was almost 0500 hours—time to get moving and head for Las Vegas. Word of what happened there had probably already reached the ears of Carillo and the triad, which meant that trouble was just around the corner. Grimaldi had taken the chopper to an airfield in El Paso and fueled it, so the aircraft was topped off and ready for action.

Once airborne, the Executioner used a remote telecommunications server to contact Stony Man. Brognola answered on the first ring.

"How did it go?" he asked Bolan.

"I think I delivered a clear message."

"Jack already contacted us once," the head Fed replied quietly. "He says you took a hit or two."

"Nothing too serious. I'll live."

Brognola cleared his throat, keeping silent for a time before saying, "What's your next move?"

"We're heading to Las Vegas. The Kung Lok has moved into that area in full force. I figure forty-eight hours at best to bring them down."

"I understand."

"Any word from the Man?"

"Yes. He agrees with me that Jose Carillo and the Kung Lok may be starting a war with each other. He's also suspicious, like we are, that either side might be receiving support from officials within the government."

"Do you have a clue who these officials might be?"

"Not yet. But if there are high rankers involved, they're doing a good job of keeping a low profile. Our strained relations with the Chinese notwithstanding, it's a good bet that Lau Ming Shui is the man responsible.

Being he's in Canada, it's a bit difficult at the moment to track his movements. Nonetheless, the President's gone forward and approved CIA involvement. They're going to be watching him on that end.''

"Shui won't make any move until his people are firmly in place here, Hal.''

"How so?''

"He's an experienced criminal, with lots of ties. I agree he's probably running the show, but many triad activities in the past have gone unchecked by the Chinese government. It's not good business for officials in Hong Kong.''

"True,'' Brognola agreed. "Groups like Shui's feed Chinese politicians with quite a bit of information and intelligence on our activities here. That's why it's always been important for them to maintain some kind of workable relationship.''

"Right. Which is why I think Shui is moving on his own with this one.''

"Do you think there could be any tie to this and Shui's relationship with Dim Mai?''

"Without a question.''

Brognola let out a deep sigh. "So we're getting deeper into this all the time.''

"Yeah.''

"Okay, Striker, I'm willing to play this your way. I've definitely got enough to involve the rest of the team, but I don't want to step on your toes.''

"I know, Hal, and I appreciate it. But like I said before, I'm concerned about compromising security. For the time being, I think it's better I keep moving at this on my own.'' He looked at Grimaldi, who was listening to the conversation through the headset, and flashed him a grin. "Besides, I've got Jack with me, and that's more than enough."

"All right, it's your call. But you know where to reach me."

"Understood. Out here."

After Bolan terminated the call, he fell silent and began to think about the next two days. Danny Tang had undoubtedly reached Ing Kaochu by now, and delivered the Executioner's message. With the previous night's activities, that meant the Scarlet Dragons would probably be searching for him. He wasn't too concerned that they'd reach him before he reached Las Vegas. There was no reason for Bolan to believe they knew how he was traveling or what his next step was, which gave him the advantage.

Bolan would have to strike quick and strike first. That was the only way to keep his strategic advantage and keep the Kung Lok on the run. The other issue that had him concerned was Carillo. There were probably still countless resources the Mexican drug lord had at his disposal, and with the destruction of his Brownsville-Houston pipeline, Carillo would be looking for payback.

If nothing else, Bolan would have to keep them coming at him. He could manipulate the situation in such a way that risk to innocents would be minimal. However, if the Kung Lok or Carillo's people were allowed to run rampant, lots of civilians stood the risk of getting killed. The Executioner couldn't allow that to happen, no matter what the costs, and he knew that if he fell, Stony Man would be forced to take over.

The men of Phoenix Force and Able Team were unrivaled, formidable adversaries who could keep the hands full of Carillo and the Kung Lok for a very long time. Bolan hoped it wouldn't have to come to that, simply for the sake of America at large. No, he was going to have to pull out all the stops and put this one to bed himself. It was going to get intense from here on out, and he still had a lot of territory to cover. He'd have to hit quick and hard, and then retreat. It would be a new kind of warfare, one for which his enemies probably weren't ready. This only created another advantage for Bolan. As he closed his eyes, allowing his body to rest and mend some, the Executioner's mind continued to draw closer to his objectives.

He had a plan.

Brownsville, Texas

LISA RAJERO and Noreen Zahn sat in Charlie Metzger's office, neither of them very happy to be stuck there waiting for their boss to return.

Rajero knew that telling Metzger about Zahn's near demise had probably been a mistake, particularly if he was on Carillo's payroll. But Zahn had insisted they follow official channels, and with Belasko missing in action, Rajero didn't know where else to turn. She was doing this for her team, but it was against her better judgment. She'd never trusted Metzger, and not because he wasn't a decent enough guy or because he'd mistreated her in any way. It was just a gut instinct—something she'd learned to trust over the years.

As far as the rest of the branch personnel for the Brownsville DEA office were concerned, and apparently the suits in Washington, Metzger was a model supervisor. He had an outstanding success record, had a loving wife and kids, went to church every Sunday and lived a clean public life. While there were rumors his record had recently been up for scrutiny, he was generally considered a fair and equitable boss. Still, she couldn't shake the feeling of dread as they told him the story, including the business about Belasko. Rajero couldn't find any way to back out of that, because Peter Willy had become concerned that she was in over her head, and he'd gone right to Metzger.

The return of her boss to the office shook her from her thoughts. She sat up in her chair self-consciously as he quietly closed the door and sat behind his desk. He leaned forward, folded his hands on his desk with his thumbs touching and fixed her with a puzzled gaze.

"We need to talk," he finally said.

He looked at Zahn and said, "Thanks for your time, Noreen. I'm glad to see you in one piece. It appears we owe your life to this Belasko guy, if nothing else. You're dismissed for now, but I want you to stick close until we can do a full debriefing. You're on suspension with pay until this mess is straightened out."

"Thank you, sir," Zahn replied. She inclined her head toward Rajero and said, "But what about Lisa? She's the one who stumbled on to all of this. I'm concerned that maybe the agency is looking at this all wrong."

"You're questioning my judgment?" Metzger asked in a low voice.

"I've never questioned your judgment, sir," Zahn replied. "I'm questioning whether the DEA has all of the facts here."

"We'll get to the bottom of it." He looked at a Rajero and said, "Believe me. Now, you're dismissed."

"Yes, sir. Lisa, I'll be waiting outside for you."

Rajero nodded, and then Zahn got up and quietly left the office. Once she was gone, Metzger shook his head and let out what didn't amount to much more than a sardonic laugh. The guy was obviously agitated, that much was for sure, but he was also apparently looking to keep himself in check. He finally took a deep breath and got right to the point.

"I don't understand, Lisa. When have I ever given you any reason to distrust me?"

Rajero tried not to squirm in her seat as she replied, "I don't understand."

"Cut the bull, Lisa. Okay? I know about your affiliation with this Belasko guy, and I know that he went to see Ramon Sapèdas of the Border Patrol. We're a tight-knit team down here. A team I thought you were a part of. Did you think that these little stunts weren't going to get back to me? Ramon happens to be a friend of mine."

"Well, then, maybe you ought to find some new friends, Charlie."

"What's that supposed to mean?"

"It means that your friend has ties with a known drug smuggler and member of the Mexican mafia."

It only took a moment for the expression on Metzger's face to change from that of indignation to realization. With a tone of incredulity he said, "You're talking about Jose Carillo, aren't you?"

"That's exactly who I'm talking about."

"And what proof do you have of this?"

"The proof that the guns used against us on this most recent bust were in his custody and care. The particular gun we traced was identified as the murder weapon of one Randy Lovato, a drug runner for the Rosarez family.''

''I know about the Lovato murder. The FBI ruled it a professional hit.''

''Then why isn't that weapon sitting in a federal evidence lockup instead of floating around on the streets and being used to kill our people? Those agents were ours, Charlie. That weapon spilled the blood of our own, and I want to know who put it back into the hands of those who did it.''

''You let me worry about that now, Lisa!'' Metzger snapped, slamming his palm on the desk. ''You're not like this Mike Belasko, that you can just be a law unto yourself and take on whatever cases you please. You're a federal agent, and I expect you to conduct yourself with some discretion. I also expect you to make yourself accountable to me, keep me apprised of your movements and I expect you to follow the rules! Am I being clear?''

''Yes, sir,'' Rajero whispered.

Metzger rose, stuck his hands in his pockets and began to pace. ''You know what bothers me most, Lisa? What bothers me most is that your actions aren't just suggestive of a maverick or insubordinate agent. They're more suggestive of an agent who doesn't trust her superiors. That hurts personally, and I don't mind saying it. But it also hurts the cohesion of our department as a whole. And not only can that severance of teamwork get more agents killed, but it undermines my authority and makes us look bad in Washington's eyes.''

''I'm sorry if you feel I violated your trust, Charlie,'' Rajero admitted with honesty. ''And you're right in saying you've never done anything to me to do that. But I have to ask myself if you're more concerned about what

Washington thinks, or about the fact that good men and women are getting wasted for nothing more than profit. This payroll of Carillo's goes deep. I know it does...I can feel it in my gut.''

Metzger sat again. "I understand what you're going through. I went through it myself once. God knows this agency isn't invulnerable to graft and apathy, but I have to know that everyone's on my team. I have to be able to trust that you'll watch my back, and you have to trust I'll watch yours. If that concept breaks down, we're all going to be in trouble. Am I being clear?''

"Yes."

"Now, if Sapèdas *is* working for Carillo, I'd be the first to agree we need to get him off the streets. But before we can do that, we need proof. A missing weapon from evidence isn't proof of any wrongdoing, which means we're going to have to find another way of going about this. I'm going to start the ball rolling on my end. For now, I'm lifting your suspension and restoring you to active status.'' He reached into his desk drawer and returned her shield and official duty weapon. "Don't blow it this time, Lisa. The consequences wouldn't be good for your career.''

"What do you want me to do?''

"You and Pete Willy to get over to El Paso. I'll get the okay from my end to make the investigation official. But you keep in touch with me at all times—'' he jabbed a finger at her "—and you don't make a move without my okay. You get me?''

She nodded, taking a deep breath and letting it out. Her feelings about Metzger had finally dissipated. Rajero was at last beginning to feel that maybe the guy was on their side, and that somewhere along the way she'd done him a horrible injustice. But this would finally be her chance to bring Sapèdas down once and for all—and bring her one step closer to putting Jose Carillo out of business forever.

CHAPTER TWELVE

Rajero and Willy were in a black Ford Bronco traveling Highway 83 within an hour from the time they got Metzger's approval to proceed with the operation.

Rajero didn't say much to Willy during the trip. She was having a hard time dealing with the fact that he'd ratted her out to Metzger, and even more difficulty understanding what had prompted him to betray her trust. But eventually she knew she'd have to get over it. They were going to be together for the next few days, and as such they were going to have to make the best of it.

"Anything you want to get off your chest?" Willy asked after nearly a half hour of silence.

"Not really."

"I see."

After a moment of uncomfortable tension, she said, "As a matter of fact, yes, there *is* something I'd like to talk about. I'd like to talk about why the hell you betrayed me after promising to keep quiet about Belasko?"

Willy groaned. "Oh, I knew it would come down to this eventually."

"You're damn right, Pete! Did you think I wouldn't find out? Did you think that Charlie wouldn't tell me who it was that squealed? I thought I could trust you, and you betrayed me.''

"I'm sorry if you feel that way, Lisa," Willy said, "but I was concerned about your safety. I thought maybe this Belasko had you misled, and I wasn't going to take the chance of watching you buy it, too. We lost several good people the night he blew that truck full of evidence sky-high. I just didn't know what else to do.''

"We didn't lose them because he blew up the drugs, Pete. We lost them because somebody betrayed us. I think that somebody might have been Ramon Sapèdas. I told you that during our meeting at the diner.''

"I know that, but I figured maybe you weren't thinking straight. I knew your suspension was a big blow, and despite the fact I personally think Metzger's a windbag, I wasn't about to lose you quite that easily.''

"Well, I believe your reasons were genuine, but that doesn't make it right," Rajero replied softly.

"Look, I swear it won't happen again. From now on, I'll keep my mouth shut if I say I will unless we both agree otherwise. Deal?''

She nodded. "Deal.''

"I guess the truth is that I'm having a lot of trouble buying this thing about Ramon Sapèdas. I mean, what's the motive here? This guy's got nothing to gain by burning us.''

"He's got everything to gain if he's on Jose Carillo's payroll.''

"Do you have any proof of that?''

"Not yet. That's why Charlie approved this little excursion to El Paso. Belasko was certain the guy had something up his sleeve, and I trust his instincts. If Ramon Sapèdas is playing for the other team, we'll find out soon enough—''

Three sedans and one van of varying colors appeared as if from nowhere and surrounded the Bronco so quickly, Willy had nowhere to go. The new arrivals boxed their quarry quickly and effectively.

''Who the hell are these guys?'' Willy asked, the tension heavy in his voice.

''Chinese triad,'' Rajero announced simply.

''What?''

Rajero reached into her purse and withdrew a Colt .380 Mustang pistol, a backup piece to her duty weapon, the Glock 19. She could see barely see through the tinted windows of the Bronco that the driver of the closest sedan was Asian.

''Stop the truck!'' she hollered.

Willy shrugged, then did as instructed, leaning on the brakes of the Bronco as the four sedans tried to keep him pinned to the center lane. The others shot past at the sudden slowing of the SUV, and the sedan in the rear swung to one side to avoid rear-ending them. As that vehicle came into the right lane, Rajero powered down her window, pointed the .380 through the opening and fired at the driver's window from point-blank range.

''What the hell are you doing?'' Willy roared.

''Trying to save our necks!''

She fired twice more. The second round shattered the driver's window and the third made contact with flesh. The sedan first veered into the Bronco, then bounced away and flipped off the highway as soon as the front wheels touched the soft shoulder. The vehicle began to spin, flipped twice end over end and landed on its roof.

Willy could barely keep control of the shimmying rear end as he tried to recover from the impact of the sedan.

A moment later, he didn't have to worry about it. The right front tire blew out. Willy leaned hard on the brakes and finally got the Bronco to stop fishtailing, but now the other vehicles had come to a stop. A wave of Chinese gunmen emerged from them and fanned out. They advanced on the Bronco, the Jatimatic machine pistols and AK-74 assault rifles in plain sight.

"I think we're in trouble," Rajero whispered.

Willy didn't reply, but instead jumped from the Bronco and took up a firing position behind the door. Rajero went to follow suit but there was no time. Willy got off one shot before his body was riddled with autofire. He jerked spasmodically as round after round pierced his flesh. Blood and tissue sprayed the interior of the Bronco, splattering across Rajero's exposed skin. The cacophony of gunfire caused her ears to ring, and the entire vehicle was rocking under the impact of weapons fire.

Rajero's mind screamed at her to get away, but she hadn't been prepared for that kind of vicious assault. The Chinese triad was formidable enough, but if Belasko had been right about the Scarlet Dragons, there was no question left in her mind why they had earned their particular reputation.

As suddenly as the assault started, it was over. Rajero lay in her seat, waiting for the Asian killers to get close enough. If she was going to die this day, she would at least take a few more with her. The passenger door opened suddenly, and Rajero shot the first visible Dragon. The man's head exploded as the .380-caliber slug from the Mustang drilled a path through his skull.

Before Rajero could select another target, something hard hit the back of her head. She drew her hand up to touch her head as darkness pervaded at the edges of her sight. The last thing she saw was her own blood covering her hand as the world around her faded.

AFTER WILLY and Rajero had left for El Paso, Noreen Zahn decided to do some checking herself. Word of the destruction of Jose Carillo's distribution warehouse was spreading through the Brownsville DEA office. So were rumors of a firefight that had left nearly twenty people dead in El Paso. Other than herself and Rajero, nobody had made the connection. But she knew it was the handiwork of a certain dark-haired, blue-eyed stranger who called himself Mike Belasko—it had to be.

Zahn contacted several of her friends in the FBI, along with a Company contact at Langley. Nobody admitted to ever having heard of Belasko, and there was no personnel record that anyone by that name had ever existed, as a cover or otherwise. This had Zahn nervous. She was certain that he worked for the U.S. government in some capacity, but he wasn't employed by any of the known groups that would participate in his kind of operations. She didn't know anybody in the NSA, but she quickly dismissed the idea since Belasko just didn't strike her as the type. It was illegal for the CIA to operate on American soil, and if there was anything she could decipher about her mysterious guardian angel, it was that he played by the rules. So perhaps he was a freelancer, as Rajero had told her, and perhaps he wasn't.

In either case, Zahn was now on a mission to find out exactly who Belasko was and for whom he worked, and there was only one real way of doing that. She would have to locate him and find out for herself what was really going on. She understood the guy's seemingly fanatic drive to stop the Kung Lok triad from participating in open battle against the Carillo empire. Such a war could prove disastrous for innocent civilians, and dangerous to the law-enforcement community, as well.

After almost four hours of digging, she finally hit pay dirt. One of DEA's people had been treated at the El Paso Medical Center, brought in early that morning by chopper. The wounds hadn't been serious, and the nurse she spoke with said the patient refused to stay any longer than necessary. Strangely enough, they couldn't find any record at that point, but that wasn't unusual since they had seen lots of patients that morning—and it was possible that the medical record simply hadn't been entered in their database yet. No, she had no idea where the chart was, and she didn't remember the guy's name. She did think they had left by chopper.

Okay, so Belasko had suffered some injuries in his battle with the group in El Paso. Based on what Rajero had told her, that left only a few possibilities. He would either continue west, heading toward a showdown in Nogales or Mexicali, or he would go back to Las Vegas to infiltrate the operations there. Zahn was betting on Las Vegas.

She made another phone call to a pilot friend, and he agreed to fly her out to Nevada. She packed a small bag and proceeded directly from her apartment to the airport. Tom Cantor was waiting for her. She'd been friends with the guy since high school; they'd even dated once or twice but it hadn't worked out, and despite the loss of romance there was no denying the strength of the friendship. Which was why she couldn't believe her eyes when he fell under the sudden fire of a dozen assault rifles.

The Asian gunners appeared from nowhere, the muzzles of their weapons winking with merciless efficiency. Zahn reached behind her to grasp the Glock secured in a holster, but she never got off a shot. As she cleared the weapon, the wind was knocked from her by a sudden blow to her back. Another Chinese gunner swung the butt of his AK-74 and connected with her stomach. The air exploded from her lungs and she cried out in pain. She bent and felt the white-hot pain of something strike the side of her neck, something like the rigid side of a hand connecting with her brachial-cephalic nerve.

And then all faded to black....

MACK BOLAN SAT in a motel room on the outskirts of Las Vegas and studied a map of the city spread out on the bed. His chair was positioned next to it, and he sipped coffee from a foam cup while marking areas on the map with a red grease pencil. He was developing a battle plan that would effectively target those areas known to be Carillo's hot spots. The targets themselves included two casinos, three large drug houses and a couple of known gathering places for distribution gangs.

Grimaldi was smoking a cigarette at a table near the window, which was opened a crack but covered by a shade. On the table were clips for the Beretta 93-Rs and the two H&K assault weapons.

The pair rarely spoke during their individual duties, obviously content to focus upon the mission ahead. Grimaldi obviously had something he wanted to tell the Executioner, but Bolan had to squash the pilot's oppor-

tunity to do so at every turn. The Stony Man flier knew
that this was something Bolan would have to do on his
own. He couldn't risk anyone else from the Farm involved more than they were already.

"What's the word, Sarge?" Grimaldi finally asked as
he loaded the last clip for the HK-53.

"Trouble," Bolan replied grimly. "The numbers are
running down."

The pilot stubbed his cigarette in the ashtray and said
with a cocksure grin, "That's no surprise. I wouldn't
expect anything less out of you."

Bolan chuckled. "Yeah, I guess not."

"How many of those locales do you think are still
held by Carillo's people?"

"I'd have to say most of them. The Kung Lok will
try to phase themselves in quietly. Only the heavy resistance will be met with a forceful takeover."

"Makes sense."

"Yeah. The only thing that makes me suspicious is
that I haven't seen much in the way of retaliation by
Carillo's people."

"What do you mean?"

Bolan shook his head. "He's not fighting to hold on
to what he has. Everything I know about this guy's history would suggest he'd be coming back at the Kung
Lok full force."

"Or at least at you full force."

"Right. He's taking a lot of hits, but he's not retali-
ating."

"That does seem strange."

"It's more than strange, Jack. It's almost…tactical."
Bolan fell silent, contemplating the possibilities.

"You think maybe he's waiting on Nievas's forces?"

"Yeah, I've considered that. It's possible that's exactly what he's waiting on. And if it is, that means he has a very large operation in mind."

"Well, you said before that whoever controlled the border controlled the Mexican-American drug trade."

Bolan eyed his longtime friend. "You're thinking maybe Mexicali?"

"It's possible." Grimaldi shrugged.

"Me, too. That could mean nothing short of a third world war right there in the Baja. I was concerned when Hal told me about their theory of Carillo and the FARC joining forces. Now it seems even more probable. This could go sour real quick."

"I don't know. That seems pretty intense, Sarge. What do you think?"

"I think it's going to get worse before it gets better."

Grimaldi pulled the shade aside and looked out the window. "Sunset. I guess it's about time for you to go."

Bolan nodded as he started to change into his blacksuit. "Start putting stuff together, would you?"

"You got it."

As the soldier changed, he began to run the situation through his head. He was almost out of time. Only five days had passed since his first encounter in Brownsville, and it seemed already like an eternity. The next forty-eight hours would be the deciding factor. Bolan knew that he was going to have to push himself beyond the limits of endurance if he were to bring things to a close. He'd tackle the problems here in Las Vegas in a quick and permanent fashion, and then head for Mexicali.

Nogales and San Luis Rio Colorado would have to wait for now. Local law enforcement could probably handle the issues in those areas in conjunction with the DEA anyway, if Stony Man found a way to filter intelligence to them without compromising the source. Brognola would probably already do that on his own, knowing what the Executioner was up against. Despite his talents as a soldier and covert operative, Mack Bolan knew he couldn't be in two places at once, and he certainly wasn't invincible. The scars and fresh wounds he noted in the mirror as he dressed were a testament to that.

After lacing up his combat boots, he strode to the duffel. Grimaldi was still arranging things in the butt pack attached to the military canvas belt so he handed the dual shoulder rigging to Bolan. The Executioner shrugged into it, cinched the straps and then checked the actions on both Berettas before holstering them into the rigging. Bolan quickly checked Grimaldi's pack job, made only a few minor adjustments, then sealed it and slung the belt over his shoulder.

Grimaldi handed him the gym-bag-sized duffel. "Both the SMGs are in there, locked and loaded. So is the .44, LBE, the last of the grenades and your combat knife. You're all set, big guy."

"Thanks, Jack. I'm going to have to take the car. You'll get back to the airport?"

"Yeah, I'll stay here tonight and grab a taxi back to the airport first thing in the morning. I think a hot meal and a good night sleep will do wonders. I'm tired and I don't want to risk flying back to Texas tonight."

"Understood."

As the Executioner headed toward the door, Grimaldi called to him, "Hey, Sarge?"

"Yeah?"

"Give 'em hell."

"Bet on it." And with that, the Executioner walked out the door.

ING KAOCHU SMILED with satisfaction as he entered the basement of his new home and noted the two American women tied to a back wall with leather ropes.

They wore nothing, a fact that had left them naked and absent of their dignity, as well. Kaochu had ordered this so that these whores—who obviously didn't know their place in a man's world—would realize he had ultimate power over them. It wasn't about sexual desires; he had plenty of women pure of his race on hand to do such bidding. This was about stripping his prisoners of honor and restraining their minds from entertaining hopes of escape.

They almost took on the appearance of trophies mounted against the dark brick wall of the finished basement. In the center of the room was a pool table covered with brilliant red felt. Spread fans of polished black wooden frames and hand-beaten tin painted gold cast shadows on the wall around the pair of American beauties. There were pictures of dragons and ancient Chinese writing painted on the fans, and the entire scene appeared apropos of an ancient Ming dynasty ritual or ceremony. It looked as if they were sacrificing these two women to appease some angry god.

And Kaochu had to admit that he loved it.

The Scarlet Dragon leader dropped into a nearby chair and propped his feet on the pool table. He began to take an interest in his fingernails, finally pulling a paper clip from his pocket and using one end to clean under the edges. He sat and acted engrossed in what he was doing, pretending to ignore the stares of hatred directed his way. He particularly enjoyed the fiery resolve of the dark-haired one they called Rajero. It was almost...erotic.

"You are both so obviously full of contempt for me," Kaochu told his guests. He looked up from his nail-cleaning task and added, "If looks could kill."

"Some say they can," Noreen Zahn replied.

"Set me free, and I'll show you what looks can do," Rajero snapped.

Kaochu let out a grunt of displeasure and then rose from his chair. He walked directly over to Rajero and slapped her across the face. The woman's head snapped to one side, and the basement echoed with the report of the blow. Kaochu sidestepped and delivered a similar blow to Zahn. He then turned from them and began to pace around the pool table.

"First, you will watch your tongues." He stopped and looked back at them a moment, adding, "Or I will cut them out myself." He continued pacing. "Second, you will tell me everything you know about Mike Belasko. I want to know where he is, what his plans are and who he works for."

"You'll have to drag that information from our cold, dead bodies, then," Rajero replied with vehemence in her voice.

Kaochu walked back to her and slapped her again. "You forgot the first rule. Don't speak unless I ask you a direct question. Fools chatter, but the wise listen carefully."

"Well, then, we know which category you fit into," Zahn snapped, closing her eyes and edging away from the blow she knew was coming.

It did. Both women now had cheeks red with Kaochu's brutality. The Scarlet Dragon leader returned to his pacing. This was going nowhere, and he was convinced that given their training, the more he tortured the DEA agents the stronger the resolve. Of course, Kaochu had learned the fine arts of extracting whatever information he desired. However, it would do no good to kill the American bitches.

His target was Belasko. He truly wanted that man to suffer.

"This man is responsible for the death of many good Scarlet Dragons."

"Belasko has been responsible for the death of a group of thugs," Rajero replied.

Kaochu could tell from the look on the DEA woman's face that she was waiting for him to come over and beat her to death, but he refrained this time. They wouldn't be quite so cavalier when they knew what sort of plans he had for them. Although he saw no reason to tell them—it wouldn't have done much good anyway.

"This Mike Belasko. Who does he work for?"

"I wish we knew," Zahn replied.

"Then he does not represent the DEA?"

"He represents everyone," Rajero said with resolve in her voice. "Eventually, he'll get to you. And when he does, you're going to regret ever hearing his name."

Kaochu couldn't resist flashing her a smug grin. "I do not think so. It would seem this man fancies himself a hero. But there are no heroes left in your society. This individual is by no means superior to our organization. We will find him and destroy him. Then your hope will be gone, and this Belasko will be forgotten as dust in the wind."

CHAPTER THIRTEEN

Las Vegas, Nevada

The information on Mack Bolan's first target was gleaned from Stony Man intelligence through Las Vegas police channels. It was a known drug house that doubled as a high-priced brothel, and was nestled in a secluded neighborhood just outside the Strip. As a matter of fact, it wasn't too far from Vito Rosetti's place.

The Executioner knew there wasn't time for soft probes. He would have to hit several places hard and fast, and still manage to keep bystanders out of the way. It would have been ideal to take them on the inside, but the three guards smoking on the front stoop needed attention first.

Bolan gave it to them. He put the sedan on the curb, casually exited and used the cover of the car to take down his enemy. The delivery came in the form of quick shots from the Beretta 93-R. The first round punched through the closest thug's chest and lodged in his heart. The target let out a surprised yell of pain, but Bolan had already tracked the second one even before the first fell to the ground. The gunman was obviously digging for hardware but he never got a chance to use it. The Executioner's aim was true, the subsonic 9 mm Parabellum round ripping off the top of its target's skull.

The third hood backed up the steps, fumbling for a machine pistol. He was able to clear it from beneath his suit jacket, but Bolan had already moved from his position into a clear line of fire. He squeezed the trigger three times. All three slugs landed on target, two in the stomach and a third in the face. The impact hurled the gunman against the front door and he slid lifeless to the porch stoop.

The Executioner closed the gap and vaulted the steps two at a time. The door opened just slightly, and a beefy, tanned head appeared through the opening. Bolan blew it off and put his foot to the door as the muscle man's headless corpse fell where it stood.

Bolan came through the front door, ready for action. Several Hispanic hoods were playing cards at a table, and another was watching the game from a nearby couch. He was the least threat, since a slim and beautiful brunette was wriggling on his lap. Bolan thumbed the selector switch to burst mode and took the two closest players before they had time to react. The third man stood and managed to bring a pistol into the play. He fired off two hasty shots and turned up the table for cover.

The soldier was undaunted, firing through the flimsy table and punching holes in the gunner's stomach and head. Brain matter exploded from his hiding place, showering the walls and table. The woman began to scream, holding on to her man tightly while he was trying to disentangle himself from her. The Executioner didn't wait for an invitation to get killed, but drew the other Beretta 93-R as he popped the magazine on the first and put a single round through the hood's jaw. The woman was doused with the blood of her boyfriend. Bolan clamped a hand to her throat, leveling the muzzle of the Beretta at her forehead.

"Get up and get out," he commanded.

She immediately obeyed, running out the front door without another word. Bolan turned to the sound of footsteps rushing down the stairs. Two more soldiers, pistols drawn, descended quickly as the woman vacated the house. He fired a well-placed shot to the kneecap of one, the round immediately disabling the gunman. The hardcase collapsed on the stairs and rolled to the bottom. The second wasn't as lucky. He managed to get off a wild round before Bolan shot him through groin and stomach. The gunman flipped over the far stairway railing and crashed through a glass-topped table.

Bolan inserted a fresh clip in the first Beretta he'd used and holstered it. He quickly stepped around the body of the one he'd wounded, who had obviously passed out during his fall. The Executioner made sure no weapons would be within easy reach if the guy suddenly came around, and then quickly ascended the stairs.

Without question, he meant to put this place out of business—permanently.

As Bolan reached the top landing, four gunners jumped from various rooms and began to fire wildly at him with pistols and SMGs. His catlike reflexes had saved him more times than he could count, and this particular time was no exception. In a situation like this, there was little room to maneuver. The soldier avoided the assault by shoulder rolling toward the closest gunman. He came out of the roll on his feet, grabbing the man around the throat and constricting his windpipe with well-trained forearm muscles.

The natural progression for the two with automatic weapons was to follow the target. Their aim was true, unfortunately for their comrade, and the rounds intended for Bolan ended up in his human shield. The Executioner raised his pistol and took out both of the guys toting SMGs with head shots. One staggered between the doorway of the bedroom, bounced off the frame several times like a pool ball and then collapsed to the ground. His body convulsed while his nervous system caught up to the brain message that he was dead.

Bolan dragged the limp body of his shield backward into a room and slammed the door closed with a kick. He dropped the corpse, reached into a concealed pouch on his blacksuit and withdrew a sleeveless DM-51 and pulled the pin. Moving to the door as the grenade cooked off, he quickly opened the door and tossed the bomb even as a fresh salvo of rounds spit from the weapon of his remaining opponent. A grunt of surprise was followed a moment later by a momentous blast.

Plaster rained from the ceiling, and some of the nearby drywall cracked with the concussion. It felt as if the entire house were going to fall around the Executioner's ears. Bolan had been through worse hellholes than this one, and he wasn't intimidated. He peered into the hallway and surveyed the scene there. It was a gruesome sight. The grenade had obviously landed close because the blast had been enough to dismember the gunman. Body parts lay in every corner of the wide hallway, and one leg was perched precariously at the edge of the stairway landing.

Bolan holstered the Beretta, then yanked the .44 Magnum Desert Eagle from the military holster and entered the hallway. He first checked the rooms with the open doors, but they were empty. He then began to take the closed doors one at a time. The search took him about five minutes, and the place turned up deserted.

Something was wrong here. Bolan could tell the house was just what the Las Vegas police had claimed it was—and he knew that Stony Man's intelligence was always good. Kurtzman went through that stuff with a fine-tooth comb before feeding details to the Executioner or the teams. There were some telltale signs that drugs and prostitution went hand and hand with each other in the house. There was powdery residue in one of the bathrooms and a half-dozen crack pipes in various places. Bolan also found a wad of cash in a dresser chest. Whoever used the place had left in a big hurry.

The wail of sirens was close; it was time to go. And as the soldier descended the stairs and exited to the house, he understood why the place was abandoned. Someone had blocked in his vehicle with a large panel truck. The source of the sirens became visible as the first police cruiser rounded a corner down the street at high speed, its tires squealing in protest.

Several curious onlookers had emerged from their houses, the gunfire and explosion having obviously attracted considerable attention. But it was the sound of the rear door on the panel truck rolling upward and slap of combat boots hitting the street that demanded the Executioner's attention.

A handful of hardened combat soldiers in urban camouflage emerged from the rear of the truck, automatic assault rifles held at the ready....

West Palm Beach, Florida

LAU MING SHUI SAT in the lobby of the Larouquette Pearl Suites, watching impatiently as the other guests arrived. His eyes roved through the lobby, insuring that bodyguards were in place and watchful for any signs of trouble. This was a very dangerous time for all of them. With the myth of this supersoldier called Belasko floating among the Scarlet Dragons, and the war with the Mexicans, he should have been up in Toronto keeping a low profile. Coming to the United States had been a matter of great risk to his personal security and his assets.

The truth of the matter was that he didn't really have time for this meeting anyway. Nonetheless, it was necessary to keep up appearances, and despite the power he wielded it was *not* acceptable to reject an open invitation by the Kung Lok triad's council. Especially when so many important guests were here. This was actually an important time for him.

Undoubtedly, word of his ostensible "coup" and subsequent activities in the American Southwest had reached the ears of the Hong Kong underworld. It also had most likely been the subject of discussion among the elite politicians of China's cabinet members. Some of those men he saw here now: individuals who roamed the halls of power with indifference and commanded armies with mere impunity. Yet, in Shui's mind, their power was superficial—they were little more than window dressings for the great China they preached among themselves in the bathhouses and their pitiful diplomatic circles. Most of them had no real love for their country, which disgusted Shui. Sure, they had done some great things in the area of military might, but China had always been strong in that sense. What they claimed they did for the country and what they had actually done were two entirely different things. He couldn't respect them for that, no matter how much they might wish, or even command, him to do so.

Shui had once been a part of them, but he wasn't anymore. He didn't even feel like a part of them. He couldn't be a part of them ever again, although he would never tell them as much—not because he didn't have the courage but because he wasn't foolish enough to burn his bridges. Despite disagreements, he rarely dealt with them and that was consolation enough. He was here only to make an appearance, and then he would depart directly for Las Vegas, where Ing Kaochu obviously needed him most.

"Lau Ming Shui?" the sweet, soft voice spoke in Chinese.

Shui stood, turned and immediately recognized the slender Chinese beauty standing behind him. She had sleek black hair tied behind her in a traditional bun held by wooden hair picks. She was wrapped in a thin, semitransparent gown of black silk that hung on one shoulder, interwoven with shiny gold threads, the pattern representative of a dragonlike shape. The incandescent lights of the lobby danced in her soft, dark eyes and her skin was clear and soft to the touch. Lau Shui bowed deeply and smiled as the woman put a slender, electrifying hand on his shoulder.

"It is a distinct pleasure to see you again," he said.

"It *has* been a long time, Lau...too long, I think," Nyenshi Fung replied.

The two had been lovers for a brief time—very

brief—but Fung became much too demanding of Shui's time. She'd obviously grown up quite a bit, having been much younger and more impressionable back in his days as a devoted Taoist student. He'd been full of ideas and ambition then. Two traits that had eventually led him to success. As a married man, he'd never betray the trust of his devoted spouse. However, if anyone might have swayed him, it would have been this woman. She was as beautiful and graceful a China doll as she had been in the days he'd first known her.

"The years have been much kinder to you than they have to me," Shui remarked.

Fung laughed, but it was a sweet and generous laugh. She said, "And you are still a man of whom it is the duty of every woman to be cautious."

Shui inclined his head, accepting the compliment in the spirit it was given. "How have you been?"

"Most excellent," she replied, moving closer to him. She looked around and said, "I am actually here to keep up appearances for my husband."

"You are married now?"

"When he has a moment to act as a husband," she said. On afterthought she added, "Forgive me…that was very disrespectful of me. I have learned some hard lessons that it is not for me to question Dim."

"You are wedded to Dim Mai?" Shui asked with a mixture of surprise and contempt, the latter of which he hoped didn't slip out in the tone of his voice.

"Why, of course. You didn't know?"

"I had no idea."

"You seem surprised."

"You'll have to forgive my bluntness, Nyenshi, but I am overwhelmed. While I do not see Dim often, we are close enough that I couldn't see how I wouldn't know. As a matter of fact, I saw him recently and he made no mention of it.''

"Perhaps he doesn't know of our past.''

"I am certain that he does," Shui said, his voice dropping to a whisper.

"Well, there is little reason to be conspiratorial about our past," Fung replied. "This would probably come as a surprise to many, but Dim is a patient and kind man. He commands the highest respect, however, and many thus view him as a tyrant in that respect.''

Shui disagreed, but he said nothing, choosing instead to reply to her with a warm smile and bow of his head. Dim Mai was anything but patient and kind. He was the largest, most powerful arms supplier in Asia—perhaps in all of the Pacific—and Shui had heard him described as many things. Patient and kind weren't two of them. He couldn't believe that Nyenshi wasn't bright enough to know this, but he saw no reason to contradict her in a setting so public as this.

Shui made a show of searching through the lobby. "I do not see Dim. Where is he?''

"He'll be down shortly. I left him in the suite on an important call. He asked me to go ahead of him and be charming.''

"A task that is suitably worthy of you, my dear.''

"You're too kind.''

Another man joined their discussion abruptly, and Shui came to a position of military-like attention. And with good cause. General Deng Jikwan was no stranger to Shui, and neither did he command a presence easily ignored. Jikwan was known throughout the triad as a military enforcer. His rise to power had been the direct result of his move to ally political views with the present Chinese premier. As such, his influence over military affairs and the subsequent friendship with the seats of power in both the Chinese cabinet and council rendered him virtually invincible to outside interference.

Jikwan was also one of the few to whom Shui showed deference and complete respect. The general had on more than one occasion made his support and liking of the Kung Lok leader very clear, though Shui wasn't clear if Jikwan's position had changed in recent times.

"Lau Ming, my friend, it is most agreeable to see you again," Jikwan said boisterously.

Shui couldn't help but let out a sigh of relief. "And you, General Jikwan."

"Please, please, must you be so formal." Jikwan clapped Shui on the shoulder. "When is it that you stopped calling me by my first name? I grow so weary of the formalities of everyday public life. Is there no place we can't be safe to socialize with each other on a friendly basis?"

"I beg your pardon, sir. I just didn't presume—"

"You never do, and that's what I so respect about you," Jikwan interjected with a laugh. He turned to Fung and said, "Good evening, Madam Mai. You will most certainly do me the honor of dancing with you later. But I ask your pardon to steal Lau Ming from you for a short time."

"I beg your leave, then, gentlemen."

Jikwan inclined his head, put his massive arm around Shui and steered him away from Fung. "I heard of your recent incursion into this country. I would believe congratulations are in order."

"I don't know if that wouldn't be a bit premature, Deng."

"Oh?" Jikwan stopped and the bushy, gray hairs of his eyebrows rose, dispersing the wrinkles around his tiny eyes. "Is there trouble?"

"I'm not certain yet," Shui replied. "Ing Kaochu has met a problem. It isn't one that I foresee as insurmountable, but it is troublesome all the same."

"Then I trust you will handle it in time," Jikwan said with a dismissive wave. "What I have in mind to discuss with you before the start of the formal meeting is quite another matter. A recent issue has come to our attention. It is one that has the council quite concerned, and they have asked that I investigate further."

"What is it?"

Jikwan looked around and lowered his normally loud voice, the whisper almost a squeak. "My spies tell me that this competitor of yours… What is his name, Carillo? I understand that he may have enlisted additional aid as a counterstrike to your plans."

Shui, of course, knew what was coming but he chose not to let on to that fact. While he trusted Jikwan, he didn't trust him completely. He realized Jikwan was going to tell him about the alliance between Carillo and Nievas, but he decided not to disclose he already had the knowledge. Jikwan was vying for a position here, and Shui would continue to act as if he were playing into Jikwan's hand until he knew what the general was really seeking.

"In what fashion?" Shui asked.

"Are you familiar with a man named Colonel Amado Nievas?"

Shui put on an act of considering the name a moment, then shook his head.

"He is the leader of the South American guerrilla army, the Revolutionary Armed Forces of Colombia."

"I know of this force."

"Then you should know what kind of problems you might encounter were this alliance to be committed."

"Ing Kaochu's men are excellent soldiers, Deng. I think they are capable of stopping these guerrillas."

"My dear Lau, it is not about abilities," Jikwan protested. "It is about sheer numbers. Even if Dim Mai supplies your weapons in the quantities you're asking, and I have it on personal authority that he's resisting this move, you cannot possibly believe that the Scarlet Dragons are sufficient against such an amassed force of trained soldiers."

"Dim Mai doesn't like my plan?"

"Mai is an imbecile. As far as the council is concerned, it doesn't matter what he wants. I have personally vouched for you, and through various machinations I am ready to come to your aid."

"I appreciate the offer, Deng, and perhaps I may take you up on it in light of this newest information."

Shui watched for Jikwan's reaction, and it was just as he suspected. The military man's smile was one of smug satisfaction. He was up to something, although Shui still wasn't sure just what that something was. An elevated position in the Kung Lok didn't make sense—Jikwan had already attained that goal. The guy was a hardened soldier, and so he couldn't envision Jikwan had aspirations to succeed Shui's position as underboss of the Western territories. No, there was something else afoot here.

"I'm a bit concerned about Dim Mai and his lack of support here," Shui replied. "I knew that I didn't have his full support, but I'm surprised he would openly criticize me to the council."

"That was something of a mystery to me, as well," Jikwan replied. "Naturally, the council is suspicious of his motives. However, you should be conscious of the fact that he very much respects you as an individual. But he is vehemently opposed to your ideas, and launched scathing attacks against your plan to monopolize the Southwestern drug trade in America."

"Would he prefer we ally ourselves with the likes of Jose Carillo and the other Mexican crime families?"

Jikwan appeared to consider this for a time. "I don't know. I know he was against any sort of similar association with the Italian crime family and their corporate holdings. But his resistance here does not seem to stem from the feelings of racial prejudice. There is something else going on here."

"Perhaps he's driven by sheer profit motive," Shui offered.

"In what way?"

"Well, the supply of arms to the Scarlet Dragons comes at sheer expense to him. There is undoubtedly little profit in supplying Ing Kaochu's people with free weapons. But if it is as you say, and Carillo has joined forces with this Colonel Nievas, it is possible that they will need weapons. Could it be that Dim Mai sees a more direct route for profit?"

"I had not thought about it from that point of view."

"Neither had I."

It was all a lie; Shui had very much considered this. Mai was a businessman, plain and simple, and the council was compelling him to supply these arms free of charge to the Kung Lok's enforcement team. From where Mai stood, that was a considerable overhead without guarantee of any sort of return on his investment. Not that Mai wasn't already one of the richest men in the Kung Lok. Still, it probably didn't make much sense to him to fork over thousands of assault weapons just to watch the money from sales go back into the public coffers. Particularly since this was a Western territory operation.

"I don't know, Lau," Jikwan said. "I've known Dim for many years, and I find it difficult to believe he's driven by sheer profit motive. He has always been loyal to the Party and the Kung Lok."

"Riches can do strange things to men, my friend," Shui replied.

"Some men," Jikwan countered.

"I would no more want to believe it of him than you would."

"Then we shall agree for now that he has his reasons for resisting your plans," Jikwan remarked. "In the meantime, I stand ready to assist you in whatever fashion you may require it. I'm concerned about the forces being amassed in Mexico. Word has it that FARC troops are already in this country, and that certainly means war between them and the Scarlet Dragons is imminent. For all we know, it may already have begun."

"I hope you will forgive me for asking, Deng," Shui ventured, "but I'm wondering why your sudden interest in this operation."

Jikwan produced a frosty smile. "You think I'm seeking something for myself?"

"I didn't want to be blunt, as you have always been

magnanimous both toward me and my causes. And I don't wish to risk our friendship. But, yes, I am wondering what advantage you seek.''

''Naturally,'' Jikwan said in a good-natured tone. ''I wouldn't have expected anything less from you, Lau. The fact of the matter is that I'm primarily doing this under the orders of the council. However, I hope to move forward in my career. I have my eye on something extraspecial. I know your influence in the area, and I am hoping for your support when the time comes.''

''And what is this mysterious goal?''

''Let us not discuss it now,'' Jikwan said. ''I promise that you aren't committed before seeing the value of my assistance.''

Noting the general's voice had lowered again, and that he was watching the lobby, Shui observed that Dim Mai, as well as the other council members, had arrived. It would be time for them to have their meeting soon. Of course, there would be the formalities of dinner first, and then the ladies would retire and the men would have time to discuss their plans at great length. Shui wasn't sure what Jikwan had in mind, but he was already certain he wouldn't like it, and equally certain that it would cost him a great deal.

And Lau Shui wondered if perhaps it was time to start looking for some new allies.

CHAPTER FOURTEEN

Las Vegas, Nevada

The first thing Mack Bolan did when he saw the troops emerging from the panel truck was take cover behind his vehicle. The second was to let them know he wasn't just going to roll over and die.

The Executioner knew he was outgunned, and he wanted to avoid starting a firefight where bystanders might get injured. The best way to avoid that kind of trouble was to take down the newcomers quickly and efficiently, and the Diehl DM-51s promised to do the job for him nicely. Bolan extracted one of the grenades from the pouch, pulled the pin and tossed the bomb into the still emerging troops. He immediately followed it with a second and third, foregoing the sleeves to cut down on flying shrapnel that might strike the now gathering crowd.

There were warning shouts from the combat troops as they saw the grenades sail over the hood of the car. They obviously hadn't expected their lone adversary would be so well armed, and underestimated his resolve. It cost six of them their lives. The explosions ripped into the far side of Bolan's sedan, the concussion lifting it off the ground as heat melted the rear tires into bubbling rubber.

The remaining troops scattered, still confused by the sudden explosions and the felling of their comrades. Bolan immediately acted on the confusion and began to lay down a firestorm with the Desert Eagle. The huge .44 Magnum pistol bucked in his fist as he repeatedly squeezed the trigger, the weapon's thunder drowning out the shouts and screams of the panicked troops.

Thus far, the Executioner had been dishing out the better part of the destruction, but it seemed obvious the remaining soldiers had regrouped and were now taking the offensive. They began to return fire, the AK-74 assault rifles chattering with their distinctive sounds. The 5.45 mm rounds shattered the back windshield, and Bolan barely escaped the onslaught as he smashed the window of the rental with the butt of the Desert Eagle, reached inside and retrieved his munitions bag from the front seat.

The sedan was history, and there were police cruisers at both ends of the street. The officers were now EVA, taking care to stay behind the doors of their cruisers as they lined up pistols or shotguns and began to fire at anything toting a weapon. Bolan cursed to himself, anxious for their safety. He peered at the cab of the panel truck and noted the interior was empty. A break in the firefight told him the engine was still running, and the damage from the grenades appeared to be superficial.

The Executioner had an idea. He holstered the .44 and traded it for the HK-53 in the bag. He vaulted off the sidewalk and onto the hood of the sedan, took down an approaching soldier with a well-aimed burst from the SMG and landed on the other side. He accessed the cab from the passenger door and climbed behind the wheel. Bolan popped the gearshift into reverse and popped the clutch as he gunned the accelerator.

The panel truck swayed uncertainly as Bolan backed the vehicle until he had a turn radius clear of any vehicles. He swung the rear end toward the house, the driver's-side door now facing the stunned enemy troops. Bolan stuck the HK-53 through the window frame and shot one enemy gunner in the face at nearly point-blank range. The 5.56 mm slug pierced the man's forehead and blew out the back of his head.

Bolan swung the muzzle in the direction of another gunner who had turned to fight the cops and squeezed a 3-round burst that caught the terrorist in the small of the back. The impact carried him forward into the concrete base of the lamp pole that had served as his cover. His lifeless body crumpled as blood spilled onto the sidewalk.

There was a lull in the firefight as one of the gunners tried to flank the Executioner. The man jumped onto the running board of the truck and tried to shoot him. Bolan's right hand withdrew the Beretta 93-R beneath his left armpit in a blinding flash. The gunner got off one wild shot before Bolan snap-aimed and squeezed the trigger. That pistol was still set to 3-round bursts, and the slugs punched holes in the man's chest and jaw. He flew from the running board even as the Executioner set the Beretta on the seat and put the gearshift in second.

The panel truck lurched into the street, and he had to wrestle the bulky steering wheel with one arm. His shoulder was aching from his earlier injuries. He tried to ignore what he knew was the sensation of blood running freely down his arm where he had torn the stitches.

He maneuvered the truck onto a direct course for the police cruisers as he shot another enemy gunner on the fly. A burst of rounds from the HK-53 struck the guy in the hip, shattering bone and dropping him where he stood.

The police officers seemed certain that Bolan was going to ram their cruisers, which is exactly what he wanted them to think. They began to fire at him, some of the pistol rounds ricocheting off the hood while a few shotgun blasts tore holes in the radiator. Steam and fluid belched from the front of the truck as it was pounded and abused by hot lead. At the last moment, the Executioner stomped on the brakes, letting the engine die as he jerked the wheel hard to the left. He brought the truck to a stop on the sidewalk in front of a house that bordered an alleyway. The truck now served as an effective roadblock, and he was far enough away from the far intersection that those officers didn't pose a threat.

Bolan engaged the brake, grabbed his bag and jumped from the cab of the truck. He sprinted down the alleyway. The officers still probably had a few of the enemy gunners with which to contend, but the soldier knew Las Vegas's finest could handle it. The Executioner couldn't and wouldn't battle with the police. He'd never dropped the hammer on a cop, and he wasn't about to start now. Which is why the appearance of a five-man SWAT team at the other end of the alleyway entrance, silhouetted against the streetlights, triggered a moment of hesitation.

A moment that was enough to give the police the advantage they needed and left him with no place to go.

"Freeze! Police department!" one shouted.

"Drop your weapons and let's see your hands!" another added.

And as Bolan came to a halt, staring at the high fences bordering either side of the alleyway, he knew there was only one small chance remaining other than surrender. And the Executioner reached slowly into the bag slung over his shoulder.

Stony Man Farm, Virginia

"HAL, WE'VE GOT some new information," Barbara Price announced.

"What is it?" the head Fed asked.

Brognola had been sitting in the War Room for the past ten hours, sifting through information that Kurtzman was putting in front of him faster than he could read it. The Bear was damn efficient, no question there, and the Stony Man chief was buried under mounds of paperwork. File folders and historical information gleaned from FBI, NSA, CIA and other U.S. agencies had been retrieved from archives or computer data collected by Stony Man.

Price smoothed out her skirt before sitting and handing a file folder to Brognola. "There's a meeting being held in West Palm Beach right now that has some very interesting faces in the crowd. One of our CIA connections at the hotel claims that at least two dozen Hong Kong diplomats from various arenas are there. We've also confirmed that the arms dealer, Dim Mai, is present. And you'll never guess who else."

"Shui?"

"Yes," she replied with surprise. "How did you know?"

"I just received a phone call from the Man. He was very curious to know why the Chinese government hadn't advised U.S. authorities that such heavy hitters from their government would be in-country. Unfortunately, I didn't have an answer for him."

"I don't understand how they could *not* know they would be here."

"That's what we're paid to know, Barb," Brognola said flatly, leaning back in his seat and sticking an unlit cigar in his mouth.

"I wonder if these recent actions we've seen by the Kung Lok aren't tied to some larger machination cooked up by the Chinese government," Brognola continued.

"Well, it's no secret that the Kung Lok has operated in the areas they have under sanctions by government officials. Ever since the return of Hong Kong to China by the British, there are large sects of the triad that have acted lawlessly in China and Canada."

"Not to mention all of the things they've done we can't link to them."

"Exactly," Price agreed. "And that doesn't even take into account the fact there's just too many of them to be effectively handled by law enforcement at local levels. And the British intelligence services don't have time to deal with it, because in comparison to the Islamic terror groups and the continual problems with the Egyptian jihad, the Kung Lok triad is small potatoes."

Brognola nodded, then gestured to the pile of paperwork and said, "I've been mulling over this whole scenario in my brain for the past few days, and I don't mind saying it scares the hell out of me."

"In what way?"

"Well, for one thing, I wonder if Shui and the Kung Lok are aware of the recent alliance between Carillo and Nievas."

"The triad's intelligence network spreads as far and wide as its criminal influence," Price told him. "I would find it hard to believe if they didn't know."

"Okay, let's assume for a moment they do...or at least they did before moving into U.S. territory. That means Shui felt he had the manpower and resources to handle the resistance. You see, it's the timing of this whole thing that disturbs me. Based on Bear's most recent intelligence, we now can say with certainty that the alliance was formed between the FARC and Carillo crime family before Shui made the decision."

"Agreed," Price interjected.

"So let's say I'm Lau Shui, and I want to take over the Mexican mafia's drug and porn action. Where would I start?"

"Take your pick, Hal. There's at least a half dozen major networks throughout the better part of the American Southwest. Drugs run through Texas, Arizona, the Baja, California, Nevada and parts of New Mexico and Colorado. That's a big area."

"Exactly. A big area that could not possibly be controlled effectively, unless..."

"Unless what?"

Brognola felt himself go pale, and it suddenly began to come to light. "Unless someone controlled the U.S.-Mexican border."

"And how in the world could they do that? I'll be the first to admit that the Carillo crime family is large. But they're not that large."

"They would be if they had a Colombian army on their side."

"Oh, my God," Price breathed.

Brognola could tell she was beginning to see his

point. The relationship between Mexico and the United States had been friendly for the most part, with joint cooperation between U.S. and Mexican *federales* in at least stemming the flow of illegal drugs being smuggled into the country. Much of the funding had gone to the U.S. Border Patrol and other agencies affiliated with border security.

"The border and joint operations tied to it has always been controlled through mutual efforts of officials at the El Paso Intelligence Center. The only way anybody could even hope to pull off an operation like that would be if members of organized crime had their hooks into certain individuals very high in the chain of command from that organization."

"Are you thinking that this meeting of Kung Lok criminals with Chinese officials may be a play by the triads to join efforts and put pressure on U.S. officials?"

"Possibly, but I think it goes much deeper than that. In order for the Kung Lok to have any hope of defeating Carillo and his network, they would need to do two things—control all major trafficking of narcotics and control border officials. That takes money, influence and considerable resources. It's my guess that the Kung Lok triad is playing two ends against the middle."

"What do you mean?"

"Well, let's suppose for a moment that Shui and the Chinese government put pressure on Dim Mai to provide arms for sale to the Colombians. It's really no money out of anybody's pocket but Mai's. While he's got the largest stake in it, and the largest risk to his investment, he could reap a reward tenfold."

"It would definitely put him in the good graces of the triad hierarchy."

"It would do more than that, Barb," Brognola replied matter-of-factly. "It would put him at the top of the list for an official position of leadership in the government dealings with the Kung Lok. But in the meantime, Shui has aspirations of his own. He wants to reap the profit, not from the arms end but rather from the drugs and porn. If he can find a way to manipulate the situation, he stands to gain a significant foothold in the West, one much larger and more influential than he currently has."

"But Carillo and Nievas won't necessarily give up so easily."

"They don't have to. Don't you see it? The Chinese are already involved with Colonel Nievas and his FARC cronies. *They're* the ones who are supplying the arms, thanks to Dim Mai. That means they have control of a large part of the FARC, and Nievas and Carillo are obviously too ignorant to see it."

"I get it now. That leaves Carillo and this little plan of his out in the cold."

"Precisely. Which is why Striker made it so clear that it's imperative he take down the Kung Lok triad first."

"Why not send Phoenix Force down to Ciudad Juárez and let them finish the job on Carillo?"

Brognola shook his head emphatically. "No, absolutely not. Striker was very clear that he didn't want me to involve the other teams in this without official word from the President, and I have to honor his request. If I go off half-cocked and drop Phoenix into this whole thing, he could get caught in the cross fire."

"I've never questioned your reasoning or authority, Hal, but I'm very concerned that this is spinning out of control."

"You might be right, but I can't justify acting on a

whim. We're doing exactly the best we can do right now with this, and that is to feed intelligence to Striker when he asks for it and then let him handle it.''

"I understand.''

Brognola sighed, and rubbed his eyes. "I understand how you feel, Barb, and I can't say I don't agree. I know it seems like we're just sitting here on our hands, and maybe in some fashion we are. But until I hear word from Striker, all we can do is wait and watch.''

"Do you think he can handle something this big on his own?''

"I don't know,'' Brognola said. "But I'm sure of one thing. If I needed someone in my corner on it, I'd want it to be him.''

Las Vegas, Nevada

MACK BOLAN COULDN'T surrender to the Las Vegas SWAT team, and he couldn't fire on law enforcement. So the Executioner was left with only one option, and it was one that might very well get him killed in the process. But he knew there was a glimmer of a chance as he withdrew the last Diehl DM-51 grenade from his bag.

"I said let me see your hands!" one of the officers repeated.

Bolan brought out the grenade, knowing they couldn't see what it was at that distance, pulled the pin and tossed the bomb underhand down the alleyway. The lights attached to the underside of the SWAT team's MP-5s might not have allowed them to discern exactly what it was Bolan had thrown, but they got the idea and scrambled to escape a blast that wouldn't have come close enough to affect them. Nonetheless, they didn't know that and it gave Bolan the chance he needed. The soldier ran to one of the seven-foot privacy fences and bounded over it with ease just as the grenade exploded. Splinters of wood gouged his hands, but he ignored the pain and landed into a crouch on the other side.

A woman was letting her dog in and was startled as the stark figure dressed in blacksuit, toting enough firepower to start a small war, sailed easily over her fence and landed catlike among her rhododendrons. She was also taken by the surprise of the booming grenade as dirt and debris came over with her armed visitor and rained on him.

Bolan stood, took a quick inventory and then asked her, "Which way is out?"

She didn't say anything, her hand trembling as she pointed toward a swing-back gate on the far side of her well-tended gardens and lawn.

"Sorry about the flowers," Bolan said with a quick nod before heading to the gate. He passed through it, waiting until he was out of her sight before drawing his Beretta. There was no point in scaring or threatening the woman.

Bolan advanced down the walkway and then bounded over another privacy fence. He tried to gauge the distance from the police on both sides of the block. He could hear additional gunshots and the unmistakable echo of shotguns as the police continued to do battle with the few remaining hardmen Bolan had left behind.

A few more fences and Bolan was on the street. He trotted across it at an angle, making his way toward another block of houses. He was still on schedule, and his near encounters with the police hadn't upset his timetable that much. The next target was one he'd penetrated before, so being on familiar territory would make it less of a problem. As long as he could keep his operations on schedule, he'd get to Mexicali in time to stop whatever Carillo and Nievas were cooking up for Baja. At least, he hoped he could get there on time. Meanwhile, it was time to take care of business.

Bolan emerged through another block, waiting in the shadows of a large bush and watching the street in front of him. It was dark but early enough that people were still out and about. He'd been lucky to escape notice this long, and he knew that luck wasn't going to hold forever. He needed transportation to help him get farther from the dragnet he was now sure the police were implementing at that moment.

Suddenly, Bolan spotted a very familiar car cruising slowly down the block. He waited until it was close enough to his cover to view the occupant inside. Vito Rosetti sat high in the seat, Sunday driving as if it was nobody's business. Bolan smiled and shook his head, then bounded from his cover and maneuvered behind the vehicle. He came up on the driver's side, opened the back door, and dropped into the seat of the sedan. Rosetti never turned his head.

The guy was still a pro.

Rosetti accelerated now, gaining distance from the area while still obeying the law. The Las Vegas police might have been tied up with the hardmen, but they would also have traffic patrol looking for anything remotely suspicious. Not that speeding was all that suspicious; still, the heightened sense of alert across the police force probably left Rosetti with the good sense not to attract attention.

Bolan kept low as he said, "All right, how did you know?"

"You ask because you don't know?" Rosetti challenged, eyes and face remaining forward. The guy didn't even look in the rearview mirror.

"I ask because I know you're dying to tell me."

"Simple. I had a police scanner wired a long time back that's able to monitor high bandwidth and a large range of frequencies. I can listen to fire, police, EMS, SWAT, and even some local communications of the FBI and U.S. Marshal Service. Actually, it was given to me as a gift."

"Gadgets?" Bolan inquired.

"Of course."

"I should have guessed."

"The truth is sometimes stranger than fiction."

Bolan grinned. "Yeah."

"I heard about the commotion over their secured frequencies, and I figured it had to be you crashing someone's party. I don't live too far, so when I heard they had a fugitive on the loose—dressed, and I quote the dispatcher—'like a commando,' I figured you might need someone to bail you out."

"So you decided to take a chance."

"Yeah, I figured you'd squeeze through that little hole. They just weren't planning on something like this happening when the original call came through. 'Shots fired' calls come in a hundred times a day in this city. They weren't expecting guys armed with automatic weapons. And they sure as hell weren't expecting you to be there kicking ass and taking names."

"Well, I guess I owe you one for pulling me out. But

don't take another risk like that. I've got too many souls on my hands already, Vito. I don't want to add yours.''

"You know I'd do it all over again, no matter what you say. You know I would."

"Yeah, I guess I do."

CHAPTER FIFTEEN

West Palm Beach, Florida

"It would seem you have a new ally, Lau," Nyenshi Fung whispered as they enjoyed their dessert.

"And who is that?"

"Why, General Jikwan, of course."

"I think it a bit premature to consider the good general a new ally. He has always been a staunch supporter. Although do not assume I mean any disrespect toward him. I have nothing but the utmost admiration for Deng. And I guess in some small respect his support of me would make him an ally."

"I think you are being overly suspicious. The general speaks fondly of you to his colleagues in the government. And I can tell you that Dim has definitely noticed the relationship."

"My dear," Shui replied politely as he dabbed the corner of his mouth with a linen napkin, "it sounds as if you have become quite knowledgeable in Dim's affairs."

"If you are referring to the licentious lifestyle he lives, or what he does for his business, you would be correct in your assumptions."

"That is odd," Shui said with a half smile.

"What?"

"I would have thought you would be more… 'ignorant' of the situation. When we were together, you were quite adamant about staying away from such sordid affairs of men in the Kung Lok."

"People can change, Lau," Fung declared. "I have found ways to go past my ideas about those things that I once found less than agreeable. It's the capacity of woman to change her mind that moves governments."

"Or topples them," he interjected.

"I beg your pardon?"

Shui recanted the comment in the form of an apologetic smile. "I'm sorry. I should take mind to keep my opinions to myself. It is just that your abilities to remain innocent, to shy away and be untouched by these things we must do, was what I most admired about you."

Fung laid a hand on his arm and said, "That's sweet of you, Lau, but I can take care of myself." She lowered her voice, looked around conspiratorially and added, "I have to tell you a secret. The marriage between me and Dim was arranged. I really had little choice in the matter."

"Your father?" Shui inquired, feeling a pang of anger.

She nodded, not looking at him now but choosing to stare at her unfinished dessert. That only agitated Shui more because he hated her father—had always hated the bastard. He had been a repressive and domineering despot, just a wisp of a man as cancer ate his body to the bone. He died a few years ago, and Shui refused to attend the burial ceremonies and rites of his death. He wanted to be there to support Fung, but there was too much enmity between the respective families so he chose not to return to Hong Kong.

Now it appeared that in addition to the insult of her father not leaving Fung any of his inheritance, instead bequeathing the residue of his riches to his son—who had squandered the entire fortune according to rumor— she had been forced into marriage to Dim Mai. Shui was aware of the friendship between Mai and Fung's father. He just couldn't have foreseen such a tragedy as this.

"I am sorry," Shui said.

"Do not be sorry," she replied. "Dim loves me and has treated me well. I have every reason to be grateful, and not one to complain. I have had a good life."

"I know, but—"

"Let us not discuss this anymore, Lau, lest we are overheard. Besides, I do not feel like talking about it anymore."

"As you wish."

"We were discussing General Jikwan and his affection for you."

"That is a subject I would prefer not to discuss."

"I understand."

Shui nodded, but he wondered if she really did understand. Right at that moment, as a matter of fact, Jikwan and Mai seemed to be in the middle of a very serious conversation. Shui thought about walking to where they stood talking and butting right into the conversation, but then he decided against it. To intrude on them would have served no purpose, and it might have even told them he was suspicious. If there was a coup d'état in preparation, he did not want ties to the architects.

As a matter of fact, as Shui looked around at the various pairs and trios of conversation, he didn't find a really friendly face in the crowd. There was, of course, Yi-chang Shen, head of the Kung Lok triad in the whole eastern sector, but he was also a direct competitor in many respects.

Shui began to wonder if he'd allowed himself to become too isolated from his ties in the East. He was certainly friendly with most of the underbosses and ringleaders, but at the same time didn't consider a single one trustworthy. The only one he really trusted was Ing Kaochu, and even within that trust lay a few doubts. Somehow, though, Lau Ming Shui had come to both expect and accept that fact. Being a recognized leader in *any* Chinese triad carried with it a certain loneliness and isolationism that one couldn't escape.

"This atmosphere has come to bother me," Shui told his companion. "Would you join me for a walk?"

"It would be an honor."

The two rose and managed to escape the huge dining hall without being noticed. Several bodyguards attempted to follow Shui but he warned them off with a flick of his head. He wanted to be alone, and with Ing Kaochu absent, the bodyguards weren't hard-pressed to hold their vigil. They would keep an eye on their master, to be sure, but at a considerable distance. Had Kaochu been there, Shui was certain he would have never allowed it under any circumstances. Shui just had too many enemies to take risks like that. It was a bit of a relief, despite Shui's admiration of Ing Kaochu's loyalty.

But Shui's idea of getting Fung alone with him had to go on hold when two large men intercepted them as they reached the doors of the hotel that exited onto their gardens.

"Mr. Shui?" the man addressed him. "Our boss would like to see you."

He was a tall man wearing a three-piece suit as gray as his eyes. His associate wore a pinstripe nearly identical in cut and style, but this one was blue. The bodyguards started to step in, but Shui restrained them by raising his hand. He looked at the man and his eyes narrowed some.

"I do not know whom your master is, sir," Shui replied. "Moreover, I am engaged with this young lady at the moment and really not interested in discussing business."

"He said you would say that," the man replied easily. "If you did, I was instructed to tell you 'the sword of the Dragon is not nearly as sharp as the talons of the Eagle.'"

"Really? Is that supposed to mean something to me?"

It was now that Fung spoke. "No. It's supposed to mean something to me."

Shui was completely taken aback by the entire exchange, and he wasn't sure he liked it. However, he wasn't afraid and it appeared the two men were no match for his bodyguards, so he agreed to go with the man. He indicated for his bodyguards to follow, but the man would only allow one of them to accompany Shui.

"You will not be harmed, I assure you. The lady may come, as well. A gesture of good faith."

The pair followed the men to the elevator and rode it to the fifth floor. The hotel wasn't terribly crowded this time of year, but there were enough people that it would have allowed someone to remain discreet. Shui had to admit he'd been impressed with the ability of this mysterious pair to remain virtually invisible when he considered the amount of security in the hotel at present.

When they had finally reached a very plain and nondescript door—like all of the others on that floor—Shui and Fung were shown into a fabulous room that looked as if it took up the space of three or four rooms. They were seated, offered something to drink and then left to wait, entertained by soft music issuing from unseen speakers.

Finally, their host emerged from a closed door, accompanied by the two men. Shui didn't recognize him, and a brief glance at Fung told him she didn't know who he was, either. The entire situation was strange, but Shui somehow felt at ease, unthreatened and almost in some sort of trance. He had to wonder for a moment if the men had drugged him, but he was in full command of his senses. The atmosphere was just charged with a combined aura of power, security and warmth.

"Lau Ming Shui," the American announced, "welcome to my home. Thank you for accepting my invitation."

"I had the impression there wasn't a choice," Shui replied coldly, doing nothing to hide his suspicion and disdain for the circumstances. "I am not accustomed to being summoned like some common servant, sir."

"I do apologize. My men were ordered to be polite." He smiled and sat down in a chair across from the sofa on which they were seated. "However, you are not a prisoner and free to leave if you wish. I hope you consider yourself my guest."

"That would depend."

"On what?"

"On why you have asked me to come here."

The man chuckled. "Ah, now that's the interesting part. I would like to tell you a story about hostile take-overs and the Mexican mafia, and about gun battles in Las Vegas and double crosses in the Kung Lok triad. But most of all, I want to tell you how we're going to help you change all of that, and make the Kung Lok triad the most powerful organization in the world."

"And who is 'we'?" Shui asked.

"The government of the United States," the man replied.

Chihuahua, Mexico

"AMADO, MY FRIEND," Carillo greeted his military guest sadly, who was seated on the veranda overlooking the gardens of Carillo's estate, "I just received a report that the team you sent to Las Vegas was destroyed."

"What?" Colonel Nievas cried, jumping from his seat. "All of them?"

"Most of them. The rest either eluded police capture or were killed resisting them."

"Someone tipped off the American law enforcement?"

"No. They responded to reports of gunfire, apparently instigated by this slippery and mysterious American. Although we do have a name now—Mike Belasko."

Nievas waved his hand dismissively. "A cover name."

"Obviously. But he is the same man that killed several of my closest associates in Las Vegas, and questioned my man inside the U.S. Border Patrol about those weapons we tried to acquire for you. Your team was responding to help my men, but Belasko apparently caught them off guard.''

Nievas slowly sat and shook his head with an expression of disbelief. ''One man destroyed a platoon of my best soldiers. I do not believe it.''

''I have no reason to lie to you,'' Carillo said frankly. ''This man is very dangerous—of this I have no doubt. We must eradicate him and quickly.''

''I agree. It will be done before sunset tomorrow.''

''No, I do not think it wise to send any more troops. I believe an alternative means is required to deal with this individual. He was posing as a member of the DEA, but I do not think he works for them.''

''Could he perhaps be with the CIA?''

Carillo shook his head. ''No, I don't think that's the case, either. I believe he may be working with an agency we know nothing about. It is hard to say. However, I have an idea that has worked in the past. There are other means to deal with such men.''

''And those would be?''

''I have previously used Conrado for missions just like this one. He is well trained, tough and resourceful. I do not think he will have any problem eliminating this Belasko.''

Carillo noticed Nievas's face turn a disconcerting shade of reddish-purple that was evident even through his dark complexion. He wasn't sure why, but he thought maybe the FARC leader was embarrassed. He didn't have any reason to be in Carillo's mind. This Belasko was a dangerous man, and his elimination required someone equally dangerous. Conrado Diaz was just that someone.

Diaz had learned his art in both the urban and jungle

battlegrounds of Mexico and Honduras. He was extremely quick and an efficient killer. Diaz killed solemnly, quietly, personally. He wasn't a flashy assassin or a braggart; he was a methodical assassin but not an exhibitionist. And Carillo had every faith he could eliminate Belasko quickly and effortlessly.

"I realize that this may be a matter of honor for you, Amado," Carillo argued, "but we must both set aside our pride and concentrate on the real task ahead of us. The controlling of Baja has become a priority. We must seize control while we can."

"You think that we should act immediately?" Nievas said with renewed interest. "To move up our timetable?"

"I don't think we have any choice, my friend," Carillo said. "It wouldn't be the ideal method, but I'm concerned that with the footholds we've already lost in Texas and Las Vegas, we might lose the Baja-California border, as well."

"I cannot argue with your logic, Jose," Nievas admitted. "That much is sure."

"Good, then we're in agreement. The time to act is now."

"How do you wish to proceed?"

"I will send Conrado to find this Belasko immediately. That should eliminate that liability. I have heard rumors that some of our remaining areas of control may fall under attack by these Chinese vermin. You must regroup your forces there, and instruct them to render whatever assistance and protection they can in conjunction with my own teams."

"They're at your disposal."

"Let's hope that word will remain strictly a figure of

speech. If Belasko isn't working for the Chinese, and he's only one man, then I dare not think about what multiple men could do. I am not sure why we're having such trouble defending our positions.''

''Because you could have never foreseen something like this,'' Nievas replied simply. ''You have neither faced a group of this size before, nor had to battle against this kind of fanatical resolve. However, I have many well-trained men at my disposal. I will bring in a thousand troops if that's what it takes. But we will not be defeated by these Chinese slime.''

''I admire your mettle, my friend,'' Carillo said with a smile.

''And I, yours. Now tell me of your plans for the Baja.''

''I believe our first step should be a quick, decisive strike against any Mexican or American law enforcement that may not be on the payroll. We have identified certain areas that should be under control before we make the move to transport our shipment across the border.''

''I thought you had all of those angles covered with the Mexican and American police?''

''As far as unmolested passage across the border is concerned, yes. But that doesn't take into account agents from the BATF, DEA or the local cops in Mexicali. They could prove to be quite troublesome if we don't take security measures.''

''What is your plan to deal with them?''

''Oh, that is the most pleasurable thought,'' Carillo said, grinning and clapping his hands in unabashed glee. ''I already have my own men in place who will create a diversion. They're going to bomb the central police station in Mexicali. It's where all prisoners arrested are brought for processing before being shipped out to more isolated jails until trial.''

''That is quite a diversion,'' Nievas admitted.

''Absolutely! The bomb will not be large, but it will be enough to bring their police and other agencies running. In light of the new antiterrorist measures created by the U.S., the aid will come pouring into the area. This creates a media circus and also focuses attention on what's happening at the local area.''

''I see what you're saying. This will allow us to quietly slip through the cracks.''

''Precisely. There are always holes, and I have spent considerable amounts of money to bribe U.S. Border Patrol officials. Not to mention my trump card.''

''What trump card?'' Nievas asked with interest.

''Oh, no,'' Carillo said, ''I'm not quite ready to reveal that yet.''

''I thought you trusted me.''

''I do, but I promised not to weaken this individual's position or status until the time was right. You see, many years of experience have taught me that it makes little difference if an operation is planned down to the most minute details. Something can still rear its head and bite one in the ass when attention is focused on the battle. I have had to learn this lesson the hard way. So when the time is right, I will reveal this plan to you.''

''I understand.''

''Now,'' Carillo said, picking up his glass of iced tea and holding it toward his companion, ''let us toast our future.''

''And the future of our enemies,'' Nievas added.

Las Vegas, Nevada

DESPITE THE DESTRUCTION of Carillo's drug house and Bolan's subsequent escape, the Executioner felt as if he'd only won a hollow victory. He was also disturbed at something that had bothered him since cleaning up and leaving Rosetti's place. It was something he couldn't put his finger on yet, but he trusted his intuition. There was a lot more here than met the eye, and he planned to be there when that something manifested itself.

Rosetti had loaned Bolan his car, and the Executioner promised to leave it parked at an arranged spot. The Executioner now approached Danny Tang's house from the rear. He'd warned the man to skip town, get out of the business of flesh peddling, but he was fairly sure the criminal hadn't followed through. It was time for Bolan to help point him in the right direction.

The soldier eventually worked his way to the backyard of Tang's house and stopped to study the layout. The guys guarding the house weren't the regular types Bolan had seen on his previous visit. They were totally professional and wore markings of the Scarlet Dragons. Nobody was talking, nobody was smoking and joking and every single one of them exuded an attitude of alertness.

Bolan did a quick estimate and gauged he probably needed to take five to six soldiers before even gaining entrance to the house. The Executioner wanted to try to pull this off quietly. He planned to get in, take care of Tang and his men and then get out.

He stripped himself of all but the Berettas and his combat knife and then moved to an adjoining yard before moving closer to the house. A flank movement would be the best approach because the thick wall of mortared flagstone that surrounded the property wasn't as much made for security as a matter of decorative taste. Tang obviously had faith in his security force.

Bolan ducked and moved silently along the wall until he reached a point he judged would be a blind spot to the guard force. He came over the wall and moved into the shadows of the house, cast by the streetlights and decorative lamps scattered at regular intervals along the top of the wall. The Executioner couldn't help wondering why the Scarlet Dragons were present. Tang hadn't given Bolan the impression he was friendly with them.

Then again, perhaps Tang wasn't there anymore. Maybe he was dead and somebody had moved into his action. Well, whoever it was wouldn't live to see sunrise. Bolan started to move quickly past a basement window when something caught his eye.

Lisa Rajero and Noreen Zahn were tied to a wall, naked, their faces bleeding and bruised. Someone had tortured them, and Bolan stared grimly at their condition. Rajero seemed to be in much better shape than Zahn. She was still conscious, at least semiconscious. The Executioner immediately knew that his odds of getting in and out quietly had just dropped to about nil.

Bolan tried to access the wide, short casement window, but it was shut and locked from the inside. He didn't want to risk breaking any glass—at least not until he'd verified Zahn's and Rajero's condition. He wasn't even sure they would have enough strength to escape, which meant he'd have his hands full if he got into a firefight.

He continued onward, moving toward the front of the

house, and crouched when he reached the corner. A guard was leaning against the side of the house, not moving and a little too busy watching everything happening on the street. It proved fatal as Bolan took a deep breath, let out half and then jumped up and encircled his forearm around the smaller man's neck. The guy struggled to break free, trying to elbow Bolan, but the effort was futile. All the man's training in martial arts couldn't compare with the cold, hard experience of the Executioner.

As the guy lost consciousness, Bolan drove the combat knife into his kidney. He deposited the corpse quietly on the lawn and then ventured toward the front door. Just over the hedges covering the front of the house, Bolan could see the top of squad-car lights. They had obviously beefed up patrols and watches since his last visit to the neighborhood. Well, he was going to avoid an encounter with them at all costs this time.

Bolan reached another casement window, jumped into the semicircle culvert and shoved the window aside. He squeezed his frame through and dropped quietly onto the carpeted floor. He was in what looked like a recreation room, and he saw two doors. The one to his left he surmised led to the room where Zahn and Rajero were held captive, but he wanted to check the other one. He would need a couple of ways out.

The soldier went to the door and tried the handle. It moved smoothly, and he cracked the door, peering through the opening. The door led onto a wide hallway that was vacant at the moment. A few doors lined one side, but they were open and Bolan didn't hear anything. He closed the door and moved over to the second.

Bolan opened this one in the same fashion and saw

he was right. Two woman were bound to the wall, and the extent of their suffering was much more obvious from his vantage point. The Executioner glanced quickly around the room, then moved through the doorway, Beretta held in front of him and ready for any threat. No one emerged to challenge him as he walked slowly toward the women. He checked Rajero first, feeling for a pulse at her neck and the lifting her head. Her eyes snapped open suddenly and she started to scream, but Bolan clamped a hand over her mouth.

"Keep still," he commanded her gently. "It's me, Belasko."

Tears began to flood her eyes. Bolan released his hold and tried to comfort Rajero as she started to sob softly. He moved over to Zahn and checked her pulse—there was none. He cupped her bruised and swollen chin in his hand and put his ear to her nostrils. No breathing either. Her eyes were sightless when he lifted the lids and the Executioner could taste the rage in his mouth in the form of bile.

"Is she okay?" Rajero finally managed to ask.

"No, she's not," Bolan said.

"Oh, God, why?" Rajero whispered. "Why would they do this to us? We didn't know anything."

"What did they ask you?" Bolan said as he untied her and found a quilt to throw over her.

"He wanted to know about you and the operations you had planned," she said.

"You didn't know that," he murmured, as he reached to a chair, retrieved an afghan throw from it and tossed it around her shoulders, "and neither did Zahn."

"What are we going to do?"

"Get the hell out of here. Did you recognize any of the men who questioned you?"

She shook her head as they moved over to the casement window. "It was just one man."

"One man did this to you?"

She nodded, obviously not wanting to talk about it. She looked as if she wanted to pass out but assured Bolan she could press onward when he studied her with concern. It was a damn tragedy, the death of a good woman like Noreen Zahn, and Bolan was thankful he'd arrived in time to pull out at least one of them alive. He silently vowed that he would come back and destroy whoever was responsible for her death. As he assisted Rajero out the window and started out after her, he heard the noise of the door to the hallway burst open behind him.

As he turned to face the threat, he knew he would get the chance to repay them much sooner than originally planned.

CHAPTER SIXTEEN

Las Vegas, Nevada

All of the Executioner's rage over the death of Noreen Zahn was poured into the initial hail of gunfire he rained on the Scarlet Dragon troops who burst into the room.

Bolan was still shoving Rajero through the opening when they appeared, one hand on her and the other extending death to the new arrivals. The subsonic 9 mm Parabellums bullets took the first pair of Dragon soldiers high. Two rounds of the first 3-shot burst punched holes in the chest of the lead Dragon, and the third took his backup man in the face, blowing apart his skull and showering the Scarlet Dragon troops with blood and brain matter. The second trio of rounds tore through the stomach of a third man, punching him to the floor.

The bodies of the hasty were now stacked in front of the door, preventing any of the other troops from gaining a clear shot. Bolan used the moment to climb through the casement window and get to high ground.

Rajero was waiting impatiently, huddled in the shadows and trembling. Bolan decided to take her mind off it by handing the Beretta to her.

"Kill anything that moves," he advised.

She nodded, and they started to return via the path Bolan had taken coming into the property. The house suddenly went bright, the grounds coming alive with the stark glare of searchlights and security lamps that had been hidden in the dark recesses of the house.

Bolan and Rajero were immediately flooded with light. The Executioner gestured to the wall, holstering his pistol and then kneeling to offer Rajero a leg up. She immediately took his cue and scrambled over the wall with the assisted height. Bolan followed behind her, going over the wall and shoulder rolling to his feet. He urged her to move immediately toward the rear of the lawn.

They stayed low, crouching as they ran and keeping close to the wall. The sudden start of police sirens in the near distance signaled the police were alerted.

So much for quiet, Bolan thought.

A shadowy form appeared to challenge Bolan, but the guy didn't have a chance under the sights of Lisa Rajero. The DEA agent shot him before he could reach Bolan. She walked forward to put another four rounds into him after he'd fallen, then kicked his body and finally spit on him. She muttered something under her breath and then turned to face the Executioner. Dirt-streaked tears were evident across her worn and weary face.

"Let's get out of here," he whispered.

And with that, Bolan grabbed Rajero's hand and led her into the safety and cover of darkness.

WITHIN AN HOUR of their escape, Bolan had managed to get them into a small motel near the airport. The cabdriver thought the couple was pretty strange, but a hundred dollar bill ensured no questions now and the promise of complete silence thereafter. The guy even waited in the cab with Rajero while Bolan checked in, which would avoid any uncomfortable confrontation with the motel staff over bringing a bruised, half-naked woman into the building.

Bolan waited until Rajero had showered and then used a first aid kit from his pack to treat her wounds. Once she was cleaned up, her injuries didn't look quite so bad. He offered to take her to a hospital, but Rajero adamantly refused. They were safer playing it quiet and lying low until she had a chance to recover.

"You can stay here as long as you want," Bolan told her. "I'm going to have to catch the next flight to LAX."

"Los Angeles?" Rajero asked. "Why L.A.?"

"Two reasons. One, I know there's a major air operation going on at a private airstrip just outside the city. Carillo is smuggling drugs across through the Baja pipeline, and from there they go to the airstrip. They then come directly here, and were being sold through one of Carillo's major houses, which no longer exists."

"You shut it down?"

"Permanently."

"What about the Kung Lok triad?"

"Who do you think was holding you? They're definitely involved in this. A guy named Lau Ming Shui is running the operation, and they're taking over big time. My actions against Carillo to this point have barely made a dent."

"How can that be?"

"Because while they could have proved disastrous to Carillo, it's no loss to Chinese organized crime. To a group like the Kung Lok, this is small-time stuff. You saw the force we were up against back there. That wasn't ordinary muscle. It was the Scarlet Dragons, which are feared and renowned as some of the toughest enforcers in the business.''

"Okay, but what do you think is going on behind all of this, Mike?" she asked. "And how does any of this tie into Sapèdas?"

"What do you mean?"

"Well, somebody told the Kung Lok that my partner and I were going to see Sapèdas, because they hit us on the road. We were under orders by Charlie Metzger to go to El Paso and pick up the investigation of Sapèdas where you left off. Oh, by the way, my boss knows about you. He also knows you've passed around fake ID as one of our agents, and he may have assigned somebody to find and arrest you for questioning.''

"Story of my life."

"I just don't get any of this. It's too much for coincidence.''

"You're right, it's definitely not coincidence. The Kung Lok has been planning this operation for a while, and I think it knew exactly how much control Carillo had over these operations.''

"So the triad decided to take it over for itself."

"Why not?" Bolan replied with shrug, dabbing at a cut on her forehead with some antiseptic. "It's nothing but pure profit, and the Kung Lok has little left to exploit in Canada and Hong Kong.''

"And that's not to mention its political ties."

"Especially with its political ties," Bolan interjected. "I have a feeling there's a lot more going on here than seems to be the case. And I think there's some political maneuvering that figures in. I just haven't figured how it ties to Carillo and his connection with the Colombians. Not yet, anyway.''

''What about the Kung Lok?''

''If it had dibs on Tang and its hooks into Mario Ibanez, than it's obvious the triad would have to take the major air shipment operation going on in L.A. That's why I have to go there. In the meantime, you can stay here until you feel strong enough to go back to Brownsville.''

''I'm not going to Brownsville. I'm going to El Paso and complete my mission, just like Metzger ordered me to do.''

''You're kidding, right? Metzger might have been the one to set you up.''

''I don't think so. And I need to do something, and since it's obvious you're not going to let me help you, then I'm going to be involved some other way. I have to, Belasko.'' Tears welled in her eyes now. ''For me and for Noreen. Those bastards killed her, and I want some payback.''

''I'll make sure you get payback,'' Bolan said firmly. ''Trust me on that.''

''Maybe so, but you can't be everywhere at once, and eventually, when and if you're finished with the Chinese, you're going to turn to Carillo. I might as well start being useful for something other than a punching bag, and start finding out what's going on. If Ramon Sapèdas is on Carillo's payroll, than I have to assume he's not the only one.''

''Fair enough,'' Bolan said. ''But you watch your back, Lisa. I can't promise I'll be around to pull you out of the fire next time.''

''Let's just say there won't be a next time. From here

on out, they either take my dead body or they don't take me at all. I won't wind up like Noreen did." She paused and added in a quaking voice, "I refuse to wind up like that."

Something in her voice, or perhaps just the conviction with which she said it, told Bolan that Rajero meant every word. There was no reason for Zahn to have died, but that thought only increased the pain. There was no dignity in her kind of death, and Bolan knew that it would change Lisa Rajero forever. She wouldn't be quite the same, and possibly the DEA wouldn't, either. They had watched one of their own fall today—Bolan understood that concept better than almost anyone.

The animals and savages had scored a victory today, but they had also endured incredible loss. And if the Executioner had anything to say about it, it would continue that way.

West Palm Beach, Florida

THE STORY THE MAN took more than an hour to recount was fascinating, if not bordering on complete fantasy. But there was something genuine and congenial and motivating about the man, and the way he told the story, that left Shui with the impression he had no choice but to accept it as the truth. At least until he had time to check with his own sources and verify the story.

This man appeared genuine, although he had offered neither his name nor an explanation for how he knew so much about Shui and the Kung Lok. It had been his understanding that the meeting was secret, and forbidden to anyone except members of the Kung Lok. Non-Asians weren't allowed—then again, he hadn't seen the man at the dinner party, or even in the lobby of the hotel, so perhaps he had kept to himself.

He had blond hair and blue eyes; the dark complexion of his skin wasn't the result of natural pigmentation as much as regular exposure to the sun. He was almost a Hollywood dream boy, had the kind of southern California good looks that Shui had seen hired again and again for the porn films they made in Canada. Shui guessed he was from the south somewhere. Perhaps the immediate area, or possibly the American Southwest.

"How much again did you say that this deal you've made was worth?" Shui asked.

"Five billion U.S.," he replied.

"Impossible," Shui snorted.

"Fact."

"And how exactly do I fit into all of this? How much is it going to cost me?"

"Nothing more than you didn't already spend. You just need to keep the pressure on Carillo. The more pressure that's on him and Amado Nievas, the more desperate they get. Pretty soon, they're expending troops and money like never before, and suddenly it's all for naught. They walk away with nothing, the Kung Lok walk away with half."

"And the other half?"

"It goes into various other coffers," the man replied quietly.

"And just exactly what other coffers are those?"

"The ones that are on a need-to-know basis. Look, you can do this or not. It makes no difference to me, but you've opened the door on the Carillo crime family, and that's not something you can just back out of. Even if you don't choose to be part of this alliance, you cannot withdraw, either. You try to back down now and Carillo will convince his Colombian cronies to come after you. There's already a small war brewing between the Carillo-Nievas faction and the Kung Lok. Why not profit from this in a way even you had not imagined?''

"Your words sound good in theory, but I have never trusted the Americans," Shui told him. "Kung Lok doesn't need the United States to fulfill its place in history against men like Carillo. Not to mention the fact, I am unable to bring myself to trust a man who claims to represent the American government but would sell out from under them for a quick U.S. dollar or two.''

The guy broke into a fit of laughter. Between his guffawing, he said, ''You're kidding, right? We're not talking a few hundred thousand or even a few million here, pal. We're talking two and a half billion dollars. Now that might not seem like a lot to Bill Gates or John D. Rockefeller, but it's more than adequate to get the attention of a profiteer like myself. Or you for that matter.''

"Do not pretend to know me," Shui warned his arrogant host. "You do not know me. You are impetuous and presumptuous, and I do not think we should continue this conversation.''

"Well, now, that's too bad because Dim Mai indicated you would be much more amicable to accepting assistance from outside sources.''

That caused Shui to give pause for a moment, and he could feel Fung's hand come to rest on his arm. He looked at her, and although she didn't return his gaze but stared straight ahead, he could tell she was fighting to keep her face impassive. It was probably her way of telling him that she hadn't been aware of her husband's plans to ally himself with American officials. Then again, maybe she had known about it and she was cautioning him. He decided to play out the line, act interested and see what turns the conversation took.

Shui made a show of looking out the window of the hotel on to the twinkling skyline of West Palm Beach and with marked disdain said, "I don't trust the Americans. I don't trust you."

"I don't trust you, either, Shui, but you have to admit that what I'm telling you is true. And let me tell you something else you may not know. The American government doesn't want the embarrassment of a war right on their own streets. You know what you're up against, taking on Carillo and his Mexican mafia, and you sure as hell know what kind of price you could pay."

"My people are ready to pay that price for the greater good."

The man snorted and let out a sardonic laugh. "Do you really think that your people in Hong Kong give a rat's ass about the pride of China? Can you honestly say you care about it yourself? You got into this to make money, Shui, and the fact of the matter remains that you won't make a cent without the help of others.

"And here's something else you probably don't know. Everybody in this little deal is doing nothing more than looking to carve a name for themselves in the financial annals of history. This isn't about pride in China or Hong Kong or the might of the triads, my friend—it's about money, plain and simple. It's about profit, and we all have our little piece of the pie. I'm offering the Kung Lok triad, and everybody in it, an opportunity to have both."

"You sound more to me like an opportunist on a mission to make as much money as you possibly can," Shui observed icily.

"You're damn right I am." The guy rose, waved the air to encompass the room. "Look around you, Shui. You think this is the way I want to build my own empire? Surround myself with meager furnishings and second-rate room service? I've been renting this hole from the hotel for months under an assumed name. Those idiots think I'm some pedantic businessman with an ego too large for my own good, and I've been doing everything I can to maintain that image. I knew about your little powwow here months before it happened. Where do think I got that information?"

"I do not know," Shui admitted. "I was wondering about that earlier."

"I'll bet you were," the guy said easily. He sat down again. "And you're probably wondering just who the hell I am and who I work for."

"Yes, Mr....?" his voice trailed off.

"That shall remain unimportant for now. Or at least until you've decided whether to accept my offer."

"I have no reason to trust you, then, if you will not even tell me your name."

The man shrugged. "None of your associates know my name either, but that hasn't stopped them from seizing the advantage. You see, Shui, now is the time to ask yourself what you believe. I can tell you that if you're doing this thing against Carillo because you feel it will put you in better graces with the Hong Kong syndicate, you're gravely mistaken. They don't care if you carve a niche for yourself. Hell, they've been expecting it, and Dim Mai's been running your name down to everyone he can, including your pal, General Jikwan."

"So you put the feelers out through the general?"

"Yeah, in a manner of speaking. Jikwan and I have done each other favors on more than one occasion. I like the guy, and I like his ideas. "You see, Shui—" he looked at Fung "—and you'll have to forgive me for saying so, Mrs. Mai, but Jikwan doesn't like Dim Mai that much. He especially doesn't like the way the guy is always lording it over everybody that he controls the Pacific arms network. He may be a big gun dealer, but that's all he is. He has no real political power, and the Hong Kong politicians hate his guts. I can definitely tell you that Yi-chang Shen doesn't think anything of him."

"It is true," Fung said, apparently having found the courage to speak for the first time since entering the room. "Shen and Dim do not get along. They are as different as night and day."

"Exactly," the stranger replied, inclining his head in Fung's direction respectfully.

He turned to Shui and added, "So you can see why an alliance with someone like myself would be of tremendous advantage to you."

"It would seem you stand to suffer nothing in this 'alliance,' as you call it, while the rest of us stand being put to considerable inconvenience."

"My intelligence told me you were a skeptic."

"So you have been spying on me?"

"It's my job to spy on everyone who poses a potential threat to the United States."

"And I am one of these people?"

"All six billion of you Chinese are a threat to us," the man said pointedly. "You've stolen our military secrets, bribed our public officials and put gangs of unrivaled force onto our streets. The Chinese triads are still one of the most feared crime syndicates in this country, surpassing the power of the Sicilians, Mexicans, or Japanese Yakuza. There are more Chinatowns in more major cities in this country than any other single icon of ethnic demographics.''

''That sounds like a stereotype.''

''Hardly. Try a well-known fact. And don't preach to me about stereotyping, Shui, because you stereotyped Americans earlier. You and your pals aren't as inscrutable and proper as you'd like the rest of the world to think you are, and I'm not so impressed by the Kung Lok that I'm intimidated. However, I *am* a wise man and a man of opportunity. I hope you're the same.''

''And if I do not accept your offer?''

The guy shrugged and looked at his fingernails. ''It's no skin off my nose. The fact of the matter is, you have nothing to fear from me. I'm not in the business of rubbing out those who don't want to play ball for me. It's not good business and it's not profitable. A man needs allies in today's world. On one side of the fence, I've got the faith and loyalty of the American government. On the other hand, I've got the Kung Lok triad.''

Shui could feel his face go flush with anger and disgust for the slime that sat in front of him. He cared for nothing, wanted for nothing. All the man could see was his greed and his power. All he could obviously envision was a virtually unlimited source of monetary funds and whatever imagined power it would bring him. This man was nothing short of delusional, and he was so confident in himself that it wanted to make Shui vomit. He knew that such a man might seem beneficial at first, but eventually he would be a liability.

Nonetheless, Shui knew that what he was saying

about the Carillo crime family was true. If he backed off now, or for some unlikely circumstance he was unable to seize the action in the American Southwest, there would eventually come a time where his life wouldn't be worth any more than the filth on the bottom of his shoes. That wasn't a good position in which to be when it came to the Kung Lok. So he would bide his time, make a pact with this nameless stranger and when all seemed right—and he had used the man for what he could—he would destroy him. And anyone else who got in his way.

"I have decided," he told the man.

"And?"

"I will accept your offer."

The stranger smiled, leaning forward to offer his hand which Shui took reluctantly. Then the guy said, "Now, I shall tell you a little more about myself. And just how I can help you succeed in destroying Carillo *and* the Colombians."

CHAPTER SEVENTEEN

Los Angeles, California

Mack Bolan took a red-eye flight from Las Vegas to LAX, procured a rental car and was soon headed toward the outskirts of the city. Thanks to one of Cowboy Kissinger's contacts, fresh firepower awaited him in the trunk of the rental. Stowing his weapons aboard checked luggage would have been virtually impossible on such short notice, and even if he could have acquired clearance documents in a timely fashion, it would have drawn way more attention than he wanted.

Bolan found a new bag in the trunk, complete with a Beretta 93-R and .44 Magnum Desert Eagle. There was also an M-16 A-2/M-203 with a thousand rounds of SS109 ammo, ten 40 mm high explosive grenades and four handheld smokers. A Remington 7 mm sniper rifle with 30-power scope completed the kit.

Lisa Rajero didn't bat an eye when the Executioner told her he had to go. The lady was tough, and she would survive. In a way, he felt guilty for leaving her behind, but he knew the numbers were running down and there was little doubt Rajero could take care of herself. She didn't act like the helpless damsel in distress, so Bolan put her troubles out of his mind and focused on the work ahead of him.

After about an hour, the Executioner stopped at a vacant rest stop off the highway and dropped coin to Stony Man. Aaron Kurtzman answered.

"We clear?" Bolan asked.

"You bet, Striker. How's it going?"

"Could be better, but I'm still on schedule. Anything new on that end?"

"Well, Hal left less than hour ago for a meeting with the Man," Kurtzman replied. "Barb's at NSA headquarters, using her contacts there to run down some additional information on recent FARC movements. Able Team's still on standby, ready to help if you need them. Unfortunately, we couldn't send Phoenix to help now, even if we wanted. They just left for Costa Rica."

"What's brewing down there?"

"I'm not exactly sure yet. Haven't had time to talk to Hal about it. Seems the natives are restless down there, though, so I'm sure I'll find out soon enough."

"Check that. Listen, tell Hal there may still be some loose strings in Vegas, and he might want to send the Feds to check it out. You remember my little message to Tang?"

"Yeah."

"Well, I think the receivers weren't happy with it. I'm sure Tang and most of his gang are no longer with us."

Kurtzman sighed. "I hate to sound cold, Striker, but that's no loss in my humble opinion."

"I hear you. But there's still a major pool of Scarlet Dragons trying to hold their position in Las Vegas. I'd advise Vegas PD to proceed with caution and do what they can to curb the problems. I'm in blitz mode, and there's one more thing to take care of here in California before I head to Mexicali.''

"Do you need anything?''

"No, Cowboy already helped me out on this end. Jack headed back to Texas, and he's waiting there for further instructions. I imagine he'll be checking in soon.''

"Already has. We've got him on standby there until we know how this is going to play out.''

"Good enough.''

"Hey, that reminds me, we have something else you might find interesting.'' Bolan could hear Kurtzman rustle some papers. "Some Company guys reported a major meeting down in Florida. Looks like we've got a whole slew of Hong Kong politicians sponsoring some sort of major shindig. Most of them have known ties with the Kung Lok triad. Seems there are a lot more fingers in this pie than we'd originally thought.''

"Interesting.''

"We thought so, too, since not one of these guys bothered to inform the Man they were in town.''

"I hope he plans to continue playing ignorant,'' Bolan ventured.

"He was originally going to make it an issue, but I think Hal talked him out of it.''

"That's probably the best way to play it. It's not like they believe we don't know they're here.''

"I agree,'' Kurtzman said. "But we're hoping that the President will come off unconcerned and they'll be off guard.''

"Not likely.''

Kurtzman let out a grunt of assent. "Yeah. Anyway, we've identified some interesting faces in the crowd. Not only are some major political players on the guest list, but also Lau Ming Shui, Dim Mai and Yi-chang Shen. And check this out. Are you familiar with a Chinese general by the name of Deng Jikwan?''

Something tingled in the pit of the Executioner's stomach. Yeah, he knew the name all too well. Jikwan had been responsible for the deaths of thousands of innocent people in his time. He'd offered arms and troops to at least a half-dozen known terrorist organizations throughout Southeast Asia, and was a major contributor to continued warfare in the Middle East countries. Much of Jikwan's funding came from official sources, but Bolan also recalled some intelligence related to his unofficial ties with the Red Mafia and al-Qaeda. Jikwan had an unusual talent for playing two ends against the middle with various warring factions throughout the world, and he was wanted by the Israeli Mossad in connection with attempted marketing of nuclear devices to Hamas.

''It sounds like some heavy hitters, Bear,'' Bolan remarked. ''If Jikwan's involved, I'd start looking for supporters from inside the U.S.''

''You think this goes that deep?'' Kurtzman asked with incredulity.

''I can almost guarantee it. Jikwan never does anything on his own, and if he has a green light from his masters in China, that means there are big plans for conquest on the part of the Kung Lok. They've already shown they're not afraid to start a war right on the streets of this country. I think Jikwan knows the FARC is involved, and I think he'll be looking to manipulate the situation to his advantage.''

''Roger that, Striker. I'll start digging up what I can on his most recent activities.''

"I'll be in touch again. Out here."

Bolan returned to his car and continued toward his target. He kept an eye on the rearview mirror, conscious of any change in traffic flow. It was light—as light as could be expected for L.A. suburbia that hour of the morning—so Bolan knew any tails would be easy to spot. He'd experienced a foreboding sense since leaving Las Vegas. No potential threat had presented itself thus far, but the warrior had learned to trust his judgment. He rarely left things like that to chance when his good sense told him different.

Still, if someone was watching him, they were doing one hell of a job staying inconspicuous. Another ten minutes elapsed before Bolan exited Interstate 405 where it met Highway 73. It was a short jog southeast to where the road intersected Highway 55. The airstrip operations were actually taking place within the control of John Wayne Airport in Orange County. The Executioner had to admit that there was some poetic justice in that fact, and the thought brought a smile.

Bolan parked his car on a side road, stripped his street clothes off to reveal his blacksuit and then retrieved his bag from the trunk. He jogged the half mile to a fenced area on the southwest perimeter of the airport. The Executioner had obtained aerial reconnaissance photographs from DEA records, and he knew which section was held by the drug runners. He'd planned to tackle this part of Carillo's organization in conjunction with his offensive on the Brownsville pipeline, but his encounters with the Kung Lok had changed all of that.

Bolan wasn't even sure if this part of the California pipeline was still under Carillo's control, but he couldn't believe the Kung Lok could move so fast in such a short period of time. Carillo's operations in the Southwest spread far and wide; he still controlled the major drug action on the other side of the border, and the Executioner had no solid evidence that had changed. Especially since he'd been working on stamping out the Kung Lok's territorial claims faster than it could make them.

Bolan studied the quiet airstrip on the other side of the fence. Planes took off in the distance, but he could remain relatively invisible. This side of the airport wasn't well-lit, and the shadows kept the soldier virtually invisible to any ground observers.

He retrieved his M-16 A-2/M-203 and several spare clips, which he shoved into the hidden pouches in the suit. He stuck the Desert Eagle into a special horizontal shoulder rigging beneath his left arm, and then folded the bag over and latched it with clip straps. To most it would have looked like an ordinary gym bag, but it actually converted into a hip satchel for quick access to the grenades. Bolan secured the makeshift pouch to his military belt and then climbed the chain link fence in one easy motion. The Executioner crossed the expanse of the airfield in a flat run and dropped prone at the far end of an asphalt strip. He eased his breathing as he studied the area ahead.

Three adjacent buildings, erected in an I-formation, stood off the airstrip. No light emanated from the windows, but Bolan suspected this was by design. He was confident that most of the drug runs took place at night when departures and landings from the main terminal were at a minimum. Most of the inbound and outbound flights from the airport were business commuters consisting of private express flights to other airports in neighboring states or business jets. None of the major airlines operated at the airport, either, as it wasn't designed to handle commercial traffic. Thus, the irregular comings and goings of private planes at odd hours wasn't unusual.

Bolan noticed a lone Learjet positioned near the buildings in a taxi lane. He couldn't tell exactly what type of craft it was, but an inspection of the exterior markings visible in the illumination by a tall light pole didn't reveal anything out of the ordinary. Bolan was about to move closer to the jet when the reflection of light on metal caught his eye. Two men dressed in slacks and light jackets exited from the central building and stopped outside the door. The soldier lay motionless in the damp grass, watching carefully. There was a sudden flare of a lighter, and moments later he discerned the pinpoint glows of cigarettes as the men talked and smoked. From this distance, Bolan couldn't hear what they were saying. Not that it mattered—he wasn't there to gather intelligence.

Slowly Bolan began to crawl the width of the airstrip. Given the two men were silhouetted and partially visible from the illumination on the jet, the Executioner knew it unlikely they would have seen him even if he chose to stand and walk toward them. Still, he couldn't risk it. The element of surprise was needed in this instance, since he had no idea of the numbers or firepower stacked against him. Those things would have to be evaluated once he'd penetrated the building.

Bolan continued to crawl until he reached what he knew would be a blind spot to the men. He then rose and sprinted, sidling up to the building as he turned the selector switch on the M-16 A-2 rifle to full-auto. After popping an HE grenade into the launcher, he slung the weapon onto his right shoulder, muzzle down to allow easy retrieval if needed. He drew the Beretta and moved along the side of the building, keeping his back to the wall but not in contact, the muzzle of the 93-R held at the ready. The voices were now discernible, carried easily along the chilly early-morning wind that blew across the airfield. The pair was speaking Spanish.

Bolan emerged from the darkness and pointed the Beretta at the two men.

They turned unexpectedly and their eyes widened at the sight of the ghostly wraith who now stood before them.

"Stay still," he ordered in Spanish. They obeyed. He inclined his head in the direction of the building and asked, "How many inside?"

Neither man spoke. They looked at each other for a moment and then stared at him, careful to keep their hands away from their bodies. Bolan instructed them to turn and kneel. Once they complied, he struck one behind the ear, and the man landed unconscious on his face.

Bolan pressed the muzzle of the Beretta to the back of the second man's head. "I asked you a question. How many inside?"

"N-nobody," the sentry stammered. "Just us two."

The Executioner didn't buy it. Even if his enemy was telling the truth, Bolan wasn't going to risk walking into a hornet's nest. That might have been exactly what the guy was hoping for. He wondered why the man would risk death to protect anyone inside, since loyalty wasn't exactly an earmark among his kind. Nonetheless, Bolan couldn't bring himself to murder the guy in cold blood.

He pistol-whipped him, meting a similar punishment to that of his cohort.

Bolan then turned and concentrated on the door. Nobody would be expecting a fully armed assailant to come strolling through the front door, and he realized that would give him the advantage he sought. The Executioner had learned through experience that taking certain calculated risks was part of the business. His intuition had paid off before—and it did again. As he suspected, the place was filled with trouble.

The first pair to spot him clawed for guns, barely able to see above a table containing hundreds of kilos of cut product and pills. The bags of cocaine weren't thick enough to repel Bolan's justice, which came in the form of 5.56 mm rounds on full-auto. The high-velocity slugs punched through the bags, continuing onward to pierce the tender flesh of the two gunmen. One man spun under the impact of the rounds and slammed face first into a support pillar. The second man was lifted off his feet, his finger curling around his pistol as he was drawing it. The round fired from the pistol lodged in his chest, but he was already dead. Clouds of crystalline narcotic rained on the table and floor, thousands of dollars lost in the twinkling of an eye.

And the Executioner was just getting started.

As Bolan reached into the satchel and withdrew one of the smokers, three more hoods with weapons drawn appeared from a nearby room. They were ready for a shoot-out, but not expecting Bolan's alternative as he yanked the pin on the smoker and tossed it underhanded onto the table. The heat from the fuse began to melt the plastic, and smoke immediately filled the area between the soldier and his opponents. Bolan knew the smoker wasn't enough to stop them from trying to kill him, and dropped to the linoleum in time to avoid a firestorm of pistol fire.

Bolan rolled under the table and came up on their side of the smoke, M-16 A-2 held at the ready. He sprayed the trio of shooters with a burst of autofire in a corkscrew pattern. The 5.56 mm hardball ammunition ripped flesh from the bodies of the three surprised gunners. Several of the rounds actually blew off the head of the closest man. The other two died just as quickly, the slugs drilling their chests before the corpse of their headless comrade hit the ground.

The Executioner got to his feet, starting to choke on the toxic fumes filling the vestibule area where the battle had joined. The fuse on the smoker had obviously ignited the meth powder in the pills. Combined with the melted plastic and heated cocaine, Bolan wasn't sure if asphyxia or overdose would kill him first. Either way, it wouldn't kill him as quickly as another trio that arrived to investigate the sounds of gunfire.

Two of these men carried some of the Jatimatic machine pistols. Bolan had seen entirely too many of them already. He delivered a blitzing firestorm, staying low and on the move as he triggered short, controlled bursts. The gunmen tried to get out of the way, but two of them ran into each other in their haste. It was a fatal mistake, and the pair fell under the merciless and unerring accuracy of the Executioner's marksmanship. The remaining target managed to evade Bolan's first couple of bursts, but the fate of the pair with him proved too much a distraction.

By the time the guy realized that his adversary wasn't going to just hit and git, it was too late. The soldier had loaded a new magazine, and now unleashed a fresh salvo of high-velocity rounds. The slugs ripped through the gunner's belly and caused vital organs to implode. The man collapsed as blood spewed from his mutilated abdomen.

Bolan rose from his kneeling position and continued through the winding complex. He kept the over-and-under in front of him, ready for any resistance. He figured maybe five or six minutes remained before he had to make his exit, assuming someone had heard the gunfire coming from the outbuildings. It was more likely nobody had heard a thing, given the distance to the enclosed main terminal and the majority of ground crews outside wore ear protection. However, there would be no hiding the plane and buildings when he destroyed them. But by that time, the Executioner would be gone.

The soldier finished checking the first building, then made his way out a rear door and proceeded to checked the second. It was empty. He moved on to the third, and it was vacant, as well. The Executioner had to admit he was a bit puzzled. It was possible that someone had warned his people, or perhaps they had left only a skeleton crew to watch the place. That didn't make any sense either, though. It seemed that Carillo was just rolling over to the Kung Lok, and the Executioner couldn't understand it.

Bolan was about to leave the third building when a light in the corner caught his eye. It was just a glowing sliver, like light spilling through a partially closed door. The soldier approached with caution when he realized that was exactly what it was. He pushed the door open with the muzzle of his rifle and immediately noticed a gray metal desk and chair—like the kind issued to many government offices. There was a small lamp on the desk, the source of the light, and then Bolan noticed the open safe. And the open window that looked on to the main terminal.

The Executioner stuck his head through the window in time to see a man running for the plane. Bolan jumped through and took up pursuit. The guy reached the Learjet and got up the ramp. Reaching the jet just as the man struggled to lift the stairway ramp on his own, Bolan managed to shove the muzzle of his M-16 A-2 through the opening before the guy could close it. He then reached up, grabbed the top of the ramp and yanked hard. The vinyl-coated, heavy-tension cables holding the ramp nearly dislodged from the mounts.

The guy stepped backward, obviously surprised by the ferocity of the Executioner's attack. He was a puny little man with bifocals, and thin hair. Bolan had seen his kind before, and there was something about the guy that was slimy and putrid.

The Executioner made a show of pressing the still warm muzzle of the M-16 A-2 to the man's forehead, making sure he got a particularly good view of the gaping escape chamber for the grenade launcher.

"Who are you. I—"

"Shut up," Bolan snapped. "I'm asking the questions. Who are you and what are you doing here?"

"I—I can't tell you that," the guy stammered. "They'll kill me."

"You're dead anyway, if you don't start answering questions." It was a bluff but an effective one.

"I don't know what I can tell you."

"Start with who you are and why you're working for a man like Jose Carillo."

The man's expression betrayed that he was appalled, even offended, by the very suggestion. "I don't work for Carillo."

"Then who?" the Executioner demanded.

And as the man began to talk, Bolan could hardly believe what he was hearing.

UPON HEARING the would-be escapee's story, Mack Bolan knew that the situation was much worse than he could have ever imagined. The story was so unbelievable, the Executioner wasn't sure he could trust his own ears. But the man knew too much and had too many details readily at hand in answer to Bolan's questions, which left no doubt his story was true.

Once he had secured his prisoner, and let loose a volley of grenades onto the jet and buildings from the perimeter of the airport, Bolan made arrangements for a pickup. The operator for the local FBI office was certainly puzzled by a phone call from a DEA agent claiming they could find a former government official who had something important to say about drug-running in southern California.

"You can find the guy tied to a lamp pole behind a deserted gas station off Highway 55," the caller told her. Then he gave her the mile post number and hung up.

After Bolan had concluded his call to the FBI, he contacted Stony Man.

"Brognola," the gruff voice answered.

"It's me."

"Good God, man, are you okay?"

"I'm fine. Why?"

"We heard there was all kinds of trouble in Las Vegas, and reports are coming in now about California. Bear said you sounded, well…strange.''

"Don't worry, Hal,'' Bolan replied wearily. "Just running out of steam, and I've still got a long haul.''

"I'm not worrying. I never worry, Striker. You know that. I just manage.''

The Executioner smiled at Brognola's verbal parrying. "Whatever you say, Hal.''

"What's next on your agenda?'' the Stony Man chief asked.

"Mexicali. I think that's going to be the center of Carillo's final play. The guy's pulled out all the stops.''

"Really?''

"Yeah. He's left skeleton crews behind at most of his major sites.''

"Or at least the ones the Kung Lok haven't taken over.''

"Yeah. I also ran into a very interesting character on my assault against Carillo's operation here in L.A. It seems my hunch about U.S. government officials tied up with the Kung Lok may have some merit.''

"Yeah, Bear mentioned something about that. He and Barb are working about six or seven different angles on this, but we haven't gained much ground. We also don't have the first clue as to who within the government might benefit greatly enough to risk treason and deal with the likes of the Chinese triads.''

"Well, the guy I stumbled across didn't have any names, but he had documents that definitely put Ramon Sapèdas of the Border Patrol on the top suspects list. There may also be someone even higher than him working this whole deal. Someone closer to Justice. But I'll get back to you when I know more about that. In the meantime, I have another angle you might find interesting.''

''What's that?''

''It seems the motive for hostile takeover isn't centered on the U.S.''

''Where, then? Don't tell me this is about Mexico or Colombia.''

''No. It's about money and Hong Kong.''

''What do you mean?''

''Think about it, Hal. The FARC needs guns and Carillo needs to control the border because the competition is getting fierce. That's scenario one. Scenario two is the Kung Lok, who think they can play two ends against the middle. Let's say Shui gets ambitious and decides to go after all of the drug-and-porn action in the Southwest. But he knows he doesn't have the resources to do it on his own, so he cooks up this elaborate scheme to start a war.''

''I think I see where you're going,'' Brognola interjected. ''He's got the manpower, but he doesn't have the firepower.''

''Or the strong political ties with Hong Kong. It's no secret Chinese officials look the other way in times like these, because the information passed back to them is invaluable.''

''And they don't want to lose their little spy network,'' Brognola concluded.

''Right,'' Bolan said. ''So they decide to have a meet, and Shui recruits major players like Dim Mai. Then because of the political maneuvering, you get people like Jikwan and Shen into the act. Before long, someone in the American government sees where this could be a strong advantage. Drugs for weapons, weapons for power and power for political anarchy. Someone looks to profit from all sides of the coin while stirring the pot. Then they step back and watch the show."

"It's an old story," Brognola said with a deep sigh.

"Yeah, but a profitable and deceptive story if all who stand to gain some major advantage play their cards right. And if a U.S. official is pulling the strings here, I'm going to deal with them my way."

"You think it's Sapèdas?"

"Doubtful," Bolan replied immediately. "I've met the guy and he's not that bright."

"Well, it sounds like you're quickly getting this under control." On afterthought he added, "It's just too bad that innocent people have to pick up the pieces when tragedy strikes."

"Not this time," the Executioner said, making no effort to hide the rancor in his tone. "I'm about to shut down this operation. Permanently."

"How?"

"I'm going forward with the mission as planned and turn off the pipeline at its source. Carillo and the FARC pose a significant threat to security, much more right now than Shui. The Kung Lok is still licking its wounds after our last bout."

"But it sounds like the Kung Lok is the real threat."

"Agreed. But destroying the drug source destroys demand for weapons or territories."

"Okay, but then what?"

"Then I finish the remaining rats as they retreat," the Executioner replied.

CHAPTER EIGHTEEN

Brownsville, Texas

Lisa Rajero didn't waste any time returning to her headquarters after Belasko left. She wanted to talk to Metzger.

Despite her short but traumatic ordeal, Rajero wasn't feeling too badly. And it wasn't as if she'd never had someone rough her up before. Her ex-husband used to regularly beat the hell out of her, but she learned very quickly that she didn't have to be a victim and put a stop to it. He went to jail, she went to divorce court, and that had been the long and short of her six-month marriage.

Rajero grabbed a taxi from the airport and within an hour of her arrival she was seated in Metzger's living room and reporting the events of the past twenty-four hours. She'd decided not to wait until he got to their offices. Rajero had a plan she wanted to run by him, and she didn't want anyone else to know about it.

Metzger listened with interest and when Rajero had finally concluded her narrative, the DEA chief took off his glasses, rubbed his sleepy eyes and sighed.

"Why is it that every time this Belasko's around, people start to die?'' He looked at Rajero and added, ''Did you ever ask yourself that question?''

''Probably because every other federal agency is sitting on its respective fat ass and doing nothing, Charlie.''

''You think I'm doing nothing about this?'' he snapped. He waved at the phone and continued, ''I spent three hours on that damn thing last night trying to console Pete Willy's widow as she wailed in my ear! Not to mention I put out a search party for you and Noreen while agonizing over where you might be or what happened to you. Now I have two agents dead, one who looks like she got run over by a semi, and some maniac who's flying around and killing anyone who looks Hispanic or Chinese. And he's doing it in the name of the DEA!''

''He's not a maniac and he certainly isn't doing anything in the name of the DEA,'' Rajero countered, trying to keep her voice calm and respectful. ''He's out there doing something while we do nothing. He single-handedly destroyed that manufacturing plant on the end of town that we've been trying only God knows how long to put down, and he also took out Jose Carillo's Houston connection.''

Metzger's rancorous expression changed to one of surprise. ''Belasko was behind that hit on the plant?''

''Yeah.''

''I didn't know that.'' He scratched his chin. ''Maybe he's not such a bad guy. That place had been generating coke and MDMA in quantities I wouldn't even venture to guess. I think our stat guys estimated somewhere in the neighborhood of five hundred keys of processed junk a week running out of that place.''

"Well, now it's a smoldering pile of ash."

Metzger appeared to think about the situation for a minute. Rajero didn't say another word, respectful of the silence. Actually, she was preoccupied with her own thoughts of Belasko. He was one hell of a guy—that much was sure. He was out there risking his life, and putting it on the line to help everyone. Belasko cared about everyone—he actually cared. He was responsible in what he did, and Rajero didn't believe he killed indiscriminately.

Sure, she didn't agree with all of his methods, but then she didn't have to. They were alike and yet different in so many ways. She had to operate within the boundaries and rules of the DEA—Belasko ran his own game. Her movements and actions were sometimes held up by the red tape and politics of the federal bureaucracy—Belasko did what he had to when he had to do it. She was restrained because these scum suckers had "rights"—Belasko cared nothing for their rights, believing them forfeit when they dealt drugs and killed American teenagers.

"Okay, Lisa," Metzger finally said, "I'm through fighting with the higher-ups about this. It's time for us to start kicking ass and taking names and letting Carillo know we're not going to take it anymore. Tell me what you think we should do."

Rajero smiled and nodded a thanks to him. Then she said, "Belasko is fairly convinced my theory about Sapèdas is true."

"You still think he's dirty?"

"I'm sure of it, Charlie. I'm more sure about this than I think I've ever been sure about anything in my whole life. I don't know if he's working for Carillo or the Kung Lok, but I know he's a filthy traitor.''

"Well, I ran a check on his whereabouts after you disappeared, and found out he was nowhere near you when the hit on your vehicle went down. I'm sure he didn't even know you were coming, so that probably rules out any connection with the Kung Lok. But, Ramon and I have worked in conjunction on a couple of cases. His office is always cooperative with us, and there's never been any problems I've heard of. Still, I know that the recent events have opened my eyes a little more, and it does seem he's a little too clean for my tastes.''

"Well, I'm glad you think so, because I believe he's on Carillo's payroll.''

"What do you propose to do about it?''

"I'm going to go to El Paso, like we tried before. I owe that much to Pete Willy and his widow. But this time, I don't want to advertise the fact. I want only you and me to know about this, Charlie. I think we need to keep things quiet until I can get to El Paso and question Sapèdas myself.''

"And what if he doesn't want to answer any of your questions?''

"Well, I can be pretty persuasive,'' she said with a wink. "But if he's uncooperative, then he's probably got something to hide.''

"Not necessarily,'' Metzger counseled her. "Just because he won't answer your questions doesn't make him a criminal, Lisa. Whatever you do, I want you to be careful. Don't lean too hard on this guy, because if he's clean and you push him we could end up with the proverbial egg all over our faces. I refuse to see my own career go down the tubes because I stepped on another agency's toes when I shouldn't have. So you make sure there's some solid evidence there before making accusations. And I want you to check in hourly.''

"Hourly? Come on, Charlie, I can't get—''

"It's not open for negotiation, Lisa. You check in hourly, or you forget it and I send someone else. I've lost two good people in the past day, and I'm not going to add to that number. No more deaths, Lisa. I couldn't take that.''

There was something somber and serious in his voice—and coupled with his expressionless look, convinced Rajero it was wiser to do what he asked and not argue the point. She wouldn't do Belasko a damn bit of good if she aggravated Metzger to the point that he got nervous and changed his mind. No matter what she might think, Metzger had the authority to pull the plug quickly and permanently.

"Okay, every hour. I give you my word that I'll check in every hour.''

"Good.''

Rajero knew it was time to get moving, so she started to leave. She had to get some things packed because she knew this little excursion to El Paso was going to be more than just an overnight jaunt. She figured to be gone at least four days, possibly the whole week. As they walked toward the front door, something in Metzger's expression seemed to fall.

"What is it?'' she asked him.

"I have a really awful feeling about this whole thing.''

"Why?''

"I don't know,'' he said with an eerie tone in his

voice. "I just feel...I feel like there's something very wrong. But I can't put my finger on it."

"Well, I wouldn't worry too much about it." She added on afterthought, "You know, you might be totally right. There might not be a thing to this theory of Belasko's."

"But then again, there might," Metzger said. "This mercy angel of yours has been three-and-oh so far, and he's probably right about the other stuff where Sapèdas and Carillo are concerned. The guy obviously has access to intelligence we don't."

As Metzger opened the door for her and she started to leave, Rajero said, "Well, I know that whatever happens it's all going to be okay."

"I hope you're right."

"Trust me on this," Rajero said, smiling sweetly. "I'm always right about these things."

Metzger chuckled and said, "Get out of here."

Las Vegas, Nevada

ING KAOCHU AND SEVERAL of his Scarlet Dragons were waiting to greet Lau Ming Shui on the tarmac of the private airfield outside the city. The Chinese crime lord had concluded his meetings in West Palm Beach and immediately departed for Las Vegas.

Shui was exhausted, having spent most of the night talking with his new partner. Despite his earlier reservations, Shui had come to like the triad's newest benefactor, and he foresaw a long and fruitful relationship with the man. Of course, he still planned to fully investigate the man. He needed leverage on every business contact, and Shui had found that the easiest way to do that was through information. And if things didn't work out like the stranger had promised? Well, he would simply have to let it leak to the Americans just exactly what was happening in their own backyard.

But first, he needed to know who the guy was and everything he could about his position inside the U.S. government. That had become Kaochu's number-one priority; Shui told him as much during their ride to Shui's hotel.

"Why aren't we going to your new house?" Shui asked.

"Security reasons," Kaochu said dismissively.

"I find your tone disrespectful, Ing," Shui said. "You will explain yourself and your actions, and you will do so now."

Kaochu took a deep breath. Whatever it was, Shui knew immediately it was a topic of discussion the Scarlet Dragon leader would have preferred to avoid. Shui didn't give a damn. He was used to having men that served without hesitation and obeyed without question. Kaochu had always been that kind of man, and something had obviously changed his mind. Shui wanted to know what it was.

"It is this Belasko again."

"I thought I told you to eliminate him."

"We tried, Lau, but he is extremely elusive. This is no ordinary man."

"Bah!" Shui waved with a disgusted expression. "That's a feeble excuse for the weak-minded, Ing. Every man is an ordinary man until someone tries to make him extraordinary. It seems this man is becoming some sort of myth among the Dragons, and you're letting it happen. He has walked into and out of the hands of your best soldiers, snuffing their lives as if it were nothing, and he has done so with repeated impunity. Why have you let him do this, Ing? He's undermining your authority and my reputation, and it has to stop. Is that clear?"

"Yes."

Shui considered something and then said, "I think that for the time being, I don't want you to concern yourself with this Belasko. Leave him to me. Your newest priority is to find out everything you can about the man I spoke with. I've arranged to secure copies of the hotel video cameras so that we can get a picture of him."

"You think he would be foolish enough to allow someone to take his photograph?"

"I don't think he believes we are smart enough to utilize those kinds of resources. I spoke with Dim Mai and General Jikwan after talking with this individual, and they don't trust him any more than I do. So we have decided to find out who he is, and then if things do not come about as he predicted, we will know who he really is and how best to deal with him."

"As you wish. And what about Belasko? How are you going to deal with him?"

"I have already told you not to worry about him." Shui looked out the window and nodded to himself. Yes, he knew exactly how to deal with Belasko. Shui added, "His day of atonement is coming."

Chihuahua, Mexico

"THE TROOPS ARE in position," Colonel Amado Nievas announced. "I just received word from Captain Mirada, and he is standing by for my orders. We're ready to implement your plan."

Carillo nodded and looked at his watch. "We still have a few hours before the trucks will arrive."

"Where is the shipment coming from?"

"I have a processing plant just north of San Felipe. It has served as a great central point for that entire area. The product will move up through Mexicali, and they'll cross the border tonight during the, shall we say, festivities?"

"It sounds like you have things well in hand, my friend," Nievas said.

Carillo tried not to look impressed with himself, although he couldn't help gloating a little bit. This had been a long time coming, and he was finally going to see all of his work pay off. Nothing could stop the disaster that was about to befall the city of Mexicali. Carillo knew that some Mexican people—his own blood—would perish tonight, but it was for a greater good.

The Americans had always been smug, looking down their noses at the "wetback." Well, that was about to change because Carillo was going to give them the monkey for their backs they always desired. The whites—and particularly those in America—had an unusual propensity for drugs, and they would pay through the nose to get them.

Teenagers loved the effects of the meth, because the entire crowd scene, where most of that product sold, offered them a place where they felt they could belong. The whites had brought it on themselves with their business deals over golf and parents who gave more of a shit about their careers than their kids. Carillo hadn't been blessed with children yet, but he knew that one day he would find the right woman and she would bear him many kids. And he would teach them the right way, and pay some attention to them.

It was always funny to him how on American television they had to tell parents to talk to their children about drugs. Carillo found that almost sad. What, the parents didn't already know that? They needed their government to tell them to keep their kids away from the perverts and the junkies and the dirty old man that ran the corner liquor store that sold smut magazines to grade-school kids.

That was the entire problem with U.S. society: they were too damn ignorant of their own problems. From the time he'd found how easy it was to mule dope over the border, Carillo had always wondered why the Americans bemoaned all of the drugs coming over. First, a large majority of Americans readily bought and used drugs, whether legal or illegal; second, others ignored those who readily bought it and used them. So it was only a natural business move to act on the demand and create the supply.

Nonetheless, Carillo feared the day when the white man might actually consider legalizing drugs in his home borders. Just enough for personal use, because if it were legalized it would be readily available. Naturally, supply would go up and demand would go down, and as a result that would cut into profits. But now, when it was hard to come by and illegal, and had to be piped up from Mexico, the risk and the forbidden fruits thereof justified the price.

Carillo considered himself nothing more than a businessman. He knew what they said about him, but he didn't really care. The whites could have their half-million-dollar homes and green lawns and dreams of successful companies. Carillo knew that after tonight his profits would be secure and that was all there was to it.

"What exactly is going to be the timing here?" Nievas asked.

"The bomb is scheduled to go off at seven-thirty their time. I have calculated that it will take approximately twenty minutes for emergency crews to respond. I've also arranged to insure that in addition to the injuries that will flood the local hospitals, the blast will allow a way of escape for prisoners they might be holding. That will keep the law-enforcement and emergency services busy."

"What about the border itself?"

"That's the beautiful part about this. Any time that such an act has occurred before, they have closed the border. It is approximately eighteen minutes from the main precinct where the bomb will go off to the border. In previous incidents that have occurred, one of the first things to happen is the border is closed. The trucks will be going through at that time. There are special lanes designated for commercial semis, and when the order comes through to shut the border down, they like to have those lanes cleared."

"So you're counting on the fact they will move the trucks through quickly?" Nievas interrupted.

"Yes."

"And if they don't?"

"They will," Carillo said proudly. "You see, I've already told you that I had a trump card to play. First of all, I have firsthand information coming from Sapèdas. But I also have a man inside the border station between Mexicali and Calexico. He has promised to insure the transfer goes smoothly.''

"And if it doesn't?''

"Then there will be many dead men before the next dawn,'' Carillo said coldly. He was becoming a little agitated with his new ally's skepticism. "I've been planning this for many months. I can assure you that it will work. It has to work or I am through. I can no longer afford to hold my assets without regaining control of some larger part of the drug trade between my country and America. And if the drugs don't get through, you don't get your guns and I have no way of fighting my Chinese competitors. You will be embarrassed, and I will have to go into hiding.''

"Perhaps, but it wouldn't be the Americans you would have to worry about hiding from as much as my own people,'' Nievas said quietly.

"What do you mean?''

"My superiors took a chance on you solely at my recommendation. If this does not work, and we cannot continue our revolution in Colombia, they will find and dismember both of us. Starting with our testicles.''

Carillo nearly gagged on a mango he'd been eating. "You are suggesting they would do something like that to their own?''

"Don't doubt what I'm telling you,'' Nievas replied. "The people's revolutionary army plays for keeps, Jose. Our cause is our life, and the blood of many good men has been spilled in the name of freedom. And one day we *will* rid Colombia of the democratic scourge that threatens us. We're not just fighting for an ideal, but for our very survival.''

"You can be sure that I understand your struggle,

Amado. And you can be equally sure that I understand the repercussions of failure.''

''I hope you understand what's at stake.''

''Do not worry, Amado. After tonight, the face of the entire American border will change forever. And nothing will be able to stop it.''

CHAPTER NINETEEN

Mexicali, Mexico

The Executioner reached his destination by sunset, and soon found his way down a main thoroughfare in the heart of the city.

Mexicali wasn't like the other cities in the Baja such as Ensenada, Tecate or Tijuana. Although Mexicali was officially part of Mexico, the obvious influence of American trade and tourism coursed through its neighborhood streets, as well as its commercial districts.

The area through which Bolan was driving was alive with activity. People walked down the streets, boldly crossing in front of slow-moving cars. A group of college kids coursed past the Executioner's slower-moving sedan, and the driver honked at him, a friendly hello, one American to another. The driver was accompanied by another male, and there were five blond vixens of various shapes and sizes, dressed in bikini tops and jean cutoffs, seated in the back. A couple of the girls actually perched on the edge of the trunk where it met the back seat, holding on to the black cowboy hats they wore and making eyes at Bolan.

The soldier flashed them a half smile and then returned to business. He was driving slowly because he was looking for something in particular, and the stunning beauty of the blondes almost caused him to miss it. Hito's wasn't the kind of place Bolan imagined when he'd first entered Mexicali. It was a hole in the wall, nothing in comparison to the other places along this part of the strip.

Bolan found a parking spot on a side street and had to backtrack three blocks on foot in order to reach the place. He'd changed into more casual attire, which consisted of blue jeans and black khaki shirt hanging outside the jeans to conceal the Beretta he'd secured at the small of his back.

The government guy he'd snatched at the airport indicated this was where "the meetings" took place between Carillo's people and the American contact they had inside the local Border Patrol office. The only problem was that Bolan had no idea who or what he was looking for. He just knew they were scheduled to meet here at 1830 hours—he had about twenty minutes to spare.

Bolan entered the dark, smoky bar and was immediately approached by two guys who looked right at home. They were short, stocky and stank of beer mixed with cigarettes. The Executioner immediately noticed one of them wore a boot knife, and the other had nothing more than a leather vest covering his hairy chest and beer belly. Tattoos adorned the two like craters on a moon, and the one with the boot knife had several teeth missing by a mechanism Bolan didn't even care to guess.

"Are you looking for trouble, my man?" the fat one asked. "Because we don't want no trouble in here."

Bolan hadn't come to brawl with the two bouncers.

At least he was assuming they were bouncers, whether officially serving in that capacity or not. The Executioner really needed information, and he knew that if he challenged their authority he would not only draw attention to himself but it was likely he'd spook whoever was supposed to be meeting.

He whipped out a fifty and said, "No trouble. Just someplace to drink."

The two men looked at the money, and then Toothless smiled, snatched the bill out of Bolan's hand and the two disappeared into the darkness as quickly as they had appeared.

Bolan made his way to a corner booth where he could see every person who came into the place without being easily noticed himself. One couple danced to a Mexican tune, and several locals hung over the bar. Everyone appeared either too tired or too drunk to care much about Bolan one way or another. A waitress showing way more of her goods than necessary, even in a place like that, took his order for a bottled beer and wiggled away. She returned a minute later, accepted the ten he dropped on her tray and then departed to make change.

As she left, a newcomer walked through the door. He was native, dressed nice in comparison to rest of the crowd and acting totally relaxed. Bolan had to wonder for a moment if he was the owner, since neither of the brutes that had stopped Bolan even appeared to challenge this man. But rather than disappear into a back room, the guy sat at a corner table and lit a cigar.

Almost a half hour went by, and the waitress hadn't returned with Bolan's change; neither had she offered him another beer. He was nursing this one for all it was worth, but it was about empty, and Bolan was beginning to wonder if he'd been misled. Before he could reconsider his options, though, another man came through the door and joined the first. This one sat with his back to Bolan, and he couldn't tell if the guy was American or not. Five minutes ticked by and then the man rose, tossed something on the table and turned to leave.

And the Executioner recognized Ramon Sapèdas.

Bolan was out of his chair in moments, crossing the dark expanse and almost in arm's reach when he was intercepted by his two muscle-bound friends from earlier.

"You *are* looking for trouble. *¿Sí, señor?*" Toothless asked.

"Move," Bolan said as a look of horrified recognition crossed Sapèdas's face.

The Border Patrol chief said something in Spanish and the two men made their move. Unfortunately for them, the Executioner was ready. Bolan sidestepped the attempted grab by Toothless and got his partner between them. If the soldier had learned anything in his time, it was that two men trying to attack one in a confined space was awkward, and generally they got in each other's way. Bolan just decided to help that process along a little bit.

Once he had the chubby one between them, Bolan snapped an elbow strike to the guy's throat. His voice box snapped. The guy reached up to his smashed throat and let out a bloody gurgle. Bolan reacted before the guy could do more and smashed his chin with the palm of his hand. The guy bit his lip. Bolan finished with three hammer blows to the solar plexus, and his would-be assailant dropped to greasy wood floor.

The second man now had hold of his senses and obviously realized he wasn't dealing with some amateur brawler. He reached down to his boot and pulled the knife. Bolan watched helplessly as Sapèdas broke for the exit and the guy he'd met headed for the rear of the place, probably bound for some rear door Bolan couldn't see. He knew time was a commodity, and there was no point in trying to fight the guy.

Bolan withdrew the Beretta from beneath his shirt, aimed between the eyes and squeezed the trigger. A half cry escaped the bouncer's lips just before the 9 mm Parabellum round split open his skull like a sledgehammer on a watermelon. The Executioner was moving toward the exit before the corpse hit the ground. He concealed the weapon beneath his shirt before venturing out the front door.

He stopped on the sidewalk and looked both ways several times, but Sapèdas was nowhere in sight. Bolan knew he couldn't have gone far, but he wasn't about to search for him because something more pressing nagged at him. As Sapèdas was leaving the table, he'd tossed something to the other guy. Some hidden force whispered urgency in the Executioner's ear, and he knew that Sapèdas wasn't the real threat. It was the native who'd met with him.

Bolan lurched down the sidewalk, shoving people out of the way and never breaking stride until he reached the end of the block. He immediately spotted his target. The guy was walking casually toward him, acting as if he didn't have a care in the world. Obviously, he overestimated the abilities of the bouncers to stop Bolan. The look of surprise on his face when the soldier stopped him short, locked arms and concealed a gun beneath them made it apparent he realized the error of his assumption.

"Walk straight until I tell you otherwise," Bolan warned.

The man nodded and smiled as the Executioner steered him away from the main street. Clearly, the guy understood the gravity of his situation, and Bolan knew he'd made the threat imminent enough. He also knew that if he'd been dealing with some religious fanatic or suicidal terrorist, he would have had a fight on his hands. However, this guy was calm and collected, which meant he had desire to live and he wasn't out to kill himself for any crazy ideals.

Within minutes, they reached the Executioner's car. The sun had now disappeared, and darkness enveloped the immediate area. Nobody could see them from the main street, and that particular area was visibly devoid of observers. Bolan didn't release his hold on the prisoner, choosing instead to jam the pistol into the man's ribs.

"Start talking and be quick about it," Bolan snapped.

"I not know what you want," the man replied in broken English. "You want money? You take wallet. Take my money, but no kill me *señor*. I have children."

"Cut the act and listen to me," Bolan said. "I know the man you met is a U.S. Border Patrol officer, and I know he gave you something before he escaped. What was it?"

"I not take anything from—"

"Listen carefully," the Executioner growled. "I don't have time to play games. Now you either cough up whatever it was he gave you, or I'm going to kill you here and now. You ready to die for a cutthroat like

Sapèdas? You think he would protect you? He's looking out for his own interests, pal, so why don't you get smart and start looking out for yours.''

The man flinched as Bolan jabbed the gun into his ribs during his little impromptu speech. The Executioner waited another moment and was about to put a hole through the guy's stomach when the man finally broke into a sweat. Quite suddenly, his peasant accent disappeared and he spoke English quite well.

''Okay, okay. Just don't get nervous with that heat, man.''

''What were you and Sapèdas meeting about?'' Bolan asked. ''And what did he give you?''

''I guess it doesn't matter if I blow the whistle now. Whoever you are or whatever your business is with Ramon is none of my affair. But if you're trying to stop what's about to go down, you're too late.''

''What are you talking about?''

There was something almost prophetic in what the guy was saying. Bolan knew somewhere in the back of his mind that Carillo had something horrendous planned, but he hadn't known where or what.

''Tell me what's planned,'' Bolan said with a hard edge in his voice.

''Well, right about now our trucks are arriving at the border checkpoint and will very shortly be in the U.S., and once they get out of Calexico they'll be home free.''

''What are they carrying?''

''Oh, not too much,'' the guy answered. ''Just enough processed smack and Adam to supply every junkie in L.A. for a year or better. And it's going to make every one of us rich.''

''Don't count on it.''

"Oh, I forgot to mention that part about the diversion."

"Stop playing games and tell me," Bolan said, "or you're dead here and now."

"You know the central processing facility for the local roughnecks?"

"In the downtown area. You're talking about the main holding area for arrestees."

"That's right."

"What about it?"

"Well, it's fixing to go sky-high, my man."

Bolan looked at his watch. It was 1851 hours. "What time?"

When the guy didn't answer, Bolan repeated the question.

"At 7:00 p.m. sharp. And you won't never make it."

"Neither will you," the Executioner said as he thumbed the selector to 3-round bursts and squeezed the trigger. A surprised look crossed the man's face just before he collapsed to the pavement. His body twitched a few moments and then went still.

Bolan could feel the bile rise in his throat as he considered the horror of his predicament. He had a choice: let the drugs go through or let potentially dozens of innocent people die.

He didn't have to think twice.

The Executioner jumped into his car and put it in a wild turn. He headed straight for the main thoroughfare, taking the corner on two wheels and nearly flipping the lightweight sedan in the process. Bolan accelerated, pushing his speed and his luck to their respective limits. He risked another glance at his watch—he had six minutes to avert a catastrophe. And the numbers were ticking off in a way Bolan could never remember they had before.

"WHY ARE YOU CALLING me here?" Carillo's voice demanded.

"Because Belasko showed up to our little meeting," Sapèdas said into his cellular phone. "You want to try explaining that to me? You assured me you would take care of this, Panchos."

"Shut up," Carillo said. "You know better than that. How did he find out?"

"How the fuck should I know? All I know is that I made the payment to the guy who planted our little package for tonight's show. Then I turn and Belasko is there in my face, heading right toward me. If it hadn't been for those two drunk bouncers of Ivan's, he probably would have iced me right there."

"Stop being so dramatic," Carillo replied. "The guy's not going to kill you in cold blood in front of the public eye. He operates in secret."

"You tell that to your boys at the Brownsville plant, or maybe Mario Ibanez."

"Don't take that tone with me," Carillo said. "I'm paying you very good money to do what you're told to do, and keep your mouth shut. So show me some respect, or I will make it my life's pursuit to track you down and cut off your family jewels personally. You hearing me, Ramon?"

Sapèdas calmed himself. "I hear you. But now what do we do?"

"We do exactly as planned. There are only a few minutes remaining before show time. You do your part, and make sure you get to the checkpoint on time. And then get your ass on a plane. I want you in El Paso by tomorrow morning. I don't want any foul-ups this time, like those in Brownsville or Vegas.''

"I'll handle it," Sapèdas said glumly. He hung up and muttered, "Asshole."

Ramon Sapèdas was Hispanic, sure, but he didn't buy into all of Carillo's bullshit. The guy thought himself to be some sort of great spokesman for the Spanish people. Yeah, whatever. If the guy wanted to consider himself a revolutionary, Sapèdas wasn't going to argue the point with him. The truth of the matter was that he'd dealt with Carillo's kind on so many occasions, it no longer impressed him. As a matter of fact, he didn't give a shit one way or the other. The guy was nothing special. Just another mindless hothead with a loud mouth, loud clothes and so much cash he didn't have the good sense to know what to do with it.

But that was okay because as long as Carillo kept that cash flowing, Sapèdas would act the stoolie. He sort of liked his role as the poor American trying to survive on a cop's salary, and oh, wasn't it so good of the high-and-mighty Jose "Panchos" Carillo to elevate Sapèdas and free his poor, oppressed Mexican brothers and sisters. What a load of crap!

Here and now was the important thing. Sapèdas lived in the present, lived life to the fullest. He enjoyed his fancy cars; he enjoyed wearing nice clothes—like the silk shirt and two-hundred-dollar slacks he had on now—and he loved to spoil his wife with diamond rings and pearl necklaces. His kids attended the best private schools in El Paso. In a couple more years, his youngest son would be headed for a military academy. And then he and Carmen could retire to Bermuda, and they could fly the kids home in the summer and around the holidays.

Yeah, life would be real good then, and he would no longer have to do Carillo's bidding.

Sapèdas looked at his watch and smiled.

Two minutes!

That was all the time Mack Bolan had when he walked through the front door of the Mexicali police station house and drew the Beretta. He pointed it at the ceiling, fired a warning shot and immediately gained the attention of everybody in the room.

"There's a bomb in the building! Get out now!"

People responded with surprising swiftness, and they actually filed out in an orderly fashion. Granted, they were running their asses off but they were moving out efficiently. The Executioner turned and noticed one of the prisoners hadn't moved. He was trying to escape, but the officers had obviously handcuffed him to an old wall-mounted radiator and he wasn't going anywhere.

The guy threw Bolan a helpless look. He was red-faced and practically gibbering in what could have marginally passed for Spanish. The Executioner didn't really know if the guy was a drunk or convicted child molester, but he didn't entertain the idea of spending time to find out. He might have been guilty of a dozen horrible crimes, but Bolan couldn't judge that here and now. The Executioner ordered the man to lean as far back as possible, aimed eight inches from the cuff chain and squeezed the trigger.

The subsonic 9 mm slug broke the link and the guy was free. The smell of alcohol on his breath was nearly overpowering, and Bolan reeled from it as the guy threw his arms around the Executioner and hugged him. The soldier disentangled himself and gruffly escorted the guy to the nearest exit. He managed to get both of them across the street where the rest of the evacuees stood in time to escape the first blast.

The explosion rocked the ground beneath them, and the thunderous report from its effects rolled down the street. Glass flew out from the windows of the single-story structure, and a second blast followed a moment later. It wasn't so large that it posed a disastrous effect outside, but had the building been occupied there would have been many deaths and many more injuries. Not to mention the number of potential criminals that would have been loosed on Mexicali and areas all along and perhaps on the other side of the border.

Bolan used the commotion to escape the crowd and got around the block to where he'd left his car on the off chance he'd get away alive. The gamble had paid off because he was certain that nobody really thought to stop and get a good description of him in the aftermath. It was probable that most of the law officers who would now go home alive to their families in the morning would certainly feel a measure of gratitude toward him—that could prompt people to forget the details pretty easily. It wouldn't be important why the nameless stranger knew about the bomb.

It was more important that he'd done something about it.

The Executioner now concentrated on the task ahead. The guy from Hito's had mentioned that there were trucks headed through the border checkpoint. Bolan now understood Carillo's plans, and he had to admit that the guy was damn sharp. He had to give credit where it was due. Jose Carillo had planned the perfect diversion.

Sure, it all made perfect sense now. Turn over a few assets and let your conscience be your guide that there were acceptable losses for the greater good. The whole time, while the Kung Lok was trying to squeeze him out and Bolan was trying to shut him down, Carillo was planning the smuggling operation that would secure his position as a man in complete control of all drug trafficking. Once word got around that it was Carillo who had masterminded the diversion in Mexicali and bribed every high-ranking Border Patrol officer from Calexico to Brownsville, he'd be immortalized as monarch of the U.S.-Mexican border.

Bolan knew, probably just like Carillo and Sapèdas and all their allies, that the minute word of an emergency got out the Border Patrol would close down the border station. Those big semis couldn't block the lanes in order to affect security, so they'd push them through in a hurry. After all, hundreds of trucks passed through that point every day. And the explosion didn't take place anywhere near the trucks, so who could possibly think there was any link between the two? So they would move the trucks through quickly and then close up the port. And nobody would go anywhere.

In the meantime, each truck carried a ton or more of drugs into the U.S., free to make deliveries to every major dope runner in the country. Profits would skyrocket, demand would be met and Carillo would become the ultimate in a drug-distribution empire of monumental proportions. And every penny would go back into his pocket so he could find more sick and twisted ways to smuggle his death-dealing junk across the border.

Well, the Executioner wasn't about to let that happen. One way or another, he was going to shut down Carillo's operation, and he had some idea of what to watch for. He knew that Carillo could no longer move the stuff down the highways and up into L.A., so the next-best step was to get it into the hands of somebody who was connected on the other side. Bolan was certain he knew where that trail led.

Based on the intelligence he'd gathered so far, Ramon Sapèdas remained the one constant in an equation growing more complicated by the moment. It was more than likely the Border Patrol chief was either appointed to oversee the safe delivery of the shipments to their destinations, or they were planning to rally the trucks somewhere, and then they could do smaller distributions from there. The latter plan seemed the safest and most reliable, and it was a tactic commonly deployed by drug runners to prevent discovery of drugs at weigh stations or random state police checkpoints.

Bolan was betting that rally point would be El Paso. It left the smallest margin of error, and with attention now focused on the activities in Mexicali, it was the last place anyone would think to look for major quantities of drugs. But one person came to mind—a dark-haired, dark-eyed firebrand who had believed from the beginning that El Paso would become a major point of focus in the whole sordid mess.

And Rajero had been right.

It all made sense now. Of course, Bolan still hadn't figured the meeting of the politicians in West Palm Beach, but he was certain that the presence in-country of Dim Mai and Deng Jikwan were sure signs that the trouble had only begun.

The Executioner was feeling exhausted. He made a mental note that as soon as he was safely across the border, he'd have to catch a few hours' rest before continuing to El Paso. He also needed to touch base with Stony Man and let them know of his suspicions about El Paso.

And whatever Lau Ming Shui and the rest of the Kung Lok had planned, it was bigger than blowing up a couple dozen innocent civilians in order to move tons of drug product across the U.S.-Mexican border. They were hellbent on eradicating the Carillo drug cartel and manipulating the Colombian arms shipments in a tailor-made plan to further their foothold in the United States.

But they were seemingly ignorant of the fact that the Executioner had entered the fray. And he was hell-bent on eradicating the Kung Lok in a game where there could only be one winner. It was a game the Executioner had played time and again.

And he'd gotten damn good at it.

CHAPTER TWENTY

Security would be tight at the border.

People rarely brought weapons into Mexico, and an American headed into Mexicali wasn't considered nearly as suspicious by the Border Patrol as one headed the other way. Especially at this time of night, when work traffic had pretty much died down. Many people traveled between Calexico and Mexicali—Americans living in the Baja while working in the U.S., and vice versa. It was another world, and since Baja California was ostensibly as much U.S. as Mexican territory, things were a bit more lax.

So Mack Bolan was only less than five miles from the Border Patrol checkpoint, considering a plan to get through with his weapons, when the road ahead suddenly erupted in flame. Chunks of concrete rained onto the sedan, pebbling the windshield and denting the hood. Bolan jerked the wheel to his right, avoiding the gaping pothole left by the blast. With the windows down, he caught the familiar smell of plastique and high explosive. Someone had planted a cratering charge in the road.

The Executioner tried to weave his way around another obstacle, only to run into a third. Someone had covered all the bases, and the Executioner was betting he knew who: the Revolutionary Armed Forces of Colombia. This was one of the encounters Bolan would have preferred on his terms, but sometimes a soldier didn't get to call the shots. Still, he'd planned for this eventuality all the same, and he was ready to answer their challenge to battle.

The soldier grabbed two smokers from the bag next to him and lobbed them out the window to provide cover. He then snatched the bag as he popped the trunk and went EVA. Retrieving the M-16 A-2/M-203 from under the spare tire, he headed for the hole his attackers had just blown in the road. He kept low, running in a crouch as the first rounds of autofire burned the air above his head. Bolan reached the crater and jumped into it. It was the only decent cover on the open street, and through the smoke and haze he couldn't see a better opportunity. It would also provide a clear field of fire.

Bolan focused on the priorities, realizing he had to take out the deafening machine gun the enemy was using to blanket the area with .50-caliber shells. The heavy rounds hadn't found their mark, but they were doing a good job of kicking up dust and debris.

The smoke cleared just enough for him to see the muzzle-flash. The gunners were on the second floor of a burned-out building, and Bolan already had the M-203 loaded for action. The Executioner adjusted the special range sight on the grenade launcher, aimed just above the muzzle-flash and squeezed the trigger. The 40 mm HE round arced gracefully through the air, landed dead center and was followed by a tremendous explosion. Bits of mesh wire, concrete and rebar fell to the ground, but there was very little left of the two bodies that had occupied the emplacement.

The machine gun was silent.

Bolan knew as the air began to clear the enemy would either use snipers to pick him off or simply flood his position with autofire. He climbed from the crater and headed for the area he'd just destroyed. There was still enough of the first floor of the building remaining to provide adequate cover. Bolan needed time to regroup, reload and get an estimate on his odds.

The autofire he'd been expecting came immediately, eating a hot trail behind him as he sprinted to shelter. He dived through an open window, shredding his shirt-front on some glass shards still lodged in the frame. The fragments missed his flesh by centimeters. As he landed on the floor inside, Bolan could feel the stitches tear again. He cursed as he rolled out of the fall and took up a position in the dark interior.

He reached into his bag, loaded another grenade, then converted it to a satchel and tied it around his waist. His blacksuit was inside, along with one remaining smoker and plenty of magazines. He'd left most of the 40 mm grenades stashed at a hotel room in Calexico, but he still had enough to mount a decent defense.

Bolan moved to the edge of the window frame and risked a glance onto the street. He marked three soldiers, barely visible in the light of a full moon, on the roof of a hotel directly across from his position. Another pair was positioned at the corner of a deserted bar. Sirens were the only sounds the Executioner could hear, and it didn't sound as if they were headed in his direction. The street was otherwise devoid of people or activity.

From what was visible in the darkness, it looked as

if this particular block was composed of a mixture of local businesses and a few apartment buildings. Bolan surmised this part of town had been condemned long ago, abandoned as the result of destitution or social depredation. Some of the structures were unkempt or neglected, while others were broken down altogether. If it had been occupied by human civilization, those occupants were long gone. And with the police and emergency services focused on the bombed processing center, it was the perfect place for an ambush.

In any case, the Executioner knew he'd be run to ground unless he started taking the offensive. He changed positions, edging carefully to a neighboring window, and carefully sighted on the area of the roof where he'd spotted the trio of FARC troops. He triggered the M-203 and was satisfied a moment later by a thunderous blast. An orange ball of flame took out the parapet of the building, and Bolan spotted the shadow of a body as it fell from the hole.

He retreated to the rear of the building and found a doorway leading onto a gravel path overgrown with weeds. He kept his back to the adobe wall as he moved along the building perimeter. He reached the corner a minute later and peered around it, spotting the other pair of FARC soldiers. They had emerged from cover and were headed in his direction, but they obviously didn't see him. He also noted that two more took their place.

Bolan guessed that there were additional troops, and they probably had the idea he was trapped, which wasn't far from the truth. The Executioner knew that a frontal assault wouldn't be possible, so a flanking maneuver was his best option. He turned and moved back along the edge of the building, passing the doorway and continuing until he reached the other corner. The street appeared to be clear. He made a quick study of his surroundings. A large statue of a Mexican bandit on a horse stood next to the building on this side.

Bolan advanced on it, sprinting the length of the building and coming to a crouch behind its base. He spotted four pairs of soldiers moving on his last known position, and they were armed to the teeth. They wore jungle-camouflage fatigues and military equipment suspenders. Grenades dangled from their harnesses, and they were toting AK-74s. The Executioner grimaced. He'd been up against greater odds, but reminded himself that these were combat-hardened FARC soldiers and not just terrorists.

Bolan raised the M-16 A-2/M-203, pressed the stock to his cheek and sighted on the closest pair. He squeezed the trigger repeatedly, his weapon set to 3-round bursts. Both enemy soldiers fell, screaming and twisting as he hammered them with the 5.56 mm ball ammunition.

The soldier fired on a second pair. One man's head nearly exploded from his body. The second's body did a spasmodic dance in the wake of the rounds as they slammed into him. Bolan broke cover and beelined across the street. The other soldiers were moving for cover, and he triggered another salvo to keep their heads down until he could make his goal. He reached a low adobe porch wall of a single-story house and vaulted over it.

AK-74 fire resounded a moment later, a hail of 5.45 mm slugs peppering the wall. The ricochets couldn't be heard over the cacophony of gunfire, and Bolan's ears rang as the remaining quartet of FARC soldiers flooded his position with steel-jacketed bullets.

There was a lull, and Bolan took a moment to load another 40 mm HE shell. He locked the breech back on the M-203 and then yanked the pin from his last smoker and tossed the grenade over the wall. He counted off ten seconds as the firestorm started again, then got to the door of the house without compromising his cover. The smoke might have disguised his movements, but it wasn't bulletproof.

Bolan reached up and whispered a word of thanks to whatever deity might have been listening. The door opened freely, albeit on rusted hinges, and the soldier crawled through the opening. The interior of the house was as black as night. He knew he had about a minute to find an exit before the FARC troops advanced on his position. He kept low, moving slowly as his eyes adjusted to the gloom. He quickly located a half-open door and eased through it noiselessly.

The rear of the house opened onto a dusty backyard overgrown with bushes and sagebrush. Bolan moved to the corner perimeter and spied a wooden ladder mounted against the neighboring building. The ladder had probably served as a makeshift fire escape. He crossed the alleyway from the yard and tested the ladder with his weight. Satisfied it would support him, the soldier slung his M-16 A-2/M-203 and quickly scaled the rickety structure. He reached the top of the building and charged to the front of the roof.

He drew near the gaping hole created earlier by the 40 mm grenade he'd used to take out the enemy troops, and it was still smoking from the heat of the HE shell. Bolan knelt and peered over the parapet. The four FARC troops, now joined by an additional dozen, leapfrogged toward the porch he'd been using as cover. The Executioner aimed his M-203 and waited. When about a half-dozen reached the outside of the porch wall, he triggered a shell into their midst. The entire porch erupted with the explosion and the overhang collapsed. The soldiers were decimated by the blast. Dust and smoke rose in the aftermath of the fireball produced by the PETN-filled grenade.

The remaining troops scattered for cover, and Bolan realized he now had the advantage he needed. He adjusted his selector switch to full-auto and began to rain 5.56 mm bursts on them. The troops were unable to find cover, and one after another began to fall under the Executioner's assault. One trooper back-flipped with the impact of the ball ammo, and another lost his leg at the knee joint. Bolan conserved his firepower by switching to single shot, aiming carefully with the sniper precision that had earned him his name and reputation. Only two managed to find cover and escape Bolan's fire.

The Executioner broke position and headed for the rear of the building. He looked over the edge and spotted a shed attached to it about five feet below. Bolan knew the jump might be risky in the dark, particularly since he had no idea if the roof would hold him, but now wasn't the time to be choosy. He leaped on faith and was rewarded with a solid thump. Another leap and he was on the ground.

Bolan moved along the back of the hotel until he reached an adjoining building, then crouched in the darkness and waited. The place seemed like a ghost town now, and he didn't hear any further activity. The road ahead was blocked, but the Executioner was counting on eventual escape. He knew that his only options at this stage would be making the border on foot. It was only a couple of klicks to the border, give or take, and he knew of some areas where he could get through.

But then he would have to get into Calexico, find transportation and then try to locate the trucks that were probably crossing through the border patrol checkpoint at that very moment. Still, he felt strange about just leaving the FARC troops to wreak havoc on unwary civilians, or leaving this situation where it was at. And he especially didn't want to risk having them pick up his trail and trip him up later when he had his hands full with the triad or Carillo's people.

Unfortunately, he'd eliminated somewhere near forty of the Colombian guerrillas, and while he had no viable intelligence on the actual numbers, he knew that his battle plan called for a tactical retreat. He was probably still outnumbered and outgunned, and he saw no point in aggravating the situation when a more serious one took place on the border right at that moment. There would be other opportunities to deal with the FARC— better opportunities. For now, he needed to get to the border and stop the drug shipments before they got through.

Stony Man Farm, Virginia

"WE'VE GOT TROUBLE with a capital *T*," Price told Brognola and Kurtzman. She dropped her handheld electronic organizer on the War Room table, and as she shrugged out of her pantsuit jacket and draped it over the back of a chair she added, "And it's related to Uncle Sam."

"What's going on?" Brognola asked, shoving aside

the intelligence briefs he and Kurtzman had been assessing.

Price sat and crossed her legs. She took a deep breath to collect her thoughts and began, "About six months ago, a meeting was held between several known members of the Scarlet Dragons and an undercover DEA agent in Miami. The deal was for guns, which the Dragons agreed to supply."

"In exchange for what?" Kurtzman asked. "Cash?"

Price frowned and shook her head. "No, drugs. They wanted a piece of Carillo's drug action in Miami. The problem is, Carillo has no drug connections there, at least none worth speaking of. So they still went ahead and agreed to supply the guns, but they asked for some new incentive."

"Let me guess," Brognola interjected. "This is where these people within the government come into it."

"Yes, unfortunately." Price nodded. "Apparently, the Dragon the DEA agent dealt with knew all along he worked for the DEA. When the offer came about like it did, the DEA was naturally suspicious. But they decided to go ahead and recruited some agents from the BATF to help them. They got blown. Both agents from the BATF, and the DEA officer who had initially made contact, were killed in a bombing of the building where the meet was supposed to happen."

"Any suspects?"

"Well, my contacts at the NSA and FBI both have their suspicions. Naturally, the DEA and BATF aren't working together on it. Each is conducting a separate investigation in a sort of hostile peace, and there's more concern at this stage about assigning blame than actually finding out the real source behind it. Nobody wants to admit that maybe they blew it."

Kurtzman shook his head with disgust and brooded. "That's teamwork for you, the way these federal agencies look out for one another. My God, Hal, you'd have thought they learned something by now, considering the change in American policy on terrorism and federal crimes in the past few years."

"I understand the frustration, but that's just the way it is," Brognola replied sadly. "Sometimes it seems there's no tragedy large enough to overcome the bureaucracy and politics that seem to override good common sense."

"That aside," Price reminded them gently, "we still have this other problem."

"Sorry," Kurtzman muttered.

"Go ahead, Barb, we're all ears," Brognola added.

"What anybody fails to see about this whole thing is the other side of the coin." Price pulled a black-and-white still from a folder she'd brought and placed it in front of Brognola. "That picture was taken several months ago by INS agents. The man in the picture is Ing Kaochu, who is a known illegal Chinese alien and overall head of the Scarlet Dragon gangs all through the country. There are some splinter factions and wanna-be outfits, but for the most part the group has an extensive network, as we already know, that answers to this man."

"He works for Shui, right?" Brognola ventured.

"Exactly right. Very good, Hal."

"I get one right every now and then."

Brognola jerked his head in Kurtzman's direction and said, "We can't all have that steel-trap mind like the Bear, here."

"So what does any of this have to do with the meeting in West Palm Beach?" Kurtzman asked.

"It has everything to do with it," Price said. "Kaochu's last known location was in Miami, but he hasn't been seen operating in the area for at least a month. There are some reports he was spotted in Toronto a couple of weeks ago, but that's unconfirmed. Where it gets interesting is that every single one of these agencies has a major stake in capturing Jose Carillo, and the same kind of stake in capturing the Kung Lok triad leaders."

"Yet when they hold an open meeting in our own backyard," Brognola finished for her, "nobody moves a muscle."

"Right. And I think that's because we have a traitor within the government who's pulling the strings on both ends."

"You know something, Hal," Kurtzman said, rolling over to his computer, "I think she's on to something. I remember a recent set of financial reports on known Kung Lok bank accounts. Dim Mai, Yi-chang Shen, Lau Shui and some Hong Kong politicians have all made recent withdrawals and the cash just disappeared. We don't have any record of payments being made or checks being cut. No transfers to other accounts—just simple withdrawals and that's it. Money's gone and nobody sees it again."

"You think they're paying somebody inside the government to help them out?" Brognola asked Price.

"That's exactly what I think. And what is really amazing is that nobody seems to know who this mysterious person might be or what affiliations he or she might have within the U.S. government."

"Well, let's try first ruling out who we know couldn't possibly be involved."

"Nobody high profile," Kurtzman said immediately.

Brognola nodded. "Agreed. Too risky for both sides."

"That rules out cabinet officers, representatives, senators, the President and heads of federal intelligence agencies."

"It's interesting that this all occurred within federal agencies at a local level, though," Kurtzman said blankly.

"I'm not sure I follow, Bear," Brognola said. "What are you getting at?"

Kurtzman wheeled around to face them. "Well, it just seems that a blatant and open move by agents within the Miami area would be too heavily scrutinized. Somebody would figure something was up, and they'd catch their proverbial rat. However, that doesn't mean we couldn't be dealing with someone who works with all of these agencies."

"I see what you're saying," Price said matter-of-factly.

She turned to Brognola and explained, "In every instance since Striker first hit the drug shipment in Brownsville and stumbled on to the Kung Lok's plan, there have not been less than two federal agencies involved with closely related cases at one point or another. The DEA and BATF at Brownsville hit. The FBI and Border Patrol in El Paso. The FBI and DEA in Las Vegas. FBI and NSA in West Palm Beach, and DEA and CIA in Ciudad-Juárez."

"Somebody has to have access to all of this information," Brognola theorized, nodding now that he was beginning to understand. "There must be some way to link all of these agencies back to a single person or agency."

"And we've already ruled out a member of congress or the presidential cabinet."

"What about judicial branch?" Kurtzman offered.

Brognola shook his head. "Doubtful. Justices and court officials don't have much of a clue about what happens outside the world of the courtroom. And there is also no viable motive I can think of when considering any of those currently on the bench."

"What if we factor out geographical locations not in border areas, Aaron?" Price asked.

Kurtzman turned to his computer and began typing faster than they could keep up with the words and search volumes pressing across the screen. He finished making his entries and then pushed a button. The built-in projection system suddenly lit up a screen with a map of the United States. Even as it focused and sharpened into view, red circles peppering every state were slowly fading. Eventually, the dissipation stopped, leaving only a few along the Canadian border, a few more along the Eastern and Western Seaboards, and the highest concentration in Florida and the Southwest.

"Okay, let's eliminate any along either Pacific or Atlantic shores, since it's highly unlikely an official involved in this would be able to effectively run the operations in this particular arena from a coastal station."

Kurtzman complied, and that left just those in Miami and the Southwest.

"Now let's filter out all those that are not multijurisdictional," Price suggested.

The computer expert put in the information, and a

considerable more disappeared, the majority in the Southwest. It didn't look as formidable as it had a few minutes earlier, and it seemed the entire mood in the room began to brighten. Price began to feel there was hope—it really seemed that they were onto something. But there was still a lot of work ahead.

Kurtzman punched up a printer on Stony Man's secured network and sent the information to begin compiling the source documents he knew would be necessary to launch their investigation. He told them, "No question about it, we've got our work cut out for us."

"Maybe," Brognola replied. "And maybe we'll get a feel for many more of them right away and be able to chop that list further until we have a few solid leads."

"It's still going to be a considerable amount of work, Hal," Kurtzman said. "I'm not trying to sound pessimistic. I'm just trying to be realistic. This is going to take a while."

"Especially since you probably don't want to involve anyone else in it at this stage of the game," Price added.

"That's because if we bring in an armload of investigators and start combing through files, records, e-mail and telephone logs, we're more than likely going to spook our spook."

"You mean our traitor," Kurtzman replied tightly.

"Right."

Brognola stood and put his hands in his trouser pockets. He started pacing the room, something that surprised both Price and Kurtzman, since they had never really known this as a manifestation of something bothering Brognola. The Stony Man chief had always been a rock—not that every single member of that team wasn't strong. Nonetheless, it was completely uncharacteristic for Brognola to be so open about it. He'd always been calm and collected, as tough as nails and uncompromising and vigilant.

"What's eating at you, Hal?" Price asked.

Brognola stopped, turned, stared at her and pointedly replied, "I'm upset that the President is forcing us to sit here on our hands while Striker is out risking everything."

"Hey, listen, Hal," Kurtzman said quietly. "The big guy knew what he was getting into from the beginning. We've never bemoaned the fact that on some occasions the powers that be tie our hands."

"Bear's right, Hal. We actually have a considerable amount of latitude," Price said.

"I know that," Brognola replied with a dismissive wave. "I'm not talking about that. I'm talking about the fact that sometimes, when it really counts, we can't just go all out and show our hand in a way these bastards won't soon forget."

"I hear where you're coming from, Chief," Kurtzman said, "but I think you're forgetting something."

"And that is?"

"If Striker's onto them, they won't soon forget it anyway."

Amen, Brognola thought. But he only nodded.

CHAPTER TWENTY-ONE

Calexico, California

Conrado Diaz knew that he had arrived too late to stop Belasko from ruining the boss's plans. He'd first missed his opportunity in Las Vegas, then Los Angeles, and now he was hearing that someone had evacuated the processing facility in Mexicali just in time.

Diaz was betting it was Belasko.

But it didn't matter because as fate would have it, he realized he could just hang out near Sapèdas and wait for the guy to show himself. And Diaz knew he would eventually show himself, because the dude was a pain in the ass and never gave up. In some respects, Diaz had to admire him. Lesser men would have thrown up their hands in defeat by now, but this guy just kept returning like the common cold virus.

Diaz also realized he was going to have to extend special caution. He'd investigated Belasko's previous movements—gathered intelligence on his methods and resources. The guy got around and he was dangerous. Diaz hadn't survived this long because he considered himself better than everyone else. He'd survived because he considered himself inferior to everyone else, and by thoroughly studying his enemy and taking necessary precautions, Diaz had produced a one hundred percent success rate and lived to tell the tale.

Diaz knew that in some respects he was considered a ruthless killer by his peers. Perhaps that was true in some cases, because Diaz believed if he was going to kill a man he had to have some personal stake in it. Wasting a bunch of kids with a machine gun or charging into a school with a bomb strapped to your ass was neither an honorable nor a smart way to die. It was stupid, and he would leave that kind of dramatic showiness to the crazies and fanatics of the world.

No, Conrado Diaz just liked to be methodical. He liked to take his own sweet time and study his enemy, so when it came to do the actual deed he'd left no margin for error. That was how he chose to do things and that was how he stayed alive. So he wasn't at all worried or feeling hurried when he found Ramon Sapèdas looking over the trucks that had rallied at a truck stop on the edge of Calexico.

Diaz climbed from his rented sports car and crushed a cigarette beneath his heel. He strolled over to Sapèdas and shook hands with him. Diaz tried to act amicable toward the guy, but the truth was he really didn't like the Border Patrol chief at all. He'd argued with Carillo more than once about keeping an idiot like Sapèdas around. He was just a waste of good cash in Diaz's opinion.

"So what do you know, Con?" Sapèdas asked him.

And that was another damn thing he didn't like, the fact that Sapèdas had taken the liberty of giving him a nickname as if they were old friends or something. He'd even told the guy on a couple of occasions to either call him Conrado or Diaz, but not Con. So in addition to being stupid, Sapèdas was also ignorant and had a hearing problem.

"Are all the drugs accounted for?" Diaz asked, ignoring Sapèdas's attempt to be friendly.

"Yeah, yeah, the shit's all here. Well, except for one truck that I'm still waiting on."

Alarm bells immediately went off in Diaz's head. He couldn't believe it. Carillo had trusted the guy to do something as simple as get the trucks across, and he couldn't even manage to get them all in one place. It had been at least three hours since the bomb went off in Mexicali, and now he decided to unload this little bit of news on Diaz. Carillo's right-hand man wasn't happy at all about that.

"When were you planning to tell me about that?" Diaz asked, trying to keep the panic from his voice.

"I didn't figure it was any big deal. I talked to my guy at the border station just a few minutes ago, and he said the truck cleared easily. It'll be here. The dumb shit driver you hired probably got lost. I'm sure he'll get here quickly enough, although I don't know how we can trust the entire load is intact."

"What do you mean?"

"Well, all you need is one of our drivers here to figure out he could make some considerable cash on his own, and next thing you know you've got a whole crap load of product missing."

"I don't think you're aware that I personally selected and vouched for each of these men," Diaz replied coolly. "They are loyal to me and Mr. Carillo, so it is neither your worry nor concern."

Sapèdas tapped Diaz's chest with the clipboard he

was holding and said, "It's my concern when I'm the one who has to unload this stuff. It's my ass if it doesn't get where it's supposed to go."

"Yes, it is. And you've been well compensated for your efforts. Now it's time to start earning the money Mr. Carillo has paid you."

There was a long and uncomfortable silence between the two men as they stood there in the shadows of the parking lot and stared daggers at each other. Diaz wasn't the least bit concerned, because he knew he could easily take the older man, and Sapèdas knew it, as well. Diaz was younger, faster and not softened by years of family life, expensive dinners and holidays spent lying around the house. Diaz doubted that Sapèdas even mowed his own lawn anymore.

The Border Patrol chief suddenly broke into a grin. "Listen to us, fighting with each other. We should be working together. We're on the same team, remember? Let's not quibble over the stupid shit. I'll make sure the trucks get to El Paso so your team can get them out. Okay?"

Diaz nodded and then went to personally inspect the trucks. He wanted to make sure the trip to El Paso came off without a hitch. Each rig was marked differently, actually bearing false markings of several major commercial companies. Small enough that they wouldn't draw too much attention but obvious enough that they would be a normal sight on the highways, day or night.

The log books were doctored but in good order. Arrangements had been made to switch drivers every five hours, and the upcoming drivers would have their own log book to mark their departure time. They were also instructed to make sure that plenty of witnesses saw them so any arrival or departure time could be verified easily enough in the event of encounters with the police.

The idea was to get the drugs to El Paso without incident. Any contact with law enforcement was to be avoided at all cost, but if detained the drivers were not to resist. If the drugs were discovered, they had instructions to cooperate to the fullest and give the cover stories supplied by Carillo's men. Ultimately, however, if trouble got out of hand, they were to respond with deadly force as necessary and escape.

And every one of the soldiers, both those waiting at the truck stop assigned to protect the shipments, and the driving teams, had orders to shoot Belasko on sight. There was no way in hell they were going to let him screw up their plans. Diaz was hoping that he'd have an opportunity to kill Belasko himself, but his ultimate job was to protect the shipment. The second priority was to find Belasko and kill him.

The only thing that made those tasks less difficult was that wherever the drugs were headed, Belasko was sure to follow. And Diaz was pretty sure the guy wouldn't make a move until he knew there was no risk to civilians. That was something Diaz had noticed almost immediately about Belasko—he actually cared about innocent bystanders. He'd proved that point when making the choice to evacuate the processing center in Mexicali over stopping the drugs from crossing the border.

After Carillo's chief enforcer had finished inspecting the trucks, he returned to Sapèdas and said, "Everything looks good except for the missing truck."

"Fine. I'll make sure we get out of Calexico and then head for the airport in San Diego. Panchos wanted me to make sure I was in El Paso by tomorrow morning so I can start rallying our mules.''

Diaz didn't trust Sapèdas but he nodded. He would put aside his differences for the sake of his boss, but when this was over he was going to ask permission to kill the little weasel.

And he doubted there would be any trouble doing that job personally.

THE EXECUTIONER SAT parked in the lot of a hotel directly across the street from where Carillo's people had rallied their semitrucks filled with drugs. All but the one the Executioner had managed to acquire just after it pulled away from the Border Patrol station. The soldier had managed to escape Mexicali and slip across the rugged terrain undetected. Probably because he'd done it so close to the station. It had then been just a matter of climbing into the sleeper part of the cab until the truck cleared customs, and then he took the driver by surprise.

Bolan could still hardly believe that they had allowed these trucks to go by so easily, but he could understand the reasoning. Apathy ran high in organizations like the U.S. Border Patrol, unfortunately. Even with heightened awareness about national security and the susceptibility of the American public to terrorist attacks, Bolan realized the reality of the situation. American border agents were some of the best in the world, but they were overworked, underpaid and sorely unappreciated. It was the kind of job that could leave the right type of person with a sense of honor, and the wrong type with either putrid prejudices or a very slanted view of professional objectivity.

He studied the situation through binoculars, watching

the movements and estimating troop strength. There was a total of six trucks, each carrying a load of one type of merchandise or another. Most of the tractor-trailers were marked with licenses from various states, which Bolan knew were probably forged, and the trailers themselves had separate markings. The entire operation looked legitimate, and Carillo had obviously made a painstaking effort to negate any possible relationship between the trucks.

Even if one or two were intercepted, that would still mean high profits and a considerable amount of drugs. But that was *if* the guy from the bar had told Bolan the truth. The Executioner had no reason to believe otherwise, and no evidence to contradict anything the guy had said. Bolan had executed him because of his involvement in attempting to kill dozens of innocents. The guy had been paid to plant that bomb; of that Bolan was sure.

The soldier considered making his move, but he was concerned about the size of his targets and the threat to bystanders. An attack in a truck stop as busy as that one had too much potential for accidental death of the unwary patrons. He spotted a couple of minivans crammed with a family, and one sedan carrying a young man and a very pregnant woman.

A second option might be to take them individually once they got on the road, but again there was the risk of high-speed collisions or accidents. There was also the off chance of bringing the law down on him, and Bolan couldn't imagine any reason worth that kind of risk. Especially when he considered his near run-ins with the cops so far on this mission.

So that left only one option: he'd have to get inside

and take them down once an opportunity presented itself. He couldn't wait until they had reached their destination. The risk they might split up was still too high. The stuff was already processed and packaged for distribution, and that meant they could take off on divergent courses. The Executioner was good, but even he couldn't be everywhere at once.

Nonetheless, something in his gut told him Carillo was much smarter than that. The Mexican drug lord wouldn't risk breaking apart his team quite so soon, especially with the Kung Lok triad looking to cut into his profits. Carillo knew, as Bolan did, that there was safety in numbers and he hadn't generated such an elaborate plan just to watch it go down the tubes because he was impatient.

No, it made sense to set up a staging area where they could break the deliveries into smaller, more manageable sizes. That would cut down on losses if the triad decided to hit the shipments, and it would certainly decrease the attention. After all, it was only a matter of time before word got out of the operation, and then the police would be looking for the semis with a fury.

But Bolan knew that by then it would be too late. So it again came back to move now or lose a possible opportunity to take them. The following day wouldn't be good enough—it had to be now and the Executioner suddenly formulated a plan that just might work.

He started the engine of the truck and turned so that he entered the road from the direction the truck would have come off the highway. He put it in second and began to give it more gas and then less gas. He was doing little short of giving himself whiplash, but that was the least of his problems. The important thing here was to make a lasting impression. And he was going to do that, without any doubt.

DIAZ AND SAPÈDAS TURNED as they heard the whining, roaring and banging of a semitruck. They saw it was their rig, and it appeared the driver was either asleep or drunk. The semi chugged inconsistently across the overpass, its engine hissing and coughing.

"What the hell is he doing?" Diaz asked aloud.

"You see?" Sapèdas said, totally ignoring Diaz's question. "I told you he would show up."

"Well, it took him long enough." Diaz squinted, trying to see what was causing all of the problems.

From that point, it looked as if the truck were having serious mechanical problems. The cab was visibly jolting as if the engine couldn't get enough gas. All of the trucks were diesels, topped off before their departure for the border, so it couldn't be low fuel. Diaz had spent much of his earlier life as a mechanic, so he knew it was too hot for the fuel to have gelled. Contamination was unlikely, since all the rest of the trucks had made it without a problem.

Well, if necessary they could probably off-load the drugs onto another truck or split the shipments. Once they had the stuff, they didn't care about all the furniture and other stuff on board. They could leave the semi parked right in the lot, and nobody would probably notice the truck parked there day after day for at least a week or better. One of the reasons they had chosen this particular truck stop was that it was one of the busiest. That allowed them to be inconspicuous parked next to eighty other semitrucks at any one given time. By the time anyone noticed the truck was abandoned, the intended targets would be tying up their arms, legs and other body parts and injecting Carillo gold into their veins.

The truck was within a hundred yards when it suddenly stopped chugging and jerking and abruptly the engine roared into full power. The truck lurched forward and began to gain speed, heading directly toward Diaz, Sapèdas and the other semitrucks. The enforcer jumped away from the truck and began screaming for his drivers and the FARC escorts to get clear.

They reached into the truck cabs and grabbed for weapons. Assault rifles, pistols, whatever they could lay their hands on as the truck plowed a murderous path directly for them. Diaz watched as a dark-haired man—dressed head to toe in black—leaped from the truck at the last minute. The semi plowed into the rear of one of their trucks, and the whole trailer shifted.

The force of the impact slammed the truck into another one, effectively neutralizing the two vehicles initially involved in the impact and possibly making the third unworthy of the road. Diaz could feel the fury as he watched all of Jose's plans go down the tubes. He was the second in command of the Carillo drug empire, next to the Carillo-Nievas alliance, and now he was watching it all go to hell.

Diaz turned from the destruction and watched the driver moving for a cover position. The guy was big, toting an assault rifle with a grenade launcher, and wearing combat rigging that bristled with all kinds of weapons of war. Based on the description he had, and something else Diaz couldn't identify, the drug enforcer was certain he was looking at none other than Belasko.

Bystanders were doing everything they could to evacuate the area quickly as the FARC escorts and Diaz's drivers took up positions to defend themselves. Diaz realized he was going to quickly be enveloped in the firefight if he didn't find some cover of his own. He yanked his pistol from beneath his jacket and looked to find some sort of protection. He'd barely reached the dual tires of one of the trailers when the first shots rang through the night.

The bullets missed their intended target, and Belasko returned fire immediately. He started with a heavy hitter, popping from cover long enough to launch a grenade. Diaz's eyes followed the graceful curves of the explosive as it headed directly for one of the trucks. The grenade hit with a metallic clank and blew a moment later. The enforcer's ears rang immediately with the tremendous blast, and he turned his head to avoid completely losing his night vision. Not that it wasn't going to be much brighter and much hotter.

Several of the FARC soldiers tried to advance on Belasko, figuring he was probably reloading a grenade. The guy did the exact opposite of what Diaz would have expected himself, and he broke cover and took the FARC troops head-on. Two died immediately, spinning and dancing under a hail of autofire.

Diaz watched with a mixture of fascination and horror as Belasko took down the other pair in similar fashion. One took a blast of high-velocity rounds square in the chest. The enforcer couldn't understand what sense there was in all of it. These guys were supposedly trained soldiers, but they didn't wear any body armor or helmets. The FARC soldier's partner suffered a worse fate, the rounds drilling holes through his body from crotch to sternum.

Diaz jumped from the tire for a moment, lined the sights of his pistol on Belasko and steadied his breath. The lashing of superheated gases and explosive force threw off his shot and slammed him to the ground. Belasko had obviously launched another grenade, this one in the enforcer's direction—or at least a lot closer than the first.

Diaz suddenly realized they had made a fatal error. They were trying to use the semitrucks for cover. What they needed to do was move away from them. Otherwise Belasko could destroy both his men and the trucks in a linear assault.

He began to scream at a soldier taking the same cover nearby to pass the word that they needed to move away from the trucks, leaving only the drivers behind.

"We've got to lure this guy out!" Diaz hollered in Spanish over the din of autofire.

"*Sí, señor,*" the soldier replied. The man turned to comply and Diaz decided to break for open ground. There was a large field behind the semi lot, and he weaved his way through the trucks as the sounds of battle started to fade behind him. He hoped his message got through. If it didn't, he would just have to hope that everyone was either dead or had disappeared before police arrived.

Another explosion resounded as another semitruck took the brunt of the guy's fury. This Belasko was hard. He was obviously well trained and, moreover, he was damn experienced. In all his work as an enforcer, Diaz had never seen anyone quite that good. The guy didn't fight like a normal enemy. He didn't cower and hide and pop off an occasional shot if he got the opportunity. He was able to kill from up close using grenades as effectively as he'd sniped two of Diaz's best friends when they were making the delivery in Brownsville.

The truth was that Belasko killed just like Diaz did. He did it quickly, professionally and without remorse. Belasko was obviously not afraid to fight up close, no matter what the cost. The rumors that Diaz had thought were just that, had turned out to be true. They weren't bad dreams or figments of superstitious imagination—this guy was just what Diaz had been told he was. He was dangerous and he was as formidable an opponent as the Mexican enforcer had ever known.

Diaz didn't want to run like a coward, and he wasn't a coward. But he realized that there was a time and place, and this wasn't it. He was going to have to pick his battle with Belasko on his own terms. He couldn't afford to get Jose's whole shipment blown to hell. He needed to find a way to protect the product at all costs. There was only one way to do that, as he saw it, and that was to retreat from the maelstrom going on behind him.

Diaz managed to get around the semitrucks and back to his car, which was parked out of Belasko's view. He climbed behind the wheel and was about to pull out when someone opened the door. Sapèdas jumped into the seat and began to scream at Diaz to do some distance from the hellgrounds.

Diaz wanted to shoot the coward right in the face, but he knew that wouldn't go over well with Jose, and he didn't have time to argue with the guy. Sapèdas wanting to split and fight the battle another day just meant he was probably a little brighter than Diaz had given him credit for. But he still didn't trust the man, and he knew Sapèdas was probably running not because it was the tactical thing to do, but because he was just a cowardly bastard.

"Was that Belasko?" Diaz asked.

"Yeah…" Sapèdas replied breathlessly. "Fuck yeah, that was him. That bastard is something else. He's one scary son of a bitch. You hear what I'm saying, Con?"

"Yeah," Diaz told him, "I hear what you're saying. And before this night is over, I'm going to make sure he's one dead son of a bitch. I swear it."

CHAPTER TWENTY-TWO

El Paso, Texas

The noonday sun beat mercilessly upon every unprotected surface of El Paso, and rendered unforgivable heat.

Settlers through the 1800s had said that if the Old West was God's country, then Texas was His desert. While not as unforgiving as its Sonora neighbor, Texas was not just a dry, arid climate as its residents might have tried to convince outsiders. This part of the state had a miserable heat during the summer—the humidity fed by Gulf currents—and there was nothing about it that Lisa Rajero could admit she liked. Having come from Maine, she didn't like this weather and never had. Although this thought had never occurred to her when joining the Drug Enforcement Administration.

Not to mention that she was exhausted from her drive straight through the night. When she got into town, she checked into a hotel about a mile from the Border Patrol office. It wasn't where she planned to start—she actually wanted to get the guy where he lived. She wanted to talk to someone who knew Sapèdas better than anyone.

It was time to have a woman-to-woman talk with Sapèdas's wife.

Rajero quickly checked the dossier file and wrote down the street address, then climbed in her rental and started across town. As she drove, the areas got to be nicer and nicer, and pretty soon she was cruising down the shaded lanes embedded between million-dollar homes situated on half-million-dollar landscapes. The place was a veritable paradise in the desert. The people who lived in this area didn't know what dust was. Rajero seriously began to wonder if she'd made a mistake, and then the address she was looking for suddenly hove into view at the top of a small incline. She turned into the drive and was stopped short by a gate. Rajero pressed a button on the small speaker attached to the pole of an adobe-style archway.

"Yes?" a clear female voice came through the speaker.

"Yes, uh, hi," Rajero said a little nervously. She shook her head, then put on her official voice and tried again. "I'm looking for Ramon Sapèdas?"

"I'm sorry, he's not here. He's out of town. You'll have to call again."

"Um, is this Mrs. Sapèdas?" There was a long pause. "Hello?"

"Yes?"

"Mrs. Sapèdas, my name is Lisa Rajero and I'm with the DEA. Listen, I really need to talk to you about your husband. It's important. Please."

There was another long silence, and Rajero wondered if she was going to get anywhere. Abruptly, a buzzer sounded and the gate swung aside. Rajero drove slowly up the driveway. It took her nearly two minutes to reach the house. A servant helped Rajero from her car and escorted her through the front entrance. The foyer was huge, lined with marble trim and some sort of glazed stone floor. The servant asked her to wait and then disappeared down a hallway.

Rajero risked a glance into an adjacent room. It looked like a living room or oversize sitting area. Hell, oversize was an understatement—the room alone was almost as big as her whole apartment. Steps led to a second floor near the entrance, and Rajero guessed a set of closed oak doors off the foyer probably led to either a study or formal dining room. Another minute passed, and somewhere a grandfather clock—or some type of clock—chimed once. Rajero looked at her watch and realized it was past lunchtime.

The servant finally returned and showed Rajero through the living room, a formal breakfast kitchen and onto a sun porch. The back lawn was scattered with large trees that swayed and cooled the entire green landscape with shade. One entire corner of the yard was occupied by an apple orchard, and the red of the fruit was visible from where Rajero was seated.

A moment passed before a dark-haired woman, slender and good-looking, arrived and seated herself across from Rajero. She was actually quite beautiful. Her skin was golden brown, hair and eyes as dark as chocolate, and she was immaculately dressed. The white slacks and pink silk shirt stood out in stark contrast to her almost bronzed skin.

"Thank you for seeing me, Mrs. Sapèdas," Rajero said politely.

"You said you have something to tell me about Ramon," she said coolly. "Is he dead?"

"Oh, no, nothing like that," she replied quickly. "I wasn't trying to imply that anything bad had happened to him. I hope I didn't frighten you."

She waved at Rajero with almost mock indifference. Her accent was almost Puerto Rican, although Rajero still couldn't quite place it. "You didn't frighten me. Is he in trouble? What did he do?"

Rajero shook her head with disbelief. She'd come to interrogate this woman, but it now seemed that *she* was the one being interrogated. That didn't sit well with Rajero, but she was trying to be patient. She tried to keep Metzger's warnings of false accusations in the back of her mind at all times. And she'd just remembered forgetting to check in with him upon her arrival to the hotel. Well, she'd call him right after this, and take the ass chewing she knew he'd dole out to her.

"What makes you think he's done anything?" Rajero asked.

She snorted, slapping her knee. "You're kidding me, right?" She encompassed the house with a gesture and continued, "Do you honestly think I believe a U.S. Border Patrol officer can afford all of this? I may be from the ghettoes of New York, Agent Rajero, but I'm not an idiot."

"You can call me Lisa," Rajero said as sweetly as she could manage.

"I'm Carmen."

Rajero got down to business. "You said your husband was out of town."

"Yes."

"You have no idea where he went?"

"Some sort of operation. Ramon doesn't discuss his every move with me, and especially not when it has to do with work. I worry about him, but I'm a good and faithful wife. I've never cheated on him, never been unfaithful in any way. He's always kept us well, been good to his kids." She paused, shook her head, then lit a cigarette. She continued, "He really is a good man, Lisa. He's just into something bad, and I'm afraid if he doesn't get out of it soon that I'm going to lose him altogether."

Rajero couldn't help but feel a pang of guilt for Carmen's sake. But she had a job to do and couldn't let personal feelings get in the way. It always saddened Rajero when she saw families torn apart by drugs. She'd seen this kind of thing in the slums of Philadelphia and the poor parts of Los Angeles. She'd seen junkies waste away on the crap pushed by neighborhood bullies—the same bullies who hung out in schoolyards and extorted local businesses. They got businesspeople hooked on cocaine, teenagers on methamphetamines and hookers on heroin. They perverted ordinarily good people.

"I don't know what he's into, Carmen," Rajero admitted. "If he's into anything at all. But now that you mention it, there are some suspicions and rumors floating around."

"And you're here to check them out."

"Yes," Rajero admitted, "but I'm also here to help you, if you'll let me. I'll be honest and admit that I'm very suspicious of your husband. However, I would like nothing better than to be able to clear him of any wrongdoing. Believe me, it would be much easier to say I was wrong than to find out I wasn't and have to arrest another cop."

For a long time, Carmen Sapèdas just stared at Rajero. The DEA agent was beginning to wonder if maybe she'd made a mistake and the woman was just going to toss her out on her ear. She wanted Carmen to be on her side, and despite what she'd told Metzger she wanted—yes, *really* wanted—to believe that Ramon Sapèdas was innocent. She didn't derive pleasure from uncovering the sins of fellow law officers; she just had a talent for it. That wasn't something for which she would ever feel the need to apologize.

"What is it you think my husband has done?" Carmen asked.

"We're not sure, but we think he might have ties with a man named Jose Carillo. Have you heard of him?"

"I know of this man," Carmen said with a frown. "He's a drug dealer. My husband may be a lot of things, but he does *not* deal drugs."

"Well, I'm afraid we already have evidence to the contrary."

"My husband hates drugs," she replied, obviously ignoring Rajero's last statement.

"Does he hate his lifestyle, too?" Rajero asked. "Does he hate his fancy house and nice cars? Does he hate providing a decent life for you, and sending his children to the best private schools?"

Carmen sighed heavily. "He is always telling me that his parents give him money."

"His father is dead and his mother is an invalid in a nursing home."

"I know that. He told me he's already received a portion of his inheritance. He deposits a check every six months that is sent to him by his parents' attorney."

"Come on, Carmen," Rajero blurted out. "There's got to be something else."

Carmen fell silent, and the tears began to run down

her cheeks. It occurred to Rajero as she stopped berating the woman that Carmen realized it was the truth. The facts were what they were, and nobody could dispute them. Ramon Sapèdas was obviously getting money from somewhere, lying to his family about the source of the income and then living like a king in the sight of God and country. It was actually quite a bold and brash move on the part of the Border Patrol chief.

The hardest thing for Sapèdas's wife to admit was that the guy really was doing something crooked, even if she'd suspected it. She'd obviously grown accustomed to enjoying the things in life he had to offer and not questioning him about it. Who knew how long Sapèdas had been working for Carillo, but Belasko had mentioned at one point he thought it was some time and Rajero had to agree. The file indicated Sapèdas's family had lived at this address for some time, and his kids attended various schools in the same area. One was even going to college next year, and Sapèdas had worked his way through the ranks of the El Paso office, so it wasn't as if he'd transferred into his position there.

That was strange in and of itself. Normally when a federal law officer was promoted, he was transferred to another office. The greatest reason for this was that leaders were less effective if they were appointed to command those people who had once been peers and associates. There tended to be politics, favoritism and a sort of cliquish environment that took hold of the administration. This caused hard feelings and unrest among those commanded, so a promoted officer was usually sent somewhere else immediately to discourage anything like that among local offices. Sapèdas had somehow managed to avoid that process, and Rajero guessed it was due to Carillo's influence.

"Listen, Carmen, it's like I've told already told you," Rajero said gently. "I'm not looking to put your husband in jail. I want to help clear his name. But I make no bones about this when I say that if he *is* involved with Jose Carillo, I'm going to make it my personal business to put him in jail."

Carmen nodded, then crushed her cigarette out and stood. "I think it's time you should go, Agent Rajero. I'm a God-fearing woman, despite what you may think of me or my husband, and I don't want to say anything else. If you feel Ramon has done something awful or broken the law in some way, I welcome you, no, I challenge you to prove it. But for the time being, I think you should go."

"¿Señora?"

The two women turned to see the servant.

"Yes, what is it, Raul?"

"Señor Sapèdas just telephoned to let you know he was back in town. He says he is bringing a guest to stay the night. He has asked you to prepare for his homecoming."

A hard edge suddenly came to Carmen's eyes. She nodded, thanked the servant and then turned her attention to Rajero. "As I said, I think it is time for you to go. Until you have proof of wrongdoing on the part of my husband, I have nothing more to say to you and I will not help you. If you believe that Ramon has done something wrong, then bring the proof back to me. If it is solid enough, I will help you in whatever way I can. I will help you not for your sake or Ramon's or even mine. I will help you for the sake of my children."

Rajero nodded. "I understand. I'll bring you your proof."

"You do that. Now get out of my house."

Rajero knew it was no time to argue. She surely didn't want to get caught in the cross fire when Sapèdas arrived, although she was intrigued by the announcement he was bringing company. Rajero entertained the idea just for a moment that it was Jose Carillo, but Rajero knew the drug lord wouldn't dare risk coming to the United States quite so boldly after his little run-in with the American justice system in Houston.

Rajero went to her car, got in and drove toward the gates. As she reached it, she wondered what had become of Belasko. And she couldn't help but wonder if he was even alive.

LI TENG-HOK WAITED in the van with seven of his best troops. The Chinese special-forces commander was not only one of Deng Jikwan's most trusted officers, but also his only nephew. His orders had been quite clear. They were to locate the U.S. Border Patrol agent working for Jose Carillo, and they were to eliminate him.

While Teng-hok never questioned orders, he knew these weren't coming directly from his uncle. Teng-hok assumed this mission was either the work of their new American ally or at the request of one of the triad leaders. The idea of using professional soldiers to further the aims of a criminal organization did nothing short of sicken Teng-hok. But then it didn't matter what he thought, because his job was to follow orders and that's what he would do. It didn't mean he had to agree with it, though, and he considered speaking to his uncle upon completion of his mission.

Nothing had really happened thus far. The house had been quiet that morning, and Teng-hok wanted nothing more than to be active. They were soldiers, and it shouldn't have been their job to watch the house and wait for their target to return. Teng-hok had no idea who their target was. He didn't have a name—just the glossy black-and-white photograph of the man in a U.S. Border Patrol uniform. Thus far, statistical analysis run on the house didn't reveal anything out of the ordinary.

Their van was parked in the drive of another house a few doors down. The vehicle looked like one of the local telephone company vans, so they wouldn't look a bit out of the ordinary parked where they were. They were watching the house through the side mirrors.

Getting in and out wouldn't be a problem. It was a standard security system. His commandos would penetrate the perimeter of the house, accomplish their mission, get out and be practically out of El Paso by the time American police arrived. Then they would return to Florida and perhaps finally be sent back to Beijing where they belonged. He desperately wanted to get home and see his wife. He didn't like America, he didn't like running military operations in America. It was beneath him to creep around peaceful neighborhoods and kill unarmed civilians like some hoodlum.

Yes, he would have to speak with Deng.

The car that had arrived earlier with a lone female occupant was now leaving. Probably a visitor to the target's spouse. When they had completed their job here, Jikwan had ordered them to find the Border Patrol officer's children and take care of them, as well, but on that point Teng-hok had adamantly refused. He did *not* condone the murder of children unless it was in a gross military action where there were acceptable losses. Surprisingly, Jikwan didn't argue the point with him.

What he didn't know was that his refusal would prompt the Kung Lok triad to send Scarlet Dragons to El Paso. The Dragons were nothing more than gangsters, in Teng-hok's way of thinking. They killed without remorse, committed warring acts without honor and carried themselves without the slightest bit of dignity. Teng-hok hoped he didn't encounter them while on this mission—he might not have been able to refrain himself from shooting each and every one of them dead.

"There is a car coming," Teng-hok's driver and second in command announced.

"I see it," Teng-hok replied with irritation.

"No, another one. And he's slowing down."

Teng-hok turned his attention from the woman in the sedan waiting for the gate to open, and looked in the direction of his lieutenant. The sapphire-blue sports car was definitely slowing. Two men rode in it. The one behind the wheel was a Mexican native, but he didn't match the description of the man they were looking for. The passenger was a completely different story. It took Teng-hok only a moment to realize that the man was coming right into their laps.

"It's him," Teng-hok announced. "Get ready."

The clacking of automatic rifles resounded through the van, the sound practically thunderous. It had been murder sitting inside that van without air-conditioning. At least they had been allowed to keep the windows down, but his men were bordering on heat exhaustion. Well, Teng-hok knew it would be easy now.

"We will have to kill the woman?" the driver asked.

Teng-hok nodded. "We cannot have any witnesses.

We cannot be seen by anyone. We will not make our move until the gate is open. If we can get behind our target's car after the woman is gone, that will be as well. But I do not think that is a realistic expectation.''

"Understood.''

The sports car started to turn into the drive and nearly ran into the sedan. The woman raised her hands and apologized, and the driver moved the sport's vehicle over just a few feet to allow her to pass. Teng-hok watched patiently as both of the men in the sports car watched her drive past. The driver suddenly stuck his hand out the window and there was a pistol in it.

The woman saw the weapon even as he discharged it and managed to narrowly escape death. She ducked in her seat as her window imploded under the pistol shot. The driver stopped the sports car, and now both men were arguing. Then the driver said something to the passenger, and the look on the man's face was one of complete surprise. They both stood up in the seat of the sports car and were taking aim at the woman's sedan. They were apparently going to riddle the vehicle with gunfire.

Teng-hok didn't care if they killed this woman, but this had provided a great distraction. It would be very easy to eliminate their target. He barked an order to his men, and they exited the back of the van. The two men were just taking up firing positions and ready to destroy the woman when Teng-hok's commandos moved toward the position in pairs, approaching in a fire-and-maneuver pattern until they were sufficiently close to implement their operation.

Just as the men in the sports car opened fire, Teng-hok felt heat that licked at his urban camouflage and heard a whoosh. He turned in time to see their van erupt into a fireball.

Someone had just blown his van to hell!

The two gunmen downrange stopped shooting and turned to see Teng-hok's forces approaching their vehicle. Most of the commandos had hit the ground upon hearing the explosion, so none was in an effective position to fire on the sports car. The driver put the vehicle in gear and spun the tires, screaming up the drive and disappearing into the trees that surrounded the house.

Teng-hok cursed and ordered his men to break cover and storm the mansion. The soldiers started to move out, but a new enemy had arrived, emerging from the hedges like a black-garbed titan. The newcomer was dressed in a skintight blacksuit and toted an M-16 A-2/M-203.

The leader of the Chinese commando unit dived for cover and ordered his men to take out the new arrival, but the soldiers were now a little confused at the appearance of a new combatant. They had last understood their orders to be the execution of a Border Patrol officer and his wife. Now they were faced with an adversary carrying automatic weapons and grenade launchers. Something didn't make sense about that.

The aggressor used the delay to his advantage. He pulled the woman from her car and disappeared up the driveway before the door could close. He also took a moment to trigger a few hasty rounds at the Chinese commandos, and Teng-hok knew that this probably hadn't been something foreseen by his superiors. This was just a damnable coincidence, and now he had two problems on his hands.

Teng-hok refused to leave the area without accomplishing his mission, and he planned to make sure that his men didn't, either. He barked a furious set of orders at his men and they immediately complied, moving forward and scaling the seven-foot wall surrounding the property with practiced ease.

Teng-hok decided to join them rather than wait. Their only means of transportation was destroyed, so perhaps escape in the two sedans would be possible. This would also allow them to split up. Teng-hok was furious and saddened simultaneously, as his best soldier had died in the van. Only six remained and that wasn't acceptable.

He tried to swallow back his rage, knowing it couldn't get the better of him or he would be dead, as well. Yes, he would accomplish his mission first and kill the targets assigned him. The execution of the stranger and the woman would be sheer pleasure. And Teng-hok would do everything in his power to make sure he got to make the kill personally.

CHAPTER TWENTY-THREE

The Executioner was at war.

After demolishing the drugs in Calexico and rendering the resistance there ineffective, Bolan contacted Stony Man. They arranged transportation on a small military jet—utilized by the commander of San Diego Air Station—to fly Bolan to El Paso. The Executioner knew with the drugs destroyed it was the only logical place for Sapèdas to go. From there, he would probably try to contact Carillo, so it was vital Bolan get there first.

The soldier had seen all of the players as they moved into position like pieces on a chessboard. First there was the arrival of the van, probably loaded with FARC soldiers or maybe reinforcements. Then the half-dozen passes performed by some Mexican gang-banger lookalikes, who were probably spies for Carillo. By now, news of the destruction of the shipment had probably reached the drug kingpin, and he might possibly have sent some of his own men to terminate the relationship with Sapèdas.

Then the last person Bolan had hoped to see: Lisa Rajero. She'd arrived just a few minutes before 1300 hours, and that wasn't good. The Executioner knew timing was everything, and he had no idea what Rajero was doing here. Maybe she had come to talk to Sapèdas, but Bolan wasn't betting on it. The woman was too smart for that. She'd find a way to take the secondary route, and probably had come to appeal to the better senses of Sapèdas's wife. Whatever the reason, Bolan could only hope to hell she got in and out before the trouble started.

But nothing could be that easy, and Bolan knew it was time to make his move when the trouble went down in Sapèdas's driveway. The Executioner had fired the grenade from nearly 150 yards away, then broke cover from his observation post in a tree above the property fence line he'd climbed before daybreak. He'd moved along the perimeter of the wall, using the shrubbery for cover, and extracted Rajero from her car just before the fireworks began.

Bolan now shoved her up the driveway and left it for the cover of a large grove.

"What are you doing here?" Rajero asked breathlessly.

"I should ask you that."

"You told me to find out about Sapèdas," Rajero snapped.

"Yeah, but I didn't expect you'd come knock on his door for the answers," Bolan shot back.

"Look, Belasko, I—"

Bolan shook his head curtly. "This is no time for conversation. Get up to the house and find Sapèdas. Try to take him alive."

"What are you going to do?"

"Never mind that now. Move."

Bolan turned and entered the thickest part of the trees as the first movements of the soldiers appeared. Based on their movements and dress, Bolan was guessing these were probably Chinese special forces. They weren't Scarlet Dragons, and they damn sure didn't work for Nievas or Carillo. That left Chinese military types, and Bolan was betting their orders had come straight from Deng Jikwan. That meant they wouldn't stop until he was dead and they had come to accomplish whatever they'd been sent to accomplish.

The Executioner was planning to make sure neither one of these things happened.

Bolan vaulted into a tree, positioned himself so he was obscured by the foliage but had a perfect view of the immediate landscape and then sighted on his first target. The M-16/M-203 wasn't the ideal weapon for snipering, but it would have to do. Bolan couldn't put down any sustained fields of fire or they would detect him. He took a deep breath, released half and let fly with the first round. The 5.56 mm NATO slug left the barrel of the M-16 A-2 at a velocity of 950 meters per second. Bolan had acquired the variant from Kissinger with the hardball ammunition known by NATO as the SS109. It had better accuracy, a greater maximum effective range and was nearly twice as accurate as its predecessor, the M-109 standard. The heavy-caliber shell slammed through the chest of one of the commandos, and the guy dropped like a stone.

But something wasn't right. Bolan lifted his cheek from the stock and watched a moment. The guy recovered and rose behind the cover of heavy bushes nearby. His enemy was wearing body armor.

The Executioner realized he couldn't take them from a distance. He'd have to get closer, engage his opponents one on one. That wasn't going to be easy, but it was the only way to insure success. Bolan changed positions, moving from one tree to another while his target recovered. He could at least attempt to snipe a few of them before trying CQB tactics. That would keep their heads down and put them on edge. Cautious soldiers were more dangerous soldiers, sure, but they could also be affected psychologically by sniper tactics.

The warrior lined up the rifle again, this time waiting for a clean head shot. He finally got a commando who poked his head over a tree trunk. Bolan settled the pinpoint sight post on the man's cheek, adjusted the height by tenths of an inch, then squeezed the trigger. The bullet landed on target, tearing off the commando's jaw. The guy let out a pitiful scream as his weapon flew from numbed fingers and he dropped from sight behind the bush.

Bolan was already panning the area with his rifle. He heard some shouting in Chinese. It confirmed the ethnic origin of his enemy, but it still didn't tie together their whole purpose for being here. This didn't make a bit of sense, and the Executioner knew he now had more questions than answers. If Jikwan was behind this, and these weren't mercenary types hired by Mai or Shui, it didn't make any sense for them to be after Sapèdas. The guy was just a pawn in a much larger game, yet it seemed he was still their target. Unless the Chinese had something else planned, or possessed some piece of intelligence the Executioner didn't.

Still, Bolan wasn't going to concern himself with anything more at this point than survival. He rallied every combat instinct and soon found his second target. The guy was trying to crawl through the underbrush, but he was unaware he was making enough noise that it was audible by the man who lay on a thick tree branch directly above him. The Executioner simply lowered the muzzle of the M-16 A-2, steadied it and squeezed the trigger. The bullet entered the base of the guy's neck and shattered his spine. The commando's body twitched a few seconds before succumbing to death.

Several rounds of autofire zipped over his head, and the Executioner knew he no longer had the advantage. He dropped to the ground and rolled out of the fall, heading into another thicket of trees and angling back toward the wall to try a flanking maneuver. He came up to the wall, then moved along its edge until he found the driveway. Bolan quickly crossed the open expanse, continuing along the other side until he had an uphill view of the entire estate.

Only a minute passed before Bolan spotted two more commandos as they converged on the southwest corner of the mansion. The Executioner raised his rifle, took careful aim and waited until they stopped. The pair halted at a tree, keeping it between them and the front of the house, completely unaware that Bolan had them dead to rights. He waited another few seconds, and just before they started to move he squeezed the trigger.

The first round landed on the mark, punching through the cheekbone of its intended target and blowing off the man's head. The second commando got lucky, jumping back and taking the SS109 hardball slug in the side instead of the forehead. The round knocked him down, and he managed to get behind the tree before Bolan could follow up with another shot. The Executioner sprinted for a large stone block hewed into a rectangle. As he dived behind it, he could see it was actually a decorative planter. From that position he had excellent cover, but he still couldn't see his opposition.

Bolan wondered if they had split their forces and were now heading for the house. He was only a secondary target. Real professionals wouldn't be deterred from their goal, and the soldier was beginning to wonder if this game of cat-and-mouse was really what he was playing. If he got his numbers correctly, there were seven of these guys. He'd scratched three, which meant four remained in the game. One was behind the tree, and Bolan doubted he could move from that position without being seen. That meant there were still three others who could be headed for the house.

He knew that neither Sapèdas nor Rajero was any match for hardened combat veterans—they weren't trained for that kind of fight and they weren't armed for it. Bolan cursed himself for having sent Rajero out of the frying pan and into the fire. Now he was pinned down, having pinned down his enemy, and there was no way out of it. He'd have to take the Chinese commando before moving to the house and engaging the remaining opposition.

A rustle of movement was all Bolan heard, but it was unmistakably the sound of someone charging from the rear. The Executioner turned just in time to see one of the commandos rushing him, a pistol in his hand. The guy was going to shoot him at point blank range, but Bolan had other ideas. He swung the stock of the M-16 A-2 in an arc and clipped the guy's wrist. The weapon was jarred from his grip.

His would-be assailant never missed a step as he yanked a combat knife from his webbing and leaped on Bolan. The warrior grabbed the Chinese commando's left wrist with both hands, then maneuvered his body so he was on his right side. He twisted away from him and forced the knife blade away from his throat. The Executioner was much larger than his opponent, but the man was wiry, deft and surprisingly strong.

The commando managed to ram a knee into Bolan's thigh, which he'd put there out of sheer instinct. Bolan had been caught off guard by blows to the crotch in times past. Men would go to great lengths to protect that area, and he was no less diligent in that regard.

Bolan ignored the numbing pain in his thigh and pushed forward even harder on his adversay's wrists. The sound of bones grinding together and fracturing under Bolan's viselike grip resounded through the air. The man howled and the Executioner seized the advantage. He swung into a kneeling position, lodging one knee at a point between the man's armpit and shoulder joint. He kept his right hand on the fractured wrist and wrapped the left around the man's throat. Bolan squeezed the guy's throat and watched as his eyes began to bulge.

Something rough caught the side of his face, scraping skin from his jaw and cheekbone. The impact from the sole of his opponent's boot was enough to daze the soldier, and he relaxed his grip on the commando's throat. It was nothing more than a distraction, but enough for the man to escape certain death. Bolan rolled away as the guy sprang to his feet and tried to launch a side kick to his head, this one intended to crack his skull. The soldier spun and landed a leg sweep at just the right moment. His enemy's balance was good enough to keep him upright, but not so good the sweep didn't have an effect.

It was all the time the Executioner needed. He saw the knife had been dropped in the grass, the oily blade gleaming in the sun. It lay there, forgotten by its owner, and Bolan seized the advantage. He jumped forward and latched on to the weapon just as his opponent realized the intent. The Chinese military specialist tried to stop Bolan, but he was a moment too late.

Bolan's first slashing movement caught the enemy's outstretched arm, cutting deep into the skin, ripping through veins and tendons. The man leaped backward but the distraction proved fatal. The Executioner feinted toward the stomach, then sidestepped at the last moment and caught the side of the guy's neck. Hot blood spurted from the jagged wound inflicted to his throat. The man clamped his hands around the gaping wound, trying to stop the spurting blood as it collected beneath his hands and began running down his chest and arms. Bolan couldn't let the guy bleed to death—it wasn't humane. He quickly and efficiently stepped forward and drove the knife through the base of the commando's neck, severing the spinal nerve. The guy collapsed and died within seconds.

Bolan retrieved his M-16 A-2 and sprinted toward the mansion. As soon as he reached the house, he spotted the fire team of three remaining commandos converging on the structure. They shot off the lock on the front door, then tossed smokers through the front windows, followed by a couple of flash-bang grenades. The threesome went through the door like the hardened experts they were.

They weren't expecting the Executioner to appear behind them. He came through the door under the cover of their own smoke, knelt so he could get better position and then cut down the first man at the hips. The autofire shattered the commando's pelvis and leg bones. He collapsed on the ground and Bolan finished him with a 3-round burst to the head.

A volley of automatic rifle fire zipped over the Executioner's head. He rolled out of the foyer and into some sort of living area. He popped the magazine from his weapon, loaded a fresh one and returned the autofire with a corkscrew pattern burst of his own. The rounds didn't hit either of the remaining pair, but it kept their heads down. Bolan decided it was no time to get creative. He needed to neutralize the remaining commandos and do it quickly before Sapèdas got away.

The Executioner popped in a fresh 40 mm HE grenade and locked back the breech. The weapon was primed for action. He stuck the weapon around the corner into the hallway and squeezed the trigger. He barely retracted the M-16 A-2 in time to avoid losing his hands. The grenade singed hairs, as it was, and cracked the foregrips of the weapon. The explosion rocked the foyer, sending deadly shards of crystal, glass and wood whooshing past him.

Bolan rolled from his position with his back against the wall and readied himself for opposition. There wasn't a sound except that of falling plaster and fire licking at the walls. A large scorch mark and what looked like human remains were burned into a stairwell. Bolan climbed to his feet and began to search the lower level. He knew that Sapèdas and whoever had been with him were probably still on the grounds.

The soldier could now hear the sound of sirens. It was time for him to either find the last of his enemy and put them down or get out while he could. He could no longer afford detainment by law enforcement. It was time to finish the job he'd started. He tossed aside the

M-16 A-2, unable to trust the fact it was still safe and drew his .44 Magnum Desert Eagle.

The Executioner moved off in search of his enemy.

LISA RAJERO WAS inside the house when she heard the first reports of gunfire downstairs. She ignored the shooting, assuming either the Chinese were in battle with Sapèdas, or Belasko was in battle with the Chinese. Rajero was betting on the latter. She continued to search each room carefully, her Glock 19 held at the ready. She was a little angry with Belasko. For the second time in a row, he'd abandoned Rajero to her own devices. It wasn't that she couldn't function without him, but it seemed that when she needed him the most he would up and disappear on her.

Fortunately she recognized Sapèdas and the man with him: Conrado Diaz. Diaz was well-known to DEA officers all over the country. He was Jose Carillo's chief enforcer and wanted in connection with at least a dozen murders of DEA agents. Now she was close to getting him, and she had no idea where they were hiding or if they were even in the house.

The arrival of the Asians wearing body armor and combat fatigues had been a surprise, as well. Yeah, things exploded quickly and violently in Belasko's world. She'd probably been maimed, shot at and nearly incinerated more times in the past week than in her entire career. She also couldn't help but wonder about Carmen Sapèdas. There was no question now Ramon Sapèdas was working for Carillo—the evidence spoke for it. What Rajero didn't want was for Carmen to get caught in the cross fire. She hoped the woman had enough sense to get the hell out while she could.

The sound of a closet door rolling aside saved Rajero. She dived away from the noise moments before bullets thudded into the carpeting where she stood. She came up behind the bed and aimed her weapon at her would-be assassin, coming face-to-face with none other than Carmen Sapèdas.

"What the hell are you still doing here?" Rajero demanded.

"Trying to stay alive."

"Get out of here."

Carmen blinked. "This is my home."

The sound of an explosion rocked the floor beneath their feet. Rajero lowered her weapon as the reverberations of the blast subsided. Obviously, she'd been right about Belasko being downstairs and probably taking care of the Chinese. That meant he'd be looking for her now, so she had to stall a little longer.

"It's also going to be your grave site if you don't get out of here."

"Where is Ramon?" she asked.

Rajero shook her head, growing impatient. "I don't know where he is. When I find him, you'll be the first to know about it. Now get out of here!"

Carmen raised the pistol and pulled back on the hammer. Rajero was completely speechless. She hadn't realized the power of love. Carmen Sapèdas obviously loved her husband greatly, so much she would risk jail or death for him. But it would be a senseless death. Sapèdas wasn't worth such devotion in Rajero's mind.

"I asked you a question," Carmen hissed. "Where is my Ramon?"

"I don't know," Rajero said quietly. "All I know is he tried to kill me."

"I do not believe you."

"I don't care," Rajero barked. "Carmen, listen to me. You can still walk away from this. You can still go on with your life. There's no reason to die here. Not like this."

"I will be with Ramon."

"Put it down, lady," an icy voice commanded her.

Belasko stood in the doorway of the master bedroom, a gleaming Desert Eagle clutched in his hands. He had the muzzle leveled on Carmen, and there was a look in his eyes that told Rajero he was about to blow her to pieces. At first, Rajero thought she might not stop the guy, but she knew that the woman was an innocent in all of this. She couldn't let Belasko cap her without at least trying to explain the situation. It wasn't fair—the woman had a right to a second chance. She didn't have to die.

"Belasko, listen," Rajero said. "This is Carmen Sapèdas, Ramon's wife. She thought I was here to hurt him."

"So?" Bolan replied, not lowering his weapon.

He pinned the woman with icy blue eyes and said, "You have any idea what kind of man your husband is, lady? You know how many people he's killed? He's been responsible for the deaths of hundreds. Every dope pusher who unloaded bad junk on a now dead teenager probably got the stuff through arrangements made by your husband."

"I don't believe it."

"Really?" Bolan inclined his head in Rajero's direction. "You think she came here on a whim? I was the one who first approached him. He lied to me about guns used in multiple drug deals where DEA agents got killed. He was bribed by Jose Carillo and this alliance he's formed with the Colombian revolution. All in the name of greed, lady. You still think he's worth saving?''

Carmen looked down the barrel of the pistol another moment, then her body began to quiver and she finally dropped the weapon. Rajero rushed forward and snatched it up, catching the woman in the nick of time before she collapsed onto the bed. She began to cry, her body trembling in Rajero's arms as she wept.

Rajero swallowed hard, unable to understand what had caused such a horrific tragedy. Fifteen minutes earlier, this woman was a proud, decent sort. Now she was weeping for the loss and suffering she knew would come about. Rajero knew that Belasko wanted to kill Sapèdas, but she warned him off with a pleading look.

''I want to take him alive, Mike. You owe me that much.''

''I don't owe you anything, Lisa. But I understand what you're saying. You take him alive. Do whatever you think you have to. What about the guy with him?''

Rajero nodded. ''His name is Conrado Diaz. He works directly for Carillo. I know him well enough to know he's ruthless and dangerous. That's who you really want, Belasko. You need to find him and kill him. He doesn't deserve anything less, for he's killed many people. Many innocent people, not to mention law-enforcement officers.''

''You think he'll stick with Sapèdas?''

''Not likely,'' Rajero said as she helped Carmen to her feet. ''He'll probably make for the border. Try to get word back to Carillo.''

Bolan nodded, then moved suddenly to a window and

looked out onto the property. "The police are here. I have to go."

"Why are you worried about the cops?" Rajero asked.

"I'm not worried about them. It's just time for me to go. Get her out of here, and start combing the place for Sapèdas. The guy's hiding somewhere on the grounds. He probably figures it's safer than trying to run. Maybe he can convince the locals he's a victim."

"Not a chance," Rajero said. "They'll find slugs from his gun in my car. And I'm sure there's enough evidence here now to hold him."

"Good luck." Bolan turned to leave.

"Hey, soldier?"

"What?"

Rajero smiled. "Thanks."

He nodded and then left the room. And Rajero whispered a silent prayer of good fortune for him.

CHAPTER TWENTY-FOUR

Bolan hit the first-floor landing of the back stairwell and looked out a window. El Paso police were arriving in droves, scouring the front lawn and moving along the sides of the property, preparing themselves to do battle.

The Executioner knew that Sapèdas would approach them immediately, but if Rajero was right about this Conrado Diaz, he would try to find a way out the back. Bolan had the same idea, and he hoped he could catch Diaz in the process. Fate or some other luck was shining on Bolan as he exited through the rear patio and quickly spotted movement on the far end of the drive where it terminated in a large outbuilding.

Bolan followed the movement in the trees, and soon realized it was a man scrambling to find a way over the huge hill that bordered a better part of Sapèdas's property. Bolan had already reconnoitered the area before taking up his observation, and he knew it better than his quarry. The Executioner picked up the pace, moving past the sports car Diaz had driven. The outbuilding was actually a separate garage, with several covered bays for vehicles. Most of the spots were empty, but they probably had used them for guests.

Well, Sapèdas wouldn't get far. Bolan decided not to

chase him on foot. Another idea struck him, and he returned to the sports car. The keys were in it! Bolan jumped into the seat and keyed the ignition. He put the sports car in a 180-degree turn and gunned the engine, tapping to second and then third. Bolan was ready to pop it into fourth by the time he'd edged around the house and was on the main drive, headed for the exit.

The police were taken completely by surprise, and Bolan caught just a glimpse of Carmen and Rajero as he drove past. Weapons came up, but no one got off a shot as the Executioner weaved between the unmarked squads and radio cars scattered along the wide driveway.

Bolan cleared the front gate, whipping the wheel left to avoid the sedans still jammed to one side and the squad car parked immediately in front of them. He turned suddenly, burning rubber as he executed a sharp turn and began climbing the hilly road. Bolan was about to put an end to Diaz's run—the guy wasn't going to get far.

He started to slow the vehicle when he reached the area that seemed most likely as an exit point, and Diaz appeared a moment later. The guy's eyes grew wide when he spotted the Executioner. A moment later, he grabbed cover behind a car parked and popped a few shots at Bolan.

Bringing the sports car to a stop and popping the clutch to kill the engine, the soldier yanked on the emergency brake. Then he was out of the car and moving up the sidewalk on the opposite side, the Desert Eagle up and ready for action. Diaz capped off a couple more hasty shots before the roar of an engine caught the attention of both men. The Cadillac Bolan had seen earlier filled with Mexican gang members roared into view.

The Executioner realized that they posed a real threat

as they jumped from the vehicle with Jatimatics in hand. The hoods immediately opened fire, not terribly concerned with hitting Bolan as much as they were looking to keep him on the move. The soldier found himself forced to oblige. The .44 Magnum was no match against a half-dozen machine pistols.

Bolan leaped into a thick stand of fern bushes and emerged to face a wall. He climbed to the top to find a monstrous backyard in a ravine below. The place was gigantic, but the fact it was secured in such a cavernous alcove hadn't been visible to the outside eye. The swimming pool was probably a good ten yards below Bolan. He knew he could make the jump, provided the water was deep enough, and he would survive the fall.

The Executioner ducked as several of the 9 mm rounds buzzed past his head. He aimed the Desert Eagle in the general direction of the hoods and triggered two rounds. The popping and chattering from the Jatimatics suddenly ceased, and Bolan hesitated a split second.

He holstered his weapon then turned and readied for the jump into the pool.

Bolan felt the sudden burn of pain in his back a heartbeat after he heard the sound of a lone pistol cracking in the still air.

But it wasn't his body toppling forward and landing in the pool that was the last sensation the Executioner felt.

It was the rush of chlorinated water into his nostrils as darkness overcame him.

* * * * *

*The heart-stopping action
concludes with BREACHED
Book II of THE FRONTIER WARS,
available in September.*

THE Destroyer®

TROUBLED WATERS

Thomas "Captain" Kidd is the new scourge of the Caribbean, and when he and his crew kidnap the daughter of a senator, CURE sets out to kick some serious pirate booty. Posing as rich tourists, Remo and Chiun set a course for the tropics to tempt these freebooters into the mistake of their career. But Remo soon finds himself swimming with sharks, while Chiun senses some illicit treasure in his future. Even so, they are ready to dispatch the sea raiders to an afterlife between the devil and the deep blue sea.

Available in October 2003 at your favorite retail outlet.

DEATH LANDS®

Devil Riders

Available in September 2003 at your favorite retail outlet.

Stranded in the salty desert wastes of West Texas, hopes for a hot meal and clean bed in an isolated ville die fast when Ryan and his companions run into a despotic baron manipulating the lifeblood of the desert: water. But it's his fortress stockpiled with enough armaments to wage war in the dunes that interests Ryan, especially when he learns the enemy may be none other than the greatest—and long dead—Deathlands legend: the Trader.

James Axler
Outlanders®

SEA OF PLAGUE

The loyalties that united the Cerberus warriors have become undone, as a bizarre messenger from the future provides a look into encroaching horror and death. Kane and his band have one option: fix two fatal fault lines in the time continuum—and rewrite history before it happens. But first they must restore power to the barons who dare to defy the greater evil: the mysterious new Imperator. Then they must wage war in the jungles of India, where the deadly, beautiful Scorpia Prime and her horrifying bio-weapon are about to drown the world in a sea of plague....

In the Outlands, the shocking truth is humanity's last hope.

Stony Man is deployed against an armed
invasion on American soil...

AXIS OF CONFLICT

The free world's worst enemy failed to destroy her once
before, but now they've regrouped and expanded—a jihad
vengeance that is nothing short of bio-engineered
Armageddon, brilliant and unstoppable. A weapon unlike
anything America has ever seen is about to be unleashed on
U.S. soil. Stony Man races across the globe in a desperate
bid to halt a vision straight out of doomsday—with
humanity's extinction on the horizon....

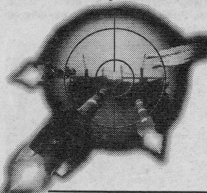

STONY MAN

*Available in
August 2003
at your favorite
retail outlet.*